Masked
in
Deception

T.K. DRAKE

SINCLAIR AFFAIRS BOOK TWO

Masked
in
Deception

T.K. DRAKE

You never needed a prince, darling.
You needed a villain.

Author's Note

Thank you for reading *Masked in Deception*! If you're new here, welcome! If you're joining us after reading Ledger and Sloane's story, *Redeemed in Crimson*, welcome back! When we started this journey one year ago, we never planned to create a series. But as the characters came to life, we knew we couldn't ignore them. The idea for Margot and Jack's story came to us almost as soon as we wrote them in book one, and these characters have had us in a chokehold since. This book remains incredibly special to us, and we hope you enjoy the ride as much as we did!

Masked in Deception

is book two in a five book series

but can be read as a standalone.

Content Warning

Please note that this is a sexually explicit romance with dark themes including BDSM scenes. These should not be taken as a blueprint on BDSM etiquette, as this is a work of fiction featuring imperfect characters.

Please visit www.tkdrake.com for a detailed list of content warnings and kinks. Your mental wellbeing is incredibly important to us! We can always be reached at tkdrakeauthor@outlook.com with any specific concerns or questions.

Chapter One

7 years old

Ledger and I tiptoe down the hall, trying to make our way past the den without being pulled into Margot duty. It's impressive how such a tiny baby can change things. The usually tidy house is cluttered, Ms. Blanche seems to be upset more often than not, and loud cries fill the halls at all hours of the day.

I've been living in the Sinclair house since my mom died two years ago. I could've stayed in my family's estate with the nannies and tutors to watch me while my dad traveled, but Ms. Blanche and Mom had been lifelong best friends, so she *insisted* on having me come live here with her two sons, Henry and Ledger.

While Henry is a few years older than me, Ledger was born the same year, and we instantly hit it off. In the two years I've been here, we've become more like brothers than anything. The only person in the family who doesn't treat me like a

Sinclair is Mr. Sinclair. He's kind enough, but his preference for his own sons is apparent.

Regardless of how comfortable they all try to make me, I can't help but feel like any day I could be sent back to my father. If I mess up, they'll get rid of me. Or now that they have a new baby, I'll be too much.

In the month that Margot has been here, I've tried to be on my very best behavior, but Ledger isn't concerned at all. As he motions for me to be quiet, I try not to feel guilty that I'm not offering to help Ms. Blanche as we attempt to sneak outside to play.

The closer we get to the door, the louder Margot's cries become. We're almost free when Ms. Blanche calls for our attention.

"Boys! Come here, please!" she yells over the screams of the newborn.

Ledger sighs and rolls his eyes before turning around to mope toward his mom and sister. I follow without any attitude as she calls out commands.

"Ledger, go grab a diaper and wipes from the nursery," she says before walking toward me, rocking the baby in her arms. "Jackie, could you please hold Margot while I go and warm up a bottle?"

Before I can respond, Ms. Blanche hands me a screaming bundle of pink and rushes out of the room.

Alone with Margot in my arms, I mimic the rocking motion her mom had done a few moments earlier, combined with some shushing, and within a few seconds, the crying stops. I look down at the tiny little girl in my arms and lose myself in her crystal-blue eyes.

"Oh Jack! You got her to stop crying!" Ms. Blanche declares, breaking my trance.

I try handing the baby back, but she steps away. "I think she's happy with you right now, Jackie." Ms. Blanche cups my cheek and smiles down at me. "From now on, you're on Margot duty. It's your job to calm her down when she's crying. Look, you've even managed to get her to sleep without a bottle. Be very gentle laying her down in her bassinet, and you can go play with Ledger."

I look down at the now sleeping Margot, and I realize I don't want to put her down. It's *my* job to hold her. "Can I hold her for a little longer?"

Ms. Blanche guides me toward a chair in the den and helps me get comfortable without waking up the baby, then hands me the remote. "Here, sit as long as you want. When you want to get up, just let me know, and I'll come get her."

I sit there until she wakes up, proud to be the one who was able to calm her. I finally have a purpose in the Sinclair house.

Margot duty.

Chapter Two

3 years old

I cry and cry, but Mommy isn't here. I ran so fast playing with Ledger, but I tripped on the stairs, and my knee hurts so bad. *Where is my mommy?*

"Hey, Princess. What's wrong?"

I look up, and my Jack is here, kneeling in front of me and looking concerned. He's not Mommy, but I love him too, so maybe he can fix boo-boos.

"I hurt my knee," I cry. I've had ouchies before, but this hurts, and it's red, and I just want my mommy. "Mommy!" I scream, crying as loud as I can and hoping she hears me.

"Hey, hey now, it's okay, Margot," Jack says, rubbing my back and wiping my tears. "Your mom is in her office, but I think a bandage and a sticker will fix you right up. You've got a little scrape, but you're such a big girl. You'll be chasing Ledger and me again in no time."

"Do you promise?" I cry, a little lighter now that I know I can have a sticker. "Can I have a pink sticker?"

"You can have whatever you want, Princess. If we don't have pink stickers, I'll find you one, I promise. Okay? Just don't cry. You know I can't stand to see my girl cry."

Jack looks like he's serious about the pink sticker, so I decide to be a big girl and let him carry me into the kitchen. He rubs a cloth over my knee, and it hurts, but before I can think about it too much, Jackie asks me a question.

"Hey, Princess, do you know what a cow's favorite dance move is?"

I sniffle and shake my head.

"A milk shake!"

Giggling with Jackie, I realize my knee feels all better, and I have a pink bandage. He puts the same one on his hand so we match.

"Now, you have to pinky promise not to tell your mom, but I have a surprise for you." Jack winks, and I giggle, watching him pull my favorite chocolate out of his pocket. "You aren't supposed to have these before dinner, so this is a very serious pinky promise, Margot. I could get in trouble. And you have to eat all your dinner tonight."

I nod and give him a big hug. "I promise I'll eat the most dinner ever, and Mommy will never know. Thanks, Jackie!"

"You're welcome, Princess."

Jack and I share my chocolate. He laughs, wiping my mouth off with a washcloth when I get it all over my lips and face. Then we're racing off again to find Ledger. Earlier, I was running to hide while he and Jack chased me, but now Jack says it's time for us to be on a team and chase my brother. I can't tell Ledger, he says, but I'm a better chaser than him, and I'm Jack's favorite to play with. Ledger sometimes doesn't want to play with me, and Henry is old and boring. But Jack never gets mad at me when we play, and he brings me chocolate and stickers and gives the best hugs.

I asked Mommy where Jack's mommy and daddy and sister and brothers are. She said he doesn't have any, and we're Jack's family. But Jack is too cool to be one of my brothers. He's better. I'm a princess, and he's my Prince Charming. As long as he's here, I'll have someone who wants to play with me and share chocolate and fix my ouchies. As long as Jack is here, I'll be a happy girl.

Chapter Three

Jack

11 years old

"Jack, you know you don't have to vacuum your room every day, sweetie. It's okay if we just do it as part of our Sunday chores. You keep everything so tidy I don't think you can have too many crumbs built up over a week." Ms. Blanche chuckles as I bring the vacuum back to the closet just outside of the den. Dinner was about an hour ago, and while Ledger went to his dad's study for one of their "lessons," I went to do the nightly cleaning of my room.

"I know, Ms. Blanche. I just want to keep everything nice." I would never admit I'm always scared a gross room will get me kicked out of this family.

She stands from her reading chair and crosses the room, turning lamps off as she goes. Placing a kiss on the top of my head, she sighs. "You can keep your room exactly as neat or as messy as you want, sweetie. It's *your* room. As long as you don't leave food in there for ants to get in my house. The episode last year with Ledger's old sandwich still gives me nightmares."

I laugh and shudder, thinking of the nasty glob that the exterminator pulled from underneath Ledger's bed, earning him a two-week grounding and double chores for a month. If I had ever brought food into my room before, that would have made me quit. "I promise, no food."

This earns me a warm smile as Ms. Blanche heads to bed. "I love you," she says, just like every night. "Come get me if you need anything."

"I love you too," I reply, knowing that it would take an absolute emergency for me to bother her in the middle of the night. The one time I had a bad dream and went to her room, Mr. Sinclair woke up before Ms. Blanche did and yelled at me to never open their bedroom door after dinner again.

Now that everything is clean and I've said good night to Ms. Blanche, I walk past Ledger's room to see he's already in bed and drooling. I'm convinced he could pass out anywhere at any time and not wake up for eight hours, regardless of his surroundings. I never sleep well, and I've always been jealous of how safe he feels to do that. Moving on to Margot's room, I see her starfished on her stomach, surrounded by an entire toy store's worth of plushies on the bed with her. It makes me smile just how much pink is in this room, and as ridiculous as it is, it's very her. Just like a princess.

Everyone is safe and tucked in, and my room is neat with tomorrow's clothes laid out, so I finally fall into bed and manage to sleep.

A terrible wail jolts me awake, and I'm out of my door and heading in the direction of the sound before I can even think. I run past Ledger's door, not surprised he hasn't woken up, and burst into Margot's room to see what's causing her to scream like this. Her plushies are all over the place, and she's thrashing around in bed, screaming, "No, Sprinkles! No!"

The pit in the bottom of my stomach loosens as I realize there's no danger and it's just a nightmare, apparently involving her favorite plush rainbow cow, Sprinkles. Still, her crying in her sleep bothers me just as much as it does in real life, and I need to wake her up so she's not upset anymore.

Moving to sit down on the edge of her bed, I gently try to shake her awake. "Margot...Margot! Wake up, Princess, it's just a bad dream. You're okay. Sprinkles is right here."

When she hears "Sprinkles," she sits up, looking around frantically as I place the ridiculous cow in her lap.

"See? She's perfectly okay."

Finally fully waking up and realizing what's going on, Margot bursts into tears all over again and throws her arms around my neck.

I can barely make out her words between the sobs. "We were on a boat and Sprinkles fell over, and she can't swim, Jack! She's only a cow! And I couldn't save her..."

Oh, my sweet Princess. What an awful dream to have, even if it's only about a stuffed animal.

"It's okay, Princess. It was a very bad dream, but Sprinkles is here, alive and well. And I'm here, so nothing bad can happen."

She looks up at me with her big blue eyes and a quivering lip. "Pinky promise?"

Looping our pinkies, I give her a kiss on the forehead. "I promise. You've got me, Henry, and Ledger looking out for you. We'll always keep you safe. But you need to get back to sleep."

She's tucked back in among her plushies, and I'm heading for the door when I hear her small voice, so quiet I almost miss it. "Will you stay with me, Jackie? I'm still scared."

Knowing there is no room for me with all those stuffed animals, I sigh. I probably wasn't going to sleep all that well tonight, anyway.

I turn, seeing her hopeful little face, and my choice is made. "Of course I'll stay, Princess. Scooch over and give me some of your guardian plushies to keep watch over me too."

She makes room, and we sandwich ourselves with stuffed animals on all sides. Finally, just as I'm about to drift off, I hear her small voice again, and her hand reaches across Sprinkles to hold mine. "I love you, Jackie."

"I love you too, Princess."

Chapter Four

5 years old

I wait ten minutes after I see the light coming in from under my door go out, letting me know everyone has gone to bed, before I quietly make my way to Jack's room across the hall.

It's just Jack and me in this wing of the house since Mommy and Daddy's room is on the other side. Ledger used to be in our wing too, but he moved to the third floor when he turned twelve. That's where Henry's room is too when he's home from school. I like being away from everyone now because nobody complains when I practice piano in my room at night. Ledger never liked it, but Jackie says he doesn't mind.

I started climbing into bed with him when I would get nightmares last year, but it was happening almost every night, so I decided to just go ahead and fall asleep with Jackie. I don't know what it is, but when he's beside me, I only ever have good dreams.

"Hi, Princess," he whispers when I slip into his room. "Come get in."

I scurry over and shimmy under the covers as he scoots across to the other side of the bed. His bed is always so much cozier than mine. And his room always feels so much cleaner.

"What story do you want tonight? *Sleeping Beauty* again?"

Jack started trying to tell me jokes to get me to fall asleep, but we would laugh so hard it would keep us awake longer. Recently, he's been telling me fairy tales, and even though I fall asleep halfway through, I love hearing about the brave princes who come to save the day.

"Ooo yes, please!" I squeal, kicking my feet in excitement.

"Shhh, calm down, silly." He chuckles. "Do you think you'll ever want another story?"

"Nope! Never!" I whisper. "Who could ever want a different story than *Sleeping Beauty*?"

"Why do you like her so much anyway?" he asks as he rolls on his side to face me.

"She's the only one with a pink dress." I think we have the same conversation every night, but I don't mind. I get my story either way.

"Alright, Princess, here we go. Once upon a time..."

"Wait!" I whisper-yell, stopping him mid-sentence. "You forgot to tuck me in!"

"Oh my, how could I forget? Alright then, lie flat," he says, tucking the covers in around my body like a mummy.

"Better?" he asks.

I nod enthusiastically. "Better."

He gives me a little kiss on the top of my head and restarts the story.

"Once upon a time…" I listen to Jack tell me the story of the princess who didn't know the stranger in the woods she fell in love with was her prince all along.

That's not me, though. I know who my prince is, and it's Jack. And one day, when I'm older, we'll live happily ever after. Just like in the fairy tales.

Chapter Five

13 years old

"Ledgerrrr! Stop skipping me! It's my turn to be the hitter, and you and Jack have to pitch and catch!"

Margot's whine echoes across the yard, and Ledger turns to me to roll his eyes. "Come on, man. Let's go inside and get something to eat. I'm tired."

They've been on each other's nerves for what feels like forever now, although I know it's ramping up as Ledger has had more and more pressure on him from his dad to grow up and take all his extra lessons seriously. I can't blame him for being stressed, but it's not Margot's fault. Besides, she's big enough now to understand more, and it's been kind of fun to teach her things I always wished I had an older sibling for. Henry was never really available to play with us, so Ledger and I figured out certain things on our own—like the best trees to climb, the fastest route from point A to point B in the house, and how to ride bikes. Margot doesn't have to worry about that, though. She's got us.

"She's getting kind of good, man. I think you're scared she'll homer off you and show you up," I say, walking up to Ledger and winking where Margot can't see. He rolls his eyes at my obvious manipulation but smiles and picks the softball back up.

"Okay, Princess, but you're getting my best pitch. I'm not taking it easy on you!" Ledger yells.

Margot steps up to our makeshift home plate very seriously and levels a stare at Ledger that makes me a little scared for whatever man she ends up with one day. *She's going to be a whole damn problem for some poor guy. And before that, she's going to be our problem for about the next twenty years.*

"Bring it on, scaredy-cat," she yells to her brother, although her pink glitter bat and helmet take away most of the sting of her taunts.

She's still growing like a weed, taller than other girls in her class, and so scrawny that looking at her, you'd wonder how she can hold up her bat. But I've learned it's never a good idea to underestimate Margot Sinclair, and as Ledger sends her an underhanded pitch that's by no means a gimme, she swings and sends the ball soaring over our heads and past the invisible boundary we had marked as our field of play.

Ledger's mouth drops open as she takes off her helmet, gives him the biggest gap-tooth grin I've seen all day, and flips her bat in the air toward the pitcher's mound.

"Loser carries the equipment in!" Her laughter rings out as she turns and heads back to the house.

Yep, six years old and Princess is already a force. *We're all in trouble.*

Chapter Six

8 years old

"Wow, Margot! You look like a real princess," Jack says, twirling me around on the dance floor at my cousin's wedding reception.

I got a couple of dances out of Henry and Ledger, but it's been Jack dancing with me for the past hour. We've all had boring ballroom dancing lessons, but I prefer either standing on Jack's feet or just goofing off.

When the band announces a thirty-minute break, I let out an exaggerated sigh, pouting at the news as Jack guides us back to the table where Ledger and Henry are fighting over who's the strongest.

This is the first wedding I can remember going to, and it's *beautiful.* I'm already making mental notes about what I would change for my own wedding. I think I would want to have it in a castle, overflowing with pink flowers. I would get a real pop star to sing at mine, though. I've never even heard of the band that's here tonight. I don't think I would serve any regular food. Instead, I would have a gigantic chocolate fountain that everyone could dip sweets into.

"We're going to get married when we're old enough, right, Jack?"

All three boys look my way, and Jack chokes on the water he was chugging down.

"Excuse me?" Henry asks. "Why on earth would you think...ow!"

Ledger elbows him in the side, cutting him off. "What makes you say that, Princess?" His tone is much kinder than our older brother's.

I roll my eyes at Henry before giving my attention to Ledger. "Well, Daddy says I can't marry him since he's already married to Mommy, and I can't marry you or Henry either because you're my brothers. So that leaves Jack!"

The three boys exchange glances before Ledger responds. "Jack is basically your brother too, though."

I look beside me at my beautiful Prince Charming. He's not quite as tall as my brothers are, but he's at least a head taller than me, and that's all that matters in fairy tales. His dirty-blond hair looks almost brown as it drips with sweat from dancing, and his chiseled jaw could cut through diamonds. I look into his deep blue eyes and have no doubts that he's the one.

"Jack is *not* my brother. Plus, he's not *gross* like you and Henry are. He's like...like a prince!" I say, noticing how Jack's cheeks have the faintest of blushes painted across them at my words.

My brothers hunch over laughing, only stopping when Jack clears his throat, pulling their attention back toward me.

Ledger is the first one to stop. "And here I thought Jack was the one with all the jokes. Margot, you don't need to worry about getting married any time soon anyway. I promise we will find you a suitor worthy of our Princess. But not until you're thirty. Or I'll beat him up. Okay?"

I roll my eyes but nod anyway. They'll see. They may not think so right now, but I *know* it's Jack.

I'm lying in my bed, looking up at the glowing stars on my ceiling and thinking about the conversation earlier. Turning to my side and propping myself up on my elbow, I look down at Jack. I stopped sleeping in the same bed as him years ago, but most nights, I still insist on him sleeping beside me on the pull-out trundle that was intended for girlie slumber parties.

"Jackie?" I whisper, trying to gauge if he's still awake.

"Yeah, Princess?" he says as he rolls over to face me. He really is the most beautiful boy I've ever seen.

"You will marry me when we grow up, won't you?"

His sleepy smile shines in the dim light. "Why do you want to marry me?"

I think about it for a minute before giving him an honest answer. "I've always just known I was going to marry you one day."

"Then do I really have a choice?"

A smile explodes on my face as I'm flooded with relief. *Of course we're going to get married one day.* "I love you, Jackie."

"I love you too, Princess."

Chapter Seven

17 years old

"Jack, when Daddy kisses Mommy, why doesn't he put his tongue in her mouth like they do on TV?" Margot asks, sitting in the den with Ledger and me while we laze around, enjoying the first day of school being out for the summer.

Ledger lets out a snort and gets up to leave, clapping me on the shoulder on his way out. "This one's all you, brother. I have to meet with Dad soon anyway."

"Asshole," I murmur under my breath, turning back to where Margot is lying under a pink fuzzy blanket in her corner of the couch with her feet in my lap.

"Why do you ask?" I hope I can say something, *anything*, to defer this conversation and avoid being the person who explains romance to this too smart ten-year-old.

"Well," she begins, "earlier we were watching MTV."

Ledger knows he isn't supposed to have that shit on when she's around. She's way too observant.

"And the couple on the show said they were in love, and they were going to get married, and then they kissed, and it went on *forever*, and then I saw his tongue! His tongue, Jack. In her mouth! And then it was all tongues. And I know Mommy and Daddy are in love, but I have never seen either of their tongues when they kiss. So what's that about?"

She looks at me so earnestly that I'm scrambling to find a way out of answering this without lying because I really hate lying to her. I swear she has a fucking sixth sense of when she's not getting the whole truth about something, and every single one of us, including her parents, has been called out by her before.

I mean, Mr. Sinclair is one of the most intimidating men I've ever been around. I've literally heard Margot say, "I don't think that's the whole story, Daddy," and he apologized to her and admitted it wasn't. *She's such a ballbuster, even at ten.*

"What else did they say on the show?" I ask, trying to buy some time.

"Well, someone else came along and asked why they were Frenching...oh! That must be it! They're French! Is that a French thing?"

I let out a sigh of relief. I don't even *really* have to lie.

"Yep, Princess, that's a French thing. And I know you know this, but you really shouldn't be watching MTV. Ledger knows better than to have that on when you're with us."

Margot rolls her eyes at me before readjusting her position on the couch with Sprinkles the cow. "I'm not a baby anymore! Besides, Mary Lee got kissed by Colt Jones last week at school, so I need to know everything I can about kissing. It's only a matter of time before I get one."

A rage I've never felt before flows from my head to my feet as quick as lightning. I don't even have time to process the feeling before I'm sitting up straight on the couch. "Someone *kissed* someone at school? You're about to be in fifth grade, Margot! That is totally inappropriate."

She can clearly see how upset I am, and deflates a little from the excited state she was in a second ago. "Are you not supposed to kiss in elementary school?" she asks.

"No!" I say, then realize I'm damn near yelling. My tone won't make her pay any more attention to me. "No," I continue more quietly, "you aren't supposed to kiss until you're eighteen."

Now it's her turn to yell.

"Eighteen! That's like, forever away!" she yells, sitting up straighter on the couch.

I smile. "I don't make the rules, Princess. Eighteen is for everyone."

She sits back on the couch, putting her feet on my lap to rub again, clearly thinking hard about this new piece of information.

"So," she says, looking at me, "that means you haven't kissed anyone, right, Jackie? Because you're not eighteen yet, and that's the rule."

Man, she's smart. I'm too far in it now, so it's time to lie to her, which sucks.

"Nope, Margot, no kissing for me. Not until I'm eighteen," I say.

"Well, when I'm eighteen, someone has to kiss me, and it's going to be you, obviously! Like in *Sleeping Beauty*!" She's happy again now, and it's impossible to deny her anything.

"Yeah, Princess, I'll kiss you when you're eighteen," I say, pecking her on the forehead and tucking her in with her fuzzy blanket before leaving her watching cartoons instead of MTV. *She's gonna be so much trouble.*

Chapter Eight

12 years old

My favorite pop star singing about heartache finishes her song, and I immediately press replay. She's the only one who understands what I'm feeling right now.

"Margot! Margot Sinclair, what on earth are you doing blaring music that loud? It's past your bedtime, and you've got school tomorrow!" my mom says, opening the door to my bedroom and looking around in horror at what I've done with the place.

I think it's a reasonable expression of my feelings. Everything *sucks*. I'm not supposed to say that word, but it's only in my head, and it's true. *Sucks, sucks, sucks.*

"Sweetie, really. What's wrong?" Mom looks concerned now, and I think maybe the song lyrics written in bold print taped up all around my room might look a little like I'm having a breakdown, which I'm not. At least I don't think so.

"I'm fine, Mom. Just sad today," I say, hoping she'll leave so I can get back to looking for my scissors. Bangs will fix this. I've watched two tutorials, so I'm ready to give it a go.

"Is it a problem with a boy? At school?" she asks, stepping into my room and closing the door behind her. I sigh, turning my music down since this clearly won't be a short conversation.

Actually, this might be a chance to get some of my feelings out. My mom is super cool, and I've never had a problem going to her with anything before. Boy problems shouldn't be any different.

"Um, yeah, it is. About a boy, I mean. Just. A boy I like doesn't know I exist, basically," I say, giving the simplest, kinda true version of the situation to Mom. I can't really say *"I've been in kid-love with my adoptive brother since I was a toddler and now I'm almost a teenager and I think I love-love him but you showed me pictures of him at college yesterday and he was hugging and kissing a beautiful girl with pink highlights and now I want to cry until I can't cry anymore."*

Even thinking this factual summary is too much, and I burst into tears.

"Oh, honey," Mom says, coming to sit beside me on my bed. "This is the worst part of growing up, you know. It's hard to feel something for someone and not have them feel the same way back. But Margot, Princess, sometimes it's just not the right time for two people to feel a certain way about one another. Sometimes you just have to live your life and know the right person will come along at the right time."

I breathe in on a sob and wipe some tears away, thinking about what Mom's saying. I mean, she's for sure the smartest person ever, but it really sounds like she knows who I'm talking about. *Nah, there's no way.* She's just being generally wise. That's it. It doesn't really make me feel better, and I kinda want her to leave so I can cut my bangs and write some more lyrics out. Maybe with some glitter this time.

"You know," she says, glancing around my room, "I've been meaning to ask you if you wanted to help me with a project."

"I'm pretty busy, Mom," I say, gesturing to my unfinished boy band collage and some jean shorts I'm bedazzling.

"Well, yes, I can see that, Margot," Mom says with a smile, "but this would be a chance for your creative side to shine. I was thinking it might be time to revamp your room. It's been ages since we've done anything to it, and since you're starting middle school soon, I thought you might even want one of the rooms with a nicer closet and room for a bigger piano area and maybe less pink zebra print."

"I want Jack's old room!" I yell before she's even finished her thought. Her raised eyebrow makes me note the volume of my voice, and I continue quietly, "I would love a new room, Mom. Maybe Jack's old room? That shower and closet are bigger, and the view is better." *It's not.* But she doesn't have to know that I'm hoping his scent will still be at least a little embedded in the mattress. Or the carpet fibers.

Mom gives me a wide smile. "You can have whichever room you want, sweetheart. We'll go this weekend and pick out wallpaper samples and some fabrics. We'll also get someone in there to build bookshelves for all these books you've been inhaling lately. It'll be perfect."

I lean on her shoulder and smile. It will be perfect. She's right. Everything will be fine. I have the right person. I just need the right time.

Chapter Nine

21 years old

"Two glasses of the best scotch you've got, neat," I say, placing the same drink order Ledger and I have had since freshman year.

We've always looked a few years older. That and a good fake ID made it easy to get around the drinking age, but I have to admit, it's nice not to have to fuss with that anymore. We attended our fair share of parties in high school, but they pale in comparison to the wild nights we've had since college. Hanging out in a bar long enough to pick up a couple of girls is actually a pretty calm Friday night for us.

As soon as we get our drinks, my phone vibrates, and I see the text from Blanche.

Mama B:

> I know you couldn't make it to Margot's recital tonight, so I recorded a few clips for you to watch when you get a chance. We miss you!

Fuck. I completely forgot about her big piano recital tonight. We never missed one when we were still living at home, but we haven't been to any since we left for school. I'm filled with guilt as I watch the video. It's too loud to hear the audio, but my little princess looks regal and beautiful as she owns the stage.

"What are you watching?"

I hold my phone out to show Ledger the video of his little sister, and I watch his proud smile grow at the sight. "Did your mom not send you one too?"

"I don't know, probably. Look at her go! She was always so much better than me," he says.

"Do you feel bad about not being there tonight?"

"Eh, maybe a little." He shrugs. "Nothing those two ladies can't fix."

I turn my attention in the direction of his gaze to find two hot blondes looking at us and giggling. Ledger waves and then motions for them to come join us. They stand to head our way, and *goddamn,* they'll certainly cure me of any guilt.

"You guys wanna dance?" the taller of the two asks, her eyes on Ledger.

"Lead the way," he says, allowing her to pull him toward the dance floor as the other girl looks at me with a smirk on her face and her hand held out.

After what feels like hours of this girl grinding on me, my dick can't take it anymore. *Shit,* I know if I'm on edge, Ledger's insatiable ass is ready to go. I pull the girl against my body, making sure she feels how hard I am, and whisper in her ear, "You girls wanna get out of here?"

When she turns to her friend to make their plans, Ledger and I exchange a wink, and I've already forgotten what I was upset about as we all pile into the car, ready to continue our night of debauchery.

Chapter Ten

16 years old

I'm waiting by the window, watching as Edward pulls up in his brand-new candy-red drop top to pick me up for my first date. We're just going to a movie, but I'm an anxious wreck. As if getting asked out by a senior wasn't a big enough deal, he's the star quarterback for the high school's football team. I'm living every girl's dream right now.

Mom comes up beside me, and as if she can read my thoughts, she gives me the extra reassurance I need to get through this night. "Remember, sweetie, *he's* the lucky one. You go out there and make sure he knows it too."

"Thanks, Mom," I say as I wait for Edward to make his way to the door. "And thank you for making sure Dad would be gone when he got here. Can you imagine?"

We're both laughing hysterically when the doorbell chimes. "Have fun! Don't do anything I wouldn't do," Mom says with a wink as she walks away.

Thankfully, my confidence decides to join me again as I greet my date and follow him to the car.

There's a reason the arguably most popular guy in school asked me out. Over the past couple of years, I've gone from a string bean to a curvy queen, or at least that's what Mom calls me. My entire family has been feeding my ego since I was born, but Mom has really gone out of her way since I hit puberty to make sure I know my worth.

Our ride to the theater isn't a long one, and the conversation is entertaining enough. I mean, he's no Einstein, but he's pretty enough to make up for it.

My eyes go wide as Edward gets us two tickets to the only horror movie currently playing. Ugh, I hate scary movies.

He must notice my hesitation as he's handed the tickets because he leans down and whispers, "Don't worry, baby. I'll protect you."

Oof. Entire. Body. On. Fire.

I'm not sure why I was worried about this movie because it's been the perfect excuse for me to cuddle up to this hottie beside me. My body is reacting in ways I've only read about in magazines. I'm pretty sure this is what it feels like to be horny. I'm totally sure I want Edward to kiss me.

We're the only people sitting in the back row of the mostly empty theater, so without anyone's eyes on us, surely he'll make a move soon.

I take advantage of all the theater classes I took as a child and grossly exaggerate my fear at the next jump scare.

"You okay?" he asks, looking down at where I'm nuzzled into his chest.

I look up at him with the biggest puppy dog eyes I can muster and nibble on my bottom lip. "It's just so scary. Can you distract me until the monster is gone?"

The smirk on his face is sinful as he realizes my invitation. "Anything you want, baby."

The kiss seems like it's taking place in slow motion as he lowers his face to mine until our lips meet. *Omg, it's happening. He's leaning down to kiss me.*

I use every tip and trick I've ever read and pour it into this kiss. I let our lips melt together for a moment before opening my mouth slightly to allow his tongue. *Okay,* this *is what it's like to be horny.*

I feel something in my core as he deepens the kiss. The hand that was cupping my face slowly makes its way down my body as our tongues dance.

Without warning, the image of Edward fades into a different man. Edward's brown eyes turn to deep blue, and his black hair lightens to dirty blond.

I pull out of the kiss and half expect to see Jack sitting beside me, but the illusion is gone. "Mmm, baby, you're an excellent kisser."

Baby. Not Princess. Baby.

The memory of Jack telling me you aren't allowed to kiss until you're eighteen flashes across my mind, and I have to force myself not to laugh out loud. What a silly little girl I used to be. All the things I used to say to him and about him. All the questions he somehow managed to answer without laughing in my face.

I wonder if he *knew* I had such a crush on him. He's never given any indication that he would think so, but God, that's so embarrassing. Not that I see him much anymore anyway. Over the past few years, he and Ledger have only ever really come home for holidays. *Sigh.* I miss those guys. One in particular.

I give my best shy smile, but don't acknowledge the kiss comment. "Thanks for distracting me."

"Anytime, you just let me know if you need some help with that again."

"I will," I say, snuggling back into him.

I don't.

I'll be spending the rest of the night thinking about what Jack's kiss would be like. Where his hands would go. *What he would do to distract me.*

Chapter Eleven

Jack

25 years old

I'm not sure what the hell I expected to be doing my first week back from a two-month-long bender in Europe with Ledger, but it definitely wasn't sitting around reminiscing with him and his mom about Margot being a whole-ass adult. We were initially supposed to leave yesterday for a deep-sea fishing trip, but Blanche realized we were going to miss prom by one day and read us the riot act about the fact that we've been gone for so many of Margot's milestones. And honestly, she's right. I didn't think Ledger and I had been *that* absent since we graduated from college, but now that we've looked at school activity pictures from the past few years, not to mention family vacation photos that we weren't there for, I feel like a piece of shit.

We're not avoiding the family, it's just that Ledger's relationship with his dad has gotten more complicated with every passing day, and I can't not be where he is. We're too codependent, so when he runs away from his problems, I follow. Tonight, though, I'm happy we're here. Blanche is in her element, showing us Margot making cheer captain, Margot wearing the first dress she designed and sewed for herself, and Margot beaming at her senior piano recital. She's clearly become every bit of the force I predicted. I wince. *We really haven't been here for a lot of it.* And now she's heading off to college in just a couple of months, and she'll be even farther away. *To Harvard.* Our brilliant girl.

But we're here tonight. We took hundreds of photos earlier—us in informal slacks and dress shirts and her in the pink dress she made herself, looking like a Barbie, as always. Ledger and I gave her little date a long talk about how to treat our princess, and he drove her off in his flashy car with too much horsepower for a high school kid. Finally, Blanche and Ledger go to bed, and I'm left alone, smiling at album after album of all of us as kids. *God, we had it so good.* And I'm an emotional fucking sap.

I pour the last of the second beer I've been nursing down the kitchen sink, ready to settle in for the night, when my cell rings, and it's Margot, calling way before I expected her to be home. I'm thrown back to how I always felt when she had nightmares and woke up screaming, or when she saw a snake in the backyard, and mine was the first name she screamed when she needed help. My skin crawls thinking she's in danger, and I'm already out the door with my keys in hand before I can answer the phone. I don't even stop to put on shoes.

"Hi, Princess. What's wrong?" I ask calmly, starting my car and peeling out of the drive.

"I'm eighteeeeen!" Margot squeals into the phone, giggling, and I slow down a little since it doesn't sound like she's in mortal peril.

"Agreed, Margot. You're eighteen. Are you okay? Why did you call me from prom? You should be dancing with your friends, not talking to an old lame like me," I tease, trying to figure out what made her want to call me.

It's quieter on the phone now, like she's moved away from a group of people, and it takes her a minute to answer. "You were supposed to kiss me when I was eighteen. But you haven't. Not very nice to lie to me, Jack. I always hated it. Butttttt..." She giggles again. "Other guys have kissed me, so it's okay if you don't want to!" She dissolves into laughter, and for some reason, unfamiliar jealousy roils in my gut at the thought of some boy's lips anywhere near my Margot.

That's new.

"Margot, are you drunk? You promised us you'd try to stay tipsy so that you can be safe tonight." I don't want to be stern with her, but her school has a reputation for wild prom nights, and she agreed she didn't want to be a part of that stereotype.

"Well, Jack. I lied," she deadpans, then hangs up the fucking phone.

That little brat. Well, two can play that game, Princess. I track her phone to the prom's location, and after explaining who I am to security, I enter the ballroom to try to find Margot so I can haul her ass home. I make a loop around the perimeter with no luck before I hear a "get *off* me" from a side hallway and take off running, regardless of who it is. But it's my princess, and her sleazy little zit-nosed date has his hand on her tit, which is fully out of her dress, as she weakly tries to push him off and stand at the same time.

If I thought the jealousy I felt earlier was a strong emotion, it's nothing compared to the red haze that falls over me at this scene. Before I'm even conscious of my actions, this fucker is on the floor with a busted lip and a broken nose, and I'm being held back by security. I tell the principal that we won't sue the senator's son for sexual assault if they don't book me for regular assault, and I'm allowed to leave with Margot, who's been relatively quiet the whole time.

We're about halfway home when Margot puts her hand on my thigh and squeezes.

"Thank you for rescuing me tonight, Jack," she says, without removing her hand. "I'm not sure what would have happened if you hadn't been there."

I look over to see that her eyes are much clearer. The bottle of water I made her drink when she got in the car helped to hydrate her and wake her up a bit. Her hand stays on my thigh, but she turns to look slightly out the passenger window, and I get my first chance to take in her profile tonight.

Her golden hair is pulled half back from her face, leaving her button nose and full lips on display. She's gone from being a pretty girl to a stunning woman, with her ocean eyes lined and accentuated with more makeup than she usually wears, and her cheeks sporting a natural blush that extends down her neck to her cleavage. She's filled out in the past couple of years, inheriting her dad's height and her mom's curves, and the pink satin dress she's designed for herself has corseted her breasts to their full advantage. She looks like the princess she is, if princesses were sexy, perfect sirens designed to bring men willingly to their knees.

When we pull into the driveway, my cock, which has been sleeping down my pants leg on the thigh her hand is on, *fucking twitches,* and Margot was always too observant for her own good. Her eyes snap to the movement, then slowly rake up my body, settling on my lips for a three-count before meeting my gaze. She licks her lips and takes in a ragged breath.

"Thank you for rescuing me as always," she says, before *squeezing* my thigh. She digs her nails in for a heartbeat, and then she's out of the car and scurrying into the house.

I release the breath I'm holding and let go of my white-knuckled grip on the steering wheel.

"Always, Princess."

Chapter Twelve

19 years old

"Whoa, Margot, are these from Brad?" my roommate Sara asks as she walks into our shared dorm room, no doubt noticing the bouquet of assorted pink flowers that takes up approximately one-fourth of our tiny space.

"No, *those* are from my boyfriend," I say, pointing at the small vase of red roses on my desk beside a tiny bear I'll inevitably throw away.

"The pink ones are from my Ja...from Jack."

Sara raises an eyebrow at me in obvious need of more explanation.

Sighing, I give her the full story. "Jack is basically like an adopted brother. Him, my two real brothers, and my dad always went above and beyond on Valentine's Day for Mom and me. It was something Dad would do for Mom, and when I came along, he roped the boys into making sure they did it for me. Of course Dad did and still does a little something for me too, but he would let my brothers take charge of my presents. Well, Henry was the first to stop, years after he had moved. When Ledger and Jack went away for college, Ledger stopped as well. Jack is the only one who still remembers. He's never missed a year."

He's really never missed a year. Note to self: remember to give Jack a call later to thank him for the gifts.

"Wow, that's so sweet. I think I need a Jack," Sara jokes, nudging me in the side with her elbow before bending over to get a better look at the bouquet.

I grab the pink diamond hanging from the necklace Jack sent with the arrangement and remember past Valentine's Days.

When I was five, we put on a *Sleeping Beauty* play for Mom. Jack was obviously my prince even though he spent the whole day poking everyone with a wooden sword.

When I was nine, they tried to make me breakfast but ended up setting off the fire alarms that, in turn, activated the sprinklers in the kitchen. Dad was so mad that he made the boys eat everything they had made. They tried to apologize for ruining my breakfast, but it was worth it to watch them suffer through soggy pancakes.

When I was eleven, they decorated the entire house to be my very own wizarding academy and convinced Mom to let us all skip real school for the day so we could undertake our magical studies. There was a potions lab where we mixed fancy drinks, a class where we used fake wands to duel, and we finished our day in the yard with flight lessons. I still can't believe they didn't drop me off the broom I was "flying" on.

"Well, are you doing anything tonight with Brad?"

My thoughts snap back to reality, and I'm reminded that my boyfriend hasn't told me his plans yet.

Sara picks up a card that I must have missed with the flowers. "I think this is for you!"

> Princess,
>
> Will you be my Valentine for the 19th time?
>
> XOXO,
> Jackie

I smile at the same note I've received as far back as I can remember, and my heart feels like it's going to explode out of my chest. I hardly think about Jack anymore, and it's usually always in a friendly, happy way.

Not on Valentine's Day, though.

Every year on Valentine's Day, he asks me to be his Valentine, and every year I let myself escape into that reality, even if only for a moment.

Me:

For the 19th year in a row, yes

I send Jack a text, not brave enough to stomach a call with him today. There's no way I could survive hearing his voice. I'm surprised when he immediately responds.

Jack:

😌 Phew. You had me sweating bullets. Getting a little late with your response there, Princess.

Me:

Well, next year you're going to have to work a little harder than a bouquet the size of my room and a custom pink necklace.

Jack:

Noted 😊

Me:

Really, thank you for the gifts. I love them.

Jack:

Miss you, Margot. I hope you have a great day for real.

Miss you too, Jackie...I would if you were here...

Me:

Miss you too, Jackie 💕

Chapter Thirteen

Jack

27 years old

It's a lovely day to bury a man I really didn't know at all. Growing up, people often assumed I was an orphan. When the Sinclair kids and I were all young enough, my hair was lighter, so I could reasonably pass for Margot's sibling. There were days when we'd all go somewhere, and people would comment, "What four beautiful children you have!" or "Two who take after Mom and two who take after Dad, how perfect." Blanche would beam, and I felt so included, but as we all grew up, it became clearer that I didn't share the Sinclair features.

I think life might have been better as an orphan, for all the good that my father did in my childhood. He existed as a specter, always hovering. An ever-present threat that I could be ripped away from the only home I ever really knew and people I considered to be my true family. The way he operated was cruel for reasons I'll never understand. I'd get radio silence on my birthday or Christmas, then a letter would pop up on a random Tuesday reminding me that if I didn't behave, get all A's, excel at my chosen musical instrument, letter in football...if any of my spinning plates dropped, John F. Carter II would swoop down and pluck me from my life for a worse one, somewhere far away.

The bottom of the bottle of bourbon I started drinking the night before his funeral didn't hold any answers as to why he was like this, and the second bottle that I began this morning isn't looking promising either. Even without answers, I was at least hoping for the numbness that liquor usually promises, but that's elusive as well. It's like I can't let myself fully slip, and I'm pretty sure I know why.

I haven't seen her yet.

My princess. Fucking Margot. Blanche. Sinclair.

Ledger and I have been back to our old ways since the fever dream that was her prom night, and I haven't really seen her since she's been off at Harvard. *God, I'm so proud of her.* She's the best of all of us. Certainly better than me, with the thoughts I've had since the night she touched my thigh and made my dick harder than it's ever been without even realizing.

I was almost certain that she was trying to come on to me that night, but by the time my brain caught up to the situation, she had already gone inside the house. She had just been sexually assaulted by her prom date, for Christ's sake. But the following morning, she was my normal Margot, and the kernel of an idea retreated into the back of my mind. Whatever happened or didn't happen, it was just enough to keep her in my thoughts. Every blonde I fucked started looking like

Margot, to the point that I've been solely pursuing brunettes and redheads for over a year at this point.

I drain the rest of my second bottle of bourbon and pop a third when I'm clapped on the shoulder. Ledger eyes me with concern and replaces my bottle with water. I scowl, but chug it as he eyes me.

"I love you, man, but the people your dad apparently associated with are all pieces of work," he says, glancing over at a group of old, lecherous men who are eyeing up one of the waitstaff passing around hors d'oeuvres.

"Yeah, well. Maybe it's a good thing he dropped me off on your doorstep and never came around," I grumble. Ledger gives me a long, searching look before he sees someone over my shoulder. "There she is! Margot, finally!"

As he's stepping around me to give Margot a hug and kiss on the cheek, I turn to see her for the first time today. She brushes right past her brother dismissively and makes a beeline for me, squeezing me into a bear hug so tight I'm a little wobbly on my unsteady feet. She notices, because *of course* she would, and pulls back to hold my biceps and look up at me. After a beat, she makes her verdict known.

"Jesus Christ, Jack. Ledger, what were you even doing if not keeping an eye on him?" She's giving her brother *the look,* and if it was cute on her as a kid, it's devastating on her now.

"Hi, Princess," I say quietly, but she barely hears me while she berates Ledger for failing to keep me functional today and leads me to a back conference room at the funeral home, shutting us in while she sends her brother on an errand to get some "food to sober everyone up" but I know everyone is just me. I'm the fuckup today. *What else is new lately?*

I feel her hands on my knees and realize she's knelt in front of me, trying to meet my gaze, which is currently trained on the floor as I lean over heavily with my forearms on my thighs and my head bowed.

"Hi Jackie, I'm sorry I was late getting here. A baby was born on my flight, if you can believe it, and it put everyone behind schedule once we landed," she whispers.

I raise my head, meeting her eyes, and imagine her kneeling in front of me in a *very* different setting, then her telling me she's pregnant, then her funeral because I'm a fuckup. I realize something concerning made its way onto my face for her to see, because she's furrowing her brow at me. Nope. Don't like that. Get the facade back up, Jack. Jesus.

I smirk and sit up straight. "It's okay, you really didn't have to come for this fucker's big day, you know. He was an ass, and now he's gone. Easy peasy."

The worry line in her forehead gets deeper as she stands up and leans on the back of the chair next to me. "I didn't come here for him. I came for you."

The bourbon must choose this moment to finally kick in, which, *hallelujah*. But also, *fuck*.

"I'd love it if you came for me, Princess," I say in what I hope is a sexy voice, but sounds kind of slurred.

"What?" Margot responds, which means my well-practiced humor must be failing me. Time to double down.

"I haven't been able to look at a blonde since your prom night without thinking of you, Margot. You're so beautiful, and I..." I trail off when I realize the look I'm getting is love, but not really sexy-love. More like pity-love. Ah, bourbon. You've let me down.

Nah, Jack. You've done that yourself.

"Jack, I love you. Today's messed up. But there's nowhere else I'd rather be than here by your side. Let's go find Ledger and go home, okay? I'll make us grilled cheeses and we can watch a movie," she says, smiling at me and reaching for my hand.

As long as you stay.

"Whatever you want, Princess."

Chapter Fourteen

Margot

20 years old

I swear to God, if I see a rat in here, living or dead, I'll scream, and Jack can just continue his journey to find new depths of depravity. I mean, *honestly.* This condo is like if a frat house had a baby with a landfill, and then the resulting mess rotted in the sun for a week. I don't even know who owns this place, or how Jack got here, but when Ledger called me frantically last night and said that Jack wasn't listening to him any more, I knew it was time to finally intervene. I don't use our private jet often, but nothing is more worthwhile than coming when Jack needs me. *Even if it means missing a piano lesson with someone who flew from Europe just to teach me.* Jack's more important.

If I walk in here and see Jack's vomit, I'm going to hurl. *If there's a woman, or women, in here, I'll do a lot worse than hurl.* I sigh, pushing *those* feelings firmly to the back corner of my mind, under lock and key. That's not a thing. It's not what

I'm here for, and it won't help anybody. I'm here to slap some sense into a dumbass man who's hurting, and even though it's stupidly stereotypical that I'm here to fix a man's mess, I'll always do anything for my Jackie.

Men really are the worst, though, I think, as I step over the remains of what was once a full rack of ribs, by the look of it.

Turning a corner into the bedroom, I finally see him, thankfully clothed and alone, lying on a mattress surrounded by take-out boxes. It's been six months since he buried his dad, and it's past time for some tough love.

Although I was prepared mentally for worse, I'll still be happy to see my prince back on his feet. He looks like shit—hair and beard too long and skin dull from an unbalanced diet. This isn't him. But he'll be back, and soon, if I have anything to say about it. It doesn't take long for me to make a couple of trips from the kitchen to the bedroom and prepare the first aspect of my intervention.

I might take a *smidge* of satisfaction in the way he pops up from the bed, shocked, when the first bucket of ice water splashes across the top of his head. I definitely smirk when he's still getting his bearings, and I toss the second bucket. By the third, which he was still not expecting, I'm full-on laughing, if only at the absurdity of the situation and to keep from crying.

"What the *fuck*?" he cries, sounding more sober than I was expecting. "I yield! I yield!"

His eyes are surprisingly clear despite the alcohol bottles and grinders around the room, so it seems I've come at a reasonable time to stage an intervention. Hopefully, he comes quietly, and I don't have to call in the big guns, a.k.a. my tears. I approach slowly, as if not to scare a wounded animal, and run my fingers through his greasy hair, his eyelids fluttering shut.

"Hi Jack," I whisper, waiting for him to give me his deep blue eyes so I know he's okay. I keep waiting and scratching his scalp. "Jack," I say a little more forcefully, tugging on his hair, "can you look at me please?"

"No," he says, leaning into my hand like a touch-starved dog. "I'm afraid to open my eyes in case you aren't actually here."

My heart breaks a little, but I roll my eyes, thinking he probably just wants a longer head rub.

"I'm really here, but if you don't look at me, I'm gonna stop rubbing your head."

That does it. His eyes snap to mine, and they're both more beautiful and more sad than I've ever seen them. "It's time to stop all this, Jack. This isn't you. The past six months have been awful, but it's time to process in a healthy way. You're booked at a sober-living grief retreat, and I'd like to take you with me today. Will you come?"

I'm not sure if it's anger, hurt, shame, or all three that I see flash in his eyes, but he settles on determination. I can already tell I'm going to have to pull the princess card to pull him out of it. I hate to manipulate him, but I'll take the guilt for that over the risk of feeling that I could have done something to stop this spiral, but didn't.

"Please, Jack," I whisper, getting down to his level so I can let him see how much I hate this shell version of him. "Please do this for me. I need my Jackie back. I can't stand seeing you like this."

The retreat specified that nobody gets help for anyone else but themselves, but I know Jack is ready for his own purposes. I'm just the little push he needs to get started.

"You owe me a kiss, you know. And honestly, I'm twenty now, so you really owe me whatever a kiss plus two years of compound interest amounts to," I say, barely loud enough to be heard in the silent room. "But I really don't want a kiss unless you're sober. My prince is a lot more charming than this."

He holds my eyes for a long few seconds before I see a smirk on his handsome face, looking more like my Jack. "I'm not sure I'll ever be able to pay my way out from under that interest. I might just have to make payments for the rest of my life." He finally chuckles, and it's the best thing I've heard in the long months that we've all been worried sick.

"Well, we can hash all that out with the lawyers once you're fully kissable again. So will you come? Not just for me, though, Jack. It has to be for you, too." I stick out my pinky expectantly, hoping he'll understand how serious I am about what I'm asking.

He rolls his neck back, giving the ceiling a long stare before bringing his gaze back to mine and offering me his pinky.

"Yeah, Princess," he says, and I get a full smile. "Whatever you want."

Chapter Fifteen

Jack

28 years old

I'm not sure how I expected Ledger to react to his father's death, but indifference was definitely not it. He resented Mr. Sinclair his whole life, and as the years passed, that seemed to turn into full-fledged hatred. After my own breakdown for a man I barely even knew, I think I certainly expected Ledger to feel *something*. But as I sit here watching Henry and Ledger casually sip their scotch on our way to the gravesite, I can't help wondering what's going through his head. For someone who usually wears his heart on his sleeve, he's as cool as a cucumber.

Henry has always been able to conceal his emotions—if he even has any to begin with these days—but not Ledger. He's never been able to channel his feelings inward like I do. Or did. If my time at the wellness retreat taught me anything, it's that keeping everything inside can lead to very dangerous six-month benders.

Ledger finally breaks his silence with a question I wasn't expecting today. "What do you think, Jack? Are you ready to start our club? Dad was really the only thing stopping us."

From the time we graduated from college and started slutting around globally, Ledger and I learned quickly that the best places for a good, no-strings-attached fuck were kink clubs. We've talked for years about opening one, but something always held him back. He would blame it on Mr. Sinclair but never give a reason. It wasn't like he needed any help financially. His substantial trust fund could run a small country, so opening a club would barely be a drop in the bucket.

"I don't think Father would've stopped you from opening a club," Henry responds, suddenly taking interest in our conversation.

As much as Ledger liked to say otherwise, the truth is that his father's approval really did matter to him. I know he would have never risked Mr. Sinclair's reputation by opening a sex club.

"Oh, trust me, he would have stopped the kind of club we're talking about," Ledger replies, a devious grin forming behind his glass as he takes a sip of his drink.

Henry raises his eyebrow, letting a smirk grow on his usually stoic face, but doesn't question any further.

Before the conversation can continue, the door opens, and we're escorted to where the remainder of the family is waiting to watch this titan of a man be lowered into the ground.

As expected, Blanche and Margot aren't handling the loss of Mr. Sinclair quite as well as his sons. I've given them both countless hugs today, but there's something different about the finality of this moment that's showing in their faces. Ledger wraps his mom in a bear hug as I feel drawn to the stoic beauty mourning her beloved father.

"How're you holding up, Princess?" I ask, walking up behind Margot and wrapping her in a hug of my own.

She spins in my arms and holds on to me like her life depends on it as her sobs begin to pick up. "Hey now, Jack hugs are supposed to make you stop crying, not cry harder."

A muffled chuckle comes from where her head is buried in my chest. I use one hand to gently tilt her head up toward me before quickly replacing it at her waist and almost melt as her beautiful eyes lock with my own. Like always, it feels like I'm programmed to comfort her.

"It's going to be okay, baby girl," I say, gently stroking up and down her spine.

Her eyes flash with something other than grief, but it's short-lived as the most annoying voice I've ever heard starts calling her name. Before I know what's happening, she's pulled out of my arms into the embrace of another man. My first reaction is to knock this guy out, but it's quick lived as she awkwardly stumbles over an introduction.

"Um, Jack, this is my...boyfriend, Brad. Brad, this is Jack, he's, erm...pretty much like my adopted brother."

"Nice to meet you, Jack," he holds a hand out to shake, but his other arm is still wrapped around Margot. I'm using every ounce of strength I have to keep my fists balled and glued to my side to keep from punching *Brad* for having the audacity to touch my princess.

Margot clears her throat, and my attention goes to her, eyes pleading for me to respond. "Nice to meet you, Brad."

That's all I can manage. I turn and head to the back of the small crowd of people. Watching as another man comforts her in her time of grief. *It should be me.* She used to want *me*. What would I give to have her want me again? I feel myself slipping into that empty pit I used to know all too well when she turns around and immediately finds me in the crowd. *Fuck me*, she's beautiful. I wink at her, and a smile lights up her face. As long as I can still make her smile, it's enough.

Chapter Sixteen

22 years old

As happy as I am about graduating from Harvard—*cum laude, thank you very much*—and as beautiful as this party is, I think my mother invited everyone who's ever known a single Sinclair. I would have been much happier with just the family having a quiet movie night in, like the old days, but Mom's right—certain things are expected to be celebrated a certain way in society. It's fine. I've been promised time with just the five of us soon, but everyone is so busy these days. Mom is always on the go, Henry has Daddy's whole empire to run now, and Ledger and Jack are still in the midst of their wildly successful club's first year.

I've always had a knack for conjuring Jack with my thoughts, and sure enough, before I know it, he's holding two drinks and a small basket and looking up at my hiding spot where I sit in my favorite tree.

"Why are you sitting in my least favorite tree, Princess?" he says, handing me the drinks and the basket and climbing up to sit next to me on my branch.

"Because it's my favorite tree, of course." I laugh, sipping the champagne he's brought me in a plastic cup and opening the basket to see he's grabbed a selection of sweets from the dessert table inside.

"This tree broke your leg!" he exclaims. "I fought hard to have it cut down after that."

"I know you did," I say, still laughing, "but I cried, and you gave that fight up immediately. This tree builds character. Every bone it's broken has been well deserved by an idiot kid."

Stealing one of my cookies, he shakes his head. "I still think if we could've kept you bubble wrapped until you turned eighteen, it would have solved a whole lot of problems."

"Well, I survived, and look at me now, a whole-ass college graduate. And not just any college, *Hahvard, dahling*," I joke, using the affected waspy accent we heard once during the admissions process and found so funny that I don't think Jack has said the word Harvard normally since.

My joking tone dies as I realize he's taken my suggestion seriously and is indeed *looking* at me. Jack has been the member of our family who has always *seen* me, but I've had a sense in the past few years that there have been times he's *looked*, too. I wonder what he sees as his eyes rake across me, sitting in my tree with my champagne and snacks. I think I look polished tonight, wearing a pale pink silk-draped top I made with my favorite jeans. My hair is in my favorite voluminous curls, the side closest to him pulled back with a crystal clip he gave me for Valentine's Day last year. Earrings from a set he gave me a few years ago complete my relatively simple look, and I wish, not for the first time, that I could read his mind.

When he finally finishes his perusal, I'm surprised to see tears not only forming in his eyes but also streaking down his face. He takes a moment and sniffles before grasping my hand and pressing a long kiss to my knuckles. "You *are* a whole-ass college graduate, Princess. I'm so damn proud of you. The past four years have been so tough. You've lost your dad, had to deal with my sorry ass. I don't know what any of us would do without you, Margot. You're the glue that holds us all together."

He's still holding my hand, and I realize what I should have already known. Jack's approval probably means the most to me of anyone in the world. Now I'm crying, and we're still holding hands and blubbering like a couple of losers in a tree.

"Jack, you know I'm proud of you too, right?" I sniffle, wiping my eyes on the sleeve of his dress shirt and making him playfully shove me off. "Your club is doing well, and you're so healthy now, running and working out and drinking your nasty green smoothies."

"Hey! Those smoothies are delicious, and you know it. I put apples and pineapples in them, not just spinach!"

Laughing, I punch at his shoulder, feeling even more muscle than the last time I saw him, which doesn't seem possible. "The taste is all spinach, and *you* know it."

I lean my head on his shoulder and sigh. "Seriously, Jack. I'm so proud of you. You're adulting goals these days. I need to get on your level when I move to New York, or I'll never be able to keep up with classes."

My reminder that I'm moving in a few short weeks sobers the mood as we both enjoy a few moments of silence before we hear my mom calling my name from the house.

Jack turns his head to kiss the top of mine. "You'll take the city by storm. I'm gonna miss the hell out of you, though. You have to text me more. I can't keep finding out about your accolades and escapades only from the group chat."

I laugh, the mood sufficiently lightened as we make our way down the tree. "I promise to text more. You'll get so sick of my life updates that you'll mute me."

"No chance. Now I want a pinky promise on that." He reaches up and puts his hands around my waist to help me to the ground, gripping my pinky with his. His gaze catches on my mouth, and he smirks, reaching to wipe the corner of my lip. "You somehow manage to always have chocolate on your lips, even now."

"As long as you're always there to wipe it off for me, Jackie."

"Whatever you want, Princess."

Chapter Seventeen

30 years old

Blanche guides Margot and me into her house as we bellow our team's fight song at the top of our lungs, still reveling in the victory.

"Yes, yes, the football team is very good this year," Blanche says in reference to Ledger's, Henry's, and my alma mater.

We used to attend games all the time, but over the past several years, making even one a season has seemed like a stretch. The Sinclairs are pretty much royalty at the university. If Henry being the best quarterback to ever come through the school wasn't enough, they could almost bankroll the program with the donations they send every year.

Margot heads straight for the minibar as soon as we get in the house and holds up a bottle of tequila. "Who wants to celebrate?"

Without waiting for an answer, she pours three shots and hands them out. We all clink the glasses together and take the shots, cheering to the big win tonight. Surprisingly, Blanche is the first to finish hers and slam it down on the counter, followed by Margot, then me.

"Alright, that's enough of that for me tonight. I'm going to head to bed," Blanche says before turning to walk out of the den. She's almost out of the room before turning back around and fixing us both with one of her famous Mama B stares. "Are you two going to be alright?"

"Yes, ma'am," I say as Margot rolls her eyes.

She squints as she stares us down a moment longer before saying good night and leaving.

Finally alone, Margot fills us both another shot and holds one out for me. "You'll stay with me, won't you, Jackie?" She may be a little tipsy, but she knows exactly what she's doing when she bats her big eyes at me. "Pleasseee."

This is probably a terrible idea. I try my best to keep my thoughts platonic, but it's not like I'm oblivious to the way my body reacts to her. The truth of the matter is that I'm just incapable of turning her down. If the princess wants it, she gets it, and that's how it's always been.

"Margot, you know I can't drive home if I take any more of those shots." We both know that's a horrible excuse. I've had a room in every Sinclair house since they took me in twenty-five years ago.

Her eyes are already gleaming with triumph. "You can just stay here tonight! Come on, you have to stay so we can discuss the fact that Ledger has a *girlfriend*! Seriously, is the world about to end? Have you ever known him to date at all?"

She's not wrong about that. Ledger's obsession with Sloane took me by surprise just as much as anyone. He had some short relationships in high school, but once we started college, he never saw the same woman twice. Neither of us did.

With a sigh of defeat, I take the shot of tequila from her hand and swallow it down in one gulp. Margot squeals with excitement before doing the same with her own.

"Oh, I know! Let's play a game!" she says, clapping her hands before grabbing our glasses and the bottle and dragging me to sit down beside her on one of the sofas, apparently forgetting all about her inquiry of Ledger. "Truth or dare. If you don't answer or you refuse the dare, you have to take a shot. But! If you take a shot, you have to go again, and you *have* to either do or answer what comes next. You go first. What do you want, truth or dare?"

"Um, truth, I guess."

She wiggles her eyebrows before looking at me. "Do you have a girrrlfrieeend like Ledger does?"

"That's funny. No, I don't."

I can't help but notice how she lights up a little at my admission. "Okay. Truth or dare."

"Hmm. Truth."

"Do you have a boooyyyfriend?" I try to mimic the way she said girlfriend, the alcohol causing her to cackle like a hyena.

"Nope, I'm a single lady." She gives a little shimmy for emphasis, which has me laughing hysterically this time.

"Okay, dare this time." Margot pauses for a moment to think before giving quite a diabolical laugh. "I dare you to text Ledger and tell him you think Sloane is the most beautiful woman you've ever s..."

I shoot my drink back before she can finish her sentence. "That was *not* fair, and you know it! I know not to accept another dare from you. Truth this time."

"Fine." She gives an exaggerated eye roll. "Who *is* the most beautiful woman you've ever seen?"

"Easy. You are, Princess."

"Ha. Ha. Very funny."

Her playful demeanor fades when she finally takes notice of my intense gaze. "I'm not laughing, Margot. Truth or dare?"

"Truth," she whispers.

There are so many things I could ask, so many I would love to ask. But for the first time in years, our relationship has been on good, healthy terms, and if I complicate things right now, I could lose one of my very best friends. "Am I still your favorite brother?"

She's silent for a moment, and I can tell she's thinking hard about how to answer this. "Jack, honestly, I've never really seen you as a brother. You've always been, well, more. So, no. You aren't my favorite brother." She's been looking down at her thumbs fidgeting during her answer, but when she looks up, she has the saddest smile I've ever seen on her face. "Still truth?"

I nod.

Our eyes are still locked on each other as she asks her truth. "Do you think of me as more than just a little sister?"

Fuck yes. I've always seen her as more. The problem is, that's changed so much throughout the years, and I don't know exactly what *that* is because I've never allowed myself to unpack those feelings. Her eyes search mine for any indication of a nonverbal answer. I should lie. I should lie and tell her no. I most definitely can't tell her yes.

Instead, I do the only other thing I can think of. I take a shot, maintaining eye contact the entire time. I couldn't look away from her if I tried. My admission causes her eyes to widen and her breath to hitch. "Jack...I dare you to kiss me."

"Whatever you want, Princess." What I wouldn't give to taste those beautiful lips of hers. Instead, I lean over and kiss the top of her head like I've always done. When I sit back, the disappointment on her face almost kills me. *God, if she only knew how disappointed I am as well.* I have to force myself to do the right thing and go to my room.

"Good night, baby girl."

Chapter Eighteen

Jack:

Please explain to me why I just found out about your recital in Carnegie Hall next week? Where is my invite?

Margot:

OMG, so dramatic...Mom was supposed to tell you!

Can you come?

Jack:

I have a business dinner that evening in NYC already...

I'll see if I can get them to push it back.

Margot:

Don't do that! Seriously, it's not a big deal.

Jack:

It is. You're playing with the Philharmonic! Even if you weren't…

No way would I miss this, Margot. You're more important than the business. Always.

Margot:

Pinky promise?

Jack:

Pinky promise, Princess. You're more important than anything.

Margot:

WHO is the woman with you in the club's post from today?

Jack:

?????

Margot:

The platinum blonde! Your arm is around her, and you look pretty cozy.

Who is she?

Jack:

That's Stella, one of our new featured performers for theme nights. She's a contortionist and is going to do some circus-themed stuff for us.

Margot:

Oh.

Jack:

Jealous, Princess?

Margot:

I just thought it was weird. I usually don't see you with blondes.

Jack:

You're the only blonde for me.

Margot:

I better be... 😊

Jack:

Why is your location in the middle of a field at 3 a.m.??

Answer your phone, Margot. This isn't funny, and I'm not laughing.

Margot:

Some of my friends invited me to a country music rave!

It honestly sucks, but they have a frozen daiquirita machine...

You should come!

Jack:

I'm in another state, Princess. You need to go home.

I just called your driver. He'll be there soon, and you're going home with him.

Margot:

I'm fine, Jack…seriously. I've had like two drinks. We're just dancing. You're not my dad.

Jack:

You're right, I'm not. If I were, I would have spanked you more and let you get away with less, and you wouldn't be such a brat, putting yourself in dangerous fucking situations.

Margot:

You want to spank me?

Jack:

At this moment? Yes. You have no idea how badly.

You can't just be out at 3 a.m., Margot. That shit isn't safe.

You should have told me you wanted to go to this thing, and I could have flown up to be with you.

Margot:

Have you ever wanted to spank me before?

Jack:

…You told me you weren't drunk.

Margot:

I'm not…

Jack:

Answer your phone, or the next time I see you, I'm absolutely spanking you.

Jack:

Who is this asshole you're hugging on your page, and why are you in Miami?

Margot:

????

Jack:

This guy. Blond. Tall. Skinny like a string bean.

Margot:

You used to call me string bean. Was that an insult??

Jack:

Don't play dumb and try to deflect, Margot. Who is this asshole?

Margot:

I've hugged a lot of guys in my time, Jack. I didn't post anyone. He must have tagged me. Sometimes I forget how old you are and that you don't understand how Instagram works.

Jack:

That's twice now you've just gone off to party with people I don't know, Princess. It's like you want to piss me off.

Margot:

Maybe I do.

Maybe I was told bad girls get spankies.
And maybe I want spankies, Jack.

Jack:

Jesus Christ, Margot. When are you
coming back to NYC?

I had meetings in the city today, and I
had hoped to see you.

Margot:

☹️ If you had told me, I wouldn't
have come to Miami.

Jack:

This is why you should stay where I know
where you are at all times, Princess.
Then I can make sure to come see you at
the right time.

Margot:

But one good thing did come out of this
trip. Look at how nice my tan is in my
new bikini!

Jack:

I'm going to spank your ass raw for letting anyone else see you like that, baby girl.

Margot:

Anyone *else* huh?

Jack:

Anyone*

Either turn your location back on on your phone, or send me your address.

We'll go to dinner and then I'll escort you back to NYC.

Margot:

Jack:

Okay, Princess. We'll do this the hard way. See you soon.

Margot:

????

Jack:

?? What?

Margot:

Can this call wait? I'm busy.

Jack:

Busy doing what? It's like 10 p.m. I wanted to tell you about the fuckup at the club tonight so you know why your brother is losing his mind.

Margot:

I'm preoccupied.

Jack:

....

Do you have a guy over? Is it that fucker from Miami?

I swear to God, Margot, you can do so much better than him.

He's not worth your time.

Margot:

NO, JACK!

Nobody is here except me.

But I was trying to masturbate, which you've now ruined with your interrogation, so thanks for that.

Jack:

Masturbate?

Margot:

Yes, Jack. Relief. Masturbation. Flicking the bean.

Battery-powered fun times. Self-love.

Jack:

Okay, I can't listen to you talk about masturbation anymore

I'm sorry. Just. Let's move on. Jesus, I wish I had never asked.

Margot:

Fine, we can move on.

Jack:

Thank you.

Margot:

Mr. Bean GIF

Chapter Nineteen

Margot

23 years old

Ugh, go away. I've been trying to ignore the knocking on my door, but whoever it is is persistent. Finally taking my eye mask off, I sigh dramatically as a glance at the clock confirms it's *way* too early to be getting out of bed on one of my precious days off. I wrap myself in a robe as I make my way to the door, wondering who in the hell would be banging on my door at nine o'clock in the morning. *"Please don't be a murderer,"* I repeat over and over until I lift my peephole and see Jack waiting with a bouquet of pink flowers.

I swing the door wide open and jump into his arms, barely giving him time to realize what's happening in order to catch me. "Jack! What are you doing here?" I scream, holding on to him as tight as humanly possible.

He walks me inside and tries to set me down, but I refuse to let go. Tears begin to run down my face, and I finally admit to myself that I was upset about not being able to go home for Thanksgiving this year. The moment Jack realizes I'm crying, he sets me down on my kitchen island and cups my face with both of his hands, using his thumbs to wipe away the tears. "Hey, hey, what's wrong, baby girl?"

He's standing between my legs in an embrace that feels more intimate than any we've ever shared.

"It's just...you're here!" I say between sobs.

"Well, I felt so bad that you couldn't make it home this year, so I decided to come to you. I couldn't leave my best girl alone on Thanksgiving."

My arms are back around his neck, pulling him closer to me as I revel in having not just anyone here with me today, but my Jack. We only stay like that for a moment before we both seem to realize the new position has his *most definitely hard dick* lined up with my *most definitely wet pussy*.

Well, at least my tears are gone.

Jack steps back, allowing me to hop down, and turns to discreetly adjust himself while I sneak away to get myself somewhat ready for the day. The urge to go full glam is hard to resist, but since Jack is dressed casually in gray joggers and a long-sleeved tee, I match the vibe with leggings and an oversized sweatshirt.

Deep breaths.

Making my way back into the living room, I watch as this beautiful man wanders around, taking everything in. This is the first time he's been in my apartment, and it's heartwarming to see him so interested in my home.

Holy shit, this is the first time he's ever been in my apartment.

We've been alone in a house before, but something about being alone in my relatively small one-bedroom space increases my heart rate. We could do *anything,* and nobody would be here to stop us.

"Well, what do you want to do today, Princess?" he asks, bringing me back to the moment.

You.

Sigh.

"I was just planning on watching the parade in my pajamas, ordering way too much food, then getting cozy on the couch and probably falling asleep watching Christmas movies."

Jack plops down on my couch and pats the seat beside him. "Let's do it, then."

I walk around the couch and sit down where he requested, allowing him to position me with my legs draped across his lap. He gets the parade turned on the TV, then starts massaging my feet just like when I was younger. It's been years since anyone has given me a foot massage, and when he hits a pressure point, I can't stop myself from letting out an involuntary, "Mmm. Don't stop."

I realize just how sexual that sounded around the same time I feel his dick start getting hard under where my ankle rests against his thigh.

Jesus, he feels huge.

I think about excusing myself again and avoiding the situation, but if we're ever going to get through this day, we've got to get past this tension. "Damn, I don't know who's getting the most out of this massage." I put the slightest bit of pressure on him where my foot rests before pulling my feet back and giving him a little light kick to the side of his head. "Do you need me to go get Mr. Bean to help you too?"

Jack grabs my foot away from his face and casually throws it off his head. "*Brat*. If you didn't sound like you were in a goddamn porno instead of getting a foot massage..."

"Hmm, I'm not sure a foot massage isn't better than sex anyway."

Jack's head snaps to mine. If looks could kill, I'd be dead. The anger on his face contorts into an expression I can't decipher. He has a brow raised, and his mouth is locked in a battle between trying to smirk and biting his lip. He opens his mouth to say something, but just shakes his head and turns back toward the TV, chuckling.

Chapter Twenty

30 years old

Fuck. *Fuck.* I must be the most masochistic asshole on the planet to think that spending a holiday alone with Margot was a good idea. This has been the best Thanksgiving I can remember, and it's all because I've spent it with my girl. I've laughed more today than I have in a month, and to end the day with my head in her lap as she plays with my hair is perfect.

I try not to think too much about the fact that she made my dick hard twice, and fully fucking knew about it both times. She was flirty as hell, and although our texts had been trending that way, I was in no way expecting our in-person interactions to be just as charged. Today was an exercise in restraint, considering how much I wanted to go full caveman and pin her down and make her mine.

I'm dozing off while she quotes Christmas movies line for line when the alarm on my phone goes off, letting me know it's time to wrap up and get back to the jet. Business never sleeps, and we have a Black Friday alternative event tomorrow for people who need to fuck out some energy after spending today with their family.

Can't relate. I'd spend every second in Margot's presence if I could. I really, really don't want to leave...*then don't. Tell her. Go full caveman.*

The devil on my shoulder has been increasingly unhelpful over the past month, especially since Margot came back for the football game. Living in NYC for her master's degree has her busy, but she's taking it all in stride, and I swear she's more confident than ever. She radiates joy and is so damn funny. I've been a little obsessed with her all my life...but the flashes of heat I've felt periodically since I picked her up from her prom five years ago seem to be getting more frequent, and I'm almost positive she feels the same way.

That way madness lies.

Yeah, thanks, angel on my shoulder. I'm totally fucking aware of the fact that this would implode my entire life as I know it. I'm also more and more aware of the fact that I can't go one day without texting her, let alone thinking about her, and every time I see her with another man, I practically lose my ability to function for hours as I stew with rage.

You dramatic son of a bitch. Use your calming techniques.

Whatever, I'm warm and I'm cozy and I'm not going to worry about feelings I can't control.

"Jack!"

I sit straight up and look around for danger and why someone's yelling, only to see Margot looking at me in concern.

"Jack! Your phone alarm has been going off for like a minute and a half, and I tried to shake you awake or pull your hair, but you wouldn't budge! Is that your alarm that you have to leave?" She looks sad at the thought, and I reach down to silence my alarm.

I turn back to tell her this is the best Thanksgiving I've ever had, and I'll always be her best friend, and thanks for hosting. I really have to go, but she has chocolate ganache from the brownies we ate earlier on the bottom corner of her lip, and my entire existence narrows to that smudge.

I slide closer to her on the couch, the length of my thigh parallel to hers, and move into her space until we're nose to nose. I can smell her undeniably Margot scent mixed with sweet chocolate.

I stay there, staring into her perfectly blue eyes until I decide.

Fuck it.

I tilt my head and lick the chocolate off, gently sucking her luscious lower lip into my mouth to make sure I get it all, before pulling back and staring again. Her eyes are closed, and her chest is rising and falling more rapidly than a minute ago.

"Princess," I whisper, and her eyes snap open again to meet mine, then briefly to my lips, and back to my gaze.

Before I can tell her I'm sorry, and I shouldn't have done that, and please don't change a thing about our relationship because you're my best friend, she speaks. She's always been braver than me.

"I think you missed a spot," she whispers, and I'm done. I reach my hand up to gently cradle her jaw, stroking her chin and committing her face, right now, to my Mount Rushmore of lifetime memories. *If I actually take time to think about it, they might all be Margot.*

There isn't anything left to be said. I lean in and meet her lips as my world tilts irrevocably on its axis, and I give my princess the kiss she's been owed for years.

Chapter Twenty-One

Jack:

I made it home safe and sound.

Thanks for letting me crash your Thanksgiving.

Margot:

I had the best time.

I wish you didn't have to leave so early.

I liked having you around.

Jack:

I can come back any time.

Just say the word and I'll be on my way.

Margot:

Will I get a kiss every time?

Jack:

Hmm, I don't know.

If you'll recall, I owed you that kiss.

Margot:

Yeah, like 5 years ago.

Jack:

Better late than never…

Margot:

Well, if YOU'LL recall, I was charging interest.

I'll have to do some calculations to see just how many.

You still owe me, but I'm pretty sure it's a lot.

Jack:

😉 I look forward to paying off my debt.

Jack:

You looked beautiful tonight, Princess.

I'm so proud that you won your class's design competition for the quarter. Not at all surprised, though.

Margot:

Thank you, Jack

I only won evening gown, though. I didn't win for the category I was most excited for.

Jack:

What did you submit that didn't win?

The judges clearly had a lapse in taste.

Margot:

selfie in mirror wearing a pink and white lingerie set

Jack:

I'm sorry you didn't win that one, Princess. But I do wish you hadn't submitted it.

Margot:

I didn't submit it. I lied.

Jack:

Margot...who did you make that for?

Margot:

You...

Margot:

Let's play truth or truth.

Jack:

Truth or truth?

Margot:

Yeah, it's like truth or dare, but since we aren't together, we can't really do dares.

Did you get off to that lingerie I made for you?

Jack:

😈 I'm going to have to take a shot, Princess.

Margot:

Ugh, no shots. Just truths.

Jack:

mr bean gif

Margot:

Ha. Ha. Ha.

Seriously?

Jack:

I've thought about that picture more than I would like to admit.

Alright, your turn...

How many other men have you worn lingerie for?

Margot:

Idk. 2 maybe 3.

Jack:

Are you telling me I have to kill 2, maybe 3 people?

Margot:

Well, it's better than the thousands I'll have to kill.

Jack:

You jealous, Princess?

Margot:

I used to be.

Jack:

Not anymore?

Margot:

Nah.

Now I'm just glad you've had all that practice so you'll know what to do if I ever let you see that lingerie in person.

Jack:

I can tell you one thing, baby girl, It'd be better than a fucking foot massage.

Jack:

When will you be home for Christmas break?

Margot:

In a few days, why??

Jack:

Well, besides the obvious fact that I want to see you...

Your brother is having a crisis with Sloane.

Margot:

Oh...and here I was thinking you had a date or something planned.

Jack:

You want to go on a date with me, Princess?

Margot:

I want to do a lot with you, Jack...

Jack:

Mmm, you and me both.

How about this? Help me get Ledger straightened out and then I'm all yours for the break.

Margot:

All mine, huh? Pinky promise?

Jack:

Pinky promise.

Margot:

That means I can do ANYTHING I want with you?

Jack:

Jesus, you're killing me, baby girl.

Chapter Twenty-Two

23 years old

"Come on, Margot, let's let the newlyweds have some alone time."

Jack congratulates Ledger as I give my new sister-in-law one last hug. "Welcome to the family, Sloane. I'm so happy to finally have another girl around. If Ledger gives you any trouble, just let me know."

"Thanks so much, I'm sure that'll be sooner rather than lat...Ah!"

My brother picks his new wife up and jogs her up the stairs. "You losers get out of here. I have a marriage to consummate!"

Jack throws his arm around my shoulders and walks me to the car.

I've always *loved* weddings. I was that little girl who kept a folder packed with her wedding plans. I wonder if Mom still has that somewhere. It would be fun to look back at what preteen me thought would be a *classy* wedding. The one thing I know hasn't changed is that I want it to be a huge to-do.

Ledger and Sloane's wedding was beautiful for how last minute it was. He literally proposed earlier tonight after winning a fighting competition. I'm sure the photographer will get a hefty bonus for all the editing it's going to take to clean up some of the cuts and bruises on his face.

He and Jack apparently spent last night decorating his house and planning the whole ordeal before he finally caved and hired someone to come in and help get things set up. Red roses covered almost every surface of his house, making it look like a sea of crimson. The only guests were Jack, a friend of Sloane's, and me. It was intimate in its simplicity and seemed perfect for my brother and Sloane too, from what I've heard about her.

A small wedding isn't for me, though. I would want the entire world to know I was married.

When we both get buckled up, I look over at Jack, and from the look on his face, I don't think I'm the only one in a post-wedding haze. "This is weird, right?"

Ledger has never even brought a girl home. Neither of my brothers has. Or Jack.

"Yeah, this is definitely weird," he says as he starts backing out of the driveway and using one hand to get the hot air turned up to full blast and my seat warmer on. "Don't get me wrong, I'm happy for my brother. But, I don't know. I guess I'm both a little sad he's not around as much and a little jealous of the reason."

"Jackie...why have you never had a girlfriend?" I ask him as he stops to check for traffic before pulling onto the road.

He turns to face me, allowing me to see a moment of sadness before switching back to his usual charm. "Well, I was under the impression I was going to have to marry your bratty ass, so what was the point?" He reaches over to pull a strand of my hair before fixing his gaze back on the road and pulling out.

"Seriously, though, Jack, why?"

Silence fills the car, and Jack shifts into a faster gear. I'm about to ask again when he answers. "Well, for the longest time, I was just fucking around with Ledger. We were young guys with no sense and too much money in our trust funds for our own good. Then my dad passed away, and you remember how I was. I wasn't in any shape for a relationship. I was barely back on my feet when Ledger and I opened the club. And then for the last little while I've been...never mind."

Jack's hand is still resting on his gear stick, so I place mine on top. The touch sends a shock through my body, barely allowing me to get out my question. "You've been what?"

"I've been hung up on someone," he says, flipping his hand around to interlock our fingers, then pulling our hands over to his thigh. The implication takes my breath away.

It seems neither of us can think of anything else to say. I turn on some Christmas music to cut the silence in the car and hold on to his hand for dear life, only letting go when he has to switch gears again. His desire for our contact seems to mirror mine because every time he has to let go, he quickly finds me again. Our hands continue that dance the entire way to my mom's house.

We walk to the house, still hand in hand, but he lets go as soon as I open the door. The confusion painted across my face is question enough.

"I can't stay tonight, Princess." He steps closer and gently wraps a hand around the back of my neck before placing a soft kiss on the top of my head. "I'll be back soon, though, I promise."

I wrap my arms around his waist and pull him into a hug. "You pinky promise?" I ask, not having any interest in letting him go to actually link our pinkies.

"Pinky promise, baby girl." He places another lingering kiss on my forehead before he turns and walks away.

Chapter Twenty-Three

30 years old

After taking the night to cool off, I'm finally able to make good on my promise and spend some time with Margot. I couldn't have gone inside with her. Our relationship has been complicated for years, but the past couple of months have taken that to new levels. Something happened in that car that we need to discuss. *Talk.* And I know without a shadow of a doubt that if I had gone inside with her last night, talking would've been impossible. *Well, for her at least.*

Watching Ledger get married last night was just too emotional for both of us. That's what it was. Today will be fine. We can catch up on things and hang out like we usually do.

"You came back!" Margot launches herself into my arms the moment I open the door, sending shivers through my body.

And removing any confidence I had that I would be able to function properly today.

I return her hug, squeezing her until she squeaks. "Of course I did, Princess. We pinky promised, remember? Where's Blanche?"

"Oh, she's still at her rehearsal. Won't be back for another hour or so."

Fuck. I was counting on Blanche being here to babysit us. Keep her adopted son from losing his mind over something as simple as holding hands like a horny teenager and fucking her daughter on every surface of this giant-ass house. *Fuck.*

Be cool, Jack. Just keep the conversation moving.

"Oh yeah, I forgot about that. I can't believe she didn't rope you into being in it like she did Ledger. You're a much better actor than he is."

Margot drops my hand, her perfect posture slacking as she looks away. "Um, well...I stopped doing that years ago."

"But you loved acting. What happened?"

"Mom and I had a big falling out over a role I had in a play she was directing when I was in high school, and we both decided it was probably best if we didn't work together like that anymore. It honestly helped our relationship tremendously, so I'm not mad about it."

How did I miss that? Of course something had to have happened for her to stop acting. But I'm such an asshole, I didn't even realize she had stopped. I missed so damn much of her life. Even now, I barely know her. We text pretty much every day, but I'm missing things. I'm practically a stranger. "Fuck, Margot, I...I missed so much."

"But you're here now." She steps into me, my hands naturally falling to her waist as hers clasp around my neck. I watch as the desire in her eyes grows as our embrace continues.

By some miracle, I'm able to step back, putting enough space between us so I can think straight again. "Margot, as much as we text, I still feel like strangers compared to how close we used to be, and that *kills me*. I can't go another day without knowing everything that's been going on in your life."

Margot sighs dramatically. *Hasn't acted since high school, my ass.* "Fine. Come on, let's get comfy."

I follow her to the living room and plop down on the couch opposite the side she's sitting on with a rigid posture. "Relax, this isn't an interview. I just want to know what you've been up to."

Time flies as I listen in awe while Margot tells me about her many endeavors. I don't know why I'm so surprised by it all. She's always been brilliant and headstrong. I feel like I've been stretched to my limit just managing the club, but here she is, navigating her time between different jobs, organizations, and projects while keeping a perfect GPA in her accelerated master's program.

Realization hits me like a ton of bricks. I'm going to be in New York very soon, getting Ledger's and my new club up and running. *I'll be so close to her.* I was planning on getting an apartment closer to the club to cut down my commute, but I would much rather be closer to her. *I wonder if there's an open apartment in her building.*

The word *Paris* snaps me back into reality like a bucket of ice-cold water. "Wait, what do you mean you're going to Paris?"

"Don't worry. I haven't accepted the position yet. I have another couple of weeks to decide."

"Why wouldn't you go? That sounds like the opportunity of a lifetime." The horror of her going to Paris is quickly replaced with the horror of her *not* going. Design has been her dream for years, and this is a crazy opportunity...

I don't even realize she's moved until she's on my lap, straddling me with her hands resting on my chest. Again, my hands find her waist like it's the most natural thing in the world. "Well, I've been hung up on someone."

She bites her bottom lip, her attention alternating between my eyes and my mouth. Any restraint I might have been holding on to goes out the window the moment she grinds down on my already hardening cock. Her eyes roll into the back of her head as she releases the sexiest moan I've ever heard in my *life*.

I allow myself to fall into whatever this is and lean in to kiss her. Our lips have barely touched when we hear the door from the garage open. Margot scurries out of my lap like I'm diseased and scoots as far away as possible on the couch, sitting as straight as a board.

"Margot! Hurry and get ready! Your brother is married and has *zero* Christmas decorations up, so we've got to...oh, Jack!" Blanche says, finally making it into the room. "Great, you can help too! Well, what are you two waiting for? Up, up, up! Let's go!"

Chapter Twenty-Four

23 years old

Mom hands us all a glass of champagne, toasting the happy couple. "To Sloane and Ledger!" she exclaims as we all clink our glasses together with a cheer. "And to grandbabies!"

It didn't take long at all to put up the decorations with five sets of hands helping, but I'm still amazed they were able to get rid of all those flowers from last night. Apparently, my brother is commissioning some kind of artwork to preserve them all.

Mom, Sloane, and I stand around the spread of food, talking about the wedding while Jack and Ledger go sit down.

"So, tell me everything," Mom requests. "I will forgive you for not inviting me but you better not leave out a detail."

Ledger chuckles from the table beside us.

"Oh, for the love, Ledger. Please leave out those details."

After getting every drop of detail we can squeeze out, Mom turns her attention to me. "You better include me in your wedding plans, missy, or I will absolutely never forgive you."

"Don't worry, Mom, you've got plenty of time to prepare. I've made it through four years of undergrad and am almost through my master's without any prospects, so I doubt there are any wedding bells in my near future."

"All the more reason to spend some time abroad!" she exclaims.

"I know, I know. I have two internships lined up between New York and Paris. I just haven't decided yet," I admit, glancing briefly at Jack to find him chewing on his lip and looking down at his plate.

"If I were a single twenty-three-year-old, I would try to find the sexiest Frenchman I could and climb him like a tree," Mom says, fanning herself with her hand for dramatic effect.

Mortification floods my mind at the thought of Jack hearing that. "*Mother!*" I hiss.

Her only response is an eye roll. "Oh, you're a boring bunch," she sighs.

Ledger walks over to grab Sloane. "Trust me, nothing is boring over here," he says, wrapping himself around his wife in an embrace I crave so desperately from the man still sitting at the table.

"Ledger!" Seriously *gross*. When did he decide I was old enough to start talking about his sex life around me?

Mom elbows me in the side. "Well, *you* give me a grandbaby, then!"

I lift my eyes to see Jack's cheeks blush as he pops a cookie in his mouth. Then I watch that slight blush darken as Ledger lays his threat. "Oh no, you don't. You're not allowed to date until you're thirty, remember? Don't think I won't make good on my promise to beat any fucker who lays a hand on you."

I roll my eyes at my brother, hoping he doesn't notice how I freeze up when Jack starts choking on the cookie. Thankfully, he doesn't have too much time to think about it before Sloane saves our asses. "Speaking of grandchildren, let's show your mom the room you had put in for the nursery."

The moment they're out of the kitchen, Jack towers over me from behind and cages me against the island with his arms. "The thought of you with another man makes me murderous," he whispers in my ear.

Chills run across my body as I try to turn in his arms, but he pushes closer, trapping me in place. He's so close now I can feel his hard length against my back. *God, I want that inside me.* I want him to know exactly what that does to me as well. "Mmm," I moan, laying my head back against his shoulder.

One arm wraps around my waist, his hand on my stomach, while the other brushes my hair to the side so he can pepper my neck with kisses. As his mouth goes lower, so does the hand on my stomach, and *Jesus Christ, I'm going to burn alive.* I feel like I'm about to combust when fingers dip into the band of my jeans, and his distraction finally allows me to turn around.

There's definitely lust radiating from him, but he's startled as well. The moment that panic takes over his expression, I grab his face with both of my hands and kiss him. His mouth opens for mine when our lips meet, he's just as hungry as I am. Jack cups my face, his giant hands wrapping around my entire head, as I lower mine to his chest. As gentle as his grip is, his kiss is the opposite. The one we shared on Thanksgiving was sweet, but this is a tidal wave washing us both away with passion.

As the kiss deepens, I lose all sense, trying to pull his shirt off like a woman possessed because *God, I need him to take me on this island, the rest of the family be damned*. He must feel it too, though, because he's grabbing my ass with bruising force, and he backs me up against the counter, pressing his even harder erection into my stomach as he devours my mouth...

Sloane's voice is the first we hear, reminding us that others are present tonight. I pull myself away from Jack, nearly losing my balance, and grab my champagne glass to hide my swollen lips.

"Alright," Mom says when everyone makes their way back into the kitchen. "Let's give these two newlyweds some privacy."

They walk us out to Mom's car, where we say our goodbyes. I'd rather sit in the back, but Jack opens the passenger door for me and insists I sit up front. We go back and forth a few times *because dealing with my mom right now is the last thing I want* before Jack discreetly motions toward the tent in his pants, and I concede. I'm trying to ground myself so I don't catch my mom's attention, but when she rolls down her window to yell "Grandbabies!" at my brother and his new wife, Jack pulls a strand of my hair.

As predicted, Mom immediately notices how flushed I am. "Margot? Are you okay, dear?" I don't miss her glance into the rearview mirror to look at Jack, but he's looking out the window.

As good as I am at fooling people, I've never been able to get things past her, but that doesn't stop me from trying. "Not really, actually. I think I drank way too much."

To my surprise, she seems to buy it, placing a hand on my leg and giving me a little pat. "I'll get you home as fast as I can, honey."

Chapter Twenty-Five

Jack

30 years old

I never had a doubt that Ledger had finally found his perfect mate in Sloane, but if I had, *fuck,* her standing up to her parents tonight would have convinced me. My life has been, for all intents and purposes, pretty damn easy. Sure, I gained a complex or two along the way, considering I had an asshole of a dad who abandoned me and a mom who died when I was young. But I knew what real parental love was, thanks to Blanche. I never had to wonder if I mattered to her or if she cared about my happiness. She proved time and time again that I was a priority, and I was only one of four kids who were depending on her. I don't know how she did it.

Sloane's parents, though. I wince, thinking about the things they said to her tonight, especially her piece-of-work mother.

Blanche wanted to have a little celebratory dinner after the Christmas play she directed, but the newlywed couple thought it would be the perfect time to tell Sloane's parents they were now married. Long story short, her mom showed up with her asshole ex, who started a crap ton of drama and effectively caused Sloane's parents to disown her.

And to think that poor girl is an only child, so she didn't even have anybody to commiserate with as a kid, or anyone to take any of the pressure off with humor, like I tried to do tonight. I take another sip of my drink, thinking again about how lucky I was to grow up with siblings. Without Henry, Ledger, and...Margot, I gulp, I wouldn't be where I am today.

I zone back in to my surroundings in time to see Margot and Sloane continuing to pass out gifts from underneath the tree. Ledger keeps trying to get Sloane to sit down and relax, but she keeps swatting him away, talking about being a good host for the first holiday in their home. Margot brings me a present and adds it to my growing pile, giving me a little wink as she bends over in front of me. God, she's beautiful. She's always been pretty, but now, in the glow of the Christmas tree, she's devastating, more confident in who she is as a woman...everything. Leave it to Margot to wear pink, even on Christmas Eve. My own personal Barbie, always.

My eyes follow her across the room, but she makes her way to Ledger next, and I remember precisely how defensive he's always been when it comes to Margot. None of her boyfriends have ever been good enough for her, according to Ledger, and while I've always vehemently agreed with him, I'm also well fucking aware that I'm not good enough for her. And I'm sure he'd agree. The thought of him being mad at me, or worse, disappointed in me, threatens to send all the holiday treats I've eaten tonight right back up my throat. He's never said anything directly to me about Margot being off-limits, but I know it's only because it probably hasn't ever once crossed his mind that I would cross that line. It would be the ultimate betrayal to have her in the ways I want.

Not to mention, Henry, who, despite being older and not around as much, has been there for me whenever I needed him. Even more so with us getting our club off the ground. And Blanche...I can count on one hand how many times she's been pissed at me in my life, and I'm pretty sure I cried like a baby every single time I thought I disappointed her. And now I want to take their princess and defile her in all the best ways.

But I also want to spoil her. Give her everything. Protect her, fight for her, be her partner...and continue being her best friend just like always. Would that be enough for the Sinclairs? Even if I'm not the man they imagined for her, could I be enough?

We could have Christmas just like this, in a bigger house because Sloane and Ledger will end up with a football team of kids. A big spread of food and a million presents under the tree. Too many stockings for one mantel to hold. Margot, wearing a pink silk dress, turning to the side to show the profile of her baby bump as she gives me a wicked smile and gestures subtly toward the staircase for us to sneak off...

That way madness lies. I know. *I know.*

The worst question that I despise myself for even asking...if it was a choice between her or them, which would I choose? She's the only true happiness I'll have in this world, I know it deep in my soul. But they're the only family I've ever had, and the only place a lonely little kid has ever felt at home. And when she inevitably realizes she deserves so much more than me? She'll leave and take them with her.

Fuck. I'd lose her too. I can't lose them. I won't.

Chapter Twenty-Six

23 years old

If my mother says "the Christmas *feeling*" one more time, I'm tying her up with garland in the attic and not releasing her until Valentine's Day. She's been so excited to have me home from school that she's continued her madness the week after Christmas, and we've been having so much mother-daughter time that I really haven't seen Jack. Mom and I have been too busy crafting, baking, watching holiday movies, and *planning next year's decorations* that I've barely had time to breathe.

I know it's been a week of getting back to work for him with a huge party coming up tomorrow at the club on New Year's Eve, but still, he's been distant. We had a great time as a family opening presents all together, and it made me realize what I've known for a while now—we're *meant* to be. He's family, and everyone loves him, so we could easily and seamlessly transition into a romantic relationship without missing a beat. No need for all the getting-to-know-you awkwardness of dating, or worrying about whether our families will vibe. I'm sure he's just busy. Plus, even if he had come around, Mom has been monopolizing my time. Maybe he realizes that, and that's why he's stayed away.

Finally, after a long-ass week, Mom informs me she's leaving for a girls' New Year's trip with her pickleball team, and before I can so much as chastise her for the short notice, she's out the door. *Well, okay then.* Monopolize my visit home, then leave, why don't you? Typical Blanche, though, so I'm not even that surprised. I *am* a little surprised when Jack finally texts me. He was sporadically available earlier in the week, but as NYE has grown closer, *the club* has had every ounce of his attention.

The club. His mysterious, highly successful endeavor with Ledger, Rendezvous, has become increasingly Jack's responsibility since Ledger has been busy with his new full-time job, Sloane. Not that I've ever been allowed to even cross the threshold of said club. Some sort of older brother bullshit has led me to be on the no-entry list since it opened even though I'm of age. *Whatever.* I can have plenty of hot sex on my own without needing a club to do it. And maybe it's better this way, since I really have no idea what Jack gets up to when he's there. He texts again, and this time, the chime pulls me from my thoughts.

Jack:

> Happy New Year's Eve Eve, Princess.

> What are you and Blanche up to tonight?

Me:

Well, well, look who finally resurfaces and deigns to give attention to us mere mortals.

Jack:

...

Me:

😐 You're no fun. Mom is gone on a trip with her pickleball team, so I'm just going to order food and binge-watch something new, I think.

Jack:

She left knowing you'd be there alone?

Me:

I'm a big girl now, Jack. I can handle staying in big houses at night alone now, no problems.

Jack:

That's bullshit. I know it, and you know it.

Jack:

> Order my usual pad Thai, and I want double spring rolls.

> I'll be there at 8.

It's the house settling, Margot. That's all it is. It's a big historic home, and they always settle at night. Or maybe it's just the wind. Either way, the creaking is perfectly natural and for sure normal and not *some terrifying murderer coming in here to get you and kidnap you and torture you.* There are fences and cameras and alarms and codes. *And one good hacker like in your books could override all that in one second and slowly creep in here to...**creak*

That's it. That's the creak that does it. Before I can even question myself, I'm out of my room like a shot and frantically scrambling across the hall into Jack's. I'm so glad he stayed tonight. Even if he was a gentleman and kept to his side of the couch despite me making it clear I was ready to take advantage of the fact that Mom was gone, we had a great night eating too much and talking about nothing.

And now, as I throw open his door and launch myself at him, practically shaking from the way I've managed to work myself up over an intruder, I'm *really* glad he's here.

"Oof...wha..." he mumbles, and I realize I've knocked the wind out of him by landing on him like an overexcited puppy. Oops.

I burrow myself all the way under his covers until his arms are around me and my face is pressed against his chest before I let myself breathe and feel safe again. Oh God, he's shirtless. My face is pressed against a warm, muscled chest that's covered in the perfect amount of soft hair, and he smells so damn good. A little like his soap, a little like his cologne, and a little bit that's just his natural Jack smell because he hasn't showered since this morning. I feel something against my cheek and realize it's a chain he has on with a small charm, but before I can reach for it to see what it is, his arms tighten around me, and he buries his face in my neck.

"Fuck, Princess, next time warn a man before you launch yourself into his gut while he's sleeping," he rasps in a sleepy voice that sounds like pure sin. Immediately, I forget all about my fears, feeling safe and warm in his arms. I'm also more than a little turned on.

I sigh as he pulls back from my neck to look at me in the soft moonlight filtering through the window. "Did you have a nightmare? I thought they mostly stopped when you got older?"

Smiling, I shake my head. "Not a nightmare, just me freaking myself out being in this big old house at night. I kept hearing little creaks and psyched myself out. I don't know why my parents couldn't have gotten a new build when they decided to move closer to the city."

"Well, I'm glad you remembered you can always come to me," he says as he tucks a piece of hair behind my ear. "You were always so damn cute when you would scamper into my room at night, scared of whatever horrors had befallen Sprinkles in your dreams."

"Hey! Some of those were extremely traumatizing, I'll have you know!"

Laughing at me, he leans a little farther back, giving me some space which I really don't want. "I'm sure they were. Now, if you're staying, get comfy so we can go to sleep. It'll be a long day tomorrow with the party at the club."

I huff, but roll over onto my preferred side, basically making me Jack's little spoon. Except, he leaves the space between us. Screw that. I shimmy my way backward until I meet his hard body and tuck myself exactly where I want to be. I give a little extra shake of my hips just to fuck with him, when...*oh.* Oh God. It's his dick. I've only let myself daydream about it a *little bit* lately, because my obsession was getting out of hand. But fuck me. It's huge, hard, and tucked up against my ass. I give another experimental roll of my hips, and the added pressure causes Jack to let out a low, pained groan behind me.

"Margot, we need to sleep, baby. It really is a long, important day tomorrow."

"Take me with you."

He sighs and tries to stop my teasing, but I'm getting something out of this little trap I've managed to set for him, dammit. If he was going to fuck me, he wouldn't have come to sleep in his own bedroom, but I'm leaving here with *something.*

"I want to see the club! I'm grown, Jack. *Please.*"

"Ledger will kill us both if he finds you there. I can't." He sighs, and he sounds so sleepy and desperate I almost take pity on him and give up my bargaining. Then I think of something I want to see even more than the club.

"Take me to your place, then. I have to have *some* fun tomorrow night, and if I can't have it with you, then..."

He snaps and pulls me back into him hard, bringing me closer than I have been all night. If I lifted my leg, his cock could slide right between my legs, and I know it wouldn't meet any resistance at all, I'm so turned on.

"You're not doing anything with anyone else tomorrow night. You're going to be a good girl, and go the fuck to sleep, and tomorrow night, I'll figure out how to do my very important job and also appease your curiosity regarding my living situation. Deal? Please say deal and stop. Rubbing. Your. Perfect. Ass. On. My. Dick," he says, punctuating each word with a mini thrust and leaving me whimpering.

"Deal," I say, when all I want to say is *please, please fuck me right now.*

He releases me with a grunt and backs up, separating our bodies but leaving one hand against my lower back, like he can't not touch me. "Get some sleep."

I don't think there's any way I'm sleeping tonight, not this close to him and with the promise of seeing his home tomorrow. *If I fall asleep, tomorrow will be here faster*, I think, and I drift off, hoping to dream of the man beside me.

Chapter Twenty-Seven

Jack

30 years old

You could cut the tension in the air with a knife as I shut the door behind me, leading Margot into my penthouse. I knew agreeing to bring her to the city tonight would be hard, but the moment she walked out of Blanche's house, I was a goner. I've never seen anyone as stunning. Her long-sleeved navy blue velvet dress hugs her body like a glove. It's a low-cut design, showcasing her ample cleavage, and her golden-blonde hair is pulled up in a clip to accentuate her swan-like neck. I've viewed her as a woman for years now, but seeing her all dolled up for *me,* well. It's the first time I've really seen her as *my woman.*

I'm not sure if taking her to dinner first made a difference. At first, I was relieved, thinking it would give me time to cool down from my initial caveman instinct to drag her to the nearest surface and impregnate her, spreading my seed to the best specimen alive. But all it's done is build up tension, so I still want to drag her to my cave and make her mine, but now, I don't ever want to let her go. At least I've been able to see her in this dress a while longer.

"Wow, Jackie. This is incredible," she says, walking around admiring my home.

There isn't much personality to it besides being a newly renovated, open-layout penthouse with floor-to-ceiling windows, boasting an impressive view of the city, especially after dark. I've always been something of a minimalist. My therapist says it's because I grew up with the lingering threat of having to leave all my things. It's the stark opposite of Margot's style. Every space she's ever occupied has overflowed with character and charm. When we were growing up, she would bring that character into *my* room. If there was ever a mess or clutter, it was from her. One I would never clean up or put away *because it was a reminder of her.*

I'm leaning with one foot propped against the wall and my arms crossed, watching her finally take notice and make her way over to the grand piano in the corner of the living room that I had craned up here before I even moved in. "Why do you have this? You don't play."

"No, but you do."

She sits down and removes the cover, running her fingers over the keys. "Do you say that to all the girls you bring up here?"

I kick off the wall and stalk toward the goddess sitting across the room from me, making a mental note not to ever be this far away from her again. Finally standing behind her, I reach down and place my hands on her shoulders, my thumbs rubbing gentle circles on the back of her neck. "Nobody else has laid a fucking hand on that piano, Margot."

A slender hand reaches back to grab one of mine, and we're frozen in a moment that seems to last forever and not long enough.

"Jackie…"

"Yes?"

"Take me to bed."

My heart stops.

Margot stands and walks around the bench so that nothing separates our bodies before weaving her hands around my neck and giving me her ocean-blue eyes. The ones I've never been able to resist. "Please, Jack. Just for tonight. Please."

I should have more reservations than I do or, at the very least, consider the reason I've been keeping my distance for the past week. There should be some concern about the consequences of taking things past the point of no return. There's no illusion that this would only be for one night. That we would be able to wake up tomorrow morning and carry on with our lives as if nothing had ever happened. But a world doesn't exist where I could ever tell her no.

"Whatever you want, Princess."

Her breath catches as she smiles and tiptoes up to kiss me, but before our mouths meet, I sweep her into my arms and carry her bridal style into my bedroom.

The lights from the city illuminate the room as I gently set my princess down on the edge of my bed. *How will I ever be able to sleep in a bed without her?*

I kneel before her like the lowly subject I am, not deserving of the air she breathes, and start unlacing her strappy heel. Her dress's high slit allows me to pull her leg up enough to kiss from her bare foot up to where her thigh meets her lacy panties before moving to the other thigh and kissing my way back down to unlace her other shoe.

"Lie back, Princess," I say, breaking the silence in the room. She doesn't hesitate to follow my command, just slowly lies back, propping herself slightly on her elbows so that she can look down at me with those beautiful blue eyes full of desire. I stare into them as I slowly pull her thong down her legs, hoping she can see from my own gaze how much I need her, before dipping my head under her dress. My first look at her pussy steals my breath. *I've never seen anything so perfect in my life.* The only thing allowing me to look away is my need to taste her.

I part her lips with my fingers before running my tongue from top to bottom. *God-fucking-dammit.* Her little moans and breaths as I worship her are rewiring my brain. I'm going to fucking die between her legs because I sure as hell can't think of anything that could make me move.

"Ja...Jack...I need you. Inside me...p..please."

Well, I guess that will do it.

As soon as I come back up, she's reaching behind her back, fumbling to unzip her dress but getting it down nonetheless. And just like that, she's clad only in that damn lingerie she made for me. I've jacked off to that image of her countless times, but the picture she sent doesn't do justice to the living, breathing woman sitting in front of me. I reach out and gently place my hand around her neck, giving her just a little squeeze, then slowly run it down her chest to her breasts, feeling the fast rhythm of her heart beating behind my touch.

She reaches behind to unclasp her bra, causing her heavy tits to fall free. I lose any confidence I might have had in my ability to make love to her. She must feel my hand tremble. "Jackie, what's wrong?"

"Just a little nervous, baby girl."

She places her steady hand on top of mine to stop the shaking. "Don't be silly. It's just me..."

Leaning my forehead against her grounds me enough to speak. "Just you? Margot, there is no *just you*. It's all you. *Everything* has always, only *ever* been you."

I pull back to look into her eyes, searching for any doubt that might finally knock some sense into me, but all I find is love, and I can't stand it anymore. Taking her mouth in a kiss, I seal the fate of our night and the rest of my life.

Chapter Twenty-Eight

23 years old

If Jack's proclamation wasn't enough to completely melt me, this kiss is. Hello, my name is Margot, and I now identify as a puddle. Because he's always been everything to me too. For twenty-three years, he's been the axis my world spun around. Always in the back of my mind. Always in my heart. And *God,* have I wanted him.

When he was a cute little boy with curly golden hair, I wanted him to hold me every time I fell and kiss every scratch. Then he grew into a heartthrob teen, lanky from growing tall so fast, but with washboard abs that stood out in the summer, when his skin was golden from being outside without a shirt every day. I was still a little girl filled with fantasies of being a princess, and I wanted him to marry me and be my Prince Charming. When he went off to college, he was hardly ever at home, but I was learning to become a young woman. Every picture posted online, showcasing how much he was filling out, would make me feel things I didn't quite understand. Somewhere along the way, he grew into the man he is today. His once unruly golden hair, now clean cut and light brown, his muscles fitting his six-foot-four-inch frame, and his style reflecting that of a man with his life together. Somewhere along the way, I became a woman, learning good and well what his pictures made me feel. And somewhere along the way, every boyfriend I had morphed into Jack when I closed my eyes.

I pull out of the kiss to finally get what I've yearned for, for years. "Jack, I need you."

And do I ever. If sex with him is anything as good as what he just did with this mouth, I'm in for a great time. It's not like I've had many sexual partners. It's just been the two long-term relationships I had in undergrad, and apparently, neither of them had a clue what they were doing.

He climbs off me, and even though I'm spread naked on his bed, his gaze never leaves my own. I might be a little self-conscious of the fact that he isn't looking at my body were it not for the fire burning in his eyes and the tent in his pants.

He starts his striptease ever so slowly, unbuttoning his shirt and letting it fall to the floor before kicking off his shoes and moving on to his pants. When he gets to his boxers, I watch in equal parts hunger and horror as the biggest dick I've ever seen springs free.

I've had nothing but confidence this whole time, but seeing how large he is makes me the slightest bit nervous. My eyes lock in on his dick as I try to figure out how we're going to get that inside me, and he must sense my apprehension. "Trust me, it'll fit."

My eyes snap up to find him smirking. *The arrogant bastard.* I hate that he knows it'll fit. God, how many women has he used to test that theory? If there has ever been anything I've been more certain about, it's that no woman has ever taken him the way I will.

And no woman ever will again.

Jack takes a step toward me before freezing in place. "Shit. Hold on, baby. I'm just going to grab a condom real quick."

"No! I mean, I'm clean, and I'm on birth control, and I trust you, and...and I just need to feel you."

A fire I've never seen before lights in his eyes before he stalks toward me, following me on the bed as I crawl backward until I hit the headboard. He pulls me to lie down before climbing over me, encasing me in his arms, and searching my eyes once again. "Are you sure, baby girl?"

All I can do is nod.

His hands roam down my body until they find my pussy, groaning when he feels how wet I am for him. The moment he sinks two fingers inside me, I release a moan of my own.

"Fuck, Princess, you're so *goddamn* tight," he says, fucking his fingers in and out of me in a slow but brutal pace for what seems like an eternity.

Eventually, he removes his fingers and grabs the base of his dick, rubbing it up and down and lubing himself with my arousal. He lincs himself up at my opening, his wide head already spreading me more than I've ever been. My eyes close in anticipation of the initial pain this stretch will cause when he cups my face with his other hand, resting on his forearm. "Open your eyes, baby girl."

I do as he says, and the view of him above me takes my breath away. *I can't believe I was about to miss this.* I've imagined this exact view countless times, but those fantasies didn't do justice to the living, breathing man above me.

"Princess, I would never *ever* hurt you. Just relax, okay? Just look in my eyes."

He mirrors my nod as he gently brushes the hair that's fallen in my face, then he's sinking into me, inch by inch. The stretch is euphoric, and he was right. The pain is barely even noticeable. He keeps going until he's deeper than I thought was possible, and when I think I really can't take any more, he finally stops with his hips fully flush against mine. I bite down on his shoulder to mask my scream as he seats himself fully inside of me. He was already trembling with the effort of holding himself still but my bite seems to threaten his resolve, and he exhales a ragged breath.

"Goddamnit, Margot. Fuck, you feel so good."

When he's given my body enough time to adjust to him, he pulls back to his tip before sinking back into me. Over and over and over, he thrusts into me, each filled with so much passion and longing. It's not frantic or rushed. He's not just trying to chase a release. No, he's savoring each time he's sheathed inside me. Praising me with his words as well as with his cock.

"Fuck, you're incredible, baby. So fucking perfect. Taking me so well. You're perfect. You know that, right, baby girl? The most beautiful, brilliant, perfect woman in the world. And goddamn this fucking cunt. I could stay buried in this tight little pussy forever. With your gorgeous body wrapped around mine. Fucking irresistible. I'll never get enough. You're a goddess, Margot."

I'm not just some girl he's brought back to his penthouse. He's not just fucking me. No, I'm his everything. He's making love to me.

I never close my eyes as he worships my body, sending wave after wave of pleasure crashing into my body. I never take them off *my Jack*.

Chapter Twenty-Nine

Jack

30 years old

My princess walks back into the bedroom, and while I would rather have her without any clothes at all, I can't deny how gorgeous and how *Margot* she looks in her pink satin babydoll nightgown. Her hair is brushed out, and her makeup-free face is glowing from her nighttime skin regimen, looking fully sated. And *fuck me* if this isn't my favorite version of her yet.

Nighttime might be a stretch since it's well into the morning. The plan was to take her to dinner, then bring her back and watch the fireworks on my balcony. *I guess we weren't too far from that. There were definitely fireworks.*

I'm sitting propped up against the headboard of the bed when she climbs in, snuggling up to me like it's the most natural thing in the world. And I guess it is.

She's barely made it into bed when she starts to doze off. I know she's tired. That's the whole reason I stopped fucking her in the first place. No, that's not right. *Not fucking.* I was worshipping her, trying with every bit of my being to show her how much she means to me. If this were the only night I would ever have her, I wanted her to feel just how deeply she's ingrained in my soul. And just in case my actions weren't enough, I told her exactly how perfect she was.

And she was perfect. *Is perfect.* Will *always* be my perfect, brilliant girl. I watched in awe as I drew orgasm after orgasm from her flawless body, delighting in the melody of every moan that came from her lips. I held off as long as I could for the first one, lost in the beauty of our bodies tangled together. But as my release came and went, I knew I couldn't stop. Not ready for our connection to end, I just kept driving into her. It wasn't like my erection was going anywhere. Not with my princess naked and writhing in pleasure beneath me. The other half of my soul.

"I love you, Jackie," she says, snapping my attention back to the present, where she's still in my arms.

God, I love you doesn't even scratch the surface of how I feel. How do I use words to tell her how I truly feel about her? *I love you too* feels like a poor imitation of the real thing. How do I put into words just how she's the axis my entire world spins around?

Before I can think of what to say, she's out, sleeping so soundly in my arms. I reach over and grab my phone to take a picture of my Sleeping Beauty, but when I see multiple texts from Ledger, panic sets in.

How the fuck does he know? I'm trembling as I open the messages, expecting the absolute worst. I told him I wouldn't be able to make it tonight, but there is no way he's found out why.

Ledger:

> The club looks amazing. You outdid yourself.

> I'm looking forward to seeing what you do in New York.

> I'm sorry you weren't able to make it, but maybe it's for the best.

> If you had been here to witness the little show Sloane put on, I would've had to kill you.

I'm finally able to breathe. *He doesn't know.* For now at least. Fuck, he's going to kill me.

It'll be fine. We can keep our relationship to ourselves for a while, at least until I can prove to them that I can do right by her. She'll stay in New York with me, and we'll be fine.

Until she realizes she made a mistake by not taking this internship. I would follow her to Paris in a heartbeat. I would tell Ledger that I couldn't do the renovation and would find a worthy replacement. But then I would have to tell him why I was bailing, and he would kill me. It's not enough time.

I've spent a decade with him, fucking our way around the world. Until he met Sloane, neither of us had even been in a relationship. Falling so deeply in love with her may make him understand that I can change too, but no way in hell is he letting me test that theory on his sister.

She would have to stay in New York, and she may be happy for a little while, but I *know* she would eventually resent me. I resent myself for even thinking about it. She would leave me, taking my entire family with her. That's the whole reason I had been avoiding her in the first place. *A week*. I was able to stay away from her for a whole week.

No, she has to go to Paris, and I have to go to New York. And then I have to pray to God that the Atlantic Ocean will be enough to keep me away from her.

Tears fall down my face as I realize what I have to do. I have to get up, but *how do I let her go?* I look down at my entire reason for existence and hold on to her for dear life, refusing to release her until the last possible second.

Trying my best not to wake her, I roll her off me and quietly get out of bed. The sun is starting to rise as I gather up enough of my things to make it until I can get to a store for more. I jot down a note, the nail in the coffin, *hopefully* assuring she goes to Paris.

"I love you too, Princess," I whisper, pressing a kiss to her forehead as I have countless times before. The memory of the way her lips felt against mine already haunts me. I grab my phone and finally take that picture of my Sleeping Beauty. A memory frozen in time. A reminder of where my heart is, in case I ever forget why my chest feels so empty.

Chapter Thirty

Princess,

I'm so fucking proud of you, Margot. You've worked your ass off, and you deserve to enjoy it. Go to Paris. Find the sexiest Frenchman you can and climb him like a tree. Live every second of your life to the fullest.

Xoxo,
Your Jack

Chapter Thirty-One

TWO YEARS LATER

If I could be less of a sap for one second, that would be *great*. Leave it to me to tear up yet again as I hang up custom bunting of tiny blue and pink boxing gloves over Mom's mantel. I just can't believe my big brother is going to be a *daddy*. Sniffling, I try to keep my hands busy, but since I arrived home yesterday, I've been so emotional thinking about how lucky we all are to be welcoming this baby.

Sloane and Ledger spent a few months in Paris last year while they were traveling, and she's become the sister I never had. I could never imagine anyone taming Ledger, but she's beyond perfect for him. As perfect as Paris was, after we got so close during their visit, I just couldn't stand the thought of being so far away from my first little niece or nephew, so it was perfect timing for my internship to end and for me to move back home. With my dream online lingerie boutique taking off enough to have stores in Paris and London, coming home to open one in New York was the perfect excuse to leave my French life behind and return to the States, at least for a bit.

Finally getting the bunting just to my liking, I turn to move on to my next task when Mom intercepts me.

"Darling, the New York store called again. Marco wanted to confirm the pop-up collaboration for Valentine's Day. I provided him with all the feedback we discussed and informed him that you can sign off on some of the visuals once you're back in town. Now, as far as the summer collection, I wanted to see if you wanted to revisit the neon moment..."

As much as I hate to say it, it's been more of a blessing than a curse to have Mom involved in my first solo business venture, La Reine. After an internship project for a department store in Paris turned into a capsule collection for another well-known brand, I realized that while lots of lingerie was *so close* to exactly what I wanted to wear, there was always a little something I'd want to change. Finally, I decided to pretend I was a man and use my unwavering belief in myself to just go for it. La Reine started with a fake name, and my family had no clue what I was up to. I didn't tell them it was my company until I was getting ready to open my second store. Now, I'm happy to have my mom's help, and we've had a ton of fun designing and brainstorming together. Sometimes we have spats that remind me of the high school play that almost broke our relationship, but for the most part, it's just been fun. She loves to meddle, though, and I realize she's still talking when I hear her say a name I haven't thought about for the better part of two years.

"So I told Jack that we had talked to Ledger and Sloane already, and he agreed it would be a perfect opportunity for us all to work together and showcase the Noir collection! They'll be setting up the logistics for the Valentine's Day lingerie date auction, and we just have to do the fittings so that all the dates feel their best when they're on stage!" Mom finally finishes, and I'm just as amazed as I was as a child at her ability to go so long without taking a breath.

Working to keep my face neutral and hide my annoyance at the fact that she even brought Jack into this, I try to get a word in edgewise. "Mom, I really wasn't aware that Jack would be involved. He didn't come up once in all of our discussions, and I don't think..."

"Oh, don't be ridiculous, Margot, it's *his* club! He's the one who's been in New York working so hard to get it off the ground. You'll be *so* impressed, darling. He's worked like a dog, and it's finally paying off, especially with how low he was after his father died..."

She continues, but if I was half listening before, I'm not paying her any attention at all now. Because the *he* that she's droning on and on about just walked in, and either I'm having a stroke or my feelings of love and hate are canceling each other out because...*Earth to Margot? Are you in there? Can we turn ourselves off and back on again?*

I feel numb? Neutral? It's like I know everything and nothing about this man. He's the same Jack I left, tall and with light brown hair that's just a little longer on top than I remember. One thing that isn't the same, though, is the fact that Jack is *jacked.* He looks like he's spent every spare moment of the past two years in the gym, more overtly muscular than the effortlessly strong Jack I knew. It's...*nice*...to see him, and honestly, *good for you, Margot,* for being such a strong woman. You're certainly not the girl who left two years ago to build a new life for yourself after the perfectly good one you already had came crashing down.

Maybe that wasn't ever actually my reality. People don't *actually* end up with everything they've ever wanted in real life. That's the stuff of fairy tales, and maybe those are better left to little kids with nightmares.

In any case, no reason to cry over spilled milk, and I'm really only in the US for a little while. Sell lingerie, spoil this baby, get dicked down by a circumcised man for a change of pace, and head back to Europe for hopefully my fourth store. Maybe Italy this time...I'm strolling swiftly into a daydream about a man I met in Venice, Antonio, when Mom's impeccable timing again disrupts me.

"There he is! My darling Jack, it's been far too long, and you text too little. I'm so glad you could come," Mom says, and I feel a looming presence behind me until Jack steps around me to embrace her.

"I wouldn't miss it for the world, Blanche," he replies, and I swear to God this man's voice has gotten deeper in the past two years.

What the hell. Why am I thinking about the raspiness of his voice? I haven't had a single thought like this since about four weeks into my life in Paris, when I decided to grow the fuck up and be an adult about a fling that obviously meant less to him than it did to me. I had fully expected to come back and just avoid him, but now Mom's giving him the full rundown about the Valentine's Day lingerie plans.

"And I told them that you would have it all handled, Jack," Mom says, beaming up at him as he smiles down at her.

"It is. Those vendors all signed last week, and we're actually ahead of schedule on the other vendors for the evening. I did book a different catering group than we discussed, which I hope is okay. It's actually led by a Michelin-starred chef who travels to different cities and establishes catering companies that employ people with nonviolent criminal histories and people recovering from addiction. He's had a lot of success, and I've been using them for quite a few events lately."

"*Of course* that's fine, Jackie," my mom says with tears in her eyes, looking up at Jack like he's St. Valentine himself. "That's just the sweetest idea. You've been working so hard for years, and for you to still find opportunities to help others is just precious." She sniffles, wiping her eyes before turning to me. "You better snap yourself up a man just like Jack while you're in New York, Margot. I doubt the Europeans can compare."

With that, and a gentle pat on Jack's cheek, she's flittering off to put up some of the finishing touches around the house before guests start arriving.

Jack has frozen and looks like he's seen a ghost, but I can feel every ounce of color that's leached out of his face rising to mine tenfold.

My mother wants me to find a man...like *fucking Jack?*

Oh, this is rich. This is just fucking *rich*. Which Jack does the great Blanche Sinclair mean? Jack Carter III, hero of my childhood? My prince and protector, always there to make me feel like the princess he called me? A man who grew up in front of my eyes and was as perfect for me at thirty as he was at ten? The nature of my love for him might have changed over the years, but it was as true on the day that he dismissed me from his life as it was from the moment I snapped into consciousness and my first memory was of his face.

That Jack Carter was a man that any woman would be proud to call hers, whether as a friend, a lover, a coworker, or in any other way she could have him. He was loyal, and brave, and strong. And I shouldn't *have* to "find a man like him," as Mom says. I had one. I had *the* one. The archetype. Or so I thought.

Too bad he was a massive *fucking fraud* who took away our chance to have it all.

If that Jack Carter *ever* existed...well. He ceased to exist two years ago, for reasons unknown to anyone but himself. The only Jack Carter I know now is a coward, and the best thing I've ever done for myself is spend two years in Paris to become the kind of strong woman who really doesn't give a fuck.

But the idea that my mother still has him on a pedestal...I can't help the red that seeps out of my pores and glazes across my eyes. A joke. What a *fucking* joke.

I can't stop the scoff, *or was that a snarl,* and the eye roll that escape, and before I even realize what I'm doing, I'm turning on my heel and stepping away from him.

He tries to stop me. "Margot, please..."

I'm saved from his annoying begging by the front door opening to Henry. I hasten to greet him, leaving Jack behind and vowing to avoid him like the plague when I'm in New York, auction be damned.

Chapter Thirty-Two

Jack

Two years and there she is. I want to take her away and never let her go again. What an idiot I was not to hold on to her in the first place. For a while, every moment of silence I had would be spent thinking about her. Until I couldn't take it anymore. I put my head down and worked seven days a week to get Rendezvous Too up and running. Whatever energy I've had left after a fifteen-hour workday, I've been burning off at the gym, making sure that by the time I get in bed, I'm too tired to let my mind wander to her. Thankfully, most nights I'm even too tired to dream because when I do dream, it's *always* of her. When I do dream, I wake up with whatever bit of heart I've regrown ripped out all over again.

It didn't take me long to realize the major mistake I made. I was in New York, Ledger was preoccupied with Sloane, and Blanche and Henry were too caught up in their own lives to make frequent visits. We were all scattered in the wind. And I missed them all, but none so much as Margot.

I realized all too late that she was worth it the whole time. That even if all she gave me was a month, it would be worth losing everything I've ever known and loved. I realized all too late that once I had her, living without her wasn't life at all.

By the time I came to my senses, finally ready to sweep her off her feet, I found that she was living just fine without *me*. If her social media and updates in the family group chat were anything to go by, she was happy.

And that was enough.

So I let her chase her dreams. I let her live her life. Live *our* life. Because the only life I'll ever have is her.

"Jack, dear, can you do the honors?" Blanche's call for help brings me back to the moment.

Right, Ledger and Sloane's gender reveal. I head into the kitchen to get the punching bag filled with either blue or pink powder and wheel it back to the expecting couple.

"We thought this would only be fitting, considering the night you, um, got married," I say, glancing at where Sloane's parents are sitting in the corner. Being careful not to word vomit like I did the last time we were all together. "Sloane, you're welcome to do the honors, I suppose, but I think this was designed for our dad-to-be."

Fuck. My brother is about to be a whole-ass *dad*.

Sloane steps back, letting Ledger take the reins. "I haven't fought since that night either, but I'll give it a go." He rips through the material with one punch, sending blue powder flying into the air.

"It's a boy!" the entire room screams in unison.

"Hey! A little Ledger!" I say, bringing the happy couple out of their little bubble of bliss after what I feel is an appropriate time to grope each other in celebration.

"Oh *Lord,* let's hope not, for everyone's sake," Blanche responds, making her way over to congratulate her son and daughter-in-law.

She's not wrong. The older I get, the more I realize how much trouble the two of us caused growing up. Ledger especially. A little boy. Wow, a little Ledger *indeed.* Poor Sloane really is going to have her hands full if he's anything like his dad.

I look over to where Margot stands with tears welling up in her eyes. With everyone preoccupied with the news of the baby boy, I allow my gaze to linger on my princess for the first time in two years, fully taking her in. This is the longest I've gone without seeing her in her whole life, and she's...changed.

She somehow looks both older and younger at the same time. Although her skin glows and her features remain as youthful as ever, her style has matured. Her long hair is pulled up in a clip instead of flowing down her back, her posture is more rigid, and instead of the pink frills she used to wear frequently, she's sporting a charcoal pantsuit.

She's still the most beautiful woman I've ever seen.

I've done my best to get on with my life since leaving for New York. It took several months after realizing we were never meant to be, but I was finally able to numb the feelings down to a slight sting. Seeing her like this, though...they're all flooding back in.

If I ever guessed Blanche would've approved of our relationship, maybe I wouldn't have left. That wouldn't have changed the fact that Margot would be sacrificing her dreams, but maybe we could've made it work long-distance until we could figure something better out.

We could very well be married by now. I certainly wouldn't have needed time to figure out if she was *the one*. *She's always been the only one.* I don't think she would've been ready to have a baby so soon, but what if she did? Or even if it wasn't planned, accidents happen. This could've been us. I wonder if that smoke would've been blue or if we would be preparing for our own little princess. One with her mother's blue eyes and free spirit.

I'm lost in my thoughts about how it would feel to be celebrating our own child when her voice brings me back. "Soooo do you have any names picked out?"

"Well, I think Ledger Jr. would be perfect," Sloane replies.

Wow, our baby boy would be a fourth if we went that route. Unless I took her last name and officially became a Sinclair.

"You know Henry the fourth is always an option," Henry says, pulling me out of my fantasy.

"Ew, you weirdo, it's not *your* son," I remind him, honestly forgetting he's not referring to Margot's and my baby.

Henry uses his hands to massage his eyes. "It doesn't *have* to be a direct father-son succession, you buffoon. But I doubt I will have any children of my own, and it would be a waste of a fourth."

Blanche hits the back of Henry's head. "Oh hush, you will absolutely have some of your own. All three of you will," she says, pointing at Margot and me in the process.

Margot turns a deep shade of red as I choke on nothing, bringing Ledger's attention to me. "You alright, man?" he asks, smacking my back.

"Yeah, yup...just all this talk of babies. I think I'm going to go get some air," I say, before going to one of the farthest bathrooms in the house to ground myself.

I close the door behind me and try to calm down. This is all too much. After two years, I figured I could keep my feelings at bay long enough to celebrate my *nephew* without losing my ever-loving mind.

Ugh, I have to get a grip. I'm over here thinking about our babies, and she hasn't said one word to me since I got here. *Fuck,* she won't even look at me.

We've gone long periods without seeing each other before, and with every stretch, it would be like no time has passed. Even when things started to get intense, we would see each other and everything would be fine. I'm not sure exactly what I expected to happen after finally crossing that line in our relationship, but I expected *something*. Anger, regret, longing, *something*.

Honest to God, the way she's been carrying on with her life like that night was just a bump in the road, I half ex pected her to see me and not blink twice, just business as usual.

At least I know it won't be two years before I see her again. She'll be in New York, working with *me* for the next two months.

Before I know what's happening, the door is thrown open, and something crashes into me. No, not something, someone. "Jack!" Margot says, pushing away as soon as she realizes she's pressed against me. "What the fuck are you doing in here?"

When I don't answer and instead just stand there, dumbfounded, she turns to leave, and my brain goes on autopilot, grabbing her and squeezing as hard as I can.

"Ugh, let go of me!" she yells, squirming in my arms.

I can't let her go. I have to tell her.

The words fall from my mouth in a blubbering mess. "Please don't leave. Please talk to me. Please, please, baby girl. I'm so sorry. I've missed you so much, Princess."

"*Don't* call me princess," she says, stomping on my foot both for emphasis and to get out of my hold.

I let her go, turning first to block the door so she can't escape. "Margot. I thought I would lose everyone. I didn't think your family would ever forgive me. That even if they didn't kill me the moment they knew what I was doing with their sister and daughter, that you would realize I wasn't worth your time, and when you left, they would leave too. I know I should've picked you, though. I realize that now, because my body's been in New York, but for two years, you've had my heart with you in Paris."

She steps back, folding her arms across her chest in the process and huffing at me for blocking her exit. *There she is. There's my princess.* "You thought what? That you could just make the biggest decision of *our* lives by yourself? That you didn't need to involve me in that? That you shouldn't at least tell me how you were feeling so that when I woke up without you in your bed after you spent the entire night *making love to me*, I would at least know why."

"Please, baby, I'm *so fucking sorry*. I thought you would always resent me if you didn't chase your dreams. I thought I was doing what was best for you. I thought..."

She searches my eyes, and for just a moment, I can see past the hatred. "Jack, *you* were my dream. You were all I ever wanted. My *whole* life. Everything else was just outside noise. Acting, piano, and design were all just hobbies. And if being with you meant I never got to do it again, I would've found something else to pour my energy into while I happily stood by your side."

That can't be right. First, I learn that Blanche always thought I would be perfect for her daughter, and now I find out that instead of ensuring *the absolute love of my life's* happiness, I ripped it away. Someone please wake me up from this nightmare where I misinterpreted everyone's intentions and, in turn, ruined my chance of ever being happy. *Ruined* her *happiness.* I mean, sure, Henry and Ledger would still beat the shit out of me, but it would be worth it a million times over to have my princess in my arms again.

"I can still be that. Please let me be that again."

"No." She hesitates but denies me nonetheless.

I reach out to touch her, any point of contact at all, but she steps back, avoiding my touch. "Then at least let me be your friend. I'm still your family. Let me..."

"No, Jack, you aren't anything to me. Now, can I go, or do you need me to write *you* a fucking *five-line* note to show exactly how little you mean to me?"

She goes to step around me, and I let her leave. *Again.*

Chapter Thirty-Three

Music blares from the speaker on my vanity as I get ready, and I welcome the positivity on a cold, dreary New York day. It's a big day for La Reine. We're preparing for our final walk-through of the staging for our Valentine's Day collaboration. It's with the most prominent jeweler in the city, and I need to bring my best efforts to ensure everything goes smoothly. I fasten my hair back in a quick chignon, *thank you, French friends for your life hacks,* and pull my vintage black tweed blazer over my black midi dress. A gold brooch and a pair of pumps complete my look, and I grab my bag before heading down to meet my driver for the short ride to the store.

Or at least, I try to head down to meet my driver. I don't make it very far before I trip over one of the rolled-up rugs stored against a wall, sticking out into the open archway I foolishly tried to walk through. *Ugh.* I really need to take Mom up on her offer to have her interior designer come and have a look at this place. Maybe I went a little crazy with the vintage shopping in France, but when the antique markets are filled with things that predate the US as a concept...what was I supposed to do? Leave the solid-gold candlesticks depicting a Grecian orgy? Leave the console table carved with scenes from *The Tempest?* I smile, thinking of the fact I made an actual "gimme" gesture when I saw it, like a desperate little hoarder raccoon.

Wincing, I flex my ankle a few times, thinking that the hoarder definition might be hitting a little close to home. Resolving myself to give Mom my permission to call the designer, I finally make my way down to the car. By the time I arrive at the store, I'm only fifteen minutes early instead of the thirty I prefer, but with one more deep breath, I enter boss-bitch mode.

I wish I could say I found being in charge tedious, but honestly, I live for this. We dive right into work, reviewing the staging for our live mannequins. Models of all colors and sizes will be wearing pieces from *La Reine* while dripping in diamonds and other pieces from the brand's Valentine's collection this year. The collection is one of my favorites that I've designed so far, featuring the store's signature color alongside my brand's classic black and white, as well as three shades of pink and red for the holiday itself. It's a little more whimsical than anything I've ever designed, and early feedback suggests that it's expected to sell out quickly, especially with the increased visibility we've gained from this collaboration. The morning flies by, and before I know it, I'm back in the car heading for my New York storefront, also getting ever closer to opening day.

From the time I click a heel down just inside the door to climbing the cantilevered staircase to our third-floor offices, I've been asked twelve questions, answered three calls, and only snapped at someone once, but really, *who* re-heats fish in a communal microwave? They're lucky I didn't fire them on the spot.

Mom arrives just in time for us to share lunch, with a thick manila envelope tucked under her arm. I jump up and let out a squeal, causing her to laugh and hold it out of my reach when I try to grab it.

"Excuse me, I know I raised you better than that!" She laughs.

Rolling my eyes, I let out a good-natured huff of exasperation. "Yes, of course. Hello, Mother, good afternoon. How are you today? How was your drive in? How is your back feeling? Thank you for gracing me with your presence."

Mom rolls her eyes back at me, but finally hands over the envelope. "I'm fine, it was fine, it's fine, you're welcome. Now let's eat and look over these final proofs."

I eat for fuel, but only have eyes for the atmospheric, delectable, titillating images before me. This collection, Noir, is one that's been burning in the back of my mind since I saw a particularly raunchy French film with one of the men I saw casually in Paris. It was a low-budget exploration of desire and, frankly, pornographic, but it depicted an entire world of sexuality I had never given much thought to. Nothing about the film changed my personal sex life, other than Michel being extra feral that night, but the *visuals* stuck with me. Leather, chains, ropes, metals...I was enthralled. Purples and blues so deep they were almost midnight black, not virginal whites but cool-toned grays. Noir was born. It's so different from my previous collections that I wasn't the only one somewhat stumped about how to adjust our advertising. Of course, my team and I fretted for far too long before Mom piped up with the solution—debut Noir in conjunction with Ledger and Jack's club.

She was right, of course. A BDSM collection debuting at the hottest kink club in New York right now is inspired. So we've been full steam ahead, and the final proofs of the collection are perfect.

"Mom, these are so beautiful I could cry. I won't. But I could," I say, still focused on my creative vision come to life in front of me.

"Yes, Jack couldn't stop complimenting them when he saw them earlier. I hope you don't mind. We had breakfast together," she replies, eyeing me with a look I can't quite decipher. I'm no stranger to the Blanche Sinclair book of machinations, however, so I give a noncommittal hum and redirect her.

"Are we still on for dinner tonight?" I ask, feeling only slightly guilty about hoping she'll cancel. Something must flash across my face because she's up, kissing my cheeks, and heading for the door before I can blink.

"Sorry, darling, but I've had something pop up. Rain check?"

"Of course, talk tomorrow. Love you." I drop back into my chair and consider another coffee before deciding to head home.

Finally, I sink into my clawfoot bathtub, sighing as the warm water soothes my sore muscles. My evening consisted of an hour-long Pilates class, a massage, some sauna time, and a quick dinner of fruit and cheese. It's almost midnight, and I still have a couple of hours of me-time before bed. I've never been a morning person, and I haven't allowed being a small business owner to change that. It's probably one of my more privileged takes—nothing is worth getting out of bed before ten o'clock in the morning—but I'll be damned if I'm going to change. *Being rich has certain perks.* Ugh, Paris turned me into a snob. I don't actually think I've changed, not really. But there's something to be said for great wine, great food, great fucking...

I smirk and think about my reminiscence of Michel earlier today, and the naughty film that led me to Noir. He was a great friend to me and an even better lover, and one of the fi rst in my lineup of tall, dark, and handsome *friends* in Paris. Michel was my age, a classical musician, and always willing to accompany me to an art gallery opening or play performance. We parted on great terms, and I smile, thinking of his black curls and dimpled cheeks. Feeling loose and relaxed in my bath, I reach for the waterproof vibe I keep in my bathroom for this exact reason, and put it between my legs as I think back to my last night with Michel.

"Ah, mon ami, then we need one last sweet memory together, non?"

He invited me to a hotel suite for our final tryst. For now, he told me earlier with a wink. Our final tryst, for now.

His suggestion was to spend the entire evening naked, and I have to say, it's erotic in a way I wasn't expecting. We haven't fucked yet, but we have eaten a three-course meal and drank an entire bottle of champagne. We're now feeding each other tiny slices of fruit as we watch the Eiffel Tower sparkle. It's surprisingly sensual to watch Michel's naked body as he eats, his lean muscles flexing and pulling as he reaches over to feed me a piece of his dinner, his cock remaining half hard but twitching when I moan as a perfect bite of dessert hits my tongue. We haven't done anything except eat and chat about nothing, yet I know the blanket I'm sitting on will have a wet spot when I stand. Something about watching his thick cock rest against his thigh is making me crazy.

When we're finished, we make our way to the large whirlpool tub in the suite and climb in, finally allowing our bodies to connect as I move to straddle Michel, trapping his cock against his stomach with my wet pussy. He loves this, and we've gotten each other off countless times making out and rubbing against each other like horny teenagers. I think that's what he has in mind for our first orgasms of the night before he stops me and pulls back to look into my eyes.

"Ma belle," he whispers, placing a soft kiss on my lips. "Have you ever used a whirlpool jet to its full effect?"

I give him a quizzical look before he repositions me on my hands and knees and backs me up to the edge of the tub. I'm considering trying to get his dick in my mouth before he presses a button and a jet of water hits my clit.

"Fuck!" I scream. Michel chuckles and lowers himself to my eye level.

"I love it when you scream in pleasure, Margot," he groans. "I want to hear you do it again when you come just like this."

I'm rocking back and forth now, looking into his eyes as he stares at me ravenously, and when he reaches down to thrust three fingers inside me and thumb at my clit, I implode.

I'm about to come just from my memory of my last night in Paris, here in my bath in New York, with my thumb on my clit and my too small vibe inside me...but I can't imagine my dark-haired Michel with brown eyes.

I shatter with a scream, and this orgasm feels even more intense than the one that inspired it for reasons I don't want to contemplate. My head falls back on the rim of the tub as I feel myself pruning and the water growing cold. I try to pretend, but I'm not delusional enough to convince myself that I saw anything in my mind when I was coming, but the truth. A brown-haired, muscled giant was looking at me with the deep blue eyes I thought I was done with.

Fuck.

Chapter Thirty-Four

I'm doing the one thing I usually make it my mission to avoid. Sitting still. In my apartment, no less. *Her apartment.* As soon as Blanche listed Margot's old New York apartment for sale, I bought it. I told Blanche I thought the layout and size would be perfect for me while I was getting myself established in a new city. But really, I was hoping her scent would still be a little embedded in the carpet fibers.

It really is a good location. It's close enough to work that I can jog there if I want to get some extra exercise, and it's centrally located for easy access to the city. Not that I go anywhere but work and the gym these days.

The problem is that every time I sit in this damn living room, the memory of our first kiss plays on repeat in my mind. *Probably the last Thanksgiving we'll ever spend together.* Which is why I'm rarely ever here.

Tomorrow, Margot will be coming to the club to start work on our upcoming Valentine's date night auction. I've been on edge since she arrived. When I flipped out on a third staff member this week for absolutely no reason, my general manager, Aaron, insisted I go home early.

He's been on my ass for a while about my work-life balance, but I've never been able to give him the real reason I was at work all the time. I know the staff can run things without me. I'm the one who would fall apart, not the club.

I tried a few hours in the gym to burn off energy before getting bored enough to start thinking, and then figured I might as well go home if I'm going to be stuck in my head regardless.

It's only been a week since the gender reveal party, where Margot took the shattered pieces of my heart and burned them to ash. I don't blame her for being angry. Leaving her a note after the night we shared? *Jesus, what an asshole move.* It felt so noble at the time, but in retrospect, wow, I want to knock myself the fuck out too.

Speaking of being an asshole, today also reminds me of why I haven't had sex in two years.

2 YEARS AGO

The hotel suite I'm staying in indefinitely is a fucking mess. The only other time I've let myself go like this is when my father died. Except this time, there won't be a princess in shining pink armor to come and save me. Goddammit, can I not have a single thought without her in it?

Think, Jack, what could get her out of your mind? Obviously, alcohol isn't going to do it, and I really can't allow myself to fall into drugs at the moment. I have a club to get up and running. A sex club. Have I forgotten what my damn job is? I'm part owner of one of the most successful clubs in the country, so I have access to any club here in the city. That's what I'll do. I'll go fuck her out of my memory.

A liter of water and a cold shower later, I'm on my way to the club we've been partnering with since starting our new endeavor in New York. It's a weeknight, but they'll be busy enough to find someone.

I'm escorted in immediately upon arrival since I've already filled out all their member paperwork. I was tested when we first started working with them about three months ago, not that I would ever fuck anyone without a condom.

No one except Margot.

I've barely been sitting in their lounge for a minute when a blonde approaches me, her intent obvious. She's an attractive enough woman. A little shorter than I would like. A little too slim. Her eyes are a little too dark, and her hair a little too light, but I'm buzzed enough to overlook all of that. We like pussy in all shapes and sizes, as Ledger used to say.

It doesn't take long for Blondie, whose name I couldn't tell you if you held a gun to my head, to invite me to a private room. I'm not drunk by any means, but there's no chance in hell I could do this completely sober, so I shoot the rest of my scotch back and follow her to the suite.

If I close my eyes, she could be anyone, that little devil on my shoulder tells me. Or is it an angel? I'm not sure which is which when both choices involve sex. I'm trying to remind myself that my goal is to fuck Margot out of my system, not back into it when she leads me into the room, and I realize, in this lighting, I don't really even have to squint to imagine she's someone else.

Blondie turns around, reaching up to kiss me, but she's too close, and the illusion fades. Before she reaches my lips, I shove her down to her knees with one hand while I work my pants open with the other.

"Open your mouth," I command as I pull my cock out.

I'm not fully hard yet, but I shove it into her open mouth until she starts gagging. This isn't really how I would imagine Margot on her knees, but I've never had her mouth before, so I have no comparison. I close my eyes and imagine it's her perfect throat I'm fucking into, and before long, I'm fully erect.

As good as this feels, I'm not here for a blow job. I pull my dick out of her mouth before telling Blondie how I want her while I grab a condom, doing my best to avoid looking at her for too long.

When I'm successfully wrapped up, she's where I told her to be, bent over the side of one of the chaise lounges, with her short skirt pulled up and no panties on. I position myself behind her and take a deep breath, the sex angel on my shoulder screaming at me to go home.

Unfortunately, the sex devil wins. I line myself up without even looking down to see the pussy I'm about to fuck, lest it ruin the illusion—because how could there ever be a pussy as perfect as my princess's?—and thrust in.

It feels wrong, but I chalk that up to the condom. Maybe the reason Margot felt better than any pussy I've ever had before is because she's the only one I've had bare...

I use my hand to cover her mouth so her annoying moans won't ruin this mirage for me as I start fucking her hard and fast, searching for that release I've needed since getting to New York.

For a moment, I'm lost in the fantasy that I'm here with my girl. "Fuck, I love you, Princess."

Her head snaps back to me, her brown eyes meeting my own, and it's all over.

Nausea floods my body, and I barely make it over to the trash can in the corner of the room before an entire day's worth of food spews from my mouth.

Blondie asks if I'm okay, but dips out the second I give her a thumbs-up. "It's just the alcohol," I tell myself, but I know deep down that's a lie. I know my limits when it comes to drinking, and I was not even close to being drunk.

No, it seems like my body just refused to allow itself to fuck anyone other than the woman it belongs to.

I was sick the rest of the night, debating whether I actually cheated on her. *Her.* I guess sex angel won because I haven't so much as looked at another woman lustfully since that night. Which means I've now been celibate for two years.

Well, *fuck you, sex angel.* Margot is done with me, and she made herself *very* clear about it. She's moved on, and it's time I do the same.

Except how?

After spending hours setting up and scouring every dating site I can find, I realize moving on is pointless. There's nobody out there for me but her. I wasn't interested in dating before Margot, so why would I imagine there would be someone after Margot?

Before Margot and After Margot. The way I've been categorizing my life for the past two years. We're technically in year 2 AM.

Okay, so dating is off the table, but I think it is time to at least end my celibacy. I own and operate a sex club, for Christ's sake. The problem is that I really don't want to start fucking around at my own club. I did that back at the old Rendezvous, and it was messier than I'd like to admit. *Especially if Margot is going to be around with the lingerie collab.*

After some research of the offerings at a few of our best competitors, I find what I think will be the perfect setup to get my guy back in the game.

Join us on January 25 for an anonymous meetup. We know everyone will have varying preferences, so there will be a questionnaire to ensure comfort. We can't wait to see you soon.

That sounds like exactly what I need. I can give my wrist some relief at least. And you know what? If I want to lean into the fantasy it's a certain princess I'm fucking, so be it.

I click through the sign-up, selecting my preferences and submitting my testing, then add the date to my calendar. It's only a few weeks away. God, why does it *still* feel like I'm cheating on her?

No, I'm not cheating on her. If she'd let me, I would whisk her away into the sunset, giving her the happily ever after she's always wanted. I'll always be ready to do that.

I don't have to fall in love with another woman. My heart can belong to Margot for the rest of my life, but I *have* to figure out how to function without her.

Sex is a primal, base-level need. This is only sex. Anonymous sex. Where I'll probably be imagining her anyway. I have three weeks to decide.

I can see how tomorrow goes with our business meeting and go from there. It had been a long time since we've seen each other, and emotions were high because of the gender reveal. Maybe she was just as shell-shocked as I was to see each other for the first time in two years, and will have had some time to think. Perhaps she'll think about my admissions and give me another chance. Maybe tomorrow will turn everything around.

Chapter Thirty-Five

Agreeing to a meeting at eleven in the morning is not something I would usually do, but I'd really rather get this initial walk-through at Rendezvous Too completed first thing so that I can move on to more enjoyable pursuits. Luckily for me, I managed to book a promotional event for our jewelry store collab just after this, so I'm in full glam and a sinful dress before noon. Nobody will accuse me of not embodying my own collections today.

My black silk dress is relatively demure from the front, with a modest neckline. It's tight, though, showing off my curves to full effect. The back, well, doesn't exist. I'll be wearing a diamond necklace reversed to hang down between my shoulders for the event, the pendant resting just above the dimples at my lower back. A little well-placed tape and I'm able to go bra-free and maintain the illusion that my tits are impervious to gravity.

Mom is away playing pickleball, so my New York right-hand man, Marco, is accompanying me to see what Jack's new club has scrounged up to present to us. Although my mother assured me that our involvement in this would be limited to the actual dressing of the models, with minor adjustments to the staging if needed, I prefer a hands-on approach when it comes to how my designs are presented. I don't spend too much time thinking about the control-freak comments I've heard growing up because if the shoe fits, I'll wear it. As the only girl and youngest child in my family, I knew what I wanted, and I consistently achieved it. I know what I like and how I prefer things, and anyone who has a problem with that doesn't stick around La Reine long.

With a sigh, I'm reminded that I need to hire a new second assistant. Really, it's not like the job is hard. I basically give them a schedule of tasks every week, and they just have to *do* them. But Val brought me the wrong lunch three days in a row last week, and I don't make the rules. Three strikes and you're out. *I guess I do make the rules, technically, but still.* If I can't trust you with my lunch order, I can't trust you with my business. As the car makes its way to the club from my apartment, *not a far enough distance in my opinion,* I feel...tired. I mean, it's early, and I shouldn't be out of my apartment yet. But still, it would be nice not to have to deal with all the fucking decisions about every aspect of my life, the designs, *and* the business every single day.

We pull up to the service entrance of the building and walk in through the back offices on the first floor. A delivery person is pushing a motorized cart full of boxes of condoms into a store room, and I smirk. That's probably the real problem here. *I need to get laid.*

I've been staring in silence for ten minutes, trying to take in the stage area of the club and think of exactly how I'm going to fix this disaster. Well, disaster might be a little unfair. Anyone who isn't an expert on women's bodies, angles, and lighting might think this looks fine. By average standards, this would exceed expectations. But I've never been average, and I'm not going to compromise now.

"All of this lighting needs to be replaced. It's too harsh, and the placement isn't going to do any of our dates any favors. It needs to be programmable, on a timer that can be paused and with the speed of the strobes adjusted manually, as I mentioned in the specs I sent weeks ago. The draping in the back is fine, but the material needs to be something less shimmery. Otherwise, it's going to reflect like a nightmare. I don't know if you thought I wouldn't notice, but these fans are the cheaper option that I specified *not* to use. They're loud and will be more noticeable in this space than the brand I requested. Replace them." I sigh, somewhat dramatically, because I was really not expecting to have to micro-fucking-manage every aspect of this. The specification sheet had *literally* all of these details. Fabrics, lighting, fans, placement, all of it. There are very few things I hate more than repeating myself.

"Princess, I'm sorry we're not up to your standards."

I don't have to turn around to know who's behind me. And I might actually hate that nickname more than I hate repeating myself.

Sighing, I turn back around to try to be civil, but my patience has really been worn thin this morning by the incompetence of Jack's team. There's the man himself, wearing tailored charcoal trousers with a pristine white shirt stretched across his wide chest, three buttons undone and still wearing the gold chain I never quite got a good look at years ago. *Jack, you slut.*

"Good morning, Mr. Carter. I've just informed your team of my notes regarding this draft of the staging. I would usually dictate them and leave them with your stage manager, but it's word for word what I sent weeks ago. I recommend that your team start from scratch and follow the instructions I sent. They're very detailed. I can't see why there would be any confusion," I say, short and to the point.

Jack opens his mouth to speak, but a man standing next to him beats him to it.

"It's nice to meet you, Ms. Sinclair. I'm Aaron, Jack's house manager."

"A pleasure, Aaron. Are you about to tell me why my spec sheet was ignored?" I ask, very politely, very demure, *taking deep breaths* until ugh, too deep, I can smell Jack's cologne.

Aaron cowers slightly under my scrutinizing gaze, and I'm reminded of the way Val looked at me just before I fired her. Jesus, I'm not that threatening, and I'm not asking too much. Just *do your job* per my very detailed directives. Aaron squeaks out something faintly resembling "family emergency," then scurries out of the room. Jack turns to watch him go, then brings his gaze back to me, head cocked to the side.

"That was rude," he says, still eyeing me with an unnerving amount of scrutiny.

"What's rude is agreeing to collaborate with a business, committing to a certain level of service to ensure the expectations of the business are met, then ignoring a line-by-line page of instructions so simple an elementary school student could follow them. It's a waste of my time when I have other things I would rather be doing," I reply, still calm, cool, and collected.

"Like Marco?" Jack asks, his gaze growing cool as he eyes my colleague, who's still close to the stage, trying to explain the color coordination system in my notes to Jack's employees. *Can they not read?*

"What about Marco?" I ask, forcing him to voice the accusation he's trying to level at me. The fact that this man thinks he has any right to be jealous of Marco after shooing me away like a stray dog is, well. Just like a man, I suppose.

"You have other things you'd rather be doing, like Marco?" he asks, and I'm impressed he has the balls to double down.

"I would never mix business with pleasure, Mr. Carter. Marco is a beloved friend and colleague, and I rely on his opinions and those of his *husband* regularly."

He has the decency to look a little sheepish, but he's not getting away with being inappropriate in our fucking workplace like that without consequences.

"If, however, I did want to mix business with pleasure..." I pause for effect and dramatically look at where Marco stands—tall, lean, and with the style and grace of a born-and-raised Italian man. I turn back to make eye contact with Jack. "If I did want pleasure, he's certainly the type of man I've been craving it from lately."

I walk to the side table where my coat and bag sit and begin suiting myself up to brave the New York weather and get on with the rest of my day. I'm not at all surprised to find Jack following me with clenched fists.

"He's half Italian, half French, you know," I say as I put on my gloves. "Individually, talented lovers, but the combination tends to be, well..." I meet his eyes once more and smirk when I see a vein in his forehead that might pop. "The combination is devastating."

My work here is *so done* for the day, and I call Marco over to shake Jack's tense hand and join me as we head across town to the promotional event. I'm sure Jack is seething, vein still pulsating. But I wouldn't know because I don't look back.

Marco, his husband Mark—they love it, and have a cute thing where they play Mark/Marco Polo when they can't find each other in a crowd—and I are enjoying a late evening dinner and drinks after a highly successful event. I don't work out for nothing, and some of the first images from the afternoon show a chic woman with killer back muscles wearing tens of millions of dollars in diamonds and a smile. It was the most fun I've had in a while, and I think the storefront and the jewelry store collaboration are both going to be perfect. The Rendezvous Too Valentine's Day auction, on the other hand, is giving me a headache and might end up being more trouble than it's worth.

My face clearly shows my change in mood, and Mark, who isn't my employee and has no qualms telling me exactly what he thinks, says, "When was the last time you got dicked down?"

Marco chokes on his martini and slaps his husband on the shoulder. Mark puts his hands up placatingly. "I'm sorry, but tell me it isn't true. You moved, you've had a ton going on since you got to New York, and you're vexed by this project. You need a really good one-night stand. At least try to establish a regular rotation like you had in France. An American Michel."

He's not wrong. I had no shortage of partners in my two years overseas, although I was just starting to explore some of my less vanilla interests. After our French film experience, Michel and I barely dabbled in some play, but he was so sensual in his daily life that passion was never something we needed any help with.

"You know, I know you wouldn't be caught dead at Jack's club as a patron. But there is another club around here that we've been to. They're legit. Background checks, testing, the works. They aren't really competitors with Rendezvous Too because instead of theme nights and kink exhibitions, they facilitate more anonymous fantasies. Glory holes and whatnot. Like a hookup app but with testing and safe rooms with panic buttons. It's really clean and nice," Marco says, and I appreciate him for trying to help me out. This sounds like it might be exactly what I need to break out of my funk. Who knows, maybe I'll get lucky enough to find someone to be regular buddies with and be in a consistently better mood. I certainly don't need a fucking relationship right now.

"Text me the info, please," I say, smiling. "And I'll see you at work tomorrow, Marco. Don't worry about your tab. Tonight's on me for putting up with my attitude." I give them a wink and head outside to my waiting driver, heading home for a bath and contemplating what I might want out of an anonymous sex club encounter.

Join us on January 25, where we will be hosting an anonymous meetup. We know everyone will have varying preferences, so there will be a questionnaire to ensure everyone is comfortable. We can't wait to see you soon.

That sounds like exactly what I need. After clicking through the sign-up, I submit my testing and then circle back to the preferences section. It's comprehensive, and the club's algorithm will match me with a partner based on complementary interests.

Thinking about what I really need, if I'm being honest with myself, is just a chance to let go a little bit. I need a good, rough fuck by someone I never have to see again. This is the perfect chance to try out new things in a safe, low-stakes environment, so I click a few of the things I've wanted to try but never have, and submit. Adding the date to my calendar, I find myself excited at the prospect of an anonymous night of fun. You deserve this, Margot. Finally home, I grab my vibe and head to the bath, thinking about a man with no face taking all my stress away.

Chapter Thirty-Six

Jack

"Sprinkles. Her safe word is sprinkles, and if she can't speak, she'll tap four times in a row," I repeat to myself as I wait for my masked woman to show up. Poetic, really, that I'll be breaking my two-year sex drought in a room that so closely resembles the one where it began. The leather furniture and dim lights are pretty standard for any club, but the faint red light casts an ominous vibe unique to this room.

I'm dressed in head-to-toe black with a matching balaclava to mask my identity. I've spent enough time in kink clubs to know that mixed with the lighting and scenery, I'm definitely a fantasy. Not a *decorated* fantasy, though, since Ledger informed me it's better not to surprise new partners with the piercings in case they aren't interested. My dick honestly feels a little naked without them. I'm a little anxious to see if whoever arrives lives up to *my* fantasy.

For two years, I've had to fight tooth and nail to stop thinking about her, but as I sit here waiting to see who steps through the door, I'm struggling to conjure my princess. Our meeting at the club was a cruel reminder of just how much two years can transform someone.

Margot has always been a spoiled princess, but also so kind and light-hearted. She showed up at Rendezvous Too as a full-fledged diva. I'm pretty sure Aaron's "family emergency" was just an excuse to get the fuck out of the room.

Any hope I might have had about us rekindling things flew out the window the moment she strutted into my club wearing that sinfully tight black dress. If her attitude wasn't enough to confirm my decision to go through with this, her casual comments about her sex escapades across Europe sealed the deal on my commitment to tonight.

Anger rises as I try and fail to summon images of the princess I used to know. I'm on the verge of giving up when the door opens, and I have to do a double take at the woman standing in front of me.

Did I actually do magic? Am I hallucinating? Am I high right now?

My apparition closes the door behind her but doesn't make a move to come any closer. She removes her silk robe, letting it drop to the floor and revealing her black leather lingerie set. I've seen my fair share of lingerie, including the set Margot made for me specifically, but nothing has made my mouth water quite like this strappy bodysuit.

I rake my eyes back up her long, elegant body to where a lacy black mask fails to cover a face so impossibly beautiful it nearly brings me to my knees. A reminder that it's the woman underneath evoking such desire from me, and not her wardrobe.

After blinking and pinching myself, I freeze, realizing that it *is* Margot Sinclair standing before me.

How is this even possible? Did she know it was me she was going to meet with? *Was she desperate for me but too angry to tell me in person, so she hacked into my computer and saw where I had signed up for this, then hacked into the club's system to make sure we matched?* Fuck, that's the wrong Sinclair. I would expect that out of Ledger, maybe even Henry, but if Margot wants something, she wouldn't mess with secret computer shit.

No, my perfect little princess wanted to get fucked by a man she would never have to see again.

Rage like nothing I've ever felt before boils inside me. *She could've had me. She could've had romance and passion and love. Like the last night we spent together.* But no. She let me make love to her all night, then went to Paris and fucked her way around Europe.

I'm pretty sure you did the same thing, Jack. Except for way longer than two years. And pretty sure you *sent her there, you incel.* Ugh, sex angel, go die in a hole.

That's fine. She doesn't want a man to live and breathe by her, praying to her with every word her body draws from his lips, worshipping at the altar of Margot. So I won't give her that.

If she wants a stranger she'll never see again to fuck her senseless, that's exactly what I'll do. If she wants us to be nothing, that's exactly what I'll treat her like. Thinking back to the preferences I reviewed once we matched, I realize I have plenty of motivation to give her exactly what the fuck she wants.

"Get on your hands and knees," I command, dropping my voice to disguise it.

Her hands go to her hips in a stance of defiance, brows furrowed in confusion, but she remains vertical.

Leaning forward, I rest my elbows on my knees and tilt my head slightly before repeating myself. "I said. Get. On. Your. Hands. And. Knees."

To my surprise, she obeys, slowly falling to her knees and then to her hands. I let her stay like that for a moment longer than I should, reveling in my victory, before leaning back in the chair and stretching my legs out in front of me as I cross my hands behind my head.

"Crawl to me."

The image of her obeying will replay in my head until the day I die. Her black pumps are still on her feet, hair down and falling over one shoulder, framing one side of her face. Her gaze is locked on mine, a mix of lust and defiance so intense I almost feel it's going to burn my mask off. She's in no hurry, hips swaying side to side, following my command but making no attempt to be quick about it.

When she makes it to where I'm sitting, she sits back on her knees like it's the most natural thing in the world, like she's done this a hundred times before. The thought of her letting even one other man fuck her reignites the anger that I had momentarily forgotten about while I watched in awe as this siren made her way to me.

She's still staring up at me, and the lace of her mask doesn't do shit to conceal those big fucking ocean eyes. I used to always be the guy to dry up any tears that would spill from them, but *fuck* do I look forward to putting them there now.

"Take out my cock."

I'm still sitting with my arms behind my head while I watch as she reaches down and makes quick work of getting my belt off and pants undone before reaching into my boxers and releasing my rock-hard dick.

Her gasp brings a smirk to my face, but she isn't looking up to see how her reaction affects me. I know her gasp isn't one of recognition, and honestly, it doesn't surprise me, since she didn't get this close to it last time. No, her surprise is either due to my sheer size or the fact that she hasn't seen a cut dick from the European fuckers she's been screwing lately. *I can definitely work with that.*

I grab my cock and slap it on her cheek, hard enough to sting a little, before bringing it back to where her full lips are closed shut.

"Suck."

When she doesn't open her mouth, I use my other hand to wrap around her throat and squeeze. *Hard.* "Either open that whore mouth and suck on my cock or I'll open it myself," I practically growl.

Hatred flashes in her eyes as she keeps them locked on me, but she slowly takes me into her perfect fucking mouth and sucks harder than I imagined possible.

Fuck this bitch for knowing how to suck a dick this good.

I'm done letting her perform for me like she has for who knows how many men.

Before she can pull back to breathe, I let go of my cock and grab the back of her head, shoving myself down her throat, and begin fucking into her. To my satisfaction, tears stream down her face, the black from her mascara staining her cheeks.

She finally manages to push herself away from me, and she's sitting on the floor, her chest heaving as she tries to catch her breath.

"Get up and present yourself for me on the couch."

My patience wavers when she disobeys me again, so I intervene this time, picking her up off the floor and tossing her down on one of the deep couches.

"I'm getting tired of repeating myself. Put your ass up in the fucking air and wait for me to get this goddamn condom on."

She's shaking as she gets on her hands and knees, pushing her ass up as she arches her back, allowing me a look at the hole cut out of the crotch of her bodysuit. I'm not sure if I'm more turned on by that or disappointed that I won't have a reason to rip it all off.

With the condom on, I fix my attention on the perfect little hole I'm about to obliterate. It's still the most beautiful goddamn pussy I've ever seen, and it infuriates me that other men have had the pleasure to do exactly what I am right now, staring at this delicacy as I line my cock up to sink inside it. *I wonder if any of them took her bare...*

She's still shaking as I ease my head in, and against every instinct I have to sheath myself completely in one violent thrust, I allow her a moment to give me her safe word, but it never comes.

So I let go, fucking into her with a force so brutal I'm sure I'll bruise her cervix. Her screams echo in the room, and for the first time in my entire life, they give me chills from exhilaration instead of horror.

"You've got a tight fucking pussy for such a goddamn slut, you know that?" I really don't want to compliment her, but I can't help myself.

Her answering moans remind me of the night she used them to compose a symphony for me, and I can't take it. I reach around her body to gag her with my fingers, suppressing her tongue so she can't make another sound to remind me that she's been in Paris screaming for God knows who the past two years.

This is the hardest I've ever fucked, but it's not enough. I need more, both for myself but for her too. I want it to hurt so much she can't finish. I want her to show up at our next meeting limping and empty.

I want to humiliate her.

I take my fingers out of her mouth, wiping all the spit that she couldn't swallow across her face, and push her down against the couch as I climb over her. One knee rests beside her while I push her face down into the cushion with my combat boot on her cheek. The new leverage allows me to finally fuck her as hard as I want, but without my fingers gagging her, she releases a tiny little squeak. I stop moving completely for a moment, my hips flush against her ass. The room is so silent, you could hear a pin drop, before I continue.

"Shut." *Thrust.* "The." *Thrust.* "Fuck." *Thrust.* "Up." *Thrust.*

"If you whimper one more time, or make one more goddamn noise, I'm taking this fucking condom off and fucking your ass raw."

Her pussy fucking *clenches*. Moving my hand to her ass, I circle my thumb around the rim of her unfilled hole as I start fucking into her again.

"Of course you want something in your ass. I forgot what a little whore you are."

She doesn't answer, remaining quiet like I commanded. I reward her for her obedience, using her wetness to slowly sink my thumb into her ass as I fuck her like a man possessed. My girl does well, though. She stays quiet, even when her body starts shaking uncontrollably, and I start feeling flutters around both my thumb and cock.

"There you go. What a natural fucking submissive you are, staying quiet while I do whatever I want to you. That's what you want, right? You came here to be used. And you're taking it like a fucking champ."

I could fuck her all night, but when her orgasm deepens, and she's milking the shit out of my dick, I can't hold on any longer. Her piercing scream finally pulls me over the edge, coming harder than I ever have in my life.

After giving myself a moment to catch my breath, I pull my leg back to where I'm straddling her ass, then get up to take the condom off and tuck myself back in my pants.

I turn to leave, but something possesses me. I pause, then walk back over to where she's flipped herself to sit on the couch. Squeezing her mouth, I wait until she opens it enough for me to pour the contents of the condom into it.

"Swallow."

She does.

"Good little whore," I say, giving her cheek a light slap before turning again to leave.

"Meet me here next week. Same day. Same time," I call into the room as the door closes behind me.

Chapter Thirty-Seven

Holy fuck. The door closes behind the masked stranger who just fucked me within an inch of my life, and I feel a trail of wetness trickle down my thigh, realizing it's my cum. I'm not sure I've ever come so hard that it literally leaked out of me. *Fuck.* I let out a laugh, feeling like a wet, cooked noodle, just flopped on this couch without a care in the world. I'm not even going to try to force any thoughts into my brain. I'm just going to lie here for a bit, then sink into the tub that I know is in the adjoining suite. I have two more hours in here to myself, based on the clock on the wall, and I intend to luxuriate in the fucking I just experienced.

I'm having a lovely soak and thinking of what a delicious monster cock my masked man has when I suddenly come back into my full stream of consciousness, and it hits me like a bucket of cold water.

What the *actual* fuck did I just do? Crawl on my hands and knees to a *man* who I then let fuck my throat and call me a slut and a whore? *Am I high right now?* Did that just happen? He put his fucking boot on my face, and I just let him stick his thumb in my ass and then came around his cock for what felt like minutes on end?

I sink under the water to try to reset myself to factory settings, but when I pop back up, not only did all of that still actually happen but I also let this man *feed me his cum from a condom. And I swallowed it.*

Jesus Christ, Margot. You were over here floating on a cloud and coming on a guy's cock while he treated you like shit. Who the fuck does that?

Well...

Wonderful. I'm having a crisis in a sex club bathroom, and my conscience decides to play devil's advocate.

You did specifically check all those things on your preferences list. In fact, you asked for a rough, dominant fuck and you ranked face fucking, cum swallowing, and degradation as highly interested to try.

I stand out of the bath and towel myself off, already seeing the physical effects of my evening. There are hand-shaped bruises basically everywhere he held me in place tonight—on my neck, shoulders, hips, waist...my traitorous pussy clenches, reminding me I had specifically listed physical marks as something I was highly interested in trying. Turns out I am, in fact, highly interested, and the fingertip pattern along my collarbone from where he held me as he fucked into me from behind is extremely arousing. I bruise fairly easily, but they also fade quickly, so before long, these should be gone. But in the meantime, it looks like I've been manhandled—which I was.

Finally, I'm dressed and I've completed the mandatory checkout process with the club, letting them know the scene was fine, everything was safe, sane, consensual, no safe words needed, no concerns regarding the other party, etc. They briefly mention aftercare, and I gloss over it, assuring them that I'm fine, and I felt in no way left adrift by my partner. It's all professional, and I hope Ledger's clubs have something like this in place to check in with patrons.

In the time it takes me to get home from the club and place a delivery order for comfort food, I've circled back to being angry with myself for being horny again at seeing my bruises, and I'm still a little shocked by my reactions to what happened today. I'm a whole-ass CEO and a damn heiress, and nobody has ever talked to me with such disrespect in my life. I would rather fucking die than crawl to a goddamn *man*. What kind of feminist icon am I even aspiring to be?

Maybe the kind who owns her desires and understands that wanting someone else in charge in the bedroom isn't a mental disorder, but perfectly normal.

Clearly, I need another creative outlet if my mind is still mustering enough energy to play devil's advocate.

One more deep breath and I set my shoulders back. Orgasm or not, this is *not* who I am, and I'm sure as shit not going back to see him "same time, same place" next week. Arrogant asshole. Fuck off. I tried something new, it wasn't for me, and that's that. I'm Margot Sinclair, and I'm nobody's "good little whore." Certainly not anyone's "natural fucking submissive."

I could've told him that in advance. I'm a boss bitch, and I'll never crawl for anyone ever again.

I feel hungover the next day, taking my sweet time with my morning toilette and carefully choosing a turtleneck to style for lunch, making sure there's no evidence of yesterday's activities for my oldest brother to scrutinize. Henry let me know last week that he would be in the city for business, and I'm always thrilled to have him here. He's coming to see my new apartment for the first time and to review some contracts for La Reine that I think have potential. One of the things I appreciate about both of my brothers is that while they are *always* available if I need a helping hand with anything, personal or business related, they mostly stay out of my business these days and let me handle things on my own. It would be all too easy for Henry to use his years of experience and training to try to push me in certain directions, but he never has.

Arriving my usual thirty minutes early for lunch, I see Henry is already seated at a corner table in the back of one of our favorite NYC haunts, wearing a three-piece brown tweed suit. I give him a broad smile when he sees me, and we quickly fall into our habit of efficiently catching up with each other whenever we're together.

"How are Sloane and Ledger?" I ask, knowing that even though we text more than the average family, there's nothing quite like being in the same city to know how someone's doing.

"They're both well. Ledger continues to somehow surpass his own world records for protectiveness and obsession when it comes to Sloane and LJ, so really nothing new."

I chuckle, having seen firsthand exactly how creepy my brother can be when it comes to his baby and his woman. "Did they officially decide on LJ, then?"

"I can't see them calling him anything else, since that's all Sloane says these days. I offered Henry again, but they declined."

Eyeing my brother, I decide to be a little vulnerable and see if I can get him to admit he wants a little Henry one day. "Do you ever feel like what Ledger and Sloane have won't be possible for us?" I ask as he eyes me warily, knowing where I'm going with this and wanting me to stop before I get there. "You *really* don't want a baby, Henry? Because honestly, I would love a Margot Jr. one day, but I'm not sure that's in the cards for me." *Since the one person I wanted that with stomped on my heart, and nobody else piques my interest.*

I see a flicker of desire shoot across Henry's face, but it's gone so fast I wonder if I imagined it.

"I genuinely don't think I'm well suited for fatherhood. I think I'm too much like Father," he says.

"I loved Daddy. He was wonderful to me. I'm sorry your experience wasn't the same," I say quietly, with a sad smile.

"None of that was your fault. And I think I had an overall neutral-to-slightly-positive relationship with him, certainly nothing so traumatic as all the complexes he gave to Ledger over the years. But a positive relationship with one child, neutral with one, and a glaring red flag negative with the third isn't really a glowing percentage of success."

I nod and turn to look out of the window at the afternoon sun peeking through the clouds.

"Is this your way of telling me that you haven't found anyone worthy of dating in your adult life, and you're starting to feel the reality that running your business at the level you prefer is incompatible with being a wife and mother? And that perhaps you're wondering if it's even worth it to try to find one when you already have a cracking success on your hands with the other?" Henry asks, and my eyes snap to his to find him giving me the tiniest grin.

This fucker has always been a smidge too perceptive for his own good, I think, rolling my eyes.

"Well, you said it, not me. So what do I do?" I'm avoiding his gaze now, unsure I want to hear what he has to say.

"Margot," he says, and I look back up at him, seeing no judgment for my insecurities. "You just have to live. It sounds trite, but my genuine advice is to enjoy every day. Enjoy the growth of your business. Enjoy the people you meet, or don't. But do try not to hold too many grudges or carry too many worries from the past forward. They'll just weigh you down. I used to have the same concerns, but that's the only real advice I ever have for you, for anything. Just live."

My sweet Henry. We part ways, rescheduling my apartment tour as he's had something come up. He's in the city for so long that I'm sure we'll have another chance soon.

Making my way home to get ready for Pilates and a massage, I think about what he said. It's great advice, and coming from him, it has a certain gravitas to it that I take to heart. But I don't think I'm ready to be that self-actualized yet. I get a reminder on my phone for my next meeting with Jack at Rendezvous Too, and I realize I'm definitely not ready. Some grudges are meant to be held, at least for a little while.

Chapter Thirty-Eight

Jack

The second hand on the clock in my office seems to tick by slower than usual as I nurse a glass of scotch, waiting for Margot to show up for our second meeting.

Aaron triple-checked her list to make sure everything requested is here and read everyone working today their final rites in the case they misbehave. Not that anyone would have in the first place. After her last visit, word spread like wildfire among the staff. Anyone brave enough to come to work today is definitely not pushing their luck to ruffle her feathers.

As always, thoughts of her fill my head. The difference now is that there are quite a few new versions. There's my sweet princess in pink from years past, there's the dreaded bitch boss who's driven terror into all of my employees, and then there's the obedient little whore who took my cock so fucking well the other night.

God, what I did was wrong on so many levels. She would've never gone through with that if she knew who was behind the mask. She thought I was a stranger, and I haven't figured out if that makes me feel better or worse. I mean, I might as well have been a stranger to myself. I've never treated a woman like that, during sex or otherwise.

In retrospect, it feels so wrong, but that doesn't negate how natural it felt in the moment. And I might be an arrogant asshole, but I think I speak for both of us when I say it was *damn good.*

It doesn't matter. I know I told her to show up for round two, but I can't do it again. I can't betray her trust like that again.

It's wrong.

When the clock finally makes it to my forty-five-minute warning, I leave my hideout and do a final walk-through to make sure things will go as smoothly as possible when the princess gets here.

Margot walks in with her entourage, strolling right past me to greet Aaron and every other employee present before turning in my direction and nodding. I give my best fake smile, biting my tongue to avoid saying something extremely unprofessional. *Because all I can think about is how fucking good she looked when she swallowed my cum.*

She's wearing another of her gray pantsuits, and it's strange not to see my princess in pink. At least it's not another skintight black dress, or I don't think my dick would survive.

"I see you were able to figure out how a line-by-line checklist works, yes?" she asks, reminding me that this really isn't *my* princess at all. This is somewhere between a monster and a queen. *One who loves to get on her knees for a mysterious masked man.*

Before Aaron loses his nerve again and abandons ship, I step in to take the brunt of her criticism. "Yes, we mere mortals finally figured it out, *Princess.*"

The hatred in her eyes still hurts, and I would be lying to myself if I said otherwise. My cock, on the other hand, grows harder by the minute with the memory of how those hate-filled eyes looked crawling to me.

"Hmm, I much prefer the Italian rendition of that pet name. *Principessa* just has a certain ring to it. Don't you think so?"

Now it's my turn to showcase my anger. Her goons shuffle forward as I stalk over to her, but she doesn't move a muscle. Just cranes her head up to meet my eyes as I step within a half inch of her.

Honestly, I don't know what I was going to say. *You weren't crawling to an Italian the other night* seems wrong, present company considered. Luckily, looking up at me caused her hair to fall back just enough for me to notice the bruises she attempted to conceal with makeup, and I'm saved.

I lean down close enough to keep our conversation private but still maintain eye contact. "Did you fall, *Princess,* or are all those bruises you're trying to hide from that Italian you seem to always reference?"

The way her skin flushes is answer enough. I allow myself a moment to stare into those eyes I've loved all my life, but I step away before she can think of a proper reply and head back to where the rest of my team stands. "Alright, everyone, let's get this show on the road. Our partners from La Reine don't have all day."

With that, the meeting continues as well as one could hope. We've nailed down most of the bigger details before our twenty participants arrive for the fitting.

Watching her in her element is awe-inspiring. I've appreciated her brilliance her whole life, but this is different. This is *more*. She's a grown-ass woman on her way to building her own empire.

If I felt guilty for our masked night before, it's tenfold now as I watch my Margot embody what she was always supposed to become. This is why I sent her to Paris in the first place.

That is, until her hair falls again, and I catch sight of those poorly concealed bruises. *I'm only a man after all.*

They trail from her neck into her blouse, a perfect replica of my hand around her throat, and before I know it, my mind wanders to what lingerie she's wearing beneath her professional attire. Would it be like what she wore to the club the other night? Surely not. It's probably a lacy bra and panty set. Maybe a matching garter like the set she made for me years ago.

"That'll do it then," Aaron says as the last participant finishes getting fitted.

Margot says goodbye to my team before finally acknowledging my existence. "Until next time, Mr. Carter," she says, holding her hand out for me to shake.

I take her hand in mine, but instead of shaking it, I pull it to my mouth and lightly kiss her dainty knuckles. "Until next time, *Princess*. Let me know if you need any cream for those bruises."

As expected, she yanks her hand back with the dramatic effect I know all too well and stomps out of the club, taking her sidekicks with her. My cock grows hard as I watch her walk away, her perfect ass jiggling ever so slightly as her hips sway, reminding me of how it shook with every thrust as I was taking her from behind. *Oh, we are definitely doing that again.*

"God, she's such a bitch," someone says as soon as the last of her posse is out of the building.

I snap around to the *soon-to-be* ex-employee and stalk toward the asshole while I lay my threat. "Do. Not. Ever. Let me hear that word come out of your mouth in regard to that woman again. Do you understand me?"

The giggling stops, leaving the room in silence as the young man cowers, bowing his head as he mumbles his apology.

I look around at the others who seemed to enjoy his comment, noticing how their relaxed demeanor stiffens. I've always taken pride in my ability to lead without making anyone feel uncomfortable, but the heat from my stare isn't inspiring anything but fear at the moment. "If I hear about *anyone* saying a single negative thing about Ms. Sinclair, they'll be fired on the spot. Do I make myself clear?"

Each employee agrees to my terms, allowing me to storm off and let thoughts of my dirty little princess calm me down.

While I was hiding away in my office to avoid biting anyone's head off, I decided to be somewhat productive.

I initially reached out to Ledger to try to talk about whatever the fuck happened last week, but he's so busy with Sloane. Plus, this isn't exactly his forte, so he recommended I text Henry.

It's no mystery to us that Henry has been a well-known Dom in the kink community for years. It seems silly now that I didn't reach out to him directly, but I honestly wasn't even thinking about how what we did would be considered part of the BDSM spectrum.

While I don't think I'm ready to go full Dom, I would like to rack his brain on how to proceed with things as my masked persona. He agreed to lunch, but he won't be free until after I told her to meet me. So I did the only thing I could do and researched on my own.

Don't get me wrong, owning a sex club pretty much comes with a general overview of at least the most common of kinks, a sex club manual if you will. But I've never been interested in any power exchange, so, Google to the rescue. I feel relatively competent now, more sure of what happened between us and why. I've at least let go of enough guilt to be able to fantasize about that night without feeling like a total jackass.

Someone might partake in such proclivities for many reasons, and from what I've found, it can be rather common with people in positions of power. I feel confident that Margot's particular inclination has something to do with how her mind always tends to run nonstop. For me, well...I never realized that sending her to Paris would take her away completely. And her submission is nice after feeling so *irrelevant* these past couple of years.

One more time. We can set a few parameters and see what this is between us. The hate fucking was crazy hot, but I think we need a more controlled environment. Hell, she might not even show up in the first place, but if she does...a world doesn't exist where I will ever let her go again. In any capacity.

Chapter Thirty-Nine

Margot, you stupid slut. One good fucking from a big dick and you can't stay away? Where the hell is the boss bitch CEO who was *sooo* not anyone's sub and would *neverrr* be talked to like that again?

I think we left her at home after she had dreams every night this week of being tied up and degraded by a man in a mask with a giant, talented cock.

Yes, thank you, subconscious. Painfully unhelpful, as always. But not incorrect in your assessment of this week, which has been hellish. My vibe and my memories of previous encounters have let me down, and I've somehow found myself staring at the door to the reserved room exactly a week after I left here pissed off and swearing never to return. I'm horny and confused, but apparently, horny is winning out.

I at least owe it to myself to see if I can get one more orgasm out of this man, and maybe we can discuss our dynamic like adults and steer it in a direction that's more consistent with my usual flings. Respectful meetings, passion, no need for all this extra...whatever it is. Not really what I would call a Dominant/submissive relationship, but a power exchange—no more. I'm the queen of my world, and I'm not going to kneel or crawl or bow or whatever else this fucker wants. If that's the only reason he's here, he'll have to find someone else.

I steel myself, take a deep breath, and open the door with my lace mask firmly in place and my black velvet robe tied around my lingerie of choice this evening. My red-bottomed heels are still on, and I have a garter belt and garters holding up my thigh-highs, currently hidden under the robe. Somehow, knowing what's on the other side of the door is more intimidating than the first time when this was totally new, and I can feel the blush heating my face, neck, and decolletage.

After closing the door behind me, I turn and lean back against it, taking in the huge, muscled frame of my masked man. He's sitting in the same chair as last time, man-spreading his huge legs out in front of him. Boots, black jeans, and a long-sleeved workout top complete his look. Plus his balaclava, which covers almost all of his face. His arms are bent behind his head as he reclines, the picture of a man who knows the world is his. *Who knows that I'm his, at least in this room.*

I want to be mad at his arrogance and the strength he's projecting, but the part of my brain descended from cave-dwellers says *this giant man will fuck you, impregnate you, protect you, and your offspring will have a good chance of surviving.*

Our biological urge to fuck is undefeated.

I open my mouth to try to set the tone for this meeting, explain that aspects of last time *cannot* be repeated, and suggest we discuss some additional ground rules to those set out by the club, but he beats me to it.

"I knew you'd come back for more, you desperate little slut."

The wind goes right out of my sails. I deflate as the reconciliatory mood I was in is replaced with disbelief and *anger.* Damn, I seem to be getting angry a lot these days. My mouth drops open, and I must stand in shock for over a minute because he finally chuckles, breaking the silence.

"Is your mouth open because you're asking for something to be put in it? We're going to have to discuss a few things, and you'll certainly be silent more often than not, but this might be a rare case when I ask you to use your words. Would you like something in your mouth?"

Oh *fuck* this guy, and fuck my misogynistic pussy for being wetter than it's been all week, just because this asshole is mouthing off. I snap my mouth shut and make a sharp turn to face the door, placing my hand on the handle and getting ready to pull it open and sprint the fuck out of here...

"Wait."

I hesitate, giving him time to rise from his chair, seemingly unbothered and unhurried, and slowly walk to me. His looming presence behind me makes me tremble with need, and I haven't felt this confused about my own desires and emotions in years. Since I was making sense of my feelings for Jack. I hated uncertainty then, and I hate it now, even as I feel myself growing wetter from this man standing over me.

He places his hands on my corseted waist, and I feel tiny standing in front of him, even in my heels. It's not so much a height difference, just the power radiating off him, and I could cry, I'm so confused. *Is it period week, and I've miscounted? What the hell is this tidal wave of emotion?* I'm still just as angry, too. Angry, horny, overwhelmed. My life story lately. Put it on my gravestone.

I feel him bend down behind me and nuzzle his nose into the juncture where my neck meets my shoulder. He inhales deeply, exhaling with a deep, masculine groan that makes my pussy clench around nothing. After holding me for a long minute, he finally speaks.

"It's not wrong to want this."

And damn him, I know he's right. It feels too perfect to be wrong. I still feel the urge to fight to be in control, though. I realize I must've said this out loud when he responds.

"You're in control, P..." He pauses after speaking the "P" sound, before giving a slight cough and continuing, "You are in control, pet. This all ends with one word or four taps from you, and you think you aren't in control?"

He spins me around to face him, and I take in his *brown* eyes? I could have sworn they were blue last week, but it was dimmer in here.

One of his large hands travels slowly from my waist, gliding with a barely there touch over my breasts and collarbone, before landing on my neck and holding me. Not squeezing, just holding me, *grounding me* against the door, and I stop trembling. His hand leaves my neck to brush across my lips before prying my mouth open. He slips his middle and ring fingers into my mouth, pressing down slightly on my tongue and holding my jaw in a firm grip. I widen my eyes when I realize I can't speak, but he immediately soothes me.

"Shh, shh. You know how to get out. Four taps, pet. But I need your attention and I need you to listen and not interrupt me, and this is the most efficient way to talk to you right now."

I must telegraph my intention with my eyes because he chuckles darkly. "I wouldn't recommend it, pet. I bite back."

Abandoning my intention of biting down on his fingers as hard as I can, I wait for him to continue. "As I was saying before I was interrupted. It's *not* wrong to want this, and as I just reiterated, you hold the control here. What *I* think is that both of us *need* this. I want to dominate you. In my outside life, things are happening well beyond my control, and I'm spiraling. I need this control. If I had to guess, I would say that in your life or career, you have to make many, *many* decisions every day, and this has become tiresome lately. You could use a break from using that brilliant brain of yours all day, every day. Nod if I'm correct."

I nod, maintaining the mesmerizing eye contact we've held this entire time and feeling the tight, comforting hold he has on my jaw. Spit is pooling in my mouth and leaking onto his hand and down onto my robe, but he pays it no mind.

"I thought so. Now, I would also guess that you're a powerful woman used to making endless decisions, being in charge, and getting your way. Correct?"

I nod. Spit drips.

"Good girl."

Fuck, are there tears in my eyes? Now I'll be covered in tears, snot, and spit...

"Pet," he says harshly, drawing my eyes back to his. "If I want you to have any thoughts or opinions other than answers to the questions I'm asking, I'll give them to you, understand?"

I nod.

"Does it scare you to feel the way you do in this room? To not be in charge of every minute decision for once?"

I nod.

"Do you want to play with me again, knowing that you're in charge, but I'll be making every decision?"

This is what he's been getting at. Reassuring me, reminding me of my safe word and my taps, and asking if I'm brave enough to engage in something that scares me but offers so much pleasure. *The last time I took this risk, I got burned.* But this isn't that. This is safe. A safe space for release with my masked man. He won't break my heart like Jack did. He can't. I don't even know who he is. *I'm safe to let go with him. He won't hurt me in any way I don't ask for.*

I nod.

Pure triumph flashes across his eyes, and he releases a fraction of the tension he was holding himself with.

"What a perfect slut you are, being brave so you can be fucked until you're mindless. I'm very proud, pet."

If he wasn't practically holding me up against the door, I might melt into a puddle right here.

"Now, I'm going to take my fingers out of your mouth, but I want you to listen very carefully. What I'm about to say is a *rule* I expect to be followed consistently when we're together at all times until a scene ends, and because it's a *rule,* there will be consequences if it isn't followed. We'll practice for today since we haven't discussed punishment yet, but nod if you understand."

I nod.

"When I take my fingers out of your mouth, you'll be able to speak again, but as a rule, I don't want you to. Forming thoughts, voicing them...that isn't why you're here. It's not your purpose here, pet. Your purpose here is to take what I give you, understand?"

I nod.

"If I ask you a direct question, you may answer with yes, Sir or no, Sir. For now, you can say please whenever you want, but if you abuse this, I'll reconsider. I look forward to hearing you beg, but I won't tolerate whining. If I *ask* you to beg, you can be more creative, but not today. Do you understand?"

I nod. He takes his fingers out of my mouth and moves his hand back to rest at my throat as I roll my jaw a couple of times and shut my mouth, relishing in finally swallowing my spit as his eyes crinkle down at me.

"Now, I want one of your approved verbal responses to the next question, and then I want to hear your safe word when I ask for it. We aren't ending our scene, but I want to make sure you know it. Do you recall your safe word?"

"Yes, Sir."

His eyes crinkle again as if he's beaming, and I wish for the first time this balaclava wasn't covering his undoubtedly gorgeous face. "That's a good girl. Now, tell me your safe word."

"Sprinkles," I whisper.

"Lovely. Mine is chocolate, for the record. If you say it again without me asking for it, we stop. The last thing I have to tell you for now, pet, is very important."

I look intently into his dark gaze as he steps even closer into my space.

"Words that aren't either of our safe words won't have any impact on me at all. We didn't mention what happens if you say no, stop, or it hurts. We didn't discuss them because you saying them means *nothing*, pet. You may say them when you're feeling what you think is too much pleasure, but what you think doesn't matter, as we've already established. You may say it hurts, and sometimes it will, but it's because I decided to make it hurt."

He's whispering now, every dark promise just between us. If anyone else were in this room, even three feet away, they wouldn't hear his filthy words to me now.

"If you want to stop, use your safe word. Otherwise, you're mine, pet. Do you understand?"

Do I understand? At this point, I'm not sure I even know my own name. But I know beyond a shadow of a doubt that I want everything this man has to give me, even if he has to force me to take it and even if it hurts. I look into the brown eyes, almost black with lust and familiar in a way I don't understand. *Please don't burn me.*

"Yes, Sir."

Chapter Forty

"Yes, Sir."

I've once again underestimated Margot Sinclair's ability to alter my perception of reality, and I'll pay for this instance just as endlessly and painfully as the others. In this moment, I don't even fucking care that she doesn't know who I am. She listened to me, felt my intention, saw it in my eyes, and decided to trust me. Am I not still myself, even under the balaclava? My princess might not know who she's submitting to, but she trusts my energy and my dominance. This version of myself doesn't even have to be a part of Jack Carter, truthfully. It certainly didn't exist in me before she and I walked into this room last week, and it exists only for her.

I decide I've heard enough for now, and I want to see if she's really ready to let go for me. I've seen how tired she's been lately. Still beautiful, still glowing, but tired. Running three huge projects simultaneously will wear anyone down, and I doubt she's had much downtime since she moved back. I can't fix all of her problems, especially while she hates me in real life, but I can take away some of her stress for a few hours at least. *And punish her for how she's been acting lately.*

Stepping back from where I've been crowding her, Margot sags a little against the doorway, as if I was structural to her verticality. I return to my chair and sit down, stretching my legs out wide in front of me. Let's see how far my horny girl will go. Based on the glaze in her eyes just from taking away her speech for a bit, I'd say she's well on her way to floating already.

"Crawl to me. Slowly. Half the speed of last time."

She doesn't even hesitate. I reach down to adjust my aching cock as she drops to her hands and knees and begins her slow approach from the other side of the room. I can see the swells of her heavy breasts as they move with her, held high by her corset but still mostly hidden by the robe I haven't removed yet. When she reaches the halfway point, I tell her to stick her tongue out, and again, she doesn't hesitate.

As she makes her way to me, hips swaying and tongue out in invitation, it takes every ounce of restraint I possess not to leave my chair, pin her to the floor, and fuck her raw. But I have so many ideas in mind for my pet, so I can't stop the fun before it begins.

Finally, she reaches me and sits back on her knees just like last time. "You may close your mouth, pet. Stand."

She glides gracefully to her feet, even in her heels, and I decide I'm going to torture her just a little while I sate a desire I've had for more years than I can admit. I'm going to inspect my princess. My *pet.*

Before I sit back down, I unbelt my jeans and pull them down with my boxers, just far enough for my weeping cock to spring free. I plan to ignore it for the next thirty minutes or so, but I'm betting on the fact that she won't be able to. I want her to see it and need it inside her so desperately that she uses one of her few words she's allowed, and *begs* me for it.

Without addressing the fact that my dick stands proudly at attention between us, I sit down, spread my legs, and pull Margot to stand just in front of me. Pulling the tie on her robe, I let it fall before tossing it away. *Fuck. Me.* She's wearing something that has to be from her Noir collection, a black corset top that's sheer except for the boning, giving me a perfect view of her nipples that look painfully hard. She's not wearing any panties...

I reach out and give a light smack to her cunt that's out and in my face, since she's wearing a garter belt, thigh-high stockings, and *no fucking panties.* She gasps but stays quiet.

"Do you make it a habit of walking around with nothing covering your cunt?"

"No, Sir."

"Only for me?"

"Yes, Sir."

"Hmm." Unable to help myself, I slide one thick finger into her tight little slit, collect a portion of the wetness gathering there, and lift my balaclava to taste her. I couldn't wait one more second, not when my dessert presented itself to me on a platter with no lid.

"Fucking delectable, pet," I say, waiting to see if she'll fuck up and say thank you. But my girl is smart and stays quiet.

Sitting straight up, I stare at her smooth cunt for so long I know she's uncomfortable, but she should get used to being observed like this. Appraised. In the same way people stare at Michelangelo's *David* for hours, Margot should be on a pedestal and admired. But only by me.

"Turn around, feet hip-width apart. Bend over and put your hands around your ankles."

Her eyes widen, but she slowly turns and does as I've asked. What a genius I am, to have her present this fucking perfect cunt to me. It's glistening, nearly dripping, and the satisfaction I have knowing I did this is otherworldly.

"Tell me, pet. Have you ever been fucked like this before? Bent in half, legs wide, completely at the mercy of the man behind you, spreading this pussy open with his cock?"

A shuddering intake of breath tells me she's just as affected by this as I am.

"No, Sir."

"And do you like the idea of it?"

"Yes, Sir."

I stand tall behind her and place my boots on the outside of her feet so that her heels can't slide any farther apart and allow her to fall, but I keep my body off hers for now.

"I think, pet, that you with your legs spread wide and with nowhere to go is my favorite position," I murmur, slowly beginning to trail my hands up and down the inside of her thighs, barely touching the wetness at her center before moving them away.

Her little thighs are trembling, and her breaths are coming faster now.

"I'm not surprised that you like it. It's perfect for such a good little whore like yourself."

I give her just one finger, all the way in, and I hold it still as she gasps.

"Whores love to be on display like this. It allows them to show off all their best assets and make themselves as useful as possible, with holes open for anyone who needs them. I think next time I'll bring a spreader bar to keep your legs nice and wide for me, so you can't close them even if you want to."

Her pussy clenches desperately around my finger, and I give her a second, then a third. No movement, just a plug to remind her I'm here. And to make sure she's ready for this cock she's about to get.

"You're being such a good girl for me. My fingers are soaked, and I have a perfect view of your tight little asshole, pet. Have you ever taken a cock this big in your ass?"

"No, Sir..." she whispers, although it's more like the world's softest sob.

"Mmm. Not tonight. But soon," I whisper, laughing darkly as her trembling intensifies. "I'm having a little trouble, though. If I take you like this, I'm not sure if I should rip your tits out of this corset and hold on to them for leverage while I fuck you, or just put both of my hands around your throat until you pass out."

She's been so distracted by my soft murmurings that she hasn't noticed the condom wrapper ripping. Poor thing. She'll be so surprised. She's not getting the moment of time to back out that I gave her last time, either. I line my head up with her tight little cunt, reach around to put one hand around her throat and one halfway over her mouth, and thrust in to the hilt in one smooth slide before she even realizes what's happening.

Her scream is ear-piercing, even with my hand halfway covering her mouth, and her legs shake as I feel her walls strangle my dick with the power of her orgasm.

"I told you that you were a desperate little slut, and you are, aren't you? Coming just from me putting my cock in you."

I haven't even given her one stroke yet, and I feel like I could come too, just from feeling her explode around me. Instead, I stay fully seated inside her, feeling every one of the aftershocks as her orgasm rolls on and on. Being deep inside her hot, tight pussy as it massages me is cathartic, and although the urge to thrust is there, I'm enjoying her being my little cocksleeve and keeping me warm. It's only been a couple of minutes—*I can't have my girl passing out from being upside down for too long*—before she trembles again and lets out a little whine.

"Something to say, pet?"

I almost don't hear her at first, and I'm starting to think she might actually pass out when I hear her faint, "Please."

Fucking music to my ears.

I laugh, delighted she's desperate enough to ask for what she wants.

"Oh my perfect girl, you only had to ask. Stand up and put your hands on your tits."

Still deep in her pussy, I pick her up by the hips and walk us over to the couch. Instead of placing her face down on the cushion like last time, I bend her over the arm and spread her legs, holding them in place at a much better angle for my height than the cushions.

Finally, I start to thrust, and it's a good thing she's already come once because I'm not going to last long like this. She's on another plane of existence right now, being such a good quiet girl for me, and I can feel her fluttering up to another orgasm while the cum from her first orgasm starts to form a ring around the base of my cock. *Jesus*, it might take even less time than I anticipated to come.

Reaching around, I find her poor neglected clit and start giving her the small, fast circles she likes. I know she's hypersensitive, so I wonder how she'll react.

"No!" she screams, writhing in my arms. *Fuck, even better than I imagined.* "Please, please no, Sir, it hurts. Please no more."

I ignore her, chasing my release and feeling her tumble over the cliff at the same time, squeezing the life out of me and making me come so hard I'm briefly afraid I'll pass out. And then who will be in charge? I make sure she hears exactly how she's affected me, groaning directly beneath her ear as I fill the condom. Taking just a second to catch my breath, I ease out as gently as possible, feeling a little smug as she winces. *Yeah, Princess. You'll be sore as fuck tomorrow.*

I'm pulling off the condom and walking to grab a blanket to wrap her in when I hear a small, "Sir?" from the couch. I turn, and my knees almost buckle at the sight of my perfect pet sitting on the couch, tongue out, obviously asking me to empty the condom in her mouth just like last week. *I am so fucked.* I could never deny her anything, and I don't deny her this. Giving her cheek a soft stroke, I help her swallow every last drop of my cum. *I mean, she's earned it. She can have it however she wants.*

She lets out a contented sigh, and I see exactly how hazy her eyes are. Kneeling in front of her, I meet her gaze.

"You were a perfect girl for me tonight. I'm so proud of you."

My heart warms at her happy little grin, and I realize that however fucked I thought I was in this situation, it's exponentially worse. But I can't find it in me to care. Now's my chance.

I retrieve the burner phone I left in the room's locker and place it on top of the stack of clothes I have laid out for her. Until this all comes crashing down, I'm going to take any scrap of attention from any version of Margot Sinclair I can get—until she unmasks me.

Chapter Forty-One

"That's literally the hottest thing I've ever heard in my life," Mark says, sipping his martini and eyeing Marco hungrily. "We need to get some masks and go back to the club, babe."

I blush, feeling a little better that the kinkiest night of my life sounds desirable and not terrifying to my friends. Not for the first time, I realize how lucky and grateful I am to have these two men in my life. Maybe New York will start to feel more like where I'm meant to be soon. Especially if my masked man continues to be a part of it.

"He sounds like a wet dream to me, cara. With the mask and the dark energy...mmm." Marco winks at me, then turns to Mark. "I think you're right, tesoro. We should spice things up a bit."

"It's not creepy, though, that he gave me this phone? For all I know, he could be tracking me, or hacking it, and planning to traffic me or hold me for ransom." I voice these thoughts even though I know they're bullshit. My masked man is *safe*, I just know it.

"The background checks are extensive at the club, and honestly, Margot"—Mark sighs dramatically and stands to leave, dropping cash on the table to cover lunch—"would being kidnapped by him really be so bad?"

My companions leave, but I order another drink and watch people mill about on the street outside, lost in my thoughts and the anonymity of sitting in a corner of a busy restaurant. The scary thing is, I've felt better this week than I have in months. The noise and upheaval of my real life have been quieted, and I've been able to keep a laser-sharp focus on all the projects currently needing my attention. Construction continues at the storefront, the jewelry store collaboration is up and running already in advance of Valentine's Day, and sales have been through the roof in all our physical stores as well as online.

I've felt...happy? My life is nice. I love my family and my job and my hobbies and my friends. Right? Maybe it's more accurate to say I've felt more alive lately. Sighing, I look again at the phone that I've kept charged since it was left on top of my clothes after my last encounter with my masked man. He hasn't reached out, and although I'm coming to terms with the psychological realities of why I enjoy our dynamic so much, I'm not ready to swallow my pride enough to text first. I pry my eyes from the phone and try to get back into my professional headspace for the rest of my day.

The last piece of the work puzzle is my final meeting at Rendezvous Too this afternoon, making sure everything is in place for their Valentine's Day date auction. It sounds like it'll be a really fun time, with both men and women in the community signing up to be auctioned off for various activities. Based on the dates' requests for their specific pieces of lingerie, the offerings include everything from a nice vanilla dinner and night on the town all the way to, well, everything.

One man was almost in tears when he saw his specially designed jockstrap and harness, saying it would be perfect to wear while performing tasks for whoever bid on his "butler for the day" package. My planning binder included a long section on how legally this isn't prostitution, and there's no promise of sex, but I mean...everyone knows what they're getting.

While the majority of the dates are to take place a few days later *on* Valentine's Day, some are for immediate play in the club that night, which should make the bidding even more exciting. My binder indicated that the last woman up has specific interests in exhibitionism and group activities, so I have a suspicion her auction will end things with a bang. In any case, members of my team will be on-site with a selection of pieces for purchase. We'll also have demonstrations of our tailoring process and answers for anyone who has inquiries about custom work. Hopefully, the staging will show off our lingerie to a large group of prospective buyers, and we can gain a foothold in the kink community.

Breathing a sigh of relief, I take in the final staging for the auction at Rendezvous Too. With minor notes, everything will be ready and as I envisioned. It's hard being right all the time and making everything perfect, but someone has to do it. *Not you when you're with your masked man.* Ugh, now is really not the time for these thoughts, especially when I see Jack making his way toward me. I give myself a little shake to clear my head.

"Good afternoon, Mr. Carter. I'm pleased to see that you and your staff have been able to complete the staging to my specifications. I have a few minor notes for Aaron, but otherwise, I think I'll be signing off on it. Everything's ready for you and your patrons to have a seamlessly romantic evening," I say, to the point. I'm ready to get home, get to Pilates, and maybe take my trusty vibe to the bathtub to think about more recent encounters.

"Are you okay?" Jack asks, head tilted to one side and a smirk on his lips.

"What do you mean, am I okay? Do I not look okay?" I look down at my outfit. Maybe the V neck of my blazer is a little more daring than usual, and *maybe* I'm wearing a partially sheer bustier underneath instead of an actual top. I've felt a little sexier this week, what can I say?

"No, no, you look fantastic. Absolutely lethal, I would say." Jack's smirk grows wider as he sees my blush bloom and travel down my neck. "You just seem different. Looser. Almost as if..." He trails off, and I already dread what's about to come out of his mouth.

"You've been getting some especially good dick," he finishes, and I'm not sure how I even want to play this. I can act indignant and tell him it's none of his goddamn business. Or I can be honest, and he can be as jealous as he was when he thought I was fucking Marco.

Cocking my head, I allow myself the tiniest of smiles and decide to just be honest. "You're right, Mr. Carter. That's exactly what it is. Truly exceptional dick."

Moving past him, I sense amusement but not jealousy. Good. Maybe he's finally understanding that my personal life has nothing to do with him anymore and moving on. Marco stands by the door with my coat, bag, and gloves, and continues to look over my shoulder as he hands over my items one by one.

"What's caught your attention?" I ask, hoping he's not noticing another aspect of the staging that isn't perfect. Following his gaze, I see him eyeing Jack like a lion salivating over an injured gazelle.

"You grew up with him, right? Has he always been so hot? I didn't really notice before, but something about the giant lumberjack look he's sporting today is really doing it for me," he says, finally giving me a wink.

He's not wrong. Jack was apparently helping with some carpentry work for one of the playrooms on the second floor of the club earlier today, so he's wearing worn jeans, work boots, and a dark green shirt. It's much more rugged than his norm, and he looks good.

"He was *not* always so hot. He actually went through quite the gangly phase before his muscles caught up to his height," I say, finally relaxing into the car and taking a sip of the coffee my driver handed me.

"Well, he's hot now. And I'll tell you one thing, Margot, that I've learned from *years* of experience," he sighs.

"What's that?"

"A man only walks like *that* if he's slinging a big. Ole. Dick."

I choke on my coffee as Marco cackles, and we drive off into the evening.

Chapter Forty-Two

Jack

"Thanks so much for meeting me, man," I say, standing up from my chair to greet Henry as he makes his way to our table.

I learned decades ago that Henry expects you to arrive at least fifteen minutes early to any appointment, so I always make a point to appease him. Out of all of us, his time is the most precious, and I really do appreciate him lending me some of it to give me the BDSM birds and bees talk.

Henry and I have always had an interesting relationship. While I was never as close to him as Ledger, I still consider him a brother. And I'd like to think the feeling is mutual.

"Anytime," he replies, returning my hug before we both sit back down. "So what is it you wanted to talk about? I will say, I'm quite intrigued. Ledger sent me a string of emojis this morning, and while I may be a few years your senior, I am well aware of what the eggplant implies, especially when paired with a peach, a tongue, and a devil. Now, I do hate to make assumptions, but considering your current profession, am I correct to deduce that you are well aware of sex?"

"Yes, *asshole*, I know about sex," I reply, rubbing my temples at the thought of how tedious this conversation might become.

Henry raises his hands in surrender. "Then proceed with your objective for this lunch."

How to say this...well, Henry, you see the thing is, your sister showed up at an anonymous sex club and matched with me. I recognized her immediately, but my disguise was foolproof, so she never realized who I was. And instead of exposing myself to her, I hate fucked her into next year.

"Um. I've sort of met someone and..."

I give him the whole spiel...*minus the part about it being our dearest Margot.* Wow. I didn't realize that when I requested this lunch, I'd be asking him for advice on how to properly dominate his baby sister.

Without her knowing it's me.

When I finish, Henry sits for a minute, stroking his chin, deep in thought before replying. "That is rather unconventional, but I'm confident that with the right parameters, you can make it work."

"Right! Parameters! I read about those online. We established some already, well, I sort of established them myself. But there was barely any time to talk, so I'm sure we need more."

"I trust safe words were included in those parameters?" he asks, raising an eyebrow.

I'm not a complete imbecile. My madness ends with secretly fucking the estranged love of my life. *Oh yes.* And then asking her oldest brother for advice on how to do it properly

"Well, yeah, of course."

Henry looks pleased and leans closer to me. "Alright, walk me through how you set your other parameters. Typically, a contract is drawn up for soft and hard limits, but I would imagine that to be somewhat of a hindrance considering your anonymity."

"We were only ever able to go over basic preferences, but the club has us fill out and sign an extensive questionnaire every time we come in."

A.k.a. I told your little sister, our princess, to shut her whore mouth and do what I tell her to or else. *Jesus Christ, Jack.*

"That's a start. I would advise you to agree on some more personal boundaries prior to your next meetup and continue to check in before every subsequent scene. Really ask to make sure she feels comfortable and safe with every task you give her, both inside and outside of the club—"

"Oh, there's no outside." I interrupt, not wanting him to give me a thirty-minute lesson on how to be a Dom. I need someone to tell *me* what to do half the time. Margot can give me all the checklists she wants. I don't mind one bit. In fact, I eat that shit up. "I don't think either of us is looking for a real Dom/sub relationship. Just a sexual power exchange, strictly within the confines of the club."

"Very well. It all boils down to setting expectations prior to the scene and sticking to them. The whole reason your submissive is allowing you to have power in the first place is generally so they can turn off their brains and really get into subspace, free of concern and the minutiae of their daily life.

"For example, if you change your boundaries within a scene without prior communication, and especially if they're already in subspace when you make that change, they might not be able to understand the changes they are agreeing to. You'll lose their trust, and they'll be hesitant to lean into said subspace again. Trust is going to be key in what you are doing."

Fucking wonderful.

"What other questions do you have for me?" Henry asks. In all my life, I don't think I've heard him say as much as he has right now.

Well, I might as well go for it. Even he would agree his sister is a disobedient little brat. "What about, um...punishments?"

"I see no reason to avoid punishments. Again, as long as the consequences have been established up front, I would actually stress the importance of following through with them. Within the scene, you provide a sense of leadership to your submissive. Keeping your word is an integral part of that illusion. Anything else?"

"Nope, I think that just about covers it."

"Just remember, maintain expectations and aftercare, what transpires between is left to preference."

What would I give to be able to hold this woman after making love...*scratch that,* after fucking the ever-living daylights out of her. "Aftercare? Um, I don't think she would be into cuddling..."

Henry massages his brows for a moment before responding. "Honestly, Jack, for someone who *owns a sex club,* for Christ's sake, how is your spectrum of aftercare so limited?

"Aftercare can be anything. It can be a hot bath, a scalp rub, taking her braid down if you've braided her hair, or cuddling. It doesn't necessarily have to be intimate, but it needs to be *something*. And as her Dominant within the scenes, I strongly recommend you give her whatever aftercare she requests. As long as you're comfortable with it as well."

"Got it," I say, making a mental list of all the things to ask when I text my *pet* tonight.

Henry sits back in his chair, taking a swig of his water in the process. "Anytime, Carter, but I do expect updates."

"Um, sure. So do you have a sub right now?" I ask, trying to deflect the attention away from my own messed-up situation. I immediately regret it when Henry's face contorts into an unpleasant expression. "Oh, um. I'm sorry if that was inappropriate."

He chuckles, a smile that seems closer to a grimace twisting his features. "No offense taken, Jack. I'm not currently contracted with a submissive, no. There isn't really enough time before..."

Henry surprises me by making the least dignified sound I've ever heard from him, a choking cough he plays off with his handkerchief at his mouth. "Quite dusty in here, is it not?" he asks, and I know him well enough to sense this topic is now over.

The remainder of our lunch is spent catching up on sports, news, business, and family, including Margot. I pull as much information about her as I can without sounding suspicious.

He fills me in on all the things she's been up to lately. As excited as I am to be meeting with her soon as my masked persona, I miss just having her in my life. "I'm proud of her."

"She's certainly the best of us all," he agrees, pride flashing in his eyes.

"It's nice to see the two of you getting so close," I say when he finishes his spiel about her recent accolades. "I feel like between all of us, you two spent the least amount of time together."

His brows furrow as that pride in his eyes changes to regret. "Well, by the time she was old enough to do anything, I was hardly home. And I was too busy keeping an eye on Ledger. Heaven knows he needed it. Anyway, she always had you to look out for her."

He's going to kill me.

Chapter Forty-Three

Sir:

Good morning, pet.

Pet:

Creepy that you gave me this phone. What do you want?

Sir:

Disappointed but not surprised by your attitude.

I was hoping that you'd want to continue seeing me at the club.

I certainly want to continue seeing you.

As such, I think it's best for us to have an open line of communication.

A place to debrief, plan, and discuss our preferences without breaking a scene to do so.

Pet:

I think the questionnaires the club provides are pretty comprehensive.

I don't think we need anything else.

Sir:

Really?

Because the club questionnaire told me you were highly interested in degradation before our first meeting. Then, after our second scene, you confirmed it as a 'five out of five' on your scale of things you have experience with and enjoy.

Pet:

I'm aware of the ranking system, and that's correct.

I gave degradation a five on purpose. I love it. Are you happy?

I still don't see the point in this.

Sir:

The point is, pet, that I might know you like degradation, but I'd prefer to know more about how you like it. Would you like it if I called you a dumb good-for-nothing slut that nobody ever loved, for example?

Pet:

...no. I can't say I would. I don't like that. It feels different. Meaner.

Sir:

But you'd like it if I told you that you're my perfect set of holes, existing only for me to use?

Pet:

Yes.

Sir:

Talk soon, pet.

Sir:

Do you have time now to text? I don't want you to be distracted for this conversation.

Pet:

Yes, Dad, you have my full attention.

Sir:

> We can negotiate if you'd like to call me Daddy, pet.

> That's a good segue into what I'd like to discuss.

> Our hard limits are well defined by the club questionnaire, but I think some of your 'interested to try' selections need to be fleshed out.

Pet:

> This still seems like overkill.

> You just want to be creepy and text me.

Sir:

> In that case, since you're "highly interested" in roleplay, maybe the next time we're together, I'll be a dragon shifter who needs a human host to incubate my eggs and continue my line. I'll bring the eggs.

Pet:

> What the fuck, dude? No.

Sir:

Now you see why I encourage communication.

Pet:

Ugh, fine. Which do you want to discuss?

Sir:

I'll send them as I think of them. Good night, pet.

Sir:

Orgasm denial, highly interested?

Do you mean edging, or if I see fit, you wouldn't orgasm during a scene at all?

Pet:

Both.

Sir:

Elaborate.

Pet:

It's tied into the idea of not being in charge.

I don't want to know I'm coming once or twice or until I pass out. It shouldn't be for me to decide.

Sir:

Too true, pet.

Pet:

Looked at the list you sent.

I think a bath and some snacks afterward feels the most like me. I love baths.

Continued petting/head rubs/massages is fine post-scene.

Sir:

Thank you for telling me, pet. Consider it done.

Pet:

Would you get in the bath with me?

Sir:

I prefer to stay as clothed as possible.

During and after.

Pet:

Okay, Sir.

Sir:

Have you finished reviewing the punishment proposal?

Pet:

It's really long.

Sir:

You strike me as a fast reader.

Is your attention span the problem?

Pet:

Asshole.

I'm just a busy, important woman.

Sir:

I recommend you review it in detail. It discusses my complete discretion over your orgasm(s), corporal punishment, specific punishments for dress code violation, tardiness, sass. I wouldn't want there to be any confusion.

Pet:

I'll read it and send it back signed.

Sir:

The pawprint next to your signature was cute, pet.

I hope you really did read it thoroughly. Our time together could be difficult for you if not.

Chapter Forty-Four

Despite my best efforts to avoid being present for the Valentine's Day auction at Rendezvous Too, Mom insisted I should be there just in case my expertise was needed or a high-profile client wanted attention. While she's correct that there are *a lot* of high-profile people here tonight, including A-list Hollywood stars, music icons, and otherwise influential people in the world, my staff is competent. Even though she conceded my point about my staff, she finally hit me with, "Well, you certainly don't have any romantic plans for this evening!"

And she wasn't wrong there. Although, *technically*, I have romantic plans for *tomorrow*, and I've been buzzing since my masked man finally texted the phone he gave me earlier this week. For tonight, though, there are worse ways to spend my evening than building my anticipation while watching my business triumph and seeing people fucking all around me.

I'm not on show tonight, so I don a simple, strappy black minidress of my own design, adding a darker eye than I normally wear and bolder lipstick. I've gone back to my classic voluminous curls, still able to curl and tease on autopilot from so many years of my signature look. Adding some shimmer to my decolletage, I realize I look damn good, and my eyes look like I have a dirty little secret. Which, I guess I do. I wonder what my masked man is doing tonight. He could technically have a partner, but I doubt that. I'm not sure why I feel so connected to him, but I'm not going to question it. With plenty of time to think about our earth-shattering chemistry, I've decided I'm young, and I'm not going to fight it.

He could be there tonight, and you would never know.

That's an interesting idea. I'm not fooled into thinking that he wouldn't recognize me if he saw me in public. My mask is a flimsy lace, designed to act as more of a seductive accessory than to preserve my identity. I'm thankfully not a celebrity by any means. My family always maintained a very private life despite my father's global business operations, my brothers' athletic pursuits, and now my budding business. Hopefully, even if La Reine is massively successful, I look enough like other blondes to blend in with the crowd.

Deciding to dress as if my masked suitor will be in attendance, I take off my opaque black tights and replace them with a garter belt and lacy thigh highs. My black heels have a platform and a strap around the ankle, giving my legs every advantage and a little extra height. Grabbing my clutch and my coat, I reach for the door when my eyes catch on a package that was delivered earlier today with no return address. Tearing open the envelope, I read the inscription on the note inside, "For you, when you're mine."

I briefly consider the lack of signature before my brain is distracted by the fact that a diamond choker has slithered out into my hand. It's gorgeous. A full circle of round brilliant stones, interrupted only by what looks like a thick, platinum ring at the back of the necklace by the clasp. It's obviously well-made but not keeping with the delicate nature of the piece overall. Staring at it for a few long moments, I finally realize what it reminds me of. A ring for a leash to be clipped on. A mental image of wearing nothing but these beautiful diamonds and being led around on a matching platinum leash flits across my mind, and I hope my arousal doesn't drip down enough to visibly shine between my thighs tonight. *But it might.*

I clasp my new necklace on and finally make my way to the idling car, ready for tonight to pass quickly so it can be tomorrow.

Seeing Rendezvous Too full of patrons, all dressed to the nines, is even more impressive than I expected. I have to grudgingly admit that Jack has clearly worked his ass off over the past two years based on the sense of excitement and community in the room. Regulars mingle with carefully chosen invitees, all sipping either their one allotted cocktail or pink mocktails, on theme for the evening. Slow, sensual beats are an undercurrent to the rising tension in the air as the auction start time approaches. Aaron informed me during our last meeting that tonight, more X-rated activities will be allowed in the main ballroom area with the stage than usual.

"So that everyone can fully immerse themselves in the sensuality of the auction," he said.

Sensual is exactly how I would describe the current energy. I see a woman being led to a chaise lounge on a leash, and absentmindedly reach to touch my necklace when I'm jolted out of my reverie by a voice I didn't expect to hear tonight.

"Margot! Darling, *where* did you get that necklace?"

Mom? My mother, ladies and gentlemen, more concerned about my new diamonds than the fact that I'm dressed like a BDSM wet dream.

"Mom, what are you doing here?"

"Well, sweetie, I had a meeting in the city, and then I wanted to see Jack while I was in town. He's been here all day, so I picked up some food and we had a little picnic in his office. Once it got closer to opening time, I just stayed to see the beginning of the auction so I could see both of my kids' visions come to life tonight. Isn't it impressive what he's done here?" she asks, finally stopping to take a breath after singing Jack's praises.

There's no reason to pretend in front of her, so I agree. "It is. I think it might be even sexier in here than the original location, not that I'd ever tell Jack that," I say, realizing too late that Mom's eyes are tracking over my left shoulder. I turn to see

Jack wearing an all-black suit with no tie, smirking as he no doubt heard what I just said. *Great.*

I roll my eyes and turn back to Mom, seeing his eyes catch on my necklace just before he's no longer in my sight. I feel him, though, coming to stand beside me.

"Thank you for the compliment, Princess," he purrs, and I roll my eyes again as Mom laughs. "I'm not sure when you managed to sneak into Rendezvous without us knowing, but I'll make sure to tell Ledger you said that at my earliest convenience."

As I'm opening my mouth to tell him exactly where to fuck off to, the lights flash twice, signaling the auction is about to start. Before we can make our way to our side-stage area, where w e had planned to observe and ensure everything runs smoothly, Aaron runs frantically up to Jack, carrying a clipboard.

"Boss, we have a problem!"
Frowning, Jack gives him his full attention. "What is it? We haven't even started yet!"

"That's the thing, we can't start. Well, we can, but the printed order of events will be inaccurate. Our first date apparently has food poisoning. She was here and dressed, but after she had a bar snack, she started throwing up. Just her, though. Everyone else who ate it is fine."

I swear I see my mom's eyes sparkle, and I internally groan, knowing that even if she didn't cause the poor woman's sickness, she's about to pounce.

"Well, this is an easy enough fix. Her date was for dinner only, right? Something light to get everything going. Margot, darling, you look beautiful. You'll simply take her place. Jack will make sure nobody unsavory bids on you, won't you, Jackie? Oh, look at the time, I have a plane to catch! I love you both, text me!" And with kisses to each of our cheeks, she's gone.

Before I can even open my mouth to protest, Aaron leads me backstage, explaining the walk.

"It's simple, just a slow sixteen-count walk to the mark at the end of the stage. Since her date isn't themed and is only dinner, there weren't any props planned, necessarily. I think there will be a chair at the end. Any pose you want to add is up to you. We'll announce you as Miss M and bidding will start. No hard feelings if you don't get a ton, I think everyone is super excited about the kinkier offerings later." Aaron is rambling now, like I'm going to bite his head off for the fact that my mother has once again meddled in my personal life.

"Aaron, this is not your fault, and this is not my first runway. It's fine."

Just like that, the music shifts even slower, and I decide to go ahead with the show, immersing myself in the beat and thinking of exactly how I'll sway my hips to match. I'm glad now that I decided to doll myself up a little extra tonight, and although my skin tone isn't exactly that of the date I'm replacing, it should be close enough to look okay in the stage lighting. *And my diamond collar should shine.* Not a collar. I'm not *collared.* My diamond *necklace* should shine.

Finally, the announcer begins.

"Ladies and gentlemen, our auction begins tonight with a dinner date featuring the utterly gorgeous Miss M."

I begin my walk, hearing more than a few approving murmurs from both sexes throughout the crowd.

"She works in design and lives right here in New York City."

I arrive at the end of the stage after sauntering my way down, feeling more empowered than I was expecting. It's a heady feeling to have the attention of a room and be desired in this way. I place a hand on the back of the chair and trail it across, beginning a slow circle while dragging my gaze across the audience. I can't see details of faces thanks to the lighting, but I imagine a massive man in a black balaclava watching. Circling the chair gives everyone a full 360 view of my Pilates-toned body, and I gladly put it on display in the dress I designed myself. Finally, once I've circumvented the chair slowly, I primly sit down on the edge and cross one leg over the other, giving half of the audience a glimpse of my toned thigh and garters pulled taut. I hear a few groans from the side with the leg on display and smile.

"Wonderful, Miss M. What do we say, folks? Shall we start the bidding on this stunning lady at ten thousand?"

The following bidding is a blur, with people from all around the room driving up and up until finally it looks like a distinguished older gentleman is going to win with a bid of one hundred and fifty thousand. He looks kind enough and seems to be here alone, so maybe he'll want to have dinner at a classic restaurant and...

"Two hundred and fifty thousand," an achingly familiar voice enunciates. My head snaps to the bidding booth to see Jack standing there in black and looking like Hades, come to drag me back with him to the depths of the underworld.

The auctioneer is thrilled. "Splendid! There you have it, everyone! Going once...going twice...SOLD the beautiful Miss M to our distinguished proprietor Mr. Jack Carter! Thank you very much, Miss M!"

I recognize the dismissal, so I rise and slowly make my way back to the backstage area with my head held high. Once I'm backstage, though, I'm fucking pissed and ready for a fight. Luckily, my fight finds me quickly and is smart enough to lead me to his office before I blow up in front of his employees and guests.

"What the *actual fuck* is wrong with you! I already had a reasonable bid. I didn't need your pity money, and I don't fucking want to go on a date with you!" I hiss at him, feeling hot all over with how angry I am. Jack, however, is utterly calm and seems unaffected by my outburst.

"I don't like that man," he says quietly, holding up a hand and giving me a pleading look to hear him out when I open my mouth to attack again. I stay quiet and give him a chance. "I don't like that man enough for him to be on a date with you, Margot. Even a fake one. He isn't a predator, or he wouldn't be allowed in my club. But he can be pushy, and I was simply afraid in the moment that once he experienced your absolute brilliance, never mind your beauty, you might find yourself with an ardent admirer you shouldn't have to deal with."

He looks at me so earnestly that it's like I'm looking at the before Jack. The one who I thought loved me before he imploded my life. I guess I can't be that mad that he protected me from a perceived threat.

"I'm not going on a date with you," I say firmly, meeting his eyes and seeing them flicker into despair and then back to neutrality in the space of a blink before he looks down to pick at a nonexistent speck of lint on his pants.

"You certainly don't have to. I'm happy to donate your bid to the charity of your choice, regardless. Or you can have it and give it to your staff as bonuses once your New York store opens to amazing success," he takes a deep breath and meets my eyes again. "But would it really be so bad, Margot? I'm aware a lifetime of apologies won't fix what was broken, but we live in the same city now. Ledger and Sloane are going to bind us all even tighter together as a family once LJ is born, and you've obviously moved on." His eyes glance at my choker, then back up. "Couldn't we have a nice dinner together as friendly business associates and soon-to-be aunt and uncle?"

As his words hit me, I feel some of my fight fade. He's right. What's broken won't be fixed, but there's no reason to continue to avoid an attempt to create a cordial new role in each other's lives. For LJ's sake, primarily, with Mom and the business as other important considerations.

Rolling my eyes, I think about the fact that tomorrow, I'll see my masked man, and none of this will matter one bit. I won't have to think about the past, or the future, or my complicated family dynamics at all.

"Fine," I sigh, standing and getting ready to watch a bit more of the auction before I plan to call it an early night. "But it better be a stellar date, Mr. Carter."

His smile is the last thing I see before I leave his office, but I'm already daydreaming of brown eyes, combat boots, and huge hands, holding a leash.

Chapter Forty-Five

Jack

Texting Margot back and forth this past week about some of our limits and preferences for our time together has had a multitude of effects on me. I've been in a constant state of arousal, and it feels like my dick has been at least half hard unless I'm actively working or asleep. It's been intimidating to see her plainly state the things that she's interested in and to know in my soul that *I'm the one* meant to be giving her these things.

If I wasn't such a piece of shit, fucking her when she doesn't know who I am, I might think it's poetic that if she hadn't gone to Paris, neither of us would've explored these aspects of ourselves. I'm also extremely excited to get my hands on her because I know she's going to break a rule, possibly on purpose, and her ass needs to be reddened for showing up to my club looking like sin incarnate last week. *Yeah, it's gonna be a good night.*

I'm dressed in my usual uniform of boots, utility pants, a dark shirt, a balaclava, and my trusty brown contacts. Quietly opening the door to our reserved room, I'm excited to see what she's up to, considering I'm, let's see, thirty-seven minutes late. Her instructions were to be kneeling on the special cushions I provided, legs hip-width apart, head bowed, and palms on her thighs. She knows I don't want her words, sounds, or eyes until I ask for them tonight, but she can answer direct questions softly with yes, Sir and no, Sir. Our last check-in was ten minutes before her arrival time to confirm safe words, our color system, and tap outs, and she asked specifically that we don't check in again until we're well into the scene, as it interferes with her suspension of disbelief.

Dirty girl.

Delighted, I see that my little setup has had exactly its desired effect. She's kneeling on two square cushions, providing memory foam support to her knees. But another cushion is in front of her, and on it, an app-controlled wand. She knew when she came in here that she was to adjust it to sit *just against* her clit, and under no circumstances was she allowed to come. I activated the wand twenty minutes ago.

She's desperate, my little princess—covered in a sheen of sweat and wearing nothing but her diamond choker. While discussing her attire for the night, she confided that her lace mask is itchy, and she knows it doesn't cover much, so she chose to forgo it. I can see the entirety of her gorgeous face. She's trembling, especially her thighs, and I know it has nothing to do with holding her position—she's in better shape than I am. No, she's just desperate and aching to be filled. I approach her as I chuckle darkly, and she stills. She's in for a long-ass night.

Turning off the wand, I move it out of my way before kneeling before her. I reach between her thighs without preamble to see how wet she is. She shakes as soon as I touch her, but she's being so strong for now, keeping her eyes down and making no noise. *She's soaked,* and as soon as I breach her little hole to release all her delicious wetness, she's dripping. I pull my finger back just to slowly circle her entrance, teasing her pussy lips on every pass.

"Good evening, pet," I say roughly, still using my extra-deep voice so there's no chance she hears Jack anywhere underneath. "We haven't even started yet, and you're dripping on my floor like a fucking whore. I think it's going to be a very, very long night for you. And that's if you find it in you to be useful, which I doubt."

No noise, but my girl has tells. Her abs clench at the degradation, and she breathes deeply, trying to control herself. I stand, licking my fingers. *Delicious.* I should make her come over and over, collect it, glaze a piece of lemon cake with it, and make her feed it to me. *Next time.*

Pulling her new leash out of my pocket, the platinum chain shines as I clip it to the ring at the back of her necklace.

"Come."

She obeys the command beautifully, crawling after me on her hands and knees as I lead her across the room to a new velvet bench that I ordered. This room is now exclusively ours 24/7 until I release the contract on it, which hopefully won't be for a while yet. It's nice to not worry about anyone else being in here between our scenes, other than the cleaning crew.

I tap the bench. "Up. On your back, head hanging off the end. Reach back and hold my thighs with your hands, that's a good girl. Bend your knees and spread your legs as wide as they can go. I want to see what the fuck I'm paying for."

She shudders but does as she's told, being such a good girl for me, although I know it's killing her not to look me in the eyes. It's a more subtle form of degradation than words, and fuck if it's not effective.

"I've had a long week, and you're here for me to use. Isn't that right, whore? Tell me."

"Yes, Sir."

"Good, now open up so I can fuck this throat. Wide, unless you want me to stretch the corners of that tight mouth so far they bleed."

That's all the warning she gets before my cock is all the way in the back of her throat. She's gagging, but she's breathing through her nose so I know she knows what to do.

"I forgot what an expert cocksucker you were," I taunt, starting to slowly thrust in and out but giving her barely any time between thrusts to breathe. This really isn't for her, but I see her pussy clenching, trying to find any relief but getting nothing. "You're getting wetter while I fuck your throat, pet. Did you know you were that much of a slut? If I played with your hard little nipple right now, would you come?"

Tears, snot, and spit stream down her cheeks, and as ruined as she is right now, I want more. Picking up my pace, I reach up and slap each of her perfect tits before grabbing both nipples with my fingers. She screams, and I pinch harder. Fuck, I'm gonna come. Releasing her, I pull out of her mouth and grab her around the waist, placing her upright on the bench with her knees wide before thrusting back into her mouth roughly. This has taken an embarrassingly short amount of time, but her mouth is perfect. *And I'll get more later. She's the one who's only coming once tonight.*

"I'm gonna come in this dirty mouth, pet, and you're not going to swallow. I want you to hold it in your mouth for me. Now. Eyes."

Her eyes snap to mine, so wet with tears and blown black with lust that I would have no idea what color they were if I didn't already know that blue so well that I'd see it in any lifetime. She's a vision, and her eyes are what push me over the edge.

Groaning, I tilt my head back but keep my eyes locked on hers, hands on either side of her head as she hollows her cheeks to suck out every last drop of my cum as I fill her mouth. When she's got it all, she sits, keeping her eyes on me as I pull away from her mouth to squat in front of her. She assumes her resting position again like a natural, knees spread and hands on thighs, but her eyes are still tracking me because I haven't overridden that command yet. So fucking smart.

I let her hold it for long enough to become uncomfortable and watch as she actively fights her instinct to swallow. Finally, my urge to see wins out.

"Show me," I growl. She opens her mouth, trying to let me see but keep everything inside. Lovely, but not what I want. "Stick out your tongue. Let me see it all."

Her eyes widen, but she complies, and immediately a torrent of my cum mixed with her spit gushes from her mouth, down her chin, and drips down onto her breasts. She's wet from a variety of our fluids now, and looks as debauched as I've ever seen a woman. Her eyes are on me, her tongue is still out, and she's just waiting for me to tell her what to do.

I could cry. Later, I will. Later tonight, when she's taken care of and I know she's home and safe, I'll go home, remember how she trusted me in this moment, and sob like a baby. But that has to wait because my pet still needs to be fucked.

I reach to where most of my cum trails between her breasts and use two fingers to spread it over every inch of her chest and stomach, paying special attention to her nipples and seeing fresh tears fill her eyes when I do. This will dry and hopefully be uncomfortable—one more layer of insurance that she won't be thinking of anything but me all night. Once she's coated, I put my fingers back in her mouth.

"You've gotten my fingers dirty, pet. Clean them."

She sucks them like it's her job, and when they're clean, she sticks her tongue back out. Now she's just being a teacher's pet, wanting extra credit.

"Put your tongue back in your mouth, slut. You're not a dog. Eyes down."

I can feel her sadness at losing the right to look at me, but she squirms as I degrade her. Perfection.

"What's your color?"

I've barely even said the c before she answers me.

"Green, Sir."

Chapter Forty-Six

"Green, Sir."

My throat hurts as I speak, and I'm glad there's not an expectation that I'll have to say much more. I felt nothing but neediness and the overarching desire to pleasure my Sir over the last...however long it's been, and I just want to get back to it. I'm wide-awake, but I feel floaty and sleepy, and it's taking everything in me to stay engaged enough to listen to him. It was nice to have my eyes on him for a while, seeing how much I affected him and how much pleasure I brought him, but I like having my eyes down too, unfocused and relaxed. I don't really even want to listen. I just want to take whatever he gives me *and feel*.

A sharp slap to my face, enough to gain my attention but not enough to hurt more than a sting, brings me back to reality.

"Pet, I know you want to float like a mindless whore, but you have to stay with me for a few more minutes," my Sir says firmly. "I was saying that I'm going to re-leash you, and you are to exit the bench arms first and follow me on your hands and knees."

I keep my eyes trained on his big shiny boots as I hear him click my dainty leash back into place before taking a big step back. Luckily, the bench isn't too high, so I carefully place one hand and then the other on the floor. I'm moving to lower my first leg when he stops me.

"Hold there, pet."

At this angle, I'm presented obscenely, not unlike the way he fucked me last time with my hands on my ankles. With my knees still on the bench and my hands on the floor, my pussy and ass are begging to be taken. Sir agrees, letting out a hum of approval.

"Mmm, you look delicious like this. Ready to be mounted like the bitch you are, hmm? This angle is everything, pet. Pussy open and weeping, ass puckered and primed. You're strong, but I don't think you could hold yourself in this position for as long as I'd want to play with you and fuck you. Maybe I'll commission a piece of furniture for you to rest on in this position. Would you like that? You may answer."

"Yes, Sir." Please, *please* let me just lie like this so you can go about your day, but come back to tease my pussy or fuck me once in a while.

"I'll consider it if you're well behaved. Now, come."

I keep my eyes on the floor and follow him to an area of the room I haven't paid much attention to. I can't see anything but the area rug I'm looking at, and the legs of a desk chair that Sir is standing next to.

"Eyes."

They're his immediately. I'm in my resting position, and he's looming over me taller and broader than ever. God, nothing could ever hurt me with him around. My cavewoman brain kicks into overdrive.

"This is my office area, pet. You can see my new desk chair, desk, and laptop. I have some work to do this evening that can't wait, which is why you took the edge off for me so I can focus. If you're good while I work, you'll come later. Do you understand?"

"Yes, Sir."

"I'm going to secure your wrists behind your back with one of my ties and use another as a blindfold for you. I don't want you listening to any of my business calls, so you'll have noise-canceling earbuds in. Your mouth will be free, but I don't want to hear a single sound out of you, word, whimper, or otherwise. You'll sit in my lap until I'm finished. Understood?"

"Yes, Sir."

"And if you make a noise, what happens?"

"I'll be punished, Sir."

"How?"

"Ten spanks per transgression, Sir."

"Good girl. Now, I'm going to bind you, blindfold you, and set you on my lap while I work. I don't want to hear a peep starting now, unless you feel your circulation is compromised, in which case I expect you to tell me immediately."

True to his word, he gets to work securing my arms behind my back at the wrists and checking to make sure they aren't too tight. It's comfy, with no tension on my shoulders, allowing me to fully relax into the binds of the tie. My blindfold is next, and I can't see a thing. Finally, with the noise-canceling earbuds in, I'm in my own little sexual sensory deprivation chamber. If I thought I was helpless before, now I feel completely at his mercy. I know my mouth is free to safe word, but there's no way in hell I'm not about to love everything he does. He leaves me kneeling on the floor for a few long minutes, and when he plucks me off the ground by my waist to set me on his lap in the armless desk chair, I realize he's naked.

I've never felt his skin before, not like this, and the pleasure is almost unthinkable for something so simple. He's so fucking *warm,* with muscles on top of muscles, like I knew he had, but feeling their hardness against me is special. His chest hair is rough against my abused nipples, and as he sits us both down, his bare cock is pressed into his abs by my wet pussy. I open my mouth to gasp before remembering myself, and I don't make a sound as he arranges my legs around his waist like a koala bear. Finally, he has me like he wants me: legs wrapped around, trapping his hard cock between us, arms behind my back, eyes covered, ears closed, torso leaning against his with my mouth and nose tucked into the crook of his neck. *His balaclava is gone too.*

He slides the desk chair closer to the desk and...works, I guess. I can't hear a keyboard click with my ears plugged, but I can feel the ropey muscles in his arms flex in a rhythmic pattern. His heartbeat is fast, but steady—not racing the way mine is. His breathing is even, and I'm rapidly falling right back into that place I was approaching earlier. Like sleep, but better. A floaty half nap, on a cloud-shaped magic carpet. I'm faintly aware of him still—his heat, the smell of his cologne, and the musk that's so uniquely him—but I float off, my tether to the world as thin as my platinum leash.

I'm jolted back into reality by a searing pain that quickly dissolves into pleasure, and I realize the high-pitched whining noise I hear is me. My next series of realizations come one after the other. While I was in float-mode, Sir covered himself with a condom, then just picked me up and slid me right down onto his cock, to the hilt. This clearly surprised half-conscious Margot and made me squeal out involuntarily. My noise must have led him to remove one of my earplugs, allowing me to hear myself and also hear him now.

"That's ten, pet. I'm not finished working yet. Go back to being a quiet slut who's seen and not heard, or we'll have to add more to your total."

With that, my earplug is back in and I'm back where I was, except better. But also so, so much worse. Sir's cock is massive, I know this. It was down my throat earlier. I felt every damn inch. And he's fucked me deeply with it before, at angles that had him hitting my cervix with every thrust. But now, he's sat me on it, and he's not moving a muscle. Still typing, but there's no indication that being buried inside me is affecting him at all.

It *hurts,* this position. He's deep enough to make my stomach ache. My pussy feels every inch of girth he's stretching me around. I want to grind against him, pull my feet out from around him, and ride him into the next century. I'm trying to stop myself from even clenching around him, afraid if I do so, I'll come and add more spanks to my punishment.

Would that be the worst thing?

Stop. Yes. It would be. You've been almost perfect tonight, earning ten spanks. Not bad for your first test. Don't give up now. With nothing to focus on earlier and his dick not inside me, I floated. Now, speared on this monstrosity with nowhere to go, I'm sinking. I can feel the itchy dried cum all over me, I'm thirsty, and the ache between my legs is intensifying. God, this is torture. He has to know this is torture. How is he calmly working right now? *What is he even working on, a fucking novel?* Okay, if I just breathe and think about how comfy I am, maybe I can float again. In through my nose, out through my mouth. As my exhale washes over his neck, I feel Sir tense. *Oh.* Did he like that? Trying it again, I swear I feel a shiver. Oh yes. I need to make this man's control snap, then he'll fuck me. I'm not allowed to move or make noise, but he didn't specify anything about my mouth.

At this point, if this is against the rules, fuck it. Slowly, I stick my tongue out and run it along the crease between his neck and shoulder. I feel his dick pulse within me, so I do it again. After my third pass, I pull the skin between my lips and suck hard. *Oh my God, he just gave me a little thrust. Fuck yes.* I suck harder and harder, unable to fully reach his neck. He's thrusting into me consistently now, if a little shallowly. I'm not going to be able to come like this unless I get friction on my clit. Deciding to push my luck one more time, I dig my teeth into the meat of his shoulder and bite as hard as I can, until I taste copper.

He pulls me all the way off his dick before thrusting in once more, so hard it's mostly pain and little pleasure. I feel my throat vibrate with my scream even though I can't hear it. He pulls me off again and lays me on my front on the desk, knees bent wide and all the way up by my waist so that I'm as spread as I can possibly be for him. He rips out my earplugs, and I realize he's panting. *He's just as affected as I am.*

He leans forward in his desk chair and gives me one long lick from my clit up to my ass, kissing my tight hole before spitting on it and pressing a finger into me. It hurts before it feels good, and I let out a breath instead of another scream purely by accident. He lets out a low, sinister laugh.

"I won't count that one, pet, but only because you've already earned twenty spanks by my count. You know how to stop me. Otherwise, you'll take what you deserve."

That's all the warning I get before the first sharp hit lands on my right ass cheek. He's hitting me with his dick deep inside my pussy, not moving, just holding me in place like prey on a spear. His left thumb is in my asshole, using it as an anchor for his hand to hold me. That leaves his dominant right hand free to spank me, and he's not going easy. He didn't ask me to count them, only to take them. By the fifth spank, I can feel my tether on reality slipping, and by twelve, they feel better and better. Each one hurts worse but takes me one step closer to ecstasy. He slows down the spanks and thrusts again, but now, each time he hits me, it's harder and on flesh that's already tender. My eyes are closed behind the tie, but I know if they were open, I'd be seeing spots.

Approaching eighteen, I realize he's started to mumble under his breath—not for me to hear, just subconscious revelations meant for his mind alone. I'm too far gone to even know if I'm hallucinating them or not.

"Fucking perfect girl, always mine. Wearing my collar, my ring. Gonna fill you up with my babies. Won't be able to get away from me now. Keep you on this leash. Keep you on my lap, on my dick at my desk. Everyone will know. You'll understand. Mine. Just. Gotta plan. *Fuck*. That's my girl. My P...unggh. My. Pet! *Mine*."

Twenty. A slap to my clit. His roar. His throbbing dick as he comes. My orgasm. Pain. Black.

I come to in a warm bath, smelling honey and vanilla and leaning back on a soft pillow. I open my eyes, wincing slightly even though the lights are off. Only flameless candles provide a soft glow. Sir kneels behind the tub, based on the arms that are wrapped around me, softly rubbing a soapy washcloth across my chest. He's redressed himself, and the long sleeves of his shirt are wet from the elbow down as he washes me. I roll my eyes when I notice *particular attention* being paid to my nipples, which are surely clean by now.

"Hi," I say softly, breaking the perfect silence of the room. He freezes, then shuffles around to the side of the tub, resting his arms on the edge so we can see eye to eye.

"Hi," he says, deeply but softly. "How are you? Does anything hurt?"

I let out a sated laugh. "I think everything hurts."

He starts assessing my body for injuries, picking up one of my arms to see if the tie did any damage.

"I don't mean it like that. I mean a good hurt."

"Oh. Okay. I...good. That's good. I know we'll debrief tomorrow, but I have cold water and then a fruit and cheese plate. Will you eat something?"

I smile. "Only if you feed it to me."

He nods, then moves to rise.

"Feed it to me, in the tub with me?"

He freezes.

"I know it's not what we said, but please? You can put my blindfold back on if you want. So I won't see you."

After a pause, I hear him move to cover me with the tie, then start to undress again, and open a fridge before settling things onto the tubside table. I scoot forward, giving him room to slide behind me. He brings the glass of cold water to my lips first and I take three deep gulps before pulling back.

"All of it," he grumbles. Although I don't have to do what he says anymore, I drink it all anyway.

"Good girl." Ah, *fuck me.* I have nothing to say to that right now. I open my mouth, and a strawberry slice makes its way onto my tongue, followed by a piece of mango and a raspberry. After I've had a few bites, I scoot back until I'm flush with his body so that I can lie against his chest.

I feel him bend his head down to inhale my hair, then press a kiss to my temple. Only, it's not a real kiss, because I don't feel his lips, only soft material. He got naked with me again because I asked him to. But this time, he didn't take his balaclava off. He left his mask firmly in place.

Chapter Forty-Seven

Remember, you're real Jack, not masked Jack, and this is a platonic date to finally spend some time with an old friend. I repeat my mantra until the doors to the private veranda open to reveal the woman who will always take my breath away.

Fuck an old friend. She's everything, and you know it.

She looks like sin and money in her fitted cream dress and matching tailored coat. Her hair is pulled half up with voluminous curls falling down her back. *Why on earth did I send this goddess to Paris two years ago?*

After an embarrassing episode of stumbling out of my chair, I make my way to meet her with an awkward hug and lead her back to her seat.

I'm not looking too shabby, either. I made sure to groom myself particularly well tonight and donned the most flattering black suit I own. I was expecting her to show up in one of her black dresses when I chose my outfit, but with her lighter option, we're kind of giving off a devil and angel vibe. I'm starting to understand why Ledger likes to role-play like this with Sloane.

"This is lovely, Mr. Carter." She looks around at the city lights below us, her reaction filling me with a mix of pride and relief.

I booked this reservation the night she agreed to go out with me. A private table at a restaurant with three Michelin stars and a 360-degree view of New York is exactly the kind of thing my princess would consider a *stellar date*.

Don't get me wrong, she likes a laid-back diner with greasy fried food as much as anyone, but my girl has always enjoyed a nice night out. She's never been that caged princess who was forced to sit all prim and proper and sip her tea with her pinky up but longed to run and play. No, not Margot. She's always *loved* getting dressed up for a fancy meal.

To be fair, she loved to climb trees and play ball as well, so maybe that's part of what makes her so special. She's always been the most well-rounded, brilliant person I've known. She would've enjoyed a fun activity tonight, but I want as much time as I can get just talking to her. Who knows when she'll ever give me that chance again.

"Margot, please just call me Jack. I can't take this distance between us anymore." I raise a trembling hand over the table for her to shake. "Can we please call a truce between us? You were my best friend. I know I fucked it all up, and I know there will be a you-sized hole in my heart for the rest of my life, but the animosity is killing me."

The candlelight reflecting in her beautiful eyes threatens to wash me away, but I've been fighting for my life in those eyes for as long as I can remember. I hold my ground, meeting her stare as the storm brewing deep within her gaze calms, her walls finally dropping to let me in.

She places a steady hand in mine. "Alright, *Jack*. Truce."

I continue to shake her hand until she clears her throat and pulls it back as properly as she can with my tight hold. Our server comes to pour us a glass of wine and walks us through the prix fixe menu to see if any adjustments are needed. There aren't any, of course. I know this woman like the back of my hand. No amount of time away from her has ever changed that, and no amount of time ever will.

"My apologies, " I say when he's left us alone again, my rejected hand rubbing the back of my neck. "Um...Did you get your flowers this morning?"

I never stopped sending her that ridiculously large arrangement of assorted pink flowers for Valentine's Day. Even when she was in Paris, although she never responded to let me know she would be my Valentine for those two years. Due to the nature of the auction date being specifically for February 14th, she's mine for tonight, though. At least for a few hours.

And that's enough.

"Yes, thank you...Jack. They were very nice. The diamonds as well." Despite our shake of truce, her demeanor is as rigid as ever.

"Please relax, Margot, this isn't a real date." *To my dismay.* "I just want to know what you've been up to lately." *I miss you.* "I've been so focused on getting the new business up and running that I'm afraid I've forgotten what it's like to live. Something you seem to have been doing to the fullest. Let me live vicariously through you."

Her pretty eyes roll as she takes in my confession. "Oh please, Jack, your business is a *sex club*. Don't act like you've been living this boring existence since you've been in New York."

I give her the best smile I can summon, which is apparently just a sad side smile. *No, Princess, it's been a very gray, boring existence indeed.*

"Well, it's certainly not as exciting as that one summer you decided you were done waiting for your *pee pee* to come in and would just take one of ours instead. You even had *Henry* watching his back. I can't tell you how many times I caught him hiding from you."

For the first time in over two years, my princess laughs at me, spitting her sip of wine back into her glass in the process. This time, the smile that spreads across my face is genuine.

"Oh my God, I completely forgot about that! I was *five*. You can't hold that against me forever!"

"Oh, I can and will. I still see a phantom five-year-old Margot coming after my *big boy bits* from time to time." Although, she can certainly take mine from me now. Any time she wants.

"Speaking of Phantom, do you remember when Mom took us all to see *Phantom of the Opera* for the first time?"

I should've guessed that saying *phantom* would lead to this.

"Do I ever! Ledger got to fuck off while you made me play both Raoul *and* the Phantom so you didn't have to choose. *That way, you get them both at the end.*"

"Well, that is on brand. I still enjoy a good why choose." She winks, swirling her glass around before taking a drink.

"Do I even want to know what that is?" I raise a brow as I take a drink of my wine as well.

"One would hope so," she answers with a raised brow of her own, accompanied by a sinful smirk adorning her perfect little painted mouth before moving along. "Can you believe Marco has never been to see *Phantom of the Opera*?"

I make a mental note to google what a *why choose* is when I get home, before teasing her a little. I know I told myself this was supposed to be completely platonic, but I can't help it. "By Marco, you mean the one Italian man you haven't slept with?"

She takes my insult as well as I could hope for such a low blow, her eyes narrowing just slightly. "Excuse me, sir, you did tell me to go to Paris and fin..."

"Find the sexiest *French* man," I interrupt before grumbling. "I didn't mean all of Europe."

This time her reaction is one of actual annoyance. "Oh please, Jack Carter, I didn't do anything you haven't done. And tenfold at that."

Even if I move a decimal, *fuck,* I hope she didn't sleep with that many men...Okay, she has a point. *Stop being a misogynistic asshole, Jack. She hasn't done anything wrong by exploring her sexuality.* She wasn't yours anyway. Remember, you let her go...

"When do you want to go?" The confusion written on her face is question enough, so I elaborate. "To the play. When can you, Marco, *and his husband,* go to see *Phantom of the Opera* with me?"

My sweet, beautiful girl just stares at me with an inkling of adoration taking over the anger in her expression. She's lost in her head, and I've seen her do this enough in my life to know I'm going to have to ask again.

"I asked you a question pe...princess."

Shit, I need to channel back to those days she had me playing both parts before I blow the cover of my actual, real-life masked persona.

"Um, I don't know. Let me look at my schedule." She gets out her phone for the first time tonight to look at her calendar. "I think I can fit it in sometime next week, but I'll have to double-check with them."

I'll get four tickets for every performance from tomorrow until she's free. I'll even become besties with Marco in the process. Anything to see her again.

"Just let me know, and I'll get the tickets. There's no way someone as close to you as Marco can continue without experiencing what it's like to sit through *Phantom* with Margot Sinclair."

This time, a smile accompanies her cute little eye roll. "Yes, sir. I'll let you know."

Be right back, choking on air. My dick is suddenly as hard as a rock, and she didn't even mean that sexually.

"You pinky promise?" I ask, holding out my hand to seal the deal like we have our whole life.

She lifts her hand over the table, as dramatic as ever. "I pinky promise to go with you to *Phantom* as long as you pinky promise not to embarrass me in front of my friends." I loop our little fingers together, knowing that she would never stand me up now. "I'll be good, I promise. I won't even bring up Sprinkles."

The mention of that damned cow she used to love so much seems to do wonders for her mood. *Go figure.* As our evening rolls on, so do our conversations. With each story, the air gets lighter and lighter. Glimpses of the Margot I used to know so very well peek through her guarded exterior with every passing course, and I realize that as fun as our sexual encounters have been, *this* is what I crave the most from my princess. I want to take her on dates. I want to laugh and tease. I want to...I want her to be mine.

And while there is no way in the world I could let go of the one masked hold I have on her, I refuse to carry on without having her as a whole.

I'll just have to find a way to win her back. *Whatever it takes*.

Chapter Forty-Eight

Good morning, pet. How does your ass feel today?

Pet:

Some asshole reddened it. It hurts.

But I did put some of the cream you gave me on it, which helped, so thank you.

Sir:

You're welcome. Hopefully, this pain makes you rethink how you behave the next time we're together.

Doubt it.

Pet:

I never properly thanked you for my necklace.

It seems a little excessive, but it's beautiful and I feel cherished when I wear it. Is that dumb?

Sir:

You're welcome, pet.

Although I think we can both agree it's a collar, particularly since you've been on a leash for me.

Pet:

Sir:

Glad to see your ass is fully healed, since you obviously aren't afraid of any further punishment.

Pet:

I'm sorry, Sir.

Sir:

Apology accepted. As far as it being excessive…

I don't think any piece of jewelry other than my hand will ever deserve being around your neck. That collar is the best I could have made on such short notice.

Pet:

You had it made just for me? Why?

Sir:

Because in the club, you're mine.

I enjoy seeing you in things only I can provide.

My collar, my bruises, my cum.

Pet:

Speaking of which, your hand print is still visible on my ass.

Sir:

Girls who tease get teased back tenfold.

Go to bed, pet. You need to start stocking up on your sleep. You'll need it.

Pet:

I think you've permanently altered my ability to sit at a desk.

Sir:

Hmm...I'm not sure I understand what you mean, pet.

Please explain. In detail.

Pet:

You know exactly what I mean, asshole.

Sir:

Humor me. I think it would be a nice exercise to hear it from you. In your own words.

Pet:

Sir:

I really don't have all day.

Pet:

Fine. Sitting at my fucking desk makes me wish you were here so I could sit on your dick while you work and just worry about not coming, instead of having to worry about doing my own damn work.

Sir:

You wouldn't have to worry about that, pet.

Pet:

Pretty sure I would.

Sir:

On the contrary, darling. I've been thinking that the next time I have you warm my cock while I work, I'll let you come as many times as you want. In fact, I think I'll insist on it.

Pet:

Sir:

Get back to work, pet. Your job is very important, I'm sure.

Pet:

Yes, Sir.

Sir:

Were the snacks to your liking after our last meeting?

Pet:

Someone's desperate to talk to me, I see.

You know they were. I couldn't gobble them down fast enough.

Sir:

You are, across the board, an exceptional gobbler.

Still. Answer my question, pet.

Pet:

Hmm…

More chocolate.

Sir:

Can you expand more on your '5' ranking for sensory deprivation?

Was that specifically for touch, sound, and sight, the way we played last time? Or are you interested in other ways?

Pet:

It's 4 am. What the hell, dude?

Sir:

Silence your phone if you don't want alerts.

That's not my problem.

Although I do like the idea of you with the volume up, waiting to hear from me. When the phone chimes, does your pussy get wet, like a good little slut?

Pet:

Really pushing the boundaries of our relationship outside of the physical location of the club, asshole. Why are you even awake?

Sir:

Between sets at the gym. The sooner you answer me, the sooner you can go back to bed.

Pet:

Fine. As long as I have my taps and/or safe word, I don't think there's any sensory deprivation that I wouldn't want to try...

Sir:

You'd be open to a full gag in addition to being bound and blindfolded?

Pet:

Yes.

Sir:

That's a lot of trust, pet. I could do anything to you.

Pet:

That's kind of the entire point, isn't it?

And...I trust you. We have our parameters, and we've discussed our expectations and rules.

I feel safe with you.

Sir:

Thank you for your honesty and for the gift of your trust, pet. Such a good girl for me, using her words.

Pet:

Here's a word.

Jack:

Were you able to talk to Marco about going to Phantom?

Margot:

They're still free Saturday.

I have plans that night, but a matinee should be fine.

Jack:

Oooo Saturday night plans...Do you have a big date?

Margot:

That, sir, is none of your business.

Jack:

Sir, huh? That's a new one, but I have to say, I could get used to it...

Margot:

No.

Jack:

Well, I'm just excited you texted me back.

I half expected you to ghost me.

Margot:

I never go back on my pinky promises.

You should know that by now.

Jack:

I used to…

You came back from Paris a whole new Margot.

Margot:

I'm not THAT different.

Jack:

Still, I'd like to get to know the new you.

I had such a great time the other night and…I've really missed you.

Margot:

Yeah…

Let's just start with Phantom and go from there.

Jack:

I've already got the tickets.

Margot:

Chapter Forty-Nine

It's been years since I've seen *The Phantom of the Opera*, and at this point, I've likely seen it in person over twenty-five times, not counting recordings. But I'm not sure when I've *sobbed* at the ending like this. Maybe never. God, am I getting old and sentimental like my mom? I need to get it together. Then again, the entire evening has been more pleasant than I had hoped for. Despite the fact that I was hoping to sit on one side of Marco and Mark with Jack on the other, we sat next to each other, which was...fine. It was nice to feel his warm hand on mine when I wept during "Wishing You Were Somehow Here Again," and the handkerchief he handed me saved me from snotting all over my dress. I hadn't prepared myself to hear that piece live for the first time since Daddy died, and having Jack there, knowing how special our relationship was, was...nice.

As I finish wiping my eyes and we stand to make our exit, Jack's hand finds my elbow, the pressure causing me to look up. His concern is plain on his face, and I'm glad we've called a truce, but nothing has *really* changed. I'm not his business. My reasons for crying are my own.

"Are you okay, Princess?"

I sniffle and pull my elbow from his grasp as we follow Mark and Marco to the coat check. "I'm fine, just tired and overly emotional. I haven't seen the show in so long that it affected me more than usual."

"Well, Jack, we have to thank you for these amazing tickets. I'm not sure how I've managed to go thirty-five years without seeing this show, but I don't think I'll make it even one more before seeing it again." Marco has red-rimmed eyes of his own, and I'm glad I could be a part of popping his *Phantom* cherry.

"It was my pleasure. I was hoping the three of you would be up for an early dinner and drinks? I know how much Margot craves comfort food after a good cry, and there's a soul food restaurant not too far from here," Jack says. As delicious as a good piece of fried chicken sounds right now, I have some work to do before I meet with my masked man tonight.

"No, I don't think I have time today, actually." I pull out my phone to call my driver. "But it was lovely, Jack. It brought back so many nice memories."

Before I can press call, Marco snatches my phone out of my hand and locks it.

"What the hell, Marco?" I hiss, displeased that my phone is in anyone's hand, even locked. *The tabs open in the browser right now...*

"Sorry, cara," he purrs, and I see Jack's fists clench. Glad I'm not the only one who respects people's privacy. "I happen to think food sounds lovely, or at least a drink. Come on, don't you want to tell me all about how this staging differs from the original? Tell me how wrong I am that I think Raoul really was perfect for Cathleen?"

Snatching my phone back, I roll my eyes as Jack snickers. It's annoying how predictable I am, and also endearing how well Marco knows me.

"I'm not even going to dignify that with a response. You know perfectly well her name is Christine. And as Jack can attest to, the happiest solution to the ending by far would be a sordid threesome." I sigh as Marco smirks, having successfully baited me. I swear I'm not that easy to rile up, but if you talk shit about *Phantom*, I'm coming for you, no questions asked.

Marco glances behind me at Jack, then gives me a wink. "You and Jack have firsthand experience with sordid threesomes, then?"

I choke on my own spit, and Jack very unhelpfully smacks me on the back before I bat his hands away as he laughs.

"Sorry, sorry, I promise I've trained him better than this," Mark says, giving Marco an eye that tells me he's in trouble when he gets home. "But he's deflecting attention away from himself because he cried in public, and he hates being vulnerable."

"It's true, I hate being vulnerable," Marco says softly. "But in the spirit of vulnerability, I really would like to have at least one drink with my friends and discuss the overarching themes of my new favorite musical."

"It's the only musical you've ever se...ow!" Mark rubs his arm where Marco has pinched him.

"Please, Marge."

"You swore you were never going to fucking call me Marge again, you ass!" I hiss.

"I made that promise under duress! You had me at knifepoint!"

"Well," Jack says, "we've just so happened to arrive at one of my favorite cocktail bars near the theater. Since we're already here, why don't we order at least one drink and a few tapas?"

I look up and furrow my brow, confused at how I didn't notice Jack shepherding us five blocks like a fucking border collie. Was I that distracted by sparring with Marco? My focus hasn't been great lately, although it hasn't affected my work yet. I've been fixated on my masked man, though, to an obsessive degree that's a little concerning. I've been excited all week to see what he's got planned for me tonight.

"Two fingers of your oldest scotch for me, please, and she'll have a gin mule," Jack orders as Marco and Mark say their drinks of choice.

Before long, we have a fruit and cheese platter in front of us and our second round of drinks.

"It's completely unethical!" Mark cries, popping another samosa in his mouth. "First, he totally is in a position of power. He's her music teacher!"

"Not officially," I say, already seeing where this is going.

Marco continues, "Well, I was going to mention the age gap, but that's low-key hot as fuck. You can't deny that it's creepy that he's watched her for so long, though, and he knows everything about her while she knows nothing about him."

Jack is still, observing our arguments with intense interest. Or he's thinking about whatever excitement he has planned at his club later. Maybe his own sordid threesome. *Why does that make me feel...something?*

Shaking it off, I admit I'm well on the side of full-on Stockholm syndrome. "I think it's cute. Endearing. I mean, yes, he knows everything about her, and she knows nothing about him, but he loves her! And she doesn't *need* to know much about him, just take the music lessons and get dicked down!"

Marco finishes off his third drink and stands as Mark closes out their tab. "I'm just saying, cara. At the end of the day, Christine didn't deserve to be in the shadows like that! With someone who wasn't willing to reveal themselves. I think it was fine for an affair for a while, but in the end..." He gives me a secret smile. "Team. Raoul!" He punctuates Raoul by howling like a wolf, and before he can continue his antics, Mark collects him and shuffles him out with promises to do this again. I'm left giggling as they wobble down the street. They look so happy and in love, and I feel a tiny, deep longing and worry that I've missed my chance for that.

Jack interrupts me from gathering my things to leave by placing another drink in front of me, only my third, and my ultimate weakness. A plate of fried mac and cheese balls.

"Oh my God, I haven't had one of these in years! The French don't know what they're missing!"

He laughs, deep and low, and has a sparkle in his deep blue eyes when he looks up. "Do you remember when you practically berated a server at the restaurant-which-shall-not-be-named when they were out of these on my half birthday one year?"

I blush before failing to stop a belly laugh. "Oh my *God*, I had completely forgotten about that! I must have been all of what, ten years old?"

Jack gives me a wistful smile that I ignore. "You were *seven*, I'll have you know. I think every table in the restaurant was impressed with your vocabulary and how eloquent you were in telling the manager that you were going to sue them for false advertising, seeing as the mac and cheese balls were on the sign right outside the front door of the restaurant!"

Groaning, I finish off the bite. "I just don't understand why Mom always took us there. It's such a weird restaurant. I know you and Ledger always requested it because she let you order one of every slice of cheesecake, but you always made yourselves sick and had a massive sugar hangover the next day."

He chuckles. "I think she always hoped we would have some sense, and it would be a sign we were maturing when we stopped asking to gorge ourselves on cheesecake for our half birthdays."

"And when did this maturing finally happen?"

"I'll let you know when it does." He winks. "Last year, I managed eleven slices before I threw up. Ledger's only ever gotten to ten."

"The two of you are a literal problem, I swear," I sigh, full of fried cheese with zero regrets. Sipping the soda I switched to a while ago, I'm about to check my phone for the time when Jack interrupts me softly.

"Do you really think the Phantom is a romantic figure, not just a creep taking advantage of a young woman's passion?" he asks, swirling the same scotch he's been nursing in his glass.

I'm not sure I have a full answer for him. It's complicated. *What isn't?*

"Well, his mask isn't necessarily only to fool her. He feels shame over his disfigurement, and he worries she won't be accepting of him if she knows who he really is. I think that it's pretty hard not to feel sympathy for that. His obsession would be creepy in real life, maybe, but between you and me...in books, that shit is hot."

Jack stares at me intensely, but I meet his gaze and continue. This isn't the first philosophical discussion he and I have ever had, although hopefully this one won't result in me kneeing him in the balls. I can't help but snort a laugh.

"What?" He cocks his head to the side.

"Remember when Mom had us play 'debate team,' and you had to defend the patriarchy, and I kneed you in the balls and yelled fuck the patriarchy?"

Jack runs a hand down his face. "God, that hurt. You were eleven! You shouldn't have been yelling fuck about anything."

I exhale, cheeks hurting from laughing more today than I have in a while, before changing the subject back to my favorite play.

"I guess. It always bothered me when people loved Raoul, just because he had loved her when they were children. It had been years! People change! And he just assumed they would be together, without giving her a whole lot of say in the matter, necessarily."

Sitting back in my chair, I come to the same conclusion I always have when trying to decide between the Phantom and Raoul.

"Christine might've actually wanted to be a dirty girl with a masked man in a dungeon! Nothing wrong with that. Masks, forced proximity, age gap—lots of super-hot kinks in there. Maybe she *did* want to be with her childhood love, and Raoul wasn't being pushy or misogynistic. He just wanted her to have everything she needed."

Jack is totally still now, and I appreciate him paying so much attention to my diatribe.

"I think, if it were me, I would simply choose...both!" Slurping the rest of my soda, I move to stand and stretch, getting blood flow back after being stationary for longer than I thought. "I've been team masked man plus childhood sweetheart equals hot threesome since Mom told me Christine could choose them both if she wanted. There's no reason not to have it all, Jack!"

Satisfied that I've thoroughly made my point, I look down at my phone only to see that Marco must have turned it on do not disturb when he had it earlier. Which means my alarms didn't go off. Which means we've been sitting here talking for hours. Which means I'm *already ten minutes late to meet my masked man, and I'm a fifteen-minute cab ride from the club.*

"Fuck!" I yell, jolting Jack out of his reverie and earning me a few concerned glances from the rest of the bar. I don't say bye or thanks as I waste no time getting outside to hail a cab.

I don't care how rude I am. All I can think about is how late I am. And how much *fucking trouble* I'm in with my own Phantom.

Chapter Fifty

Jack

When I walk into the room, my girl is kneeling on her cushions, wearing nothing but her collar like a good pet. Like she wasn't thirty minutes late. Technically, I'm late too, and technically, I'm the reason we're *both* late in the first place, but I've been fantasizing about this particular punishment from the moment we established this *pet and Sir* dynamic.

I watch her chest rise and fall dramatically, no doubt from the adrenaline rush of making it here before me. She thinks she's off the hook. *Oh, do I have news for you, Princess.*

"You were late," I say, stalking over to stand in front of her.

Her posture slacks but only for a fraction of a second, and if you didn't have a graduate degree in her tells, you would never know. Lucky for me, I've spent my life studying Margot Sinclair, so I know she's already accepted her defeat. She doesn't say anything, though. No, my good girl keeps that perfect little mouth closed as she stares down in front of her like she was instructed to do.

I crouch down in front of her and take her chin in my hand, gently pulling her face up to look at me. "Did you think I wouldn't know you were late?"

She stares up at me but doesn't make a move. *God, she's so perfect. I almost hate to do this to her.* "You may answer, pet."

"I'm sorry, Sir. I thought when I got here before you that you were late too, and it wouldn't matter—"

"It always matters." I cut her off and squeeze her jaw for emphasis. "You do understand that the punishment for being dishonest is going to be much worse than the punishment for being late?"

"Yes, Sir."

She's probably imagining a series of spanks and a rough fuck. The anticipation in her eyes alone is enough to have me fully erect. I could give her that. I could spank her ass raw, then sink into her perfect fucking pussy. My little pain slut would be so wet from her punishment, I could sink to the hilt with one thrust. Or I could finally take her ass. I could tie her so that she couldn't squirm away from me as I fed her tight hole inch after long inch.

Deciding to go with my original plan, I use my thumb to gently rub her lips before standing up to go get the supplies for the night, laying one of her cushions down in front of my desk, and sitting in my chair.

"Do I need to walk you over here on your leash, or can you crawl to me by yourself?"

My good girl slowly crawls over to her cushion and sits up on her knees between my spread legs, waiting for my next command.

"That's a good girl," I say, petting her hair back from her eyes before gently taking her arms and pulling them behind her body, using a satin rope to tie her wrists behind her back. "Color?"

"Green, Sir."

When I look into her eyes again, her pupils are blown with lust. *I forget how much my dirty girl loves bondage.*

"Good. Open your mouth and stick out your tongue."

She obeys my command beautifully, pulling her red painted lips into an O and sticking her tongue out, just the way I imagined. It takes everything in me not to take out my cock and slide it so far down her throat she can't breathe. But I fight the temptation, pulling my balaclava up to above my mouth and leaning down close enough to spit onto her tongue. My good little whore doesn't even flinch, just hollows her tongue to hold what I gave her and waits for her next order.

"Now, I'm going to set a timer for three minutes. Hold that there until the timer goes off, then you can swallow. Since you were thirty minutes late, we're going to do that ten times. That's your first punishment."

Between each round, I spend my time typing like a madman to make her think I'm really working, when, in reality, I'm just pouring my heart out to her in a confession she'll probably never see.

She takes her first sentence like a champ, just as I expected. I'm the one who's struggling to keep it together. Each time I pull my mask up to reveal my mouth, it's harder and harder not to claim hers with my own, and when she licks her lips before my last spit, my resolve is gone. I crash our lips together with a force that steals her breath. She can't reach around to touch me with her hands bound together, but mine are free, and they latch on her waist with a bruising grip as I explore every inch of her mouth. I allow myself a moment to indulge in the fantasy where this is real Jack and real Margot alone in the house we share, before pulling away, leaving a mouth full of my spit behind in the process.

"You did so well taking your punishment for being late," I say as she swallows for the last time. "Color?"

Her bright blue eyes are almost entirely black as she looks up at me. "Green, Sir."

"Good, now place your head on my thigh and keep it there, pet. Are you ready for the punishment for not being honest with me?" I ask as I begin petting her hair back from her face.

"Yes, Sir."

The longer I run my fingers through her hair, the more she relaxes on my leg.

I'm about to order her to take out my cock, when I remember I have her hands tied. I use one hand to make quick work of my pants, allowing my weeping dick to spring free, while the other continues petting her. The precum dripping out of my head is hardly enough to cover my length, but I'm positive she'll be dripping with arousal. Reaching down, I dip two thick fingers inside her pussy and find the lube I was looking for. The intrusion causes her to shiver, and chill bumps erupt across her body. I don't intend to let her come tonight, but I can't help myself from rutting my fingers in and out a few times before I take them away. I didn't think it would be possible to get any harder, but as her eyes roll back in her head, my already rock-hard dick proves me wrong.

"Mmm, my little whore is dripping for me tonight."

On the last thrust of my fingers, I scoop out as much of her wetness as I can to lube my cock up before stroking my hand up and down my length. Her brows furrow in confusion as I continue to pet her with my other hand. I know she wants to take me in her mouth, and *God* do I want that too. I'm starting to wonder who this is punishing more.

I stop petting her momentarily to click play on my computer. It's just an audio of some random porn, but she'll be none the wiser since she can't see my screen. How could I ever get off to a poor imitation of sex when the archetype of desire is kneeling at my feet? And completely naked sans the diamond collar I gave her, with her arms tied behind her back, at that.

"Let's see here, who do I want to watch today? Ah yes, Dakota. She *never* would've lied to me." I couldn't point you to a Dakota if you held a gun to my head, but she doesn't have to know that. All she has to know is that her deceit displeased me.

The moment the audio begins, she tries to lift her head, but I replace my hand to pet her, keeping her on my thigh while I jack off with the other. I can practically feel the anger radiating off her as I use my best acting skills to tease her.

The truth of the matter is that I haven't gotten off to the image of any other woman since the night we slept together. And if I'm being honest, it was Margot I'd envision long before that night.

By the time I'm close to coming, I've completely drowned out the phony audio, my mind homing in on the only woman I care to hear moaning. My hand stills where I've continued petting her, as I aim my cock down, spilling my cum onto my boots.

After taking a second to catch my breath, I click the audio off and dare to look at her. Just as I assumed, a fire rages in her eyes, but she still says "green" when I ask for her color.

"What's wrong, pet? Did you want my cum?" I ask as I continue petting her hair back. I watch as her anger simmers down, her face donning the most seductive pout I've ever seen. "Yes, Sir."

"If you want my cum, lick it off my shoes."

I hope that she can see the challenge in my eyes even through my brown contacts because if there's one thing I know about this woman, it's that she never turns down a dare. I would much rather strip naked and hold her flush against my body, feeling her soft, warm skin against my own. But alas, when in Rome.

She widens her stance so that she can bend over more easily with her hands tied behind her back, and *licks my fucking cum off my boots.* My cock, which had been half hard and flopped over onto my thigh, is now back at full attention.

"That's my good pet. *Goddamn,* you're such a good fucking whore," I say, releasing the tie around her wrists and allowing her the use of her arms. Even as strong as she is, I know how hard that position must be without the support of her hands.

By the time she's got my boots squeaky clean, I've managed to tuck my still hard cock back into my pants. I really want nothing more than to sink into her perfect little cunt and fuck us until we've both lost count of our orgasms, but I was told to always follow through with punishments, and I'm sure she'll learn her lesson. She's such a good fucking girl already, so I shouldn't have to deny us that fantasy many more times.

She's back in position, kneeling on her cushion with her hands on her knees, when I crouch down again to see her.

"You did so well tonight, pet," I praise, stroking her hair back from her face. "How would you like your bath?"

"Excuse me?"

"I said how would yo.."

"No, I heard you, Sir. What do you mean *how would I like my bath*? I haven't come yet." Her head is no longer hung in submission as she stares up at me, demanding so much respect, even from her knees.

"You agreed to this punishment weeks ago, pet. I'm only doing what we agreed."

This time, when I reach down to run my fingers through her hair, she swats my hand away, standing to her full height with a grace women around the world would kill for. Her dominance takes over the room as power radiates from where she's standing.

"In that case, *Sir,* I will not be requiring a bath tonight." She grabs her personal items from a locker in the corner of the room and wraps her trench coat around her still naked body, then she's out the door, mumbling something about *asshole* and *just wait.*

If I didn't know how to handle her meltdowns, I might be scared that I'd ruined things for good. Lucky for me, I've been dealing with Margot Sinclair's tantrums all my life, so I'm not the least bit defeated.

Chapter Fifty-One

Are you okay?

I understand that this is a new dynamic, but you cannot just leave us both emotionally hanging at the end of a scene like that. It's not healthy for either of us.

I have to know you're okay. You've got one more hour before I break my own rule and activate the tracking feature on your Y hone.

Pet:

Are you fucking kidding me??

Lose this number, asshole.

Sir:

Glad you're okay.

Pet:

I am NOT okay. I signed up for whatever this is to get off, that's what you're good for, and you didn't fulfill your promise.

I'm as horny and as frustrated as I've ever been in my life.

I don't know why you treated me so callously and wouldn't let me explain myself or apologize.

Sir:

This is why I would have preferred that you stayed for aftercare. We could have calmed down and then discussed this. Now we're relegated to doing this by text, which is impersonal. But it's what we've got so, listen to me, pet.

As to your accusation that I treated you callously, if you truly think that, I'm sorry. If it's the emotional release talking, I would have sincerely liked to have been there to help you ride it out. I want to be very clear.

Letting you explain yourself would have served no purpose.

There was no reason you could have given that would have made tardiness acceptable. You did apologize, and I accepted, but that doesn't change your punishment. You took your punishment and that means it's over now and in the past.

As to fulfilling promises, the punishment for tardiness was explicitly detailed in section 24 b of the contract you signed so prettily and assured me that you had read.

I don't want apologies. I want corrected behavior, and if I don't enforce our contract, then it's useless, on both ends.

Pet:

I...

It was really long. I was tired that week, and I kinda skimmed the punishment section because I had no intention of misbehaving.

Sir:

I'm sure you didn't, because you're a very good girl.

But everyone slips up, so it was bound to happen.

I'm extremely disappointed that you didn't read everything.

It could have led to a much worse outcome than this, particularly if I had attempted to punish you in a more severe way that I thought you had consented to.

Based on your lack of response, perhaps you need more time to think about things. You know where to find me.

Pet:

I'm sorry.

Sir:

You've already been forgiven, pet.

Pet:

I don't want my mistake to affect our next time together.

Feeling the things I do when we're together has opened up another aspect of myself I didn't know existed.

I don't want to be awkward and stifled now.

Sir:

The punishment structure exists to ensure clean slates. We'll move forward as if this never happened.

In fact, I have a present for you.

Pet:

Please not another necklace worth the GDP of a small country?

Sir:

Small is a relative term, but no. This is a decidedly more sexual present. But you only get it if you're a very good girl.

Pet:

Jack:

How did Mark and Marco like Phantom?

Margot:

They loved it, obviously!!

Jack:

Obviously.

So, did I also make a good impression on your friends?

Margot:

I'm not sure why that matters at all.

And why do you think I would know what they think?

Jack:

It matters because you're important to me, and they are important to you.

And I know you well enough to know you would've talked about me.

Margot:

 They like you fine.

That doesn't mean anything, though.

Jack:

It's good enough for now.

Margot:

What's that supposed to mean?

Jack:

If they hated me, I doubt you would give me the time of day.

Jack:

And I'll take whatever I can get right now.

Margot:

Jack…I can't promise I'll ever be able to give you more than a casual friendship.

Jack:

I know, Princess…and I will happily take just this forever, as long as I get to be in your life.

Margot:

Guess what I just saw an ad for?

Jack:

???

There are literally a million things this could be.

Margot:

You're no fun.

The *Sleeping Beauty* ballet will be playing in two weeks!

Jack:

I haven't been to see that in years! We have to go.

Margot:

Let's do it! I'm free for a Sunday matinee.

Jack:

Say less. I'll get the tickets.

4?

Margot:

Just two this time, I think.

Jack:

Even better, Princess. I can't wait. 😊

Margot:

Me either 😊

Jack:

😊

Chapter Fifty-Two

"Agreed. These renderings are much better. If they can fabricate the displays within the next two weeks, we should be able to salvage the opening date." I sigh, finally heading to my office for the lunch meeting with Mom I've been excited for all week. After basically floating around in my own little happy sex haze for so long, my last encounter with my masked man has left me ruffled. We've texted, and I feel settled and reassured about what happened. It's just not something that I'm used to. Pretty sure the last time I didn't get my way was literally two years ago when...nope, not going there. We're in a truce, and we're friendly acquaintances. I'm not forgiving him, but we're being adults. LJ will be here soon, and he'll need an aunt and uncle who are a united front.

Luckily for me, the company contracted to provide some displays for the store completely mangled them and delivered a truckload of hot garbage to my doorstep two days ago. I wouldn't display dog food on them, no offense to dogs, let alone my custom lingerie pieces. We've gotten another bid to have them all remade, and it's taken every bit of my energy to solve this issue. I haven't been able to sulk once. I also haven't gone to Pilates, or enjoyed a soak in my tub, or read a single page of a book. My meals have all been takeout, and not even the healthy kind. I'm not feeling very girl boss. My spinning plates are starting to wobble.

"Darling, if you insist on being introspective, at least unfurrow your brow. You'll get wrinkles!" My mother breezes into my office, carrying our lunch with her and closing the door behind her with her hip. Kissing my cheeks, she unpacks and sets up our salads and fries, lining up all five of our favorite dipping sauces from this particular burger joint.

"It's disturbing to know that you can tell when I'm being introspective."

She rolls her eyes and launches into a spiel about how disturbed *I* would be if I knew the things she knows, and how it's her job to know everything about all four of us.

"Even Jack?" I ask, although I already know her answer.

"Of course, darling. You know I consider him just as much my child as the three of you. I'll have you know my will is split evenly four ways, although I might have to amend that now that I have grandbabies on the way."

I choke on a fry, then cough it up, sending it flying across my desk toward my mother, who is sitting undisturbed, with one eyebrow arched.

"GrandbabieS?" I rasp out before sipping water. "Is someone else pregnant? Did Jack get someone pregnant?"

"First of all, are you really surprised I consider him one of my own? I had rather hoped it was clear based on how I treated him all these years. Second, no, to my knowledge, only LJ is technically cooking right now. But! I have quite the intuition, you know, and I just *feel* that this is going to truly open the floodgates. I think Christmas in a few years will be quite different from this past one," Mom finishes her explanation of her inconceivable choice of plural noun, and daintily goes back to eating her fries.

"Well, I mean, I know you love Jack like a son. I guess I just never saw him as a brother, so it's hard to think of him as your son," I say, unsure why I brought this up or why I even care.

"No, I never did think that he was really a brother to you, although he was always so sweet the way he looked after you," she says, and I roll my eyes. "Well, he was, Margot. I don't know what to tell you. I'm not surprised you didn't see him that way, though. He was always such a handsome little guy, and now, well. He's quite the catch these days. I'm not sure he's done much over the past couple of years but work and work out."

"Yeah, he mentioned that's just about all he's had time for since he came to New York, but I didn't really believe him," I mumble, moving on to eat Mom's fries since mine are long gone.

"You've been talking more?" I swear my mom's eyes are sparkling right now. I'm surprised she's not rubbing her hands together like a cartoon villain based on the look on her face.

"Uh, yeah. We've been catching up a bit. Went to see *Phantom* last week with Marco and Mark. Going to see *Sleeping Beauty* next week. It's been nice," I say. I'm a little bit flummoxed as to why exactly she's so invested. It's not even like she would've known much about my falling out with Jack, and me being an ocean away was really lucky. If I had been Stateside, there's no way in hell I could've kept our mortal enemies status a secret.

"You went to see *Phantom* and didn't invite me!" she pouts, and I'm more convinced than ever that I've inherited all my dramatics from her.

"Well, you had a pickleball tournament. You weren't even in town! And besides, it was a very last-minute thing. Marco had never been, and Jack mentioned tickets, so we went. It was nice! That's all." I sigh.

Mom studies me thoughtfully, and usually nothing good ever comes from these looks.

"Whatever you're thinking, you might as well go ahead and say it now, Mother."

"I was just thinking about how happy I am to see you wearing this lovely cream sweater dress, darling. It was a couple of years of all sleek Parisian black and chignons. Your hair looks wonderful down in your curls again," she says primly, then continues in a soft voice. "I was also thinking about how much you loved *Sleeping Beauty* when you were younger. You were so fixated on Jack being your prince. He really handled that well for your entire childhood, you know. Such a good friend and protector for you. Henry was of course always busy, and Ledger was going through so much with your father, but it felt like Jack was just for you and me. A darling child, never causing me any trouble. And I could count on him to play with you and never complain."

I give her a soft smile and indulge her in her reminiscence. "He told me that he and Ledger still gorge themselves on cheesecake every year. I can't believe you still go!"

At this, she throws her head back and lets out a hearty laugh. "We all still go, darling. You'll have to join us now that you're back."

Clearing my throat, I deflect a bit. "Yes, well. Back for now. If this shop does well, I'm not sure how long I'll stay. I had built quite a happy little life for myself in Paris, you know."

"You also had quite a life here when you left," Mom says.

I had nothing here when I left, I want to scream at her. *Less than nothing, actually. Not zero but an unfathomably huge number in the negative, a hole the likes of which I didn't expect I would ever meet the bottom of. That's what I had here when I left.*

"I'm just ready for the baby to be here. I can't imagine how Sloane and Ledger feel," I say, not even pretending that I'm doing anything other than shifting the conversation to safer waters.

Mom takes my bait, at least momentarily. "I think they're going crazy with excitement at the moment. Both of them just feed into each other's energy. It's like having two individual balls of chaos merge into one supernova. Sloane is nesting and made an offhand comment about how she felt like nothing was clean enough. Ledger offered to burn down the house and build a new one, to which Sloane said the smoke particles would be even worse for the baby. After that, your brother had a state-of-the-art air filtration system put in the entire house. It's actually clean enough and with fresh enough air that you could make sterile products! He had it tested!"

We both laugh and dig into the chocolate cake Mom brought for dessert.

"Are you happy, darling? I know you mentioned one suitor in particular quite a few times in the last months before you moved back. I'll admit I've been worried that perhaps you've been missing him since you've been home. Michel, was it? He was rather handsome in the photo you sent of the two of you at the opera."

Aaanndddd there it is, folks. I knew she hadn't been reminiscing and making grandbabies plural for no reason. I'm not sure what she knows or suspects, and I'm not giving her an inch. I'm definitely not broaching the subject of my favorite friend with benefits with her right now.

"What even is happiness, Mom? I'm creatively fulfilled, I have my health and a wonderful family. I'm making more friends in the city, and I listen to podcasts. What am I supposed to do to check the box that is happiness?"

This earns me a wan smile, like she was expecting exactly that answer. I swear, if she just knows what she wants us all to do, she should just come right out and tell us instead of her meddling machinations. Although her interference did work out well for Sloane and Ledger...

"I think it depends on what you want, sweetheart. Let me just say this, and then I'll leave. My happiness came from having all of you kids while still helping your father run the company. I couldn't have reached my full realization as a human without both. As much as I hated to miss a single game or recital, my time away from you all when I was working made me happier and a better mother when I came back. And now, as an older woman with children who have flown the coop,

I'm lucky to still have those friends I made and contacts in the industry to dabble in projects now and again. It was a very privileged thing to be able to do."

She's gathering her things now, and I have no clue where she's going with this.

"Ledger has now basically devoted himself to a domestic life with Sloane, and he's happy. They work out, try new recipes, read, putter about in their garden, and he's perfectly content. That's a perfectly wonderful existence to aspire to as well.

"I want you to know that I'm proud of what you've built, Margot. It's been amazing to watch you do it all on your own without using the family name once. And if it brings you utter fulfillment and joy, by all means, continue at the pace you're going! Open all the stores! Do all the collabs. I'll be right there with you.

"But if you feel like this was something you needed to do for yourself at a certain point in your life, and now you're no longer in that place, maybe you have other things you aspire to. I think being here in the States and being around your family and the most important people from your past and present might help you feel out what happiness means for you right now."

Why are there tears in my eyes? Jesus, is it period week again?

"Shoot, I'm late for my flight. Pickleball tournament!" After kissing my cheeks and giving me a big hug, Mom pauses on her way out the door. "Just think about it, Margot! Aggressively pursue happiness!"

And with that, my own personal psychic breezes out of my office. I swear, I think sometimes she just projects her daily horoscope email in the direction of whichever kid will listen.

In any case, she's given me a migraine and an excuse to get out of this damn construction zone. Pulling up my phone, I see new texts from both of the men who have been dominating my messages this week. Rolling my neck, I ignore them both. Instead, I place a grocery order for some fresh produce for tonight and call for the car, planning a long soak alone with my thoughts. *And maybe my vibe.*

Chapter Fifty-Three

Jack

I've sat through *Sleeping Beauty* with my own princess at my side more times than I can count. The ballet as a whole is nostalgic, but the Rose Adagio in particular brings me back. Margot had just started taking ballet classes, and when she found out that her favorite animated princess was actually based on Tchaikovsky's *Sleeping Beauty*, she *had* to go. In true Sinclair fashion, Blanche loaded us all up and made Henry Sr. drive us to the ballet.

19 YEARS AGO

"Ugh, you aren't doing it right, Ledger!" Margot whines from where she sits on the floor. I've lost count of how many times she's fallen down, and with each failure, the tension in the air rises.

"Stop messing it up, son. We've been at this for hours, and some of us actually have things to be doing right now," his dad says from his place in the line. It's a rare occasion when Henry is home from boarding school, so she's got all four of us lined up, just like *Sleeping Beauty*.

I'm behind Ledger, next up to greet the young princess, followed by Henry and Mr. Sinclair. "Dad, I don't think Ledger is the problem." Henry looks over at the pouting princess who's still on the floor with arms folded across her chest. "Pretty sure it's the six-year-old who just started taking ballet last month and is trying to accomplish what is commonly regarded as one of the most challenging sequences in the art."

"Nonsense," his father replies, walking over to lend Margot a hand. "Come on, Princess, let's try it one more time."

It only takes one more failure before she's decided that not only is she done with trying to master this particular move but she's also done with ballet as a whole.

"Don't be ridiculous, sweetheart. It takes *years* to develop the skill required to stay en pointe long enough to successfully perform the Rose Adagio." Ms. Blanche tries to console her daughter, to no avail.

"If she doesn't want to do ballet anymore, I don't see a reason to force her, Blanche. Lord knows she has enough extracurriculars at the moment," Mr. Sinclair says before hugging both his wife and daughter and leaving the room, with Ms. Blanche soon to follow.

"Thank God. Let's go." Ledger slings his arm around Henry and leads him out, leaving me alone with the now crying princess.

I'm about to follow the guys to join in whatever they're about to get up to when Margot lets out her most dramatic whimper yet. Sighing, I walk over to her instead.

"Hey, Princess," I say, combing the hairs that have fallen out of her tight bun back behind her ear. "Look what I have. You want to go upstairs and watch a movie? I'll even let you pick *Sleeping Beauty* again."

She looks up at the chocolate truffles in my hand, and like magic, her tears disappear. "No!" She huffs as she grabs a chocolate out of my hand and pops it into her mouth. "I'm never watching that again."

"Oh, come on, Princess. That's your favoritest movie of all time, remember?"

"Not anymore, it's not," she huffs.

Before she can continue with some silly excuse, I pull her into a hug. "Margot, you don't have to do ballet to be as good a princess as Aurora. You're already *leagues* better than her or any other princess you come across. She can still be your favorite, even if you don't love *everything* about her. It doesn't have to be an all-or-nothing deal. You'll find so many things in life that are *almost* perfect, but just because it's not completely flawless doesn't mean you should give it up."

The feeling of Margot's hand on mine brings me back to the present, where Aurora and Désiré are performing their grand pas de deux. Electricity circuits through my body from where our skin meets until she breaks our point of contact to clap emphatically as tonight's performers take their final bow.

I take our coats from the doorman as we leave our private suite and help her into hers before putting mine on as well, savoring any point of contact I can get. With spring just around the corner, I felt we could walk a block to a popular teahouse for a light spread, the beauty of a Sunday matinee. That being said, it's still pretty chilly in New York. I wrap my arm around her for warmth, and even though she doesn't snuggle into me like she once would before, she doesn't move away. And that's enough.

"Oh wow, this place is beautiful." Margot looks around the restaurant in awe of the whimsical pastel decor as the hostess sits us at a table for two tucked away in a cozy corner of the room.

"Not as beautiful as you are, Princess." I can't help it. *God,* I can't help voicing her beauty. She's an absolute vision in her blush dress. It's not the vibrant pink from days of Margot past, but it's the most *her* outfit she's worn as of late. I worked hard throughout the ballet to pay attention to the show, but now that I'm sitting across from her, I can't help but take her all in.

Her hair is pulled back from her face, but she left her long golden curls to flow down her back. Her makeup is lighter than it has been recently, with hues to match her dress. Her luscious tits flow over the top of her satin corset.

"Earth to Jack! What are you thinking about?" She snaps her fingers to get my attention.

I bring my gaze from her chest to her sparkling eyes. "I was thinking about the fact that this is the first time I've seen you wear pink in...well, I guess in over two years."

"Well, you know it's practically a mandatory requirement of mine to wear pink to see *Sleeping Beauty.*"

"Ah, of course, your protest that her dress should only ever be pink, never blue, and that you *must* wear pink in a show of the passion behind your opinion."

"Well, yes. Exactly," she deadpans.

"Do you remember how you would make Ledger, Henry, and me be the three fairies and Blanche be Maleficent?"

She snorts from laughing so hard. "I did not do that. I refuse to believe it."

The memory reminds me of exactly how many years the entire Sinclair house lived and breathed *Sleeping Beauty.*

"Your mom will have a picture somewhere to prove it. You even had your dad playing Prince Phillip, so you must've only been two. Three was when you started insisting I play the prince in every play. It was something to watch you boss that man around. So tell me, do you still prefer the storyline of the movie to the ballet?"

"Oh the movie of course, and don't act like you don't know why!" she says as her laughter dies down. "There's no way that Prince Désiré could possibly be her true love if he had never met her."

"And you still think an afternoon frolic in the forest with Prince Phillip justifies their love?" I ask, leaning forward onto the still empty table between us.

"Well, not exactly," she says, matching my position as she props her elbows on the table to lean in as well. "But they were destined to be married! Phillip knew from the moment he first saw little baby Aurora what his purpose was in her life. He spent sixteen years with the duty to marry this princess hanging over his head and never once wavered. Then he meets her again all these years later with no pretense of who she's supposed to be, and he's ready to risk it all and give up *real* Princess Aurora to be with *forest* Princess Aurora. So you tell me that's not destiny."

We've both been drawing closer with each passing moment, and by the time she's done with her spiel, she's only a few inches away. I caress her chin, my hand like a magnet drawn to its other pole. To its home.

"I certainly know what it's like to hold a baby in my hands and know what my purpose is in life," I say, my eyes locked on hers. "But I also think that two souls can be made for one another. The fact that Prince Désiré was there at the exact moment he needed to be and overcame every obstacle to wake the sleeping Aurora should mean something as well. Maybe her soul called to him...because I also know what it feels like to have the other half of mine call to me."

I barely hear her breathe out, "Jackie..." before I'm pulling her mouth to mine, finding it impossible not to taste the lips my name just fell from so effortlessly. I've almost found my mark, only a hair's breadth away from my own personal nirvana, when our server arrives to greet us.

"Good afternoon. My name is Em...oh! I'm so sorry, I didn't mean to interrupt!" Margot tries her hardest to escape my grasp entirely, but I hold her jaw steady in my hand, running my thumb back and forth across her lower lip.

"No need to apologize. My girl just had a little something on her lip that I was helping her with," I assure, never breaking eye contact with Margot while I order for us both.

Margot slaps my hand away and sits back in her chair the moment our server leaves us alone again. "I could've ordered for myself!"

I've gone to at least a hundred teas with this woman. I know her order. *I know everything about her, for that matter.* I raise a brow as I take a drink of water, sitting back in my chair. "Would you have ordered something different?"

She folds her arms across her chest but doesn't accept her defeat. "Whatever, Jack. And I'm not *your girl.*"

"Whatever you say, Princess." This time, I give her what I hope to be a rather rakish smirk as I slouch down a bit, throwing an arm around the back of my chair.

My princess just rolls her eyes, but I can see that smile she's trying to hide. I let her off the hook the rest of the afternoon, just enjoying her company.

Chapter Fifty-Four

As I sit on my cushions, eyes down and wearing only my necklace while waiting for my Sir to come in, my mind wanders to another man for the first time ever in this room. Jack briefly flits across my mind, and the fact that I almost *kissed* him this week. Would kissing be considered cheating on Sir? I try to clear my head, slowing my breathing, so that I'm focused only on maintaining good posture and being perfect for when he enters. I'm nervous about how tonight will go after our *incident*, and even though we took a week off and texted a bit, I'm not sure what the vibes will be. Luckily for me, my Pavlovian response to being in this room and on my cushions is calming me. I know I'm already wet, and when I hear the door open, the thud of his boots making their way to the desk behind me has me dripping. He takes a few minutes to arrange things on and around the desk, opening and closing a storage room door before coming back to stand in front of me.

"Good evening, pet. I don't want any noise from you right now. But I do want your pitiful little gaze. Eyes."

I give him what he demands immediately, like the well-trained girl I am. I'm not sure I'll ever be able to ignore the word "eyes" ever again. He's especially intense tonight, and I have absolutely zero clue what I'm in for. Last time told me it could be anything. He squats down in front of me, thick thighs strong as he holds his position, head cocked to one side as he rakes his gaze over my naked body. One hand reaches out and trails slowly from my temple down along my cheek and jawline, grazing my collarbone before giving the faintest caress to my breast. Before my brain can conceptualize how heated his barely there touch is, he's grabbed my nipple and pinched, harder than he ever has, making me cry out in surprise.

"Hmm," he murmurs, back to caressing my breast before trailing down my waist and between my legs, rubbing directly over my clit on his way to toy with the wetness at my entrance. "I thought we discussed that you were going to be my good whore tonight, and here you already are, acting like a dumb bitch who I didn't train better than that."

I have to fight the urge to roll my eyes back into my head at his words, and I know he can feel the gush of wetness that just joined what he's already spreading on my inner thighs.

"I'll let you in on a secret, pet. You were already going to get that ass spanked raw tonight, just because I felt like it. So I'll have to add in those ten you just earned in a more creative way."

I'm shaking now, my body already a live wire at the idea of the pain taking me out of my own head just to float among the stars. *Please.* The click of my leash brings me back.

"Come, pet. Eyes down."

Following him slowly on all fours, I stop and present myself near the velvet bench. I can see the legs of an apparatus, but I refuse to get excited until I know for sure what it is, or what he has planned.

"You may look, pet."

I fight a smile as my wish is granted. It's my custom fucking furniture, as I've deemed it in my head, designed exactly as I imagined it when we discussed it a few scenes ago. I'll be strapped into the padded table on my front, head supported with a cushiony massage table-esque U pillow, breasts hanging beneath me through a cutout, with my knees slotted onto bent padded ledges, thighs strapped in. My pussy will be presented to him at a slight angle, and he'll have access to my clit if I'm lucky enough to have him pay attention to it.

"It's a modification of the idea of a breeding bench, and I'm not surprised you like it so much, pet." *Fuck, he reads me like a book. I didn't even move my face.* "Only the dirtiest whores like to be presented like this so that any man who walks by could grope you or fill this tight cunt up."

I tremble with the force of holding in a whine, and he chuckles darkly.

"You'll come tonight. I know you're a pouty little slut when you don't. But it *will* be on my terms, and it *won't* be anytime soon. Do you understand?"

"Yes, Sir."

"I'm going to blindfold you and plug your ears. You'll be strapped in, but your mouth will be free to release you if you need it. I won't stop for anything else. And I don't want to hear anything else from you until you absolutely cannot hold it in any longer. I'll remove the earplugs before I'm ready to tell you to come, so if they're in, don't even think about it. Understood?"

"Yes, Sir." *Fuck, he's going to put me on display and use me like a toy.* My pussy clenches around nothing. *Please.*

I thought I had an idea of what he meant when we discussed overstimulation, but I had no goddamn clue. I've been half conscious for what has to be hours, taking what he's given me, unable to see, hear, or move. Only feel. I don't know if I've been making noise, but I've gotten myself spanked regardless. I know I won't be able to sit comfortably for a long while based on how my ass and thighs feel. My tether to reality is slipping. Pieces of the night come back in fragmented flashes—when he would pull out an earplug and degrade me, only to slip it back in without telling me I could come.

Earplug out. "Look at this slutty little hole in the air for me, waiting to be mounted like a bitch in heat," *he growls, dipping one thick finger into my soaked pussy, slowly teasing in and out while I try to clench and keep him inside.* "You have the prettiest cunt I've ever seen, pet. It's not even fucking close. You have no idea how hard it is to get any work done every day when all I see when I close my eyes is this dirty little hole opening up for me, spreading so perfectly tight around my dick..."

Earplug in. I can't hear anything, even close to my face, so I damn sure don't hear the swoosh of the leather paddle coming through the air before landing hotly on my ass cheek. I know for a fact I choke on my exhale, but I don't think my noises actually matter now. I think I'm getting my ass beat regardless.

Earplug out. "Look at that perfect red ass. Goddamn, pet. You're crying so hard, did you notice? Tears and snot running down your face. Your pussy is crying, too. Are they happy tears *because it dodged the spanks that your ass got? I don't think that's very fair, do you?"*

Earplug in. He followed through on his threat to spank my pussy and my raw, tender clit, before moving underneath to redden my tits, raining down alternating smacks in a pattern I can't begin to track. My presence in reality is really slipping now, and I feel my body shake in earnest as I'm going to come, whether he likes it or not.

Earplug out. "My perfectly filthy pet. I think you're getting a little close to coming. You can't help but love all this pain, can you? Let's make sure we don't get too hasty here, hmm?"

Earplug in. He clamps something terrible, awful, sharp around both nipples, and I know I scream because I feel it reverberate out of my throat, so loud it's raw when I stop. He's right. I'm further away from coming than I have been all night, but I'm also further out in space. I'm actively sobbing, but I can't care, floating so far away from my body.

Earplug out. Laughter. "You're wetter than you've ever been, darling." He's slowly thrusting three fingers in and out of me, and I whine as he adds a fourth. "I wish you could see yourself. What a work of art. Everyone deserves to see you like this, born to be such a sweet whore for me." I clench around his hand as he barely teases, adding his thumb to my hole. "Oh, you perfect dirty girl." His other hand slaps my tender ass, and I hiccup through my sobs. "You'd love that, wouldn't you? Let me get a crowd of men in here to see you on display for me to break. They'd be so jealous of how well I've trained you, pet."

He releases the nipple clamps, and they clang to the floor, somehow hurting so much worse coming off than going on. He laughs again, his hand still practically all the way in my pussy, just staying there as he rubs my ass cheek before pushing a thumb into my puckered hole.

I'm too far gone to know what I'm saying, but I know that if I don't come back down now, I never will. I'll be too far gone, just a cluster of sex atoms in the universe with no corporeal form.

"Please..." I give the faintest whisper as I sob, throat raw from screaming and voice rough from disuse. Everything around me stills, and I beg the man on my mind for relief. "*Please, Jack.* Please, please let me come. No more, it hurts. I need it. I need you please. *Please give me your cum.* I can't..." Crying harder, I'm shaking as I feel my limbs being released from my bench, and my blindfold being ripped off, but I don't open my eyes. I'm pulled to straddle my tormentor, my savior, and I don't know what I'm saying, but I know what I want. "*Raw, please.* Please, I need it. Please *kiss* me. I can't...*make it hurt...*"

I can't even breathe. I'm sobbing so hard and on the verge of hyperventilating...

Smack. I'm slapped across the face almost enough to turn my head, and my eyes pop up to see the *brown eyes...Sir. Please.*

I'm pulled onto his thick cock in one hard thrust, pulling one more scream from my throat as I explode, only my scream is muffled by the lush lips on mine, owning me and pulling me under as I drown. My orgasm never stops as he drives brutally up into me, and I suck on his tongue before trying to bite his lip hard enough to draw blood. He pulls away and instead keeps our foreheads locked together and eyes fused. I clench once more around his length inside me, pushing him over the edge, and watch fascinated as his eyes roll back into his head, and he fills the condom with a manly groan.

*Condom? Why would he wear...*Oh God. Oh my God. *Not Jack, not Jack, fuck. No. I wasn't thinking. My Sir. Fuck. I'm sorry.*

I'm expecting to see anger in his brown eyes, like he would know who I was thinking about, and kick me out. But they're kind as always after a scene as he pets my hair and rubs my back. He lifts me and walks us to the bathroom.

"My perfect girl," he coos, kissing my temple, "you did so well. I'm so proud of you. You took it all beautifully. Such a good fucking girl."

As he draws my bath, I realize I'm not going to be able to stop my tears from returning, both from the release and endorphin rush, but also from shame and confusion and exhaustion of how jumbled I am right now.

"Hey, hey..." He crouches down once I'm in the bath, seeing how upset I really am. "What is it? Does something hurt?"

"N...no..." I sniffle. "No, I'm great. I think it's just a big crash tonight. I'm okay."

He washes my hair in silence, strong hands massaging my scalp and relaxing me enough to stop my sobs, if not my tears. Finally, he goes to get my snacks and has my fruit and cheese tray prepped, ready to feed me, when I have to stop him.

"Thank you, but...I...can you..." I take a deep, watery breath. "I think I'd like to be alone, please. I'll get out of the bath soon, and I promise to eat, but. Please? Nothing you've done, just me. I need to get my head on straight. I think the worst of the crash is over. You can have the desk worker check on me if I'm not out in twenty. But I'm okay, I swear."

I see the hurt flash across his eyes before he masks it. He gives me a searching glance before nodding. "If you're sure. But I'm sending them in here in fifteen." He stands to leave before turning back to give me a lingering kiss on the forehead. "Thank you, pet, for tonight. And for everything."

I stand from the bath, ready to get dressed as soon as I hear the outer door click shut, and make my way to my pile of clean clothes. On my way, though, I'm stopped short by another plate he had prepared for me, after my fruit was eaten. *Chocolate. All kinds.* Including my favorite truffles, and that's the last straw.

I steel myself to get past the desk without freaking them out, assuring them I was happy and healthy and nothing untoward had happened, and I collapse into my car before pulling out the truffles. As soon as one hits my tongue, my tears are back. I'm missing my masked man already and wishing he had blue eyes.

Chapter Fifty-Five

Good morning, pet. How are you feeling after last night?

I'm okay. It was a lot. I didn't expect to crash that hard.

I'm not surprised. I edged you for hours, and you took a lot of pain. Would you tell me if it had been too much?

I think so, yes. It never was. I enjoyed it all. I feel unsettled today, though.

Did you finish eating your snacks yesterday?

Pet:

Wasn't very hungry so didn't eat much of it.

Sir:

Please try to eat three good meals today and stay hydrated.

We don't want you to pass out from anything but pleasure.

Pet:

Did you enjoy yesterday? I didn't do anything wrong, did I?

I was so floaty by the end that I'm not sure what I was even saying.

Sir:

You were perfect as always, pet.

I couldn't ask for anything more from you.

I'm not convinced you're capable of being anything but perfect.

But I am a little worried about your drop.

Can you text someone you know in real life?

Maybe reminisce with an old friend or meet someone for lunch?

I'd feel better knowing you were with a friend or family member for at least a bit today.

Pet:

Yes, Sir. I can do that.

Sir:

That's my good girl.

Margot:

What are you up to?

Jack:

I just watched *Sleeping Beauty*...

You're right. Maleficent is totally more intimidating than Carabosse.

Margot:

THANK YOU!

Now you understand why I always wanted to sleep in your bed after I watched it!

Jack:

Hmm. I think it was just because you wuuuved me.

Margot:

Ugh, get over yourself.

Jack:

Look, feel free to come crawl in bed with me anytime you feel scared.

Margot:

What am I going to do with you, Jack Carter?

Jack:

Let me take you out again?

Margot:

Maybe.

Jack:

Well, what are you doing this weekend?

Margot:

This week is pretty busy but maybe next weekend.

Just text me closer to then and I'll see what's going on.

Jack:

Will do, Princess. 😊

Margot:

Do you remember the train game we used to play?

Jack:

The one where we grew an empire or the one where we were the conductor?

Margot:

Conductor.

Jack:

Couldn't tell you...

But I do remember the way you had us hunker down with blankets and provisions like we were going to be out in the wild for a month.

Margot:

It was serious business...

Jack:

Oh I recall.

I also remember that you would always fall asleep an hour into playing, and then if Ledger and I had the audacity to stop the game and do something else, you would raise hell when you woke up.

Margot:

Jack:

Spoiled Princess...

Margot:

Jack:

Jack:

Are you still free this weekend?

There's somewhere special I'd love to take you.

Margot:

I think Friday night's open. What's this special date?

Jack:

Can't tell you! It's a surprise!

Margot:

OOOO SURPRISE!! Can I at least get a hint?

Jack:

It's probably your favorite thing in all the world.

Margot:

Henry Cavill?

Jack:

No, and I still think it's weird you like him so much…

He's like a generic version of our own Henry.

Margot:

Ugh, you take that back.

😰

Maybe another hint?

Jack:

Nope! Just the one.

Margot:

Alright, fine, but you better not disappoint, Carter!

Jack:

Never 😊

Margot:

Can you at least tell me how to dress?

Jack:

To the nines!

I'll have a car come get you at 6.

Chapter Fifty-Six

"When you used to tell us that you did *super secret spy shit* for your dad's company, I didn't think for a second you were fucking serious, man. What the fuck!" I scream as the parachute finally deploys, Henry laughing brightly behind me. Luckily, he seems like an expert skydiver, so I'm basically a baby strapped to his chest, along for the ride.

When he asked me two days ago if I was available to help with a quick business trip, I was a little confused, but he's my brother. To be honest, I was mostly just excited to be included, since he usually drags Ledger on "business trips." Fuck, was this what they were doing all the time?

"Yes," he replies, and I realize I must've said that out loud. "But now that he's got Sloane, he's retired, leaving me to fend for myself. But I like having a buddy to take on these trips, and your presence hasn't been vexing to me lately. I also admit that

I've enjoyed being your sexual mentor more than I would have thought."

I must be having a fucking fever dream right now, because I *know* I'm not gliding peacefully toward a field in the middle of nowhere, strapped to Henry Sinclair's chest like his chubby little toddler, while he acts like he's the one who taught me about sex.

"I'll concede that you've been helpful during my exploration of a particular *piece* of my sexuality, but I had sex well under control before you *ooomph!*" We touch down sooner than I expected, and with more force than I really think was necessary. I wasn't ready and didn't have my feet set, so I'm face down in the grass while Henry uses me as a mattress, breaking his own fall.

"You really weren't any help at all, Carter. Did you forget you have legs?" he asks, rolling us to our sides and beginning to unhook us each from the harness.

"Well, I didn't really know we were about to land."

"It doesn't matter. Listen, we're making a clandestine approach to a cabin on the other side of this tree line. I have it on good authority that what we'll find will be excellent blackmail material for a client of ours. I have a body cam on, and I'll be doing all the talking. You can watch my back and call for backup if things get hairy." He says all this like it's a foregone conclusion, and then he's sprinting through the trees in his tactical gear. I don't even know who he would want me to call. This doesn't strike me as a 911 situation. Guess I'll figure it out as I go along. This is fine. Normal stuff. Fine.

I realize as I finally catch up to Henry, *fucking blow to my ego that this giant asshole is that much faster than me,* that he's barreling through the front door in a very *not* clandestine manner, and there's a big chance this is all about to go to shit. He's in the house and gone by the time I clear the entryway, only to have a hand cover my mouth and pull me into a chokehold.

My fight or flight kicks in, and this cannot be how my life ends. I'm getting Margot back, the club is doing well, and my hair has looked better than ever lately. Fuck all that. Getting Margot back is the only important part, and I am not about to let some prick derail my plans. I'm seconds away from spinning out of this and fighting for my life when I realize I can see just enough of the hand over my mouth to know that *I know that hand.*

He realizes that I know a moment later, and once he knows that I know, he lets out a booming laugh and unleashes me. Henry peeks around the corner where he was hiding.

"Gotcha!" Ledger says, laughing his ass off and falling backward into a chair. I want to be mad, but seeing Henry actually laugh is contagious, and before I know it, I'm doubled over, abs hurting from the effort.

"What the fuck is wrong with you two? You couldn't have just invited me to the cabin for a few days?" I ask, taking in my surroundings and realizing that it's one of the Sinclair properties in a relatively remote part of New York. Blanche and Margot hate this cabin because the water pressure sucks. We usually spend a lot of time outside when we're here, which is not their favorite pursuit.

"Nah, man. This was way too much fun. We've gotten soft on the pranks as we've gotten older. I had to get one more good one in before LJ gets here," Ledger says, pulling me into a hug and slapping me on the back to hide his sniffles. I don't think this man can even think about his son without tearing up. *Lucky bastard.*

"Come on, you two, you can hold hands and reminisce later. We've stocked the cabin with everything we need for a couple of nights, except..."

"Firewood," Ledger and I groan, knowing that Henry's favorite thing in the world is chopping firewood. I don't know if it's a meditation thing for him, or if it makes him feel like he's everyone's dad who has everything taken care of, but fuck. I already know this is about to be a few hours' worth of work before he'll let us stop.

Three goddamn hours later, we've all stripped off our shirts, and we're steaming in the chilly evening air, but we have a big-ass pile of much-needed wood. I'll admit my arms and shoulders should have a great pump tomorrow. Running a business is satisfying, but there's something about chores and maintaining a home. Maybe Ledger's onto something with his renovations and his garden.

After a dip in the cold tub Henry had ready for us, *he's such a dad*, followed by a dinner left in the fridge by the caterer, we're all in the hot tub with a beer in our hand. Well, all but Henry. He's drinking a glass of Merlot because of the day of the week, or the moon phase, or whatever.

"So, Jack, how is your Master/pet relationship coming along with your new submissive?" Henry asks in an even tone, raising one eyebrow as Ledger spits his entire mouthful of beer out.

"Your what?" he exclaims, looking betrayed. And, yeah, I feel kinda bad about not telling him *something* at least, but we've both been so busy. Him hoeing his garden, me hoeing his sister...*not helpful, Jack.*

I make my face as apologetic as possible. "Uh, yeah. Sorry man. It felt like more of an in-person discussion."

I give him a basic rundown of my initial visit to the other club and the journey I've been on since. I'm able to keep it mostly cool until Henry asks a question that he likely thought was standard.

"How does she submit?"

Ledger's brow furrows. "What do you mean? Sounds like he tells her to do something, and she does it. Pretty straightforward."

Cracking his neck, Henry tops off his glass of wine. "It's not at all straightforward. In fact, it's a wide spectrum. I'm just curious if Jack's found himself a brat to tame."

I lean my head back on the edge of the hot tub. I *really* don't want to describe the nature of their sister's submission to me, but I can't stop the cheesy fucking grin that splits my face. Ledger lets out an "oooo, Jackie is in loooove" and I have *got* to deflect. Henry is already eyeing me like he's about to give me a lecture about the importance of not falling in love with your anonymous BDSM club partner.

"She submits beautifully," I say, knowing that *if I get tears in my eyes, these fuckers will never let me live it down.* "She's powerful, magnificent, really. And there are flashes of her willfulness that shine through, but it's rare. She mostly really wants to be my good girl. She's a natural."

I already sense the follow-up questions, but I'm saved by the bell, a.k.a. Ledger's phone ringing with Sloane's custom ringtone. He scampers out of the hot tub, yelling "my Angel!"

to see whatever Sloane and Blanche are getting up to during their "girl time."

Henry moves to exit as well, clapping me on the shoulder and telling me he's happy for me.

When they're gone, there's nothing to stop my mind from wandering to the dark place I've been trying to avoid for the past few days. The place where I'm forced to sit and think about just how much I've fucked *everything* up. All over again. After I swore I would never make the mistake of letting Margot go again, I overcompensated and now I've managed to get her back twice. In two parallel lives that don't touch.

What I didn't tell Henry and Ledger was exactly how much Margot *trusts* me when we're at the club. It's obvious in all of our interactions that she trusts her masked man completely. She's outright said it multiple times when discussing ideas for scenes. The totality of that trust sinks into my gut like a sharp knife because I've *already broken it.* I've been breaking her trust in that room from the moment I realized it was her. And I'm the most selfish man alive. I didn't see a way forward for real Jack to get her back, so I chose to betray her and move forward as masked Jack, to have any piece of her I could, to keep myself alive a little while longer.

I never expected her to soften to me at all in real life, but over the course of our collaboration and our dates, I've finally gotten her to a place where I *know,* at least I think, that she remembers the true magic of our relationship. *God, I'm such a piece of shit.*

And the way she broke down at the end of our last scene and felt so guilty...I could see it. She didn't realize she said my name out loud, and I watched as she grasped what she had done, her guilt eating her alive. But while she was panicking and feeling confused, I was exhilarated. Perversely pleased. *Fucking stoked.* Because she was thinking about real life me while fucking her masked man. I don't have any idea what she's going to decide to do with both ongoing relationships, but I do know that I'm too far in this to quit now. Whatever scraps of attention she'll keep giving to me, I'm going to keep fighting for. I'll prove to her that I'm a better man than I was, and that I can give her everything she'll ever want. Nobody knows Margot Sinclair like I do.

Except you're not a better man at all, you lying fuck.

And maybe that's true. Maybe I'm not any better. But I am older and wiser, and I've learned lessons from my mistakes, including the only one that matters.

Do whatever it takes to keep Margot Sinclair.

Lying be damned.

Chapter Fifty-Seven

"Princess, I would never ever hurt you. Just relax, okay? Just look in my eyes."

"My perfect girl," he coos, kissing my temple, "you did so well. I'm so proud of you. You took it all beautifully, such a good fucking girl."

Go to Paris. Find the sexiest Frenchman you can and climb him like a tree. Live every second of your life to the fullest.

A knock on my door jolts me from my thoughts, and I take a deep breath to steady myself. My personal life is in shambles, and I feel as unsettled as I have in years. Of course the period when I felt in control of myself and my life, emotions, relationships...that lasted, God, how long? A month, tops? Of course. It's comically predictable at this point.

At least I had the bright idea to make sure I was ready for my date with Jack before I sank into my melancholy. I'm dressed in what's become my look of choice lately—head-to-toe pink.

I suppose what's old is new again, or maybe it's true that every woman goes through style cycles. When I asked Jack for our dress code tonight, he only replied "to the nines," so with *that* unhelpful bit of information, I did what I could. I've had this dress forever, waiting for an occasion to wear it, which is a stupid way to think. What if I had been hit by a bus with this dress sitting in my closet?

Then they could have buried you in it!

Jesus, Margot. Morbid, even for you.

Making my way to the door and grabbing my clutch, I take one last look at myself in the full-length mirror in the entryway, smirking. This pink is so pale it's almost white, and the tea length paired with the corseted waist overall gives a rather bridal look. I bet Jack panics and chokes.

Opening the door, I see not Jack but his driver. "Ma'am, Mr. Carter will be meeting you at the venue, if you please."

Well, if he can't be bothered to pick me up himself, maybe this isn't as much of a date as I thought.

Finally, we arrive at the destination, my chauffeur refusing to give even a hint about where we're headed.

Stepping out of the car and over a puddle because there's no sidewalk, I look up at...a big, abandoned factory? Great, the chauffeur has dropped me off in a questionable area, clearly at the wrong address, and driven away to leave me...

"Miss?"

I look up to see a man in full formal serving attire beckoning me into the wrought-iron gates of the imposing building.

"I'm Remy. Mr. Carter apologizes for the delay and hopes you'll come inside. He'll be with you in a few short minutes."

Rolling my eyes, I decide being kidnapped is less likely since everyone clearly knows who Jack is, so I follow Remy into the building. Initially, we're in a nondescript hallway, and I see cracked windows looking into the huge, disused production area. Before I know it, he's opening one more set of doors, and tears fill my eyes as I see a logo I would recognize anywhere.

L'éclat du Chocolat. The Chocolate Sparkle.

One of my many obsessions as a child was an offset of one of the larger chocolate producers in the United States. The founder and main chocolatier was the daughter of the CEO of the chocolate company, who wanted a chance to make smaller batches with organic ingredients and leave her mark on the family business. Having access to it was a real treat since the batches were so small, so Mom would conserve it for very special occasions. I know the woman who founded it moved to France years ago and stopped marketing the chocolate, so I'm not sure where I am right now.

Unlike the derelict larger facility just outside, this kitchen and workspace is immaculate. White tiles, dark green accents, and antique appliances that have been seemingly maintained all these years. It's decorated, too, with a seating area featuring a small round table set formally for two, delicate flameless candles and a bouquet of peonies completing the romantic setting.

I sniffle. Well. I underestimated Jack Carter. Again.

"Well, Princess. Maybe one day you'll stop. But I don't mind. It makes it all the more exciting to continue to hurdle your expectations of me."

Jack steps out of the shadows just beyond the table, and my confused heart clenches at the sight of him. He took his dress code very seriously, wearing a black tuxedo that fits him like a second skin. *Jesus fuck,* he's untied his bow tie, allowing it to hang on either side of his dress shirt, the top three buttons undone as always. He looks like a rake who's lured me here under false pretenses to steal my virtue in my little pink dress. *Not so sure I didn't know the pretenses when I agreed to come, though.*

"I know for a fact I didn't say a word out loud," I defend myself. I keep my internal back and forth *internal,* thank you very much.

He laughs as he reaches me, taking my hand to kiss my knuckles and take my clutch from me. "You don't have to say things out loud, darling. I see them on your face. You forget how well I know your tells."

Before I can open my mouth to scramble for a witty response, a bright, cheery voice rings out behind us.

"Bonjour, mes amis! Welcome to my little slice of paradise!"

A diminutive, distinguished woman wearing a starched white chef's coat joins us, kissing both Jack and me on each cheek.

"My name is Susanne Ferrer, and it's a pleasure to welcome you tonight. I *love* love, so when Mr. Carter reached out, it was a no-brainer to accept his offer," she says, beaming up at us with a twinkle in her eye.

I'm not even going to touch the *love* comment, deciding that despite my turbulent internal thoughts earlier today, I'm just going to go with the flow tonight. I can be breezy. I can do this.

"It's an absolute honor to meet you, Chef Ferrer," I say.

"Please, call me Susanne!"

"Thank you, Susanne, that's so kind of you. I have to ask you, where *are* we exactly? When we arrived, I was a little nervous about the state of the building, but this kitchen is so beautiful, I was surprised!" I follow as she leads us over to the cooktop.

"I'm so glad you find it as magical as I do, dear. This is my secret hideaway, as I used to call it. This was the kitchen that started it all when *L'éclat du Chocolat* was just a passion project I was trying to get off the ground. My father carved out this section of the factory for me and let me renovate it. Even once I was producing bigger batches, this remained my main test kitchen whenever I was in the city. Eventually, I moved to France to chase my wife, and I decided it was time to step back from the business, but one of our longtime employees lives here and acts as a caretaker for the property. Any time I'm on the East Coast, I try to pop in to play a bit!"

She gives us a full tour of her antique ranges and specialty chocolate-making tools, then pulls out a chocolate mold I would recognize anywhere.

I gasp, reaching just behind me where Jack has been hovering closely, paying rapt attention to Susanne's stories, and grab his hand as I extend my other reverently to the mold.

"Is that...?" I whisper.

"La petite vache?" she says, amused. "Yes, my favorite mold I ever worked with. The little cow. I loved every collection we released with this. They were so whimsical, and I've always loved cows!"

I can't stop the tears in my eyes, thinking of how thrilled I was every time the cow chocolates were released, and how

Mom hoarded them for my special occasions. Jack squeezes my hand, and I realize I never let it go after I grabbed it earlier.

I don't let go now.

After two courses of dessert, we convince Susanne to give us a short break to digest before she brings us the finale.

"There's no way that's true. I would remember locking you in the pantry. Plus, that doesn't sound like me. I was a perfectly well-behaved little girl. I would never get up to mischief like that." I laugh, remembering the exact instance Jack is describing. He wouldn't tell me what he was getting me for my birthday, so I tricked him into one of the creepier pantries off the kitchen and wedged a door stop under the door so he couldn't escape. "How old would I have even been?"

"You were eight," he says, removing his cuff links and pocketing them, then rolling up his cuffs. "The most menacing eight-year-old who has ever existed, I'm convinced. See, look at the scar I have from trying to climb out of the transom window to get out of that damn pantry!"

Sure enough, a long, thin white scar crosses underneath his forearm.

I roll my eyes. "Oh please, that could be from literally anything."

His eyes sparkle. "Come on, Princess. Would I really lie to you?"

"Princess, I would never ever hurt you. Just relax, okay? Just look in my eyes."

He realizes what he's said as soon as I do, and the playfulness from the moment before fades. I take in the soft lighting on his face, the tightness around his eyes as he thinks he's lost me, lost this wonderful night. Is that what I want?

Aggressively pursue happiness.

With a little shake of my head, I bring us both back into the lighter energy we enjoyed all night, feeling in my bones that this decision is a fork in the road for us, and hoping I'm choosing the right direction.

"No, Jackie. I don't think you would," I say, and his dazzling smile is his only response.

With a herculean effort, Jack and I finish off Susanne's pièce de résistance, a simple but decadent chocolate cake dripping with ganache, topped with a little cow chocolate. Jack has my clutch and a box of chocolates under his arm, a parting gift from Susanne. But I have her number now, and it'll be hard for her to get rid of me. *We'll have to be friends.* I have so many questions for her about her time running a small business as a woman, and...

Jack's warm hand on my lower thigh stops my train of thought. He's looking the other way, out the window on his side, almost like he's afraid to see how I'll react. I wonder briefly if he'll always think I'm going to swat him away, and resolve myself to change that.

I'm two steps above him on the stairs in front of my building, which puts me just about eye level with him. Maybe a little taller, which I kinda like.

"I like being taller than you. I feel very powerful. Dominant. Maybe I need to find taller heels. Or you could try being shorter?" I ask, playfully patting the top of his head, which I usually can't see or reach. *God, his hair is nice. Has he changed up his shampoo?*

He raises one eyebrow, trying to look speculative, but he fails when I rake my fingers through his hair once, causing his eyes to roll back into his head. When they return to mine, they're heated, and a thrill shoots down my spine.

"I'll happily get on my knees for you anytime you want, Princess. You'll be much taller than me, then. And you're welcome to dominate me, if you wish," he whispers, challenging me to take the bait. And I do.

"I'm not really into that," I admit, feeling a bit like I'm doing something I'm not supposed to by flirting with Jack. Like I'm a teenager sexting with her boyfriend while hiding her phone under the covers.

"Oh?" Jack asks, slowly advancing us up the stairs one at a time. I step up backward, steadied by both his hands on my waist.

We finally reach the landing and are on equal footing. Our usual height difference is restored, and he looms over me like a tree.

"Yeah," I whisper, both of us leaning closer until I'm almost speaking into his lips. "I've kinda found out that I rather like the other side of that equation."

Like a viper, he strikes, and in half a second, I'm pressed between the hard wall of my building and his even harder body, with one of his huge hands around my neck and his tongue down my throat.

I've never been kissed like this. I don't know if he felt the shift tonight, the decision I made...or if some tether that's been loosely connecting our souls has finally snapped taut again after years of being slack.

My clit throbs, and if I don't stop this now, I'm going to chain this man up in my apartment and never let him go. But we still have things to sort through, and this is not the night to just fall back into bed together. He's not getting the message, though, based on his hard length rising to meet me through his pants. Finally, I bite down on his tongue, hard, to get his attention.

He pulls back to look at me, eyes blown and crazed, like he'd give me the world if I asked him to. *And one day I just might.*

"Thank you for the best date I've ever been on, Jack," I whisper.

"Yet," he says in response, and I give him a questioning look.

"The best date you've ever been on, yet," he says with finality, then steps back, realizing his dismissal without me having to say it. He backs down every step without looking back, knowing when he's reached the bottom and stopping to watch until he sees me go into the building. *Did he count them on the way up? Why is that so hot? A stair-competency kink? Really, Margot?*

Moving so I don't look crazy just standing here, I give him a soft smile and wave, which he returns, before moving past the grinning doorman into my building. I'm sinking into my bath a little while later when a phone chimes, but not the tone I was expecting. Instead of a follow-up text from Jack, it's my Sir.

Sir:

> This week, I'd like you to wait for me in your collar but not naked. Wear lingerie, something bright red.

Fuck, I was not ready for how this text would make me feel. I give myself ten minutes to sit calmly, fully exploring my emotions about the situation, and make a decision. Once I do, I feel sad, but it's as if a weight's been lifted off my shoulders. Nothing is set in stone, but it's time to figure some things out.

Me:

> Sorry, I can't this week.

He responds instantly, just giving my message a thumbs-up, but before I decide how I feel about that, my real phone chimes. I smile when I see Jack's name, thanking me for the best date he's ever been on *yet.*

I'm still grinning like an idiot when I get out my vibe, and when I come tonight, a specific man is on my mind with no mask in sight.

Chapter Fifty-Eight

Jack:

I had an amazing time tonight, Princess. Thank you so much for agreeing to go out with me.

Margot:

 No, thank YOU! I can't believe you pulled that off.

I had forgotten all about *L'éclat du Chocolat*

I had an incredible night!

Jack:

Does that mean I get to take you on another date?

Margot:

1000%

Seriously, the best date I've ever had.

We didn't even get to my usual favorite part of the night! 😉

Jack:

I can be at your place in 30…

Margot:

Lol. Slow down, Jack.

I'm still in shock from that kiss

Jack:

Oh, you liked that, did you?

Margot:

Big time…

I've missed kissing you…

Jack:

I've missed kissing you too, baby girl. So much.

I've missed everything about you...

Margot:

Jack:

Margot:

Ugh. Work sucks today.

Jack:

You wanna tell me about it?

Margot:

Just a bunch of legal gibberish for the new location.

Jack:

Oh yeah, that stuff sucks. Thankfully, we have someone to deal with most of it.

Margot:

Do you like what you do?

Jack:

What do you mean?

Margot:

I mean, managing the club. Dealing with the day-to-day stuff.

Jack:

Hmm, I did when we first opened Rendezvous.

It was new and fun, but the bigger it became, the harder it was.

I mostly prefer the creative aspects of it now.

I've been training Aaron to take over the day-to-day for a while now.

I just haven't had a reason to step down

Until recently...

Margot:

Ooo... And what's this big opportunity?

Jack:

You, Margot...

Margot:

Oh...

Jack:

I was an idiot before not to chase you while you followed your dreams

This time, I want to follow them with you.

Margot:

Well. I don't even know what that is anymore.

I love designing. And I thought a storefront would be great for the business.

But it just took off so fast, and every opening has been more successful than the last.

I love that we're doing so well.

But I find myself too stressed to create new designs.

Jack:

My advice, Margot?

You seem to have a fantastic team behind you.

Let them take over the daily shit, and you do what you do best.

Margot:

You're right.

Thanks, Jackie.

Jack:

Anytime, Princess. 😊

Margot:

So I've been trying to declutter.

And you'll never believe what I just found in the back of my drawer...

Jack:

A friendship turkey made of chocolate?

Margot:

🙁 Hamish died years ago, Jack. Why bring that up?

*sends picture of pink and white lingerie set

Jack:

Is that the same set you made for me years ago?

Margot:

The very one!

Jack:

2 things

1 - don't you dare get rid of that.

2 - I'm going to need to see that on you again.

Margot:

*Sends picture wearing lingerie

Jack:

Jesus fuck, Margot!

Warn a man before you make him nearly come in his pants.

Margot:

 You asked for it!

Jack:

I meant in person!

Margot:

That can be arranged.

Jack:

Jesus Christ, Margot. You're killing me.

Full disclosure, I've just locked myself in my office

I'm about to get rid of this hard-on…

Margot:

Sends GIF of Mr. Bean

Jack:

Jack:

Are you flying with Henry to LJ's shower?

Margot:

Obviously. Why would I fly commercial when I can go on the family jet...

Jack:

Well, excuse me for wanting to make sure I'd get to see your pretty face

Margot:

Yes, Jack, I'll be there.

Jack:

Margot:

What?

Jack:

Are you trying to join the Mile High Club orrrr...

Margot:

Um, who says I'm not already a member??

Jack:

Never mind I said anything...

Margot:

You should really think that through because if Henry were to see us, you wouldn't have anywhere to go.

Jack:

Easy, I'd just jump out

Margot:

He can parachute. Pretty sure he would jump out, catch you, and then drop you, just so he could tell everyone it was by his hands.

Jack:

Fuck. No, you're right...

Another time then?

Margot:

Another time then

Jack:

Chapter Fifty-Nine

Jack

"I don't understand why we are obligated to attend yet another shower for your child," Henry says as Ledger opens the door to welcome us.

Henry was already in New York for business, so he flew Margot and me down to LJ's baby shower, and he's been a sourpuss the entire trip. As much as he grumbles, I know he would never miss anything concerning his nephew. And in his defense, he's never been wild about babies. In fact, I'm pretty sure Margot is the only baby he's ever even held, so it's pretty adorable to watch him try to hide his obvious excitement where LJ is concerned.

"Ugh, I don't know, man. Ask our mother," Ledger responds, clearly on the same page with baby parties as his brother. "I was able to talk her down from one of her notorious soirees, where she invites everyone she's ever known, but..."

"But we're celebrating that child, Ledger Sinclair, whether you like it or not." Blanche interrupts to give Henry, Margot, and me a hug. "But you're probably correct to spare Sloane from having to greet so many strangers when she's a month away from giving birth."

"Annnnd?"

"And we're more than capable of purchasing everything LJ could ever want or need without accepting gifts from others."

"Because?"

"Because it would be a bunch of things that you didn't really want, and Sloane would either feel obligated to use it or feel terrible that she was wasting it if she didn't."

Ledger finally smiles down at his mom and pats the top of her head. "Very good."

"Nevertheless," Blanche says, leading us all into the den where Sloane is sprawled out on the couch. "We're still going to have a ball celebrating our little guy as only we Sinclairs know how. And just so you know, *Henry*, the last one was a *gender reveal*. It's completely different. It's like you didn't grow up in society at all."

"Well, he sort of spent most of his adolescence in England," Margot says in defense of her brother. "I certainly recall him being absent more than present—"

"Now that everyone is here, let's go over the agenda for the day," Blanche announces, cutting her daughter off. "We're going to begin our activities with a cooking challenge. Ledger has picked out a couple of recipes that Sloane has been craving, so we're going to team up and see which she likes better. After that, we're each going to paint a ceramic gnome. While those are in the kiln Ledger had installed, we are all going to sit around and plan LJ's first Disney trip. Then we're going to lounge around with our mom-to-be and watch whatever movies she's in the mood for."

I've barely been paying attention to the itinerary, my mind fixed on how Margot's ruffled powder-blue blouse brings out the light in her eyes, until the mention of ceramic magical dwarves brings me out of my trance. "Um, why are we making the baby gnomes?"

"For his garden of course," Sloane replies matter-of-factly.

"Right...right...makes sense." My initial reaction is to make fun of this preposterous idea, but from the corner of my eye, Ledger is sizing me up like prey, and I know that any jokes will be dealt with in blood.

Sloane laughs, thankfully, not oblivious to the ridiculousness of the idea. "Look, I just wanted to eat popcorn and play Monopoly."

"No!" I yell, along with the other four Sinclairs.

"We aren't allowed to play Monopoly," Margot admits. "Mom banned that after Ledger and Jack got into a knock-down, drag-out fight because Ledger wouldn't trade Boardwalk for all three of the red properties."

"If I remember correctly, I put ole Jackie here in the hospital for a night." The man himself grabs me in a chokehold and ruffles my hair like it was an adorable bonding moment between us as adolescents and not like he broke my nose, fractured my ribs, and caused enough bruising to have the doctors concerned with the risk of internal bleeding.

"I absolutely remember," Margot responds, giving her brother one of her famous stare downs. For once, I'm not jealous not to be the object of her attention. "Because I was only seven at the time and thought he was going there to *die,* so *I* stayed the night with him and had to sleep in that horrible hospital chair."

"No, Princess, your mom was the one in the chair. *You* were starfished belly down, on top of me in the little bed and kept messing up my IVs all night."

Sloane's contagious laughter has us all coming undone at the memory. "Ohmygod stopit, you guys. I pee when I laugh now."

Blanche is the first one to pull herself together enough to rein us all in. "Alright, alright, let's get this show on the road. Ledger and Henry will be on a team, and then Margot with Jack. Sloane and I will judge."

After a full day of activities, including Margot and I almost starting a fire in the kitchen trying to make pierogi from scratch, Ledger almost leaving our baby gnomes in the kiln long enough to burn them to a crisp, and Henry getting so exhausted from planning the Disney trip he offered to rent the whole park out for the day, we're all exhausted.

"With the renovations going on, I'm afraid I only have three guest rooms ready, so you'll have to draw straws," Blanche says, after we all decide it's time to call it quits for the night.

"I'll take the couch," I concede immediately, knowing there's no way either of my brothers are giving up a bed, and there's no way in *hell* I would take one from Margot.

"No way, Ledger and I will just go home," Sloane slurs, finally coming to after passing out on her husband at the beginning of this last movie.

I wouldn't have accepted her offer, with or without Ledger's current death stare. "No, I'll be fine. This is probably more comfy than any of those beds anyway," I say, bouncing up and down on one of the plush cushions for emphasis. I'm not wrong either, I've taken plenty of naps on this couch, and it really is comfortable.

I've barely had time to get the blankets in place after saying good night to everyone, when I hear an all-too-familiar pitter-patter coming my way. The outside lights flickering from behind the curtains are more than enough to see my girl looking as gorgeous as ever in a pale pink nightgown. I've only seen her in black lingerie or completely nude recently, but something about the innocence of the soft hue is enthralling, so I'm not sure which I prefer more. *Especially knowing exactly how much she's been corrupted.* Her hair is down now, framing her makeup-free face, which is somehow even more beautiful than when it's artfully contoured.

"Jackie, why don't you come get in bed with me? We used to sleep together all the time." she says, sitting at my side on the edge of the couch. Her hand effortlessly finds my thigh, and fantasies of a domestic life with her threaten to pull me away from the moment.

I push myself up, my blankets falling to my waist, exposing my bare chest before tucking a stray hair behind her ear. "Princess, if I got in bed with you right now, there wouldn't be any sleeping."

Letting my hand fall to caress her neck, I revel in the feeling of her pulse quickening beneath it, until her hand finds mine and guides it down to her chest. When she reaches her desired destination, she tightens her grip on me, a silent request for me to do the same to the luscious breast I'm embracing, while her other hand trails up my thigh toward my hardening cock. "And would that be such a bad thing?"

This time, I'm the one who can't control their racing heart. In a blink, I've rolled her over onto her back with her face caged between my hands and my chest grazing hers with every rise and fall of my breath. "No, it wouldn't be a bad thing at all, baby girl. It would be a very. Very. Good. Thing," I say, emphasizing each word with a thrust of my hips, letting her know just how much I would, indeed, love to take her to bed. "But your brothers would kill me for the screams I would pull from that pretty little mouth of yours. So maybe we don't do the shared bed thing here tonight."

"Oh," she breathes.

I slowly pull myself off her after kissing the top of her head, then pull her to sit up as well. "Yeah, *oh*. Go to bed, Princess—" I'm interrupted by the ruffling commotion of her making a pallet beside me. "Jesus, Margot, no! You aren't sleeping on the floor."

"Well, I'm not leaving you alone!" my stubborn girl says, crossing her arms in an act of defiance I know all too well.

"Get on the damn couch, Margot!" I sigh, giving up my comfortable makeshift bed and getting onto the pile of blankets she's laid out on the floor.

"Jackie?" she asks as we both settle into our new "beds."

Rolling over on my side, I'm greeted by my own goddess, glowing in the moonlight, and looking down on me with just as much reverence as I feel for her. "Yes, Princess?"

"When we get back to New York, can we maybe find a bed to share where my brothers won't be an issue?" she asks, reaching a hand down toward my own for me to hold.

I happily accept her offering and kiss the top of her delicate knuckles before threading my fingers through hers and holding on for dear life. "Whatever you want, Princess."

Her response is a simple smile, but it's more than enough for me. She's out like a light almost instantly, but I want to savor every minute of her touch. Like I've said before, any scrap I can get. The thing is, as I lie here holding her hand in mine, I realize this is way more than just a scrap. I'd rather only ever be able to hold her hand as Jack Carter than be able to fuck her senseless whenever I want as her masked man. And I think, *I hope*, she's starting to feel the same.

If the incredible dates we've been on recently, the late-night text conversations like days of old, or her canceling on masked me weren't enough to give me hope that things with us could work, spending the day with the family sure is.

As we laughed and played together, I realized something I should've known all along. We are *meant* to be. We're already family. But unlike Henry and Ledger, who are the same as brothers, or Blanche, who's like a mother to me, Margot has always been more. I swear to God, I get the imprinting bullshit now because it's like my soul has always belonged to her, but only in the way she needed from me at the time.

Whether that be someone to console her when she cries, make her laugh when she's sad, protect her when she's in danger, hold her when she's scared, or *put a collar on her when she needs dominating*...The list could go on forever.

My purpose has always been and will always be Margot, and for the rest of my life, I'll give her whatever version of Jack she needs. I just hope with everything that I am, that what she needs in me now is her forever.

Chapter Sixty

"Yes, thank you so much for your warm wishes. I'm still not interested at this time, but if that changes, I'll be sure to consider your team," I say politely, masking how much I want to bite the head off the representative for the third giant corporation who's tried to buy me out this week. The New York store has been an amazing success, and although it's been a whirlwind, I'm having a good time. There have been a couple of moments, though, when I've considered what it would be like to take a step back from the administrative duties and solely focus on creative direction. Then the devil on my shoulder reminds me that we've only just achieved all this. Why would we give it up so soon? I don't *really* have time to unpack all of that tonight, so I shake it off as I grab my things and move downstairs to meet my driver. Milan and Berlin have both been floated as potential expansions, and I have the weekend to prepare before meetings next week.

I look up from the sidewalk to find my driver, but instead, Jack is waiting in front of a sleek SUV.

"Hi, Princess," he says, kissing my cheek and taking my things before opening the back door for me. Sliding in beside me, he places his hand on my thigh, immediately causing goose bumps to erupt across my body.

"What is this? Is anything wrong?" I ask, a little breathless from his presence.

He chuckles and shifts over to be closer, his entire body pressed against the side of mine. "Nothing wrong. A little birdie told me that you've had an extremely busy week, and I was hoping you'd indulge me with dinner at home tonight. Nothing fancy. Just to relax. If you don't want to and you'd rather be home alone and do your skincare and go to sleep, we can drop you off there. No pressure."

I release a breath I didn't realize I was holding and think about how, since I've been slowly letting Jack back into my life, I've felt lighter and more like myself than I have in years. He seems to really just want to take care of me, and as hard as it is to accept it, I really like it. After being pretty independent for over two years, I'm starting to like the idea of a partner, someone to share things with. I could fight him for taking me away from my pre-planned evening of, well, nothing. But I think I might be done fighting. At least, I think I'm getting there.

Leaning into his side and putting my head on his shoulder, I smile. "I think a quiet dinner sounds perfect."

It's a bit surreal, pulling up with Jack to my old apartment building from my time in the city while completing my master's. He usually isn't the forgetful type, and didn't he say we were going to his place?

"I don't live here anymore, Jack," I say, furrowing my brow and checking to see if he's showing any overt signs of a stroke. Trying to remember the acronym, I see his face isn't symmetrical, but I think it's due to his half grimace, half grin. He wasn't slurring his words in the car. The driver has dropped us off and left, so now we're stuck here for the time being. "Are you okay?"

"Ha. Yeah. Yes, yes, I'm okay." He awkwardly chuckles, clearing his throat and leading me by the hand into the building and up the elevator. "So, I know you don't live here, Margot. But, uh, well. I kind of do."

Too much time passes as I blink at him sheepishly.

"You live here."

"Yes."

"Since when?"

"It's been a while. I don't really remember the move-in date. I might have the paperwork around here somewhere if you want details, or we can ask Mrs. Goldsmith across the hall. You know she never forgets anything and probably has a time-stamped video of me moving all my stuff in..."

He's rambling, but I've stopped paying him any attention. As soon as he opened the door and led me in with one hand on my lower back, I made a beeline for the corner of the living room that always got the most natural light during the day. Now I'm running my hands along the beautiful grand piano from his other apartment, feeling tears fill my eyes.

"Why do you have this?" I ask lowly, not daring to turn around. He takes slow steps until he's a foot away, then he stops.

He's not going to answer me, and as I move to sit on the piano bench so I can see him, I ask him again. My voice is clear, making it obvious he's getting nothing from me until he answers. This is an answer I've deserved for a long time, I think. I'm going to hear it from him whether he likes it or not.

"Why. Do. You. Have. This?" I ask again, through clenched teeth, before I can't take it for another second. I turn on the bench, fully facing him and seeing his head bowed, eyes on the floor, jaw clenched. "Why do *you have this*? And why do you live in my apartment, Jack?" My voice that had risen falls to a whisper on his name, like I'm scared to speak it and conjure him, even though he's already here.

I see his jaw clench once more before he tips his head back, eyes to the ceiling, and then he kneels so that his eyes are level with mine. Tears stream down his face, and after a moment, his face crumples. He takes a moment to reach out and grab one of my hands, playing with my fingers before he speaks, so quietly I can barely hear him.

"The piano is here because I...I had to pretend in any way that I could that one day you'd be here, too. It's not...it's fair, it was my fault. I deserved it. But Margot, I...." He lets out a heavy breath, and his words come faster but no louder, and the tears don't stop. Jack's emboldened, I guess, by the fact that I haven't run screaming yet. He continues, playing with my left ring finger although I doubt it's intentional.

"I regretted everything the instant you left. And I knew, immediately, that I was to blame, and I deserved every ounce of pain coming my way. And I took it all, I promise you. Please never doubt that every moment you were in France was a penance for me, one that I know I deserved. But I'm so selfish, Princess. I had to have something to delude myself, deep down, that you might be back where I was, one day. So I bought the apartment. I hoped it would still smell like you." He lets out a watery, self-deprecating laugh at this. "It did for a while. God, it was heaven while it did. I could go to work, come home, sit on this couch, and think about Thanksgiving and eat chocolate like an asshole and pretend. Then it faded, and I started buying your perfumes and shampoos, but it didn't smell right, and fuck if that wasn't a dark hole to crawl out of."

He's back to staring at me now, with the most earnest, pleading look I've ever seen, and I feel my heart break along old lines and then snap back together, tighter than before.

I think he's waiting for me to say something, or give any indication that I'm internalizing what he's saying, but the glint of silver at the cuffs of his shirt has caught my eye. His cuff links are delicate and clearly custom. A replica of Sprinkles, my favorite childhood stuffed animal. He sees me notice them, but doesn't say anything, and my gaze travels up his torso before snagging on the chain I've only ever seen glimpses of. Instead of a cross or some other emblem at the center, it's a crown. *Or maybe a tiara.*

He sees me notice the necklace, too, and must decide it's time to say something, anything at all, to try to salvage how creepy he just made himself sound.

"Princess, I...fuck!"

Whatever else he was planning to say is silenced forever by my mouth as I pounce off the piano bench and onto him, straddling his waist and pushing us both to the floor. Threading my fingers through his hair, I grind against him, reveling in how hard he is underneath me, how much bigger he is. I bite his bottom lip hard enough to draw blood before sucking it into my mouth, needing him inside me in every way.

Sitting back up, I rip his dress shirt open, buttons flying, and scrape my fingernails down his chest and torso as hard as I can. *I hope I leave scars.*

Grinning down at his bewildered face, I growl out, "*Mine.* That piano is mine. This necklace is mine. You. Are. Mine."

Something about this brings him back into himself, and he gives me a saucy smirk before he sits up effortlessly to bring his forehead to mine and look into my eyes. "Yeah, Princess. It's all yours. It always has been."

He moves to stand, and I squeak and wrap my legs around his waist, convinced he'll drop me from this awkward angle, but he stands to his full height, holding me like I'm weightless. I'm expecting to be dropped softly onto the bed, or set on the back of the couch, or hell, on top of the piano. Anything except him slamming me into the wall so hard a frame falls to the floor, one hand coming behind my head to protect it from the force.

The look in his eyes is different from anything I've ever seen from Jack before. He's unhinged. Feral. I might have enough sense to be scared if I wasn't so horny.

"I'm yours, Princess. I have been, and I will be, independently of anything you could ever do in this life. Nothing can ever change that. You *have to know.*" He pulls back, eyes blown black, and moves his hand from behind my head to cradle my jaw firmly, holding me in place while he stares into my soul.

"I *am* yours and *you. Are. Mine,*" he growls. "You've always been mine, Margot. I won't let you go again. For anything."

Fuck. Yes. Yes, you stupid man who's atoned and fought for me. I want you. Yes.

"Please," I breathe, and he's on me again.

By the time we make it to the bedroom, we have more clothes off than on, and we'll both be covered in scratches and bruises tomorrow. It's like we both want to dig into one another, burrow inside so deeply that nothing can tear us apart again. Finally, my blouse is torn away, and I'm left lying on the bed in the simple matching bra and thong I wore today in soft pink lace.

"You're such a fucking vision, Margot Sinclair," he moans. I yelp as he pushes my panties to the side and plunges two long fingers into me, finding me soaked.

"Oh my God," I wheeze as he adds a third, stretching me out as if he's on a mission.

"Gotta make sure you're ready for me, baby, but worshipping you like you deserve has to wait. I have to be inside you. It's been too long." He's shaking with the effort of keeping himself off me now, and I need him.

"Please, Jack. Please. Inside me, I need you," I gasp as he gives me exactly what I asked for, ripping my panties off and slowly sliding the thick cock that I've missed so much all the way inside in one devastating thrust.

He doesn't even ask, just slides into me bare. Nobody has since him, and I forgot how much better, how much...more...it feels.

"I hope you're not on birth control, Princess."

"Don't you mean..." Fuck, he's deep, and I wiggle, trying to find a way to catch my breath as he's forcing it out of me, one long thrust at a time. "You hope I am?"

He stops thrusting, settling deep inside me and leaning down to stare into my eyes as his fingers find my clit. "No, baby girl. I really fucking don't."

I come immediately, his words and his fingers leaving me unable to resist falling apart.

"That's it, darling. Mine. My orgasms, isn't that right?" He pulls back to give me a long look full of a wild adoration that I sincerely hope I'll be seeing for the rest of my life. Pressing a sweet kiss to my forehead, he moves both of my legs to his shoulders and bends me in half. *Oh fuck, that's deep.* I wince, then moan as he drags his way out. The push and pull of the pain and pleasure is going to send me over the edge again.

"Ah, ah, ah," he teases, drawing my attention back to him and placing one hand around my neck. Not much pressure, just enough to remind me that he has me where he wants me. *God, I like this new sex Jack.* "You pay attention to me when I'm fucking you, Margot. And you damn sure look me in the eyes when you come on this cock."

I do. I stare right at him, fighting the urge to let my eyes roll back into my head but keeping them on him the entire time.

"Oh fuck," he says gently on an exhale, before giving me the same honor and holding my eyes as he comes inside me, his warmth spilling as deep as he can. "That's my girl."

He releases my legs from his shoulders, and I wrap them around his waist, eager to stay connected for as long as possible. Our kisses turn sweeter and sweeter, and I'm lost in them when I realize he's hard *again.* Or he was never soft. He's fucking back into me slowly now, our combined cum making a mess of my pussy that I can feel dripping down onto the sheet. As he picks up the pace, he gives me one more kiss before pulling out, flipping me over onto my elbows and knees, and driving back in, pausing deep with the sexiest groan escaping his mouth.

"You look confused, Princess," he taunts. "Did you think we were done?"

I whine as he refuses to thrust, staying firmly pressed against my G-spot as he teases me. "I thought...*ugh*...you came, so I thought we were done."

Wrapping my hair around his fist, he pulls me up, still speared on his cock, until my back hits his chest. Gently turning my head so that I can see him, he's giving me a confused look as his thrusts begin again, just enough to remind me that he's there.

"You thought that I would have you for the first time in years, and come inside you *once*, and that would be enough for now? That I would need a break? I hate to break it to you, darling, but we're nowhere near done for the night. You might as well settle in," he trails off into a whisper before pushing me back down onto my elbows, and I let him.

His thrusts become more punishing, and I feel his strong arms and the delicate chain dangling down to tickle my back, and I float away.

Chapter Sixty-One

There have been so many orgasms between the two of us tonight, I've lost count. *Take that, past European lovers.* I've had my girl in every way imaginable, but it's not enough. It'll never be enough. I could spend the rest of my life buried to the hilt in her sweet pussy, holding her flush to my body, her skin sending shock waves into mine, and it wouldn't be enough. Not even close.

Her poor body is already covered in bruises from my grip. I really don't want to hurt her, but I can't seem to hold on to her tightly enough. I don't bruise quite as easily as my little peach, but I'm sure if I went to check, I would find her own passion expressed in an abstract masterpiece of scratches across my back.

Breaking our languid kiss to look down at the woman below me takes almost all of my strength, but the view I'm rewarded with is worth the momentary loss of her mouth. While the glow from the city filtering through the windows is the only light in the room, it's more than enough to carve every inch of my goddess into the very core of my memory. Her skin glistens from our hours of exertion, causing her hair to cling to her neck and face. My slow but thorough thrusts into her continue at a steady pace as I brush the damp strands away, giving me a complete view of her beauty and *goddamn*.

With each orgasm, her lust-blown pupils have receded further and further to the storm of affection brewing in the sea of her light blue irises. Those ocean eyes I've adored her entire life now shine brightly with unwavering love, calling to me like a siren, to the depths of her soul. *The other half to my own.* I let go of any tether holding me to a world where she isn't mine and set out to anchor our hearts together at last.

Her exhaustion is obvious, and I know this will likely be the last time we're able to fall apart in each other's arms tonight. Her legs wrap around my back with a grip that seems impossible with how tired she must be. Supporting myself on one arm, I use the other to pull one of her legs off me and trail kisses from her ankle to her inner thigh before replacing it behind my back.

"Come here, baby," I say, sitting back on my knees, pulling her up with me by her waist, as I continue driving deep inside the paradise between her legs.

Our bodies are pressed so close together, it's hard to know where I stop and she begins. Then again, that's how it's always felt with us. I keep one arm wrapped around her waist, my hand pressed to her back to hold her against me, while the other finds her hip, guiding her down in sync as I thrust up. The new angle adds pressure to her clit, and it doesn't take long before I start to feel her fluttering around my cock, threatening to take us both over the edge.

"I love you, Margot," I breathe out, leaning my brow against hers. "So goddamn much, Princess."

Her wandering hands move to my hair, gripping it between her fingers as she holds my head against hers. "I love you too, Jackie."

We're slick with sweat as we grind against each other, seeking something so much more than pleasure in this final climax, and I'm shaking with restraint, refusing my release until we can go together. Still being held tight to her, I roll my head to the side for better access to her ear. "Come for me, baby girl."

She guides me to that spot she loves so much on her neck, already starting to bruise from earlier tonight. My teasing kisses start chaste, but as my thrusts increase in intensity, so does the attention from my mouth. I haven't even bitten her, but I'm sucking so hard I'm surprised I haven't drawn blood.

Before I know it, her body convulses, barely giving me time to pull away and look into her eyes before she sweeps us both away in a tidal wave of pleasure. Our gaze remains locked on each other as we fall apart, and I know that when we put each other back together again this time, I'll finally be whole.

"Please don't leave this time," she whispers. Her head falls to my shoulder, and she relaxes but still clings to me like a koala.

Our connection remains with my still hard dick buried inside her when I wrap my arms around her waist and hold on with all my might. "Oh Margot, I'm never leaving you. Ever again. I'm never letting you go. *Fuck,* baby girl, I *can't* let you go. I can't live without you again." I reassure her, kissing her head frantically between each statement until tears begin to well in my eyes.

"Look at me, baby." Summoning the courage to let go of her in order to grab her face, I pull her attention to me and search her eyes as my tears start falling. "Letting you go two years ago was the dumbest thing I've ever done. I'll spend the rest of my life regretting how we wasted that time, but I refuse to waste any more."

Her eyes begin watering as well, but before a tear can fall, I guide her lips to mine and let our tongues continue this heart-to-heart as they dance together. Like everything else about this woman, her kisses will never cease to amaze me. There's just something about the way she tastes that's so *Margot.*

Without breaking our kiss, I manage to get up off the bed way smoother than I thought I would be able to, and walk us to the en suite bathroom to give my princess a nice soak.

"Too tired," she says, finally pulling our mouths apart as I lean over to set her on the edge of the clawfoot tub.

"Baby girl, we need to get cleaned up a bit. I haven't been this sweaty in years, and as much as I would love to leave you covered in our cum, I would rather not have you suffer through that inevitable UTI."

"Shower," she says sleepily.

"Okay, Princess, why don't you go pee real quick and then wait for me in the shower?"

I didn't do any renovations in this apartment, clinging to as much of her as I could, so she's familiar enough with the layout to find her way around without my guidance. As she wobbles to the toilet, I quickly turn on the shower, change the sheets, and get her a clean shirt of mine to wear to bed.

When I get back to the shower, the water temp is to her liking, *scalding hot,* and Margot sits on the built-in bench, half asleep. I wash her as gently as I can, careful not to wake her, then quickly clean myself as well. I dry us both off and carry her to bed.

Fighting the urge to leave her magnificent body on display, I dress her in my shirt and tuck her under the covers, then pull on boxers and get in on the other side. She's barely been conscious since I found her dozing off in the shower, but the moment I get into bed, she scutters under the sheets until she's cozied up against my side, and drapes an arm *and* a leg over me.

"Pinky promise you'll be here when I wake up?" she mumbles, face down into my chest, making no effort to actually give me her pinky.

Rolling her over on her side so I spoon her from behind, I hug my arms around her and breathe in that pink Margot scent. "Pinky promise, Princess."

I can't see her face, but I swear I can feel her smile when she says, "I love you, Jackie."

"I love you too, baby girl."

And just like that, she's asleep in my arms again. Not a day went by in over two years that I didn't drown in regret, dreaming of the last night I got to hold her in my arms. I don't know what I did right to end my torture, but I'll take every bit of it I can.

I'll have to cease to exist as her masked man, of course. Whatever tricks I used to convince myself I wasn't a complete asshole for deceiving her in the first place won't work to justify cheating on my girlfriend with my...girlfriend. *Fuck, I like the way that sounds. Not as much as I'll enjoy my wife but nonetheless.*

the way that sounds. Not as much as I'll enjoy my wife *but nonetheless.* As sexy as it was, I don't need that exact dynamic between us. Why would I need a pet when I have a queen?

If there *was* any question of her not being able to keep me sexually satisfied without a collar and leash, it went out the door tonight. She is such a natural submissive. And while I'm still learning about my own dominating preferences, I was just as aroused, if not more, by her simple submission than with the overt Master-pet play. *Not that I would turn her down if she wanted to.*

I'll tell her about the masked man. One day. One day far away. Maybe after we're married. Or after she's just had our first kid. Or on my deathbed.

No, I really do need to confess to her that I've been her Sir all along. She'll be upset at first, but I'm sure after several years, it'll be one of our funny stories we bring up over dinner.

"Hey, remember that time you wore a mask and made me crawl to you on your hands and knees before fucking the living daylights out of me but then didn't tell me it was you!"

It'll be great.

Ultimately, it will have to be fine because I meant it when I told her I would never let her go. Masked man or not, I was never going to be enough. Even now, I don't deserve her. But for some reason, the universe chose to align my soul with that of a living breathing goddess. And for some stranger reason, she loves me. The stars gave us another chance at happiness, and I'll hold on to that with my life. I'll follow her around the world as she chases her dreams, never giving her time to resent me as I find new ways to worship her.

The sun is starting to rise as I drift off to sleep. "I love you, Princess," I whisper, pressing a kiss to her hair like I have countless times before, knowing that I can have her lips whenever I want from here on out. Tears stream down my face as I realize what an honor it is to have her in my arms again, so I look down at my entire reason for existence and hold on to her with all my strength, refusing to release her for the rest of my life.

Chapter Sixty-Two

This has to be the best dream I've ever had, and I almost don't want to wake up, only...I really need to wake up to make sure Jack didn't leave in the middle of the night. I want to believe him, that he'll stay and that he's mine forever, but if I could just open my eyes and see him for myself, I could relax and go back to sleep. There's a heavy weight on my stomach, though, and I need to move so I can get up to pee, but I can't move. *Fuck, I'm going to pee myself in my dream.*

"There's my girl. Let go for me, Princess."

I wake up just in time to see deep blue eyes staring at me from between my legs before I feel myself letting go into a slow, rolling orgasm that's clearly been building for a while. Oh my God, I'm peeing all over Jack.

He lets out a long, low groan before going back in to lap up everything I've just given to him. "Fuck me, baby. You squirting for me first thing in the morning is a revelation. Give it all to me."

And I do. He doesn't stop licking and nipping at me, working me back up quickly and scooting up my body just in time to feel me come again, this time around his cock. It doesn't take him any time at all, three lazy thrusts max, before he joins me, filling me up and sweetly kissing me as he moans my name.

New favorite alarm clock.

"I'll wake you up like that every day for the rest of our lives if you want, Margot. I pinky promise." He laughs, rolling us onto our sides but keeping our connection for as long as possible.

I have to watch what I say out loud around this man. Can't go telling him all my secrets.

I lie on my side, facing him, using his bicep as a warm pillow. Tracing his eyebrow, then his cheekbone, then his strong jaw and full lips...is this man ever going to stop getting hotter?

"I hope not, at least until I'm in my fifties for sure...but then hopefully I'll be a full-on DILF so, let's go with no. I'm never going to stop."

"I cannot keep doing that. You should have to learn to read my mind to earn access to my innermost thoughts." I smile, rubbing my nose up and down the length of his.

We lie like this for a while, just enjoying the pale morning light and each other's warmth. Finally, I have to voice my fear that didn't come true, just to get it out of my head.

"I'm so glad you stayed," I whisper, unable to keep my voice from wobbling as I feel relief at being so comfortable and safe in his arms.

Sadness colors his expression for a moment before determination takes its place. Pulling his hand up to echo the patterns I traced across his features, he gently cradles my jaw. "I'll never forgive myself for giving you a reason to doubt me," he says, so low I can barely hear him. "But I will try every day to make you as happy as I possibly can, Princess, and I'll live for the day that you don't wonder if I'm going to disappear again."

We rest in the quiet of the morning for a while, but when my bladder protests too loudly to ignore, we finally get up and get our day started. By the time I complete my morning routine, I can smell pancakes from the kitchen. I walk in to see a broad, muscular back flexing as he cooks, listening to music on his phone, flipping pancakes, slicing fruit, and pouring me what I can tell is going to be an excellent cup of coffee. It strikes me briefly that this is almost *too* perfect, but then I remember that this man does know me, inside and out. Instead of living in the past, feeling resentment and fear, new Margot is going to simply enjoy being loved by an Adonis of a man who spoils her. *Life is good.*

"I could really get used to this," I say as I sneak up behind Jack and wrap my arm around his trim waist. I can't resist trailing my fingers lightly across his happy trail and the V of muscle that frames it, causing him to groan a curse and spill coffee on the counter.

"Don't tease me like that, baby girl, or we're never going to eat anything around here."

"Oh I'm not sure about that," I tease, eyeing him up. "I think I could take a juicy bite out of...what is this?"

His smile falls as he stops to see what I'm looking at, then chokes out a laugh, clearing his throat and giving me a sly grin. "Well, uh, that is a tattoo, Margot."

"You don't have any tattoos! You never have."

I climb onto the kitchen step stool to get a better look at the tattoo of a *bite mark* on the top of his shoulder. I must've missed it last night in the dark and this morning in the pale light of the sunrise, but...I move as if to bite the same spot and find my mouth a perfect fit. *It's definitely a bite mark of* my *teeth.* Only...

"When did you get this?" I ask, already knowing the answer.

"Two years, four months, and five days ago," he whispers. "I had to keep a piece of you. It's the only tattoo I have. But if you like it, I can cover myself in them. Just say the word. They could all be your bite marks, if you want. Avant-garde, or you can sign 'Property of Margot' across my chest. Maybe we can add some of your scratch lines to the mix...mmmph."

He's cut off as I kiss him, then I burst into laughter at the ridiculousness of this man. I kind of can't believe he got a tattoo of my teeth after our one night together, but then again, I'm standing in the apartment he bought because it might smell like me. So I guess it tracks.

Allowing myself to be led to the kitchen island, I hop up and wrap my legs around Jack's waist as he feeds me breakfast, taking one bite himself for every two of my own. As lovely as this is, discussions need to be had, and I can't wait until we eat at a snail's pace to ask him. I decide that being direct is the best way to rip this bandage off.

"So, Jack," I begin, and he gives me his full attention, quirking an eyebrow at me. "I have questions, and I would appreciate your candor. I think it's better that we get everything out in the open, and these are serious considerations if we're beginning a relationship. Neither of us will do the other any favors by hiding anything. I'm going to just start with the hardest question, and go from there, okay?"

He's paler than before, but he solemnly nods his head yes and reaches for his glass of water.

"Okay. When the *fuck* did you get your dick pierced?" I ask, and he *chokes* on his gulp of water. I fall back onto the island, cackling as he coughs and tries to get his breath.

"*That's* the most important, most serious, most terrifying question you had to ask me? You had me scared as hell, Margot. Jesus. I thought you were asking something real!"

"It *is* real! You have a transformer for a penis, Jack. What the hell! You have to tell me everything. This story has got to be crazy," I plead, giving him puppy dog eyes.

He rolls his eyes to the ceiling before pinching his nose. "Well, Margot, you see...a couple of years ago...Ledger and I..."

"Ew! Fuck! No. You're not telling me my brother has a Christmas tree, too?"

"He has way more than..."

"Stop! Forget about it! I do not need to know the origin story of my new favorite toy. I don't need to associate Ledger with your dick in any way." I dramatically gag to prove my point, earning me a tickling attack.

"I tried to tell you not to bark up that tree, woman! You just didn't want to listen," he teases, still tickling me and making me laugh so hard my cheeks hurt.

"I yield! I yield!" I yell, finally making him stop. Biting my bottom lip between my teeth, I blurt out the question I have to know the answer to even though I know I'm going to hate it.

"Was it for a woman?" I whisper, averting my eyes so I don't have to see the look in his eyes as he remembers whoever convinced him to do this.

A gentle finger under my chin turns my head back to center as Jack looks at me contemplatively. "I think, deep down, everything I've done in the past two years has been for a woman. But, Princess, if anything, it's only ever been for you. It was a drunken night with Ledger, and I won't tell you the full stupid story, but I did always wonder if you would like it."

Knowing that this isn't some bitch named Candace's personal recommendation for dick jewelry makes me feel a little better, and I can't help but tease. "Well, I do like it. I would even say I might love it. Have you ever had any complaints?"

He scratches his nose and turns back to put the dishes in the sink. "Nobody else has ever...experienced it, so I can't really say."

I freeze, waiting for the punchline to what has to be a joke because this hot-ass man standing in front of me cannot possibly be telling me he's been celibate since I left for France. There's no fucking way.

"Jack—" I begin, but he turns around to lean back against the sink and looks at me, blowing out a heavy breath before interrupting me.

"I won't lie to you and say there wasn't anybody else. Just after, I tried, and it just didn't go well. She wasn't you, and I thought I needed more distance...then time just kept passing. I was busy with the club, and before I knew it, you were back in my life like a whirlwind..." His voice trails off, and I wince, thinking about all the times I threw my European adventures in his face when I came back into town, like a complete bitch.

"I'm sorry that I said all the things I did when I came back. I didn't know..."

"No. Don't even think about feeling guilty for a bit of that. You did exactly what I told you to do when I pushed you away, and I deserved to hear it." He wipes away a tear that's escaped and fallen down my cheek. "All that matters...*Look at me, Margot.* The *only thing* in the world that matters now is that we're together, okay? You and me. I'm going to make you so happy, Princess. Just let me, okay?"

I sniffle and nod, accepting a sweet kiss from him that I try to deepen, but he pulls back. "I'm going to shower and then we're going to the little bookstore you saw on our walk the other day, okay? We're going to have a great day, baby."

He kisses my temple and heads for the bathroom, while I stay perched on the island, fighting the feeling of general shittiness that I can't shake. He was here pining for me, and I was being spitroasted in Italy...*no, Margot.* He had a lifetime of sexual experiences before you, and you deserved to have your fun and get to know your own sexuality. *He pushed me away in the first place.*

And, most importantly, that's all in the past. He has all of me now, and that's what matters most. Shaking off my guilt and resolving not to let it fester, I go to get ready for our day when I think of one last piece of me that still belongs to someone else.

Grabbing my overnight bag from the bedroom, I dig to the bottom to find the phone with only one contact, not really understanding why I've still been carrying it around. It's bittersweet, but only for a moment, because I hear Jack singing in the shower and smile.

"*Hi. Thank you for everything, but I can't see you anymore. I don't even know what to say, because thank you doesn't seem like enough. I've met someone who's very special to me, and we're serious. I'll miss you, and I hope that's not wrong of me to say. You've helped me unlock a part of myself that I didn't know existed. I hope you're lucky enough to find someone who makes you half as happy as my new guy makes me. All the best.*"

Phew. Okay, that's just a little awkward. I mean, really, Margot? *All the best?* Whatever, it's over. I feel mostly excitement about Jack, relief I cut ties with my masked man, and the tiniest twinge of sadness.

I hear Jack's phone vibrate somewhere in his nightstand, and I smile, thinking of how Ledger has been spam texting him lately with his latest acquisitions for LJ. They've been hyping each other up like crazy, and a vision of a little blue-eyed boy flashes across my mind. Sneaking into the bathroom, I decide the bookstore and the rest of the world can wait a little while. I have everything I need right here.

Chapter Sixty-Three

"It's going to be fine, Jackie. Just breathe," Margot says, running her hands up and down my arms.

She looks so much like herself in a pastel pink sundress and matching cardigan, with her hair styled down and framing her face, it takes my breath away.

I can tell the moment her thoughts turn mischievous, the glint in her eyes undeniable, especially paired with the smirk growing across her face.

"Or..." She drops down slowly, her touch following her down from my chest to the waistband of my slacks, giving me chills. Her salacious intention is crystal clear as she sits on her knees, staring up at me and biting her lip. She continues the descent of her touch, finding her mark and squeezing my fully erect cock, threatening to dissolve the last thread of restraint I'm holding on to.

With my head thrown back, a groan of both pleasure and irritation falls from my mouth. "Woman, get off the damn floor," I command, my hand around her throat as she rises.

Her devious little smirk remains as she wraps her arms loosely around my neck, swaying us back and forth. "See, you're not nervous anymore!"

"No, you're right. Having a rock-hard cock is a much better alternative for when your mother arrives." I adjust my crotch with one hand in an attempt to hide the obvious dick print there, while my other hand finds the small of her back. She bypassed heels in lieu of sandals today, so our height difference is exaggerated as she stares up at me. *And I still have to pinch myself to make sure this isn't just a dream.*

After a week of absolute bliss, we decided it was time to tell Blanche. Well, more like Blanche was going to be in the city this weekend, and Margot decided for us both that we had to tell her. We both took the week off work, and after a trip to her apartment to get enough of her things, we've pretty much been living in our sheets. I don't know if it's the fact that this used to be her home and it's been home for me for the last two years, or just how naturally domestic we've been together, but it really does feel like *ours.*

My mornings have consisted of waking up by my body's alarm for once, making pancakes to bring my princess in bed, then waking her up to eat a breakfast of my own between her legs. After a few orgasms each, Margot will drag me reluctantly out of the house to hit the gym where she'll completely show me up before pulling me into the shower for another round or two. We'll get dressed, pick a spot for lunch neither of us has been to before, then head home, barely making it in the door before fucking on the first surface we can get to. When we're equal parts exhausted and satiated, we'll lounge around binge-watching TV or playing games or just talking. Then after takeout for dinner, we'll get ready for bed and make love until we fall asleep.

Needless to say, it's been the best week of my life.

We've been living in this honeymoon dreamland, but with Blanche coming over, it's back to our real life, and I'd be lying if I said I wasn't nervous. Not that I would ever stop fighting for Margot, but real life will probably mean less sex.

Margot grabs my face in her hands, lowering my attention to her, then brushes back the hair falling onto my brow. "It's going to be *fine*. I promise, you have nothing to worry about. Mom loves us both so much, I know she'll be thrilled we've finally found someone who makes us happy. And even in the one thousandth of a chance she hates it, I'm not going anywhere."

The impact of that last statement lifts a weight I didn't even realize I was carrying. *You won't lose her.* Without a second thought, I lift her by her ass and walk her over to the kitchen island, her legs wrapping around me instinctively as our mouths meet in a ferocious kiss.

It doesn't matter that I've had her so many times today I've lost count or that our company should be arriving any minute. *I need her.* With my brow against hers, I break our kiss only long enough to get out a breathy, "I love you, baby girl," before going back in to savage her mouth, biting and sucking ravenously, not stopping even when the doorbell rings, letting us know Blanche is here.

"Jack, come on, let's go let Mom in," she pants, able to pull her lips away from mine but still trapped in my embrace.

I'm standing between her legs, holding her waist to mine with one hand, while grabbing a fist full of hair with my other as I keep her head pressed against my own. "You promise you won't leave me? No matter how this goes?"

"Pinky promise, baby," she whispers, followed by a chaste kiss on the corner of my mouth.

Taking in a deep breath, I back away, allowing her to hop down. I'm shaking at the loss of her contact and frozen in place until she laces her fingers in mine and leads me toward the door.

Blanche's infectious smile calms my nerves the moment Margot opens the door. "Thanks so much for having me over, Jack! I missed you last time I was in the city!"

"Well, come in, come in. Dinner is almost ready," I say, giving her a hug and a kiss before taking her coat.

She's been here enough between the time Margot lived here and visiting me to know her way around, and immediately makes her way into the kitchen to help get the meal prepped. "Of course you didn't actually cook anything. Really, you're just heating up garlic bread? That's what you meant by dinner's almost ready? When Margot called to tell me you two wanted to make dinner for me, I imagined more than just heating up...Oh!"

Her rambling is cut short when she turns her attention back to where her daughter is now standing in front of me, her back to my front, hugging my arms around her waist and kissing one of my hands that are interlocked with hers. The moment she cocooned herself in my arms, wiggling her ass against me in the process, I couldn't resist leaning down to kiss the bare strip of skin between her hair and sweater. Which just happens to be what I'm doing when her mom turns to see us.

"Ohhhhh..." Blanche's eyes go wide in shock.

While I snap back up to my full height like a kid caught with their hands in a cookie jar, Margot remains cool as ever, swaying us back and forth. "Mom, Jack and I are together."

Tears well up in Blanche's eyes, and I'm immediately flooded with guilt. *Fuck, I'm going to break up this family.* My mind is spiraling, unable to find a future when one of the people I love most in the world doesn't end up hurt by this union in some way or another, when Blanche pounces.

"Oh my babies! Finally!" She wraps her arms around us both, creating a Margot sandwich.

"Wait, you don't think it's weird? Us growing up together?" I ask as the color slowly returns to my skin.

"Of course not! I know you didn't really see her as a sister. You know why? Because she has brothers who didn't treat her anywhere close to how you did. You were always more of a guardian angel looking after her. And I know for a fact Margot didn't see you as anything but her future husband."

"Mom!"

"Well, it's true! You've been in love with him all your life, darling." Her words steal the air from my lungs, causing me to tighten my hold on the woman in my arms, who's loved my undeserving ass for so long.

"Anywho, I knew what was going on in my own house, and if there had been anything inappropriate happening, I would've picked up on it immediately. It's perfectly normal for your love of someone to change over time, dear. What I *do* know for a fact is that nobody will ever love my daughter the way you have for so long, and I can sleep easy at night knowing she's got someone she can trust implicitly."

My internal tail stops wagging at the mention of trust. The trust I broke before she was even mine. *Fuck.* If I'm ever going to live up to that man Blanche described, I have to tell her it was me. Because she's right. Nobody will ever love Margot Sinclair the way I do, but I can't in good conscience let her love *me* without knowing everything.

The oven timer sounds, breaking our embrace in order to get the rest of the food on the table, although I doubt I'll be able to stomach anything. Not with the guilt of my deception haunting me after hearing Blanche praise my intentions toward her daughter. On the contrary, the two ladies dig in as Margot tells her mom how we came to be in a relationship. *A few too many details.*

"Jesus Christ, Margot, I don't think your mom needs to know how many times you, uh...*finished*...in one night."

Both Sinclair women look at me like I've sprouted a horn. "That is absolutely of utmost importance when choosing a partner. Eleven is definitely an accomplishment. Be that as it may, my husband had you beat, Jackie."

This time, Margot joins me in my horror, her skin flushing to the same color mine has been. "Oh God, I did not need to know that about Daddy. I'm still under the illusion he gave you three, max...ugh, let's just drop it."

"Yes, please," I agree, putting my arm around the back of my girl's chair and twirling her hair between my fingers to calm my nerves. "And when we tell your brothers, can we just avoid this whole conversation altogether?"

"Oh, don't worry, dears. I'll take care of the boys," Blanche says, pausing for a drink. "But if they aren't aspiring toward double digits, I raised them wrong."

No, I think they are just fine. I've personally witnessed one of them attempting this, and from my recent mentorship with the other, I think his women are fine too. That is, if the temperature high for the day is equal to or less than what was predicted and he finishes reading the morning paper before he's finished with his coffee, or some shit like that.

"Thanks, Mom." Margot lays her head on my chest, and before I know what I'm doing, I've pulled her from her seat beside me into my lap and nestled my face into her neck.

"On second thought, why don't we wait until after LJ is born." Blanche coughs out, reminding me that we have very important company at our table tonight and that I can't lift her daughter's dress and sink into her while we finish our dinner.

I reluctantly put my princess back in her chair before kissing the top of her head. "Now *that* I can agree. In fact, why don't we just wait until we have a baby to show them? I've seen the way they both swoon over the thought of LJ. They can't be mad at a baby."

A look of genuine sadness crosses Blanche's face, scaring the absolute shit out of me, because I *too* am excited about that little guy. "Oh God, what's wrong? Is LJ okay?"

"Oh, he's doing wonderful, last I heard! It's nothing really, I just realized if you two are together, I only get half the number of grandbabies from you."

We haven't really talked about kids, but as I look over at this perfect woman, I know I'll put as many babies in her as she'll let me. Placing my arm back around Margot, my thumb rubbing circles on her shoulder, I move my attention back to Blanche with a cocked brow and a smirk. "Oh, I wouldn't be too sure about that."

Chapter Sixty-Four

"Aren't you just a princess in pink?" Marco teases, immediately clocking that I've walked into the New York office wearing my signature color for the first time ever.

"Yes, yes, get all your little digs in." I laugh, twirling around in my voluminous skirt and showing off the bow holding back half of my voluminous curls. I haven't felt this much like myself in years, and I know exactly who makes me feel safe enough to shed my outer boss bitch veneer that I grew in Paris.

Marco makes a show of slowly circling me before stopping in front of me and pulling me into a crushing hug. "You look amazing, cara. You're glowing. I hope he's treating you right."

Sighing, I try to keep the hearts out of my eyes as I bring Marco up to speed on what exactly I've been up to since I've been spending less time in the office. Although I've been designing from home or Jack's apartment, I haven't really had the discipline to come in and take any in-person meetings.

My little love bubble hasn't popped, and it's tempting to stay within it forever. Our dates, lazy days at home, plans for a quick trip to check on the Paris store next week...by the time I'm done, Marco has hearts in his eyes, too.

"I do need to get back to Pilates class, though. If I start losing flexibility at this point, I'm likely to injure myself..." I trail off as one of the new PAs comes blustering in, dropping a file folder and flinging paperwork everywhere.

"Sorry, ma'am, Mr. Franco is on the line regarding the Milan meeting later. He asked if you would be able to move it up an hour," she wheezes, and I try to make my face as neutral as possible so I don't scare her any further.

"Yes, that's fine. Move it up." I wave a hand to dismiss her as Marco eyes me critically. "What? I don't care. If we start an hour earlier, maybe I can be home sooner."

He gathers his coffee and briefcase before coming to kiss both my cheeks. "You know I love you, Margot, and I will always give it to you straight. It's okay if you don't want to be here as much. We can run this office just as well as London and Paris, and as long as you keep the collections fresh and keep innovating, you can work from home as much as you want. Just something to think about."

Then he's gone and I'm left thinking about what the reality of opening Milan would entail, both excited but dreading the call this evening. He's right, I'm happier at home these days, no longer running from the man of my dreams but instead running into his arms at the end of every day.

I'm exhausted but feeling strong when I leave Pilates a few hours later, ready to go home, shower, and collapse into bed. Jack has a late-night meeting at the club, so we agreed I wouldn't wait up, but I'd come to his apartment. With my lavender shower mist, rainfall showerhead, and spa soundtrack, I'm zoned completely out when I see a shadow across the glass a split second before a giant body is wrapped around me, one bulky arm around my waist and a hand over my mouth.

"You should pay more attention to your surroundings, Princess," the intruder growls, and I roll my eyes.

Biting his hand hard to get him to remove it, I scoff, "I knew it was you, you jerk! I was so Zen and now you've ruined it."

Laughing, he swats my ass. "So bitey. I thought your class would've worn you out enough not to be so mean. Maybe a massage will—"

"Ugh yesss." I interrupt as his strong hands go to work on my shoulders, drawing a low chuckle from him.

"I assume that's a yes to the massage, then?"

"Yes, pleeeease, just like that," I whine, and I feel the effect of my words as his cock, half hard since he stepped behind me in the shower, rises to full attention against my ass. He ignores it, though, using my body wash to methodically massage down my back, then both arms, down my legs. Only when he's coming back up my front does he allow himself to paw at my breasts and tease my nipples. Moving back behind me again, he sits on the built-in bench and pulls me backward, the height now perfect to slide himself between my thighs until his piercing rubs my clit just right.

"Oh fuck, Jack," I breathe out as he starts giving shallow thrusts, fucking my thighs and hitting my clit on every single pass. "I'm too sore from this morning to go again, but I can finish you off if you want." He freezes behind me, and I turn my head to look at him over my shoulder.

"Does this hurt, Princess?"

"No, it doesn't. I just assumed you were gonna, you know, slip it in, and I think that would hurt, so…"

His little thrusts resume, and fuck, it's erotic to feel him behind me using my body like this, slick and soapy and overheated from the shower.

"I can lick this pretty pussy if you'd prefer, but you have to come tonight, Margot, or you're not going to sleep well. You and I both know it. So do you want me to drop to my knees and eat you out while you sit on the bench, or do you want me to fuck your thighs and get you off rubbing that sweet little clit?"

He's already got my answer, my body subconsciously chasing release, rubbing my clit up and down his hard length between my thighs. It looks obscene from this angle, sticking out way too far to believe it ever fits inside me, *but it does, so perfectly,* and I'm almost ready to beg him to fuck me regardless of me being sore when I hear him.

"Fucking perfect girl, letting me use you like this. *Shit* day at work, and I come home to an absolute goddess. *God baby,* I don't deserve you. That's it, you feel what you do to me? You feel amazing, *all mine.* I'm never letting you go, Margot. I'll chase you to the ends of the earth. *Fuck.* I feel you shaking, baby. You can let go for me. I'll catch you. I love you. *I love you I love you I love you...*"

He keeps whispering like a prayer as I do what he says and shatter, the pounding of his piercing against my clit finally setting me off. My pussy clenches around nothing, and I miss him being inside me for this evening, though I know it would hurt. I ride him until I feel my orgasm finally recede, and he picks up the pace to finish himself off. It feels oddly nice just to have him between my thighs, keeping him slick and warm. I wonder briefly where he'll want to come before he reminds me that he's *such* a caveman at heart.

Pulling back just a bit, he nudges my legs apart with his feet and notches just his head at my entrance, teasing me with just the tip. Barely a second later, he comes with a low groan of my name, tiny thrusts trying to get as much of his cum into me as possible from this position. We stay like this, his forehead pressed into my mid-back and a hand on my lower belly, until he grows soft and slips out of me.

After we've rinsed again and gotten into bed, he pulls me into him like he can't get me close enough tonight.

"Is everything okay?" I ask, pulling back to look at his weary face.

He sighs and kisses my forehead. "It really was a shit day at work. Some asshole bypassed our background checks using a fake passport and tried to assault a server. The panic button did its job, but we've started a complete review of current membership and a task force to come up with an entirely new screening protocol. We think facial recognition software is the way to go, but it'll be a tense time before it's up and running, and we feel safe again."

"That's awful. I'm so sorry, Jack," I whisper, wishing I could help.

"You help just by being here and being you, Princess," he begins. "And no, you didn't say that out loud, but I told you that I know all your tells, woman. You're an open book for me now. I know all your tricks."

I yawn before I can reply, and he pulls me back against him into our favorite sleeping position.

"I love you more than anything, Margot," he whispers as I melt into him and drift off to sleep. "My Princess."

Stretching, I feel for Jack, but he must have gotten up earlier and gone to the gym before work. I moved everything I could to remote work for the rest of the week, so I have no plans for the day except being lazy and maybe making a few packing lists for Paris. Maybe spend time at the piano, one of my favorite pastimes lately with all the nights we've been spending here at Jack's apartment. Digging through the drawers I've taken over, I realize they need a complete reorganization. I've just been shoving things here and there as I've brought them over to stay the night, and I have a mix of loungewear, workwear, and evening wear all in the same cluttered space.

Pulling out a tiny clutch that I can't even remember using lately, I tip it open, and my stomach drops as my diamond collar spills out. *Shit.* I just texted this man "bye, see ya never" as if I didn't have his multimillion-dollar necklace in my dresser drawer. I'm surprised he hasn't reported it as a theft, waiting for it to pop up in some luxury pawn shop.

Okay, stay calm, Margot. There's an easy fix for this. For whatever reason, I still have the burner phone buried too. I just haven't gotten around to deleting all the info and donating it yet. Seeing it's still charged, *the battery on these old flip phones lasts forever,* I sit on the edge of the bed and send the awkward text.

"Hi. Sorry to bother you again. I just remembered I still have this necklace, and I'm pretty sure it's real. Do you want it back? I can't imagine keeping it, it's far too valuable. I could leave it with the club desk for you to pick up or whatever works. Please let me know! Hope you're doing well."

I exhale and press send, glad the task is over even though I'm not sure why it gave me so much anxiety to send one text.

A buzz from Jack's nightstand pierces the silence of the room, and my heart lurches into my throat.

His phone in his nightstand...but he's gone for the day. Okay, maybe he just forgot it, Margot, and he's going to be back at any moment for it and apologize for leaving it.

You're stupid, Margot, but not that *stupid, surely...*

Tears fill my eyes as I start to shake, realizing that I am, in fact, that stupid.

I send a "Hello?" message to Sir's number again, letting out a harsh sob when I hear another buzz from the nightstand.

This can't be real. My breathing is too fast. The room is too quiet. I can feel my blood pumping through my veins as time slows. *Fuck, I'm either hallucinating or hyperventilating.* Hopefully the former but almost certainly the latter. I lean forward to open Jack's nightstand, and there, under his little trinkets and tchotchkes, is the twin to the phone in my hand.

I don't even try to stifle my sobs, sounding more like a wounded animal than anything else, as I open it, seeing the other side of all of my messages with my Sir. *Jack.*

Maybe it wasn't him? Maybe he just found this phone. My masked man didn't have any piercings, so perhaps he was trying to find my masked man to kill him. Picking up a velvet pouch in the nightstand, any hope I have leaves my soul as my matching leash slides out into my hand.

Why? Why would he do this? To trick me? To make a fool out of me one more time? I can't...*Jesus, I can't breathe.* Okay. Okay, Margot. No hyperventilating over a man. Any man. Fuck this. Get out. *Get out, before he comes back. Get out, get out, get out...*

If I can keep it together for ten minutes, I can be free. Gasping for air, I swallow the bile that's risen in the back of my throat and try to stand. *Come on, Margot. Just make it ten minutes.*

All I really need is my purse and my phone. Calling Marco, I give him the emergency word we came up with ages ago to signal that we needed to do whatever the other says with no explanation. "Toast," I said, and he repeated it, called the jet, and headed my way in a car.

Moving through the apartment, I ignore my piano, my shoes near the door, the flowers Jack got me two days ago, the box of my chocolates on the sofa table...I ignore it all, moving like a zombie, or a robot, or whatever bipedal being has the least of a heart.

He needs to know. He needs to know what he's done so he can be in a fraction of the pain I'm in right now. I leave both phones on the kitchen island, open, so he knows I saw the texts.

I unhook my diamond cow keychain he sent me for Valentine's Day in Paris, when I was still mad at him but couldn't resist how perfect this stupid thing was. It's been on every set of keys I've carried since. I set it down next to the phones.

Barely holding on to my robot spirit, I take down the bow from my hair and add it to the island. Pink silk with a tiny crystal J hidden in the clasp. He bought it for me last week from a street vendor who was customizing them on the spot. Jack tried to tell the man to add an M, but I told him I'd prefer a J. I remember thinking his smile could have powered a whole block for a day, it was so bright.

Finally, hands shaking, I clip my leash onto my collar and add it to my tragic little pile on the island. My offering. Or sacrifice, I guess. If I thought burning these things would cleanse me in some way, I'd incinerate them now and not blink. But there's no saving me from this pain, no ritual that can undo this damage.

Marco texts that he's downstairs and the plane will be ready by the time we get to the airport, so I leave my little collection of offerings to Jack on the kitchen island. He's joked before that it was an altar at which to worship me.

Well.

It can be an altar at which he mourns me, now. I pray he feels an ounce of my pain. I hope he sees everything, and *knows* immediately, and feels the enormity of his mistake. I hope he feels it for the rest of his days.

Amen.

Chapter Sixty-Five

After another day of dealing with the fallout from our security breach at the club, I have one more stop to make before I can get home to my girl. I've been shaving off an hour here and there, making sure her ring is resized and polished to perfection. She picked it out herself years ago in a vintage shop, some offhand comment about how she'd never settle for another ring and her true prince would *know* and find this one. In a tiny shop. Off the beaten path. Naturally, I snatched it up, thinking I could at least keep it until she found a man worthy of her, then give it to him. All I need now is the perfect time to ask. *Soon,* I think, before LJ is born. Maybe even while we're in Paris. We're meant to be together, and I'm ready to be her emergency contact. There's no reason to wait.

Well, maybe one reason. I haven't come clean about being her Sir yet. I've meant to, we've just been so fucking happy. And at this point, I know I'm a giant piece of shit, so what else is new? But now I think she'll see the positives, and see my heart, and we'll be romantic together in the City of Light. At least this is my hope. If this all blows up in my face, I'm not even entertaining that as an option.

I'm whistling with a pep in my step as I open the front door, ready to smell Margot's hair and let the worries of the day melt away before we head to our favorite Thai restaurant for dinner. Immediately, I know it's too quiet. Beyond that, it's as still as a tomb in here. Unnaturally so. Fucking creepy.

"Margot? Princess, are you okay? Are you here? What's..." I trail off as I enter the kitchen and see the items left on the counter. I freeze, waiting for anything at all to happen to make this not be my reality. But it is. She found out.

She found out about my absolute bullshit, and she's gone.

I can't do anything but fall to my knees and crawl to the island, sitting back on my heels to look at the pieces of Margot left behind. Both my Margots. Her collar and leash, the phones, the keychain. *The bow.* I lose it at the bow, crumpling to the floor in a heap of sobs, ruining the silk with my tears as I clutch it to my face. I remember how it felt when she said she wanted a J instead of an M. I thought I was going to burst with love. Now, I feel like I'm going to burst with pain.

Fuck, and I deserve it. I allow it to wash over me, sobbing until I don't have tears and then dry heaving until my abs burn with the effort. I hadn't even wanted to keep the phone, but every time I almost got rid of it, I thought of Margot feeling like she needed her masked man for something, and showing up to the room and him never coming. I convinced myself I couldn't hurt her like that, so I kept it in my nightstand just in case. And now everything's exploded in my face.

She's gone. Two years, and I had her for not even a month, and she's gone. I must literally pass out from panic and grief because the next thing I know, I wake up to a darkened apartment and a million missed texts and calls from the entire family. Immediately, I fear the worst, that they've figured out about Margot and me, and now how I've hurt her. Instead, it's just the group chat popping off with more baby stuff, work texts about the security updates, and calls from Ledger trying to confirm new hires for the clubs.

I lie on the floor, twisted uncomfortably but unwilling to adjust because I deserve every bit of this. Time passes, and I remain there until I see the first beams of the sunrise start to move through the apartment. Finally, I stand to rinse my mouth and use the bathroom, and when I come back to the living room, I see the sunlight hitting the polished top of her piano. She's played for me every time I've asked in the last few weeks. I asked her if she thought our kids would have her musical talent, and she gave a coy shrug and said, "We'll see." The tears threaten to fall again when I realize I'm not doing this again. I'm not giving up. I gave up two years ago, and it was the wrong thing to do. I knew then and didn't fight. But now I've had her again and she's magic, all the fucking good in the world. I'm not letting her go. One of the missed texts was from Blanche saying she wouldn't come for dinner tonight since we were in Paris early. Margot must have told her she was going ahead, and Blanche assumed I was with her. Clearly, Margot didn't feel like explaining, but that's to my advantage. I know where she is, and nobody else in the family knows what's going on.

I can work with this. Packing the lightest possible bag and planning to buy everything else when I get there, I'm on the next flight across the Atlantic.

I told you I'd follow you to the ends of the earth, Princess. Time for me to prove it.

After a frustrating text exchange with Ledger while I was en route, I finally land in Paris and make my way to the pickup spot for the car service. I mean, how hard is it to just confirm or deny whether he thinks a turkey baster pregnancy is a reasonable method to trap a woman with you forever? He acted like he never considered it with Sloane, *which I know he did,* and tried to be all high and mighty about it. The man hacked her medical records and put cameras in her house! His high horse is a fucking miniature pony at this point.

I'm running on fumes by the time I reach Margot's apartment, ready to beg, grovel, plead, disfigure myself, anything she wants if she'll just let me in and listen to me. My hand is raised to knock when it opens and a supermodel walks out wearing a red, skintight latex midi dress, a coat slung loosely over her shoulders, carrying matching gloves and wearing sky-high heels. Large sunglasses cover most of her face, and her blonde hair is pulled back into a tight chignon. It's not until she sweeps past me without a glance, and I catch a faint whiff of her scent that I realize it's...

"Margot?"

She freezes, before turning to give me a stare over the top of her sunglasses. Clearly not impressed by what she finds, she turns to continue strutting away.

"Margot, please. Please, Princess. I came to apologize. I need to talk to you. I know I'm despicable. I know I fucked up and it was wrong..." I'm begging as she makes her way down the hallway toward the lifts, but something I've said has made her stop and turn to face me again. Thank fuck, if I can just beg, maybe kneel and kiss her feet, maybe she'll...

"You. Fucked. Up?" she says lowly, and I realize that somehow I've already managed to say the wrong thing. *Jesus Christ, Jack, never once in your life have you managed to say the right thing at the right time.* I'm going to keep my mouth shut now, for once.

"You think that's what you did? That you fucked up? Made a mistake, came to apologize, and we would what? Go back home to our little life we were having so much fun with?" Her voice is completely calm while she's talking. I'm so happy to see her that I could cry, but I know calm is probably the worst possible reaction from her in this situation. She takes off her sunglasses and puts them in her bag, coming close enough that I can see her bloodshot eyes and the bags under them. Fuck, I did that.

"I don't think your pathetic, pea-sized man brain will ever actually understand what you did, but let me at least try to spell it out so you have a fighting chance to feel as shitty as you actually should. A little recap, just for you. I *idolized* you growing up, Jack. You were my knight in shining armor as a child, my crush as a teen, my only love as an adult. Mom wasn't exaggerating. I thought you were perfect, and I was sure you were the only man I could ever be convinced to marry."

Tears stream down my face now, but her expression remains blank.

"This is obviously too much pressure to put on one human. Nobody is perfect. But we had our night together, and I really thought you shared my feelings. Naivety of youth, clearly. You sent me away with that note and shattered my dreams, and blah, blah. Old history."

She's coming closer now, her blank gaze turning fiery when she stops inches away from me. God, just yesterday I was allowed to touch her, and now every inch feels like a thousand miles between us.

"I came back to New York, forced to work with you. And you wormed your way back into my heart. Saying all the right things, doing all the right things. The plays, the memories, *the cuff links,* God. That was so smooth. You had me fooled."

"I wasn't trying to..."

"No," she spits. "You don't speak. You don't ever speak to me again. You only listen. The entire time you were wining and dining me, convincing me you were the same Jackie I always loved, and you had made a terrible mistake...*you had me on a leash crawling to you on the floor!*"

She realizes she's screamed the last bit and takes as deep a breath as her dress will allow before continuing, again calm and in control.

"You knew who I was, and you knew full well that my consent to our activities would have changed had I known it was you, and that kind of deceit is so rotten and disgusting that I can't even stand to look at you. I went back through the texts, Jack. Playing both sides to your advantage. One Jack enjoying the sex and the power, the other being *my best friend again* when I desperately needed one. You abused an inherent position of power over me as my Dom, while literally telling me I could trust you completely and build a life with you. I would never build a life with a man who could take advantage of a woman like that and then hold her close at night. You fooled me twice. There won't be a chance for a third."

She takes a deep breath, and her eyes flare, the anger there hitting me harder than any physical punch.

"We're done. In every capacity. What we'll tell the family isn't my concern. We can cross that bridge when we come to it. You can lose my number and my address. Honestly, don't even think about me. I don't plan to exist in your world at all, anyway. I don't plan to ever direct my gaze, or my voice, or my thoughts toward you again. Hopefully, you can't do the same, and you miss me for-fucking-ever."

Looking down at her watch, she rolls her eyes. "Now I'm late for my meeting. Goodbye, Mr. Carter."

With one middle finger in the air, she's around the corner to the lifts and gone. She was right that I hadn't fully registered the depths of my betrayal, particularly the fact that she wouldn't have consented if she had known it was me. I'll carry that shame for the rest of my life, and no amount of rationalizing will make that right. Her points about me playing both sides...it had seemed like the right thing to do at the time, a means to an end, but she's right again. It was despicable.

She's wrong about one thing, though. She can't cease to exist in my world. She's the axis it turns on. I'm not fucking leaving. I let her go once and told her I wouldn't do it again, and I meant it. I don't care what she does. She can move to India, fuck a million men, or become a nun. I'll be one hundred feet away in case she needs me. I don't think that'll happen, though. I think her soul will realize I have half of it, just like she's walking around with half of mine. When that time comes, I'll be right here.

For weeks, I follow Margot as she takes Paris by storm. Or tries to. She's losing weight and looks terribly tired, with nobody to carry her bags for her and rub her feet at night. She sends back the flowers I send as mulch and donates any food to the local soup kitchen. Her schedule is too packed, and I worry that she's getting close to burning herself out. My Princess is true to her word, though, never glancing in my direction once, regardless of how close I am. She's so stubborn. *Fuck, I love her.*

Tonight, something is off. She's wearing more makeup than usual, and she had an intimate dinner with a man at a romantic restaurant, laughing and being way too tactile with him. This is clearly someone from her time here years ago, hopefully just another friend. My stomach falls when they make their way back out of the restaurant, and his hand slides past the small of her back to the top of her perfect ass. The red cloud of rage that falls over my eyes almost causes me to crash the motorcycle I'm using to follow them, earning me curses in French and getting my head back into the game.

Finally, we're back at Margot's apartment, and I watch to make sure she gets in safely before I can go upstairs to the unit I bought across the street. Instead of this asshole escorting Margot to the door of the building, though, she gives him a wide smile, and he follows her in, hand now fully on her ass.

Holy shit. I'm going to die on this sidewalk, in Paris, of heartbreak. The worst fucking part is I deserve it. I would honestly sit in a chair five feet away and *watch* Margot fuck this guy if it meant I got to be near her again. But I see the lights turn on in her apartment, and their silhouettes come together too closely to be anything but an embrace. As she closes her curtains, I realize I don't exist in her world, but she still exists in mine.

Chapter Sixty-Six

For weeks, my shadow has followed me around, navigating Paris as well as I do, a reminder of how much time he and Ledger spent fucking around Europe. A carousel of pictures flashes through my head, the memory of seeing them for the first time clear as day. I eventually stopped crying every time my brother would post a picture boasting the beautiful women he and Jack were always around, but it never stopped hurting. *It still hurts now.* Everything hurts.

I didn't just lose one man. I inadvertently lost both Jacks in my life, and the hole left behind is twofold as well. Every day, my will to keep him at a distance wavers, my traitorous body coveting his touch. My traitorous heart longs for its mate. I've tried to deter him, but nothing I do seems to even slow him down. Not until tonight. I know he's been watching. I've felt his eyes on me all night, and I can feel them now, as Michel leads me from the car to my apartment.

Tonight isn't purely to shake my stalker. It's in part for my own benefit. I held off for a while after returning to Paris before running back into the arms of my old friend and lover. Even now, I have to convince myself this isn't cheating, but I *have* to fill this void. And a sexy Frenchman I *know* will be a good, safe time just may be the answer to all my problems.

As soon as we're inside, I make quick work of closing the curtains before practically jumping Michel. "Cheri, slow down, we have all night. Plus, I want to take in as much of you as I can in this little pink dress. You're a vision, mon amour, more beautiful than any Parisian spring I've seen before."

I honestly forgot he'd never seen me wearing my signature color. In all the time I was here, I avoided it, trying to distance myself from that girl I'd left behind. Trying to distance myself from the man I left behind as well. But the more I tried removing Jack from my life, the more I lost myself. This time, I refuse to become a shell of myself even if I have to live with a piece of Jack slowly burning a hole in my heart, killing me from the inside out.

"Michel, please," I *beg*, looking up into his eyes. They don't bring me to my knees like the blue ones I love so much, but there's a familiarity there that calms my nerves. "I need a distraction. Please."

He stares down at me, searching for an explanation I'm not ready to give, before conceding. He wraps his arms around my waist and pulls me close. His embrace isn't passionate, nor does it send shock waves through my body, but I relax into his arms, just relieved to have *someone* hold me.

"How do you want me, mon amour?"

With my eyes closed in an attempt to conjure up a fantasy, all I can see is *my love...my Jackie...fuck!* Visions of our time together flood my mind, bringing up memory after memory of each orgasm he's given me both as my Sir and as my Jack. Hundreds at this point.

"Margot? Cheri?"

"Just get me out of my head, however you can," I say, hoping he didn't notice the flash of disappointment on my face when I opened my eyes to find him standing there and not the only man who's ever succeeded at my request.

Michel removes his tie as he walks me to my room, proceeding to gently place my hands on a poster at the foot of the bed and blindfolding me. He slowly unzips my sleeveless dress, letting it fall to the floor in a puddle beneath my feet and leaving me in a matching set of floral lingerie from our spring collection. He's never been a very vocal lover, or at least not like Jack, constantly whispering praises into my ears. I'm able to imagine anyone leaving chaste kisses from the small of my back to my neck. Except there isn't enough need behind the way his lips meet my skin. There isn't a fire that burns into my soul with every touch of his fingertips.

The flush that spreads across my skin encourages his perusal of my pleasure, but it's not from desire. Sweat glistens across my skin as a panic attack threatens to ruin this moment. *If I could just stop comparing him to Jack.*

On second thought, maybe I have this all wrong. Maybe thinking about Jack is exactly what could help you.

I try with all my might to welcome those memories of orgasms past back into my mind, but I can't quite conjure them. Because even with the blindfold, everything is *wrong.*

"Mmm, mon amour," Michel says, licking his way up my neck.

Mon amour. Not my love, not my princess, not baby girl. Mon amour.

I'm already at risk of losing my dinner when he moves his lips to mine, but I'm done from the moment I open my mouth. I run to the bathroom, ripping off the makeshift blindfold in the process, before spilling my guts into the toilet.

"Margot, are you okay?" Michel asks, holding my hair back with one hand and rubbing my arm with the other as I continue throwing up more than I ever have in my life. And God, I'm so undeserving of his kindness.

The moment I'm finished, I turn around in his arms and finally let myself break, sobbing as I fall to the floor, bringing him down with me. "I'm so, so sorry, Michel. I can't do this. I thought I could, but...but I..."

"You belong to someone else. I know, mon amour."

"You know? How do you know?" I ask, pulling away to look in his eyes.

"I know because I tried to make you mine years ago, cheri. You are a treasure, Margot Sinclair, but try as I may, you've never been *mon trezor*." He pauses to wipe a tear falling down my face, smiling softly. "Tell me about him, belle. And why on earth you're here and not with the man you love."

All it takes is a sniffly head nod before Michel scoops me up in his arms and carries me to the bed, leaving me there momentarily to grab a wet towel for my face, a bottle of water, and my favorite blanket. Climbing in beside me, he adjusts me so that I'm bundled in my blanket, then holds me as I spill my heart out for the first time in my life. Starting from my very first memory and ending with the perpetual shadow I've had as of late.

For hours, this beautiful, successful, *kind* man caresses me while I blabber on and on about another asshole, not once showing any signs of annoyance. He's always been like this with me, always there when I need him, but never pressing me for more than I'm willing to give.

"God, why could it not have been you, Michel? Why can't it be you *now?*" I ask as tears fall from my eyes yet again tonight.

He squeezes me a little tighter before placing a chaste kiss on my covered shoulder. "Oh, don't I wish it could be. But it seems the heavens had someone else in mind for you, mon amour."

Oh and don't I know it. I've only spent *my entire life* knowing there would never be another man for me. Even when I didn't allow myself to voice the thought in my mind, my very essence called to him. *Well, fuck the heavens.*

"No, it's over. I can't be with him, but it seems the heavens have cursed us both because I can't be with anyone else either."

"Yes, you can, cheri. You have to." He's brushing my hair now, and I realize he's been doing it for a while. "He's your Heathcliff."

"Excuse me?"

"Your Heathcliff. He's from *Wuthering Heights.*"

"I know my Brontë, Michel," I say, cutting him off with more attitude than intended. "I'm sorry, but what do you mean he's my Heathcliff?"

It's been years since I've read any classics, especially since Sloane and I started a little smutty book club, but I remember the story fairly well. Sure, Jack and I grew up together, and sure, we had a strong connection as children, but that's where our similarities stop. He is most definitely in the same social class through his own parentage, so he would've been raised alongside us regardless. And God only knows, neither of my brothers resented him. Henry never had reason, and there were moments after they left for college that I thought perhaps he and Ledger were a closeted couple, given how codependent they became on each other.

My furrowed brows must convince Michel to proceed. "Whatever souls are made of, yours and his are the same."

"Oh." Well, yeah. I guess that's another pretty significant similarity.

"Men are idiots. Take your time but hear him out. If I'm being honest with you, I'm not sure I wouldn't do the same thing just to have a piece of you again. I've half a mind to whisk you away right now."

I turn in his arms, slapping his arm lightly as my tears dry. "Stop it, you would not!" I say, laughing for the first time tonight. "But seriously, how do I ever trust him again?"

"You will just have to learn, mon cheri, but you have to forgive him. There's no reason to live a half life when you can grow old with the man picked out for you by the stars. Believe me, few are so lucky."

Michel lays my head gently against his chest and snuggles me in his arms, and I let him, soaking in the night together, both of us knowing it'll be the last time. When a tear leaves my eye this time, it's not for Jack. It seems the heavens not only gifted me a man crafted for my very soul but also sent a guardian angel to guide me back to him when I lost my way. And I'm going to miss my angel greatly.

I wake up the following morning and wiggle out of the wrong arms to look at my phone that's been dinging like crazy. Well, it's midafternoon, but regardless...

Sinclair Fam:

LJ IS COMING

"Ohmygod! Michel, wake up! LJ is coming. I have to go!"

Michel gets up immediately, helping grab my things and throwing them in a bag as I rush to get ready. I quickly get dressed in a sweat set before combing through my hair and throwing it up into a clip, all the while trying to text Mom, Sloane, Ledger, and Henry individually as well as the family group chat to get a gauge of how much time we have and coordinate travel. Which unfortunately involves me sharing a private jet back to the States with Jack. *You can do this, Margot. This is for LJ. You don't have to talk to him, you don't even have to look at him.*

By the time all the details are ironed out, the car Michel called for me waits by the street, and the bag he packed for me sits by the door.

"Come on, cheri," he says, throwing an arm around my shoulders, the other carrying my things, and leading me down the stairs.

"Are you sure you don't want me to go with you?" he asks when we reach the car, putting my luggage in the trunk before coming to open the door for me.

"No, no, that won't be necessary. Just lock up here before you go?"

We both freeze, knowing this is our final goodbye. Finally, I jump into his arms, tears falling down my face. "I'm going to miss you, Michel. So, so much."

His arms are still wrapped tight around my waist where he caught me, and when he looks into my eyes, I see tears in his as well. "I'll miss you more, mon amour. Promise me, Margot. Promise me you'll forgive him. Promise me you won't waste any more time. It's the only way I can let you go. The only way I can say goodbye is knowing that you're happy."

"I promise." With one last hug, I let him go, allowing him to help me into the back seat before closing the door.

"Pinky promise," I whisper to myself as the car takes me home.

Chapter Sixty-Seven

Jack

"If I hear one more announcement about that damn gift basket raffle fundraiser, I'm going to lose it! Come on, Henry. Maybe if we go buy all of the damn things, they'll shut up about it!" Blanche storms off, dragging Henry behind her. The atmosphere since we all arrived at the hospital has been tense, to say the least. We're all so excited, and Ledger is ecstatic, but the Sinclair family isn't exactly known for their patience, so the wait is killing us all. We're lucky to be in a semi-private wing with a large suite, so at least our tense exchanges haven't been observed by anyone other than the medical staff.

With their departure, and Ledger only coming out to give sporadic updates of how Sloane is feeling, Margot and I continue our standoff. After we both got the same "LJ is coming" text in the family group chat, she didn't even seem surprised to see that I was already at the airport waiting when her car arrived. She may not have been happy about sharing the jet with me on the way home, but she didn't speak to me to say no. Now that we're back in the States, confined to this hospital for who knows how long, it's much easier to keep an eye on her and make sure she has what she needs.

As mad as she is, she didn't refuse her chocolate croissant and iced coffee for breakfast, or the fashion magazines I picked up at the gift shop, or the fluffy blanket I had delivered when I realized how cold she was. Her feet are warm in her slippers as she sips her tea, and I think I have about two hours before she gets hungry enough for lunch. There's gummy candy in my bag for any hint of hanger I see. She's a fast reader and the magazines probably won't last much longer, but I know she's got the Kindle app on her phone, so as long as she has a charger, she should be okay...

"Do you fucking mind?"

Her voice, as acerbic as it is, is music to my ears. It's the first time she's addressed me since our encounter when I arrived in Paris, and it's completely fucked how amazing it feels to be the focus of her attention, even if it's her wrath.

"What?" I ask, knowing exactly what.

"Stop staring at me like a psychopath and stop trying to ply me with treats and creature comforts. I'm perfectly capable of taking care of myself. You're being such a creep," she huffs, and I swear I see a crack in her anger armor.

Slowly moving closer, I take what I think is my chance to plead my case again.

"Margot, please. I am begging you. I'll stay on my knees forever if you want. You were right, in the hallway, everything you said. I was so much worse than I had realized, and I know I don't deserve your forgiveness. But please, Princess. I can't stop fighting for you. It doesn't matter what you do, if you want the man from your apartment, I'll still be in your life in any way you'll let me. I won't let you go." Every time I think I've cried all my tears, I surprise myself and more form in my eyes.

"Michel," she says primly, eyes drifting back to her magazine.

"What?"

"The man from my apartment. He has a name. It's Michel."

"Did you…" My voice cracks, and I must be a masochist for how much I have to know the answer to this. "Did you sleep with him?"

She's still nonchalantly flipping her magazine pages, barely paying me any attention. "Hmm, I'm not sure. He had a mask. It could've been anyone. He said he was Michel, though, and I *trust* Michel, so…"

God, I deserve that, and it hurts more because I know I do. I can't stop the tears from escaping now. "I just, *fuck, Margot.* I know I deserve that, but please…"

"You're being a little pathetic right now, Jack. Jesus. I didn't sleep with him." She rolls her eyes and stands up, stretching and drawing my eye to the sliver of skin she shows as her shirt rides up.

She's lazily doing walking lunges across the room while I cry, and her apathy is so much worse than her anger. "I know I'm a piece of shit, Princess, but you don't have to be this cold to me."

This has exactly the effect I desired, and she rises and turns to me with fire in her eyes, crossing the room and shoving her finger into my chest as she raises her voice. *Yes. Touch me, yell at me. Anything.*

"Are you fucking kidding, Jack Carter? You ripped my heart out of my chest, *again*, and you're sad about me being *cold* to you? You should be glad I didn't kill you! You've been stalking me, not giving me an inch of space, suffocating me with your presence even after I flew across an ocean to get away from you. Now I'm anxiously awaiting my nephew's arrival, and you still won't let me out of your sight! You followed me to the bathroom!" Her chest is heaving now, and as perverse as it is, I'm not sure she's ever looked more beautiful.

"I know you don't believe me, but I was going to tell you. I promise. Before we went to Paris, I was going to explain myself. I wasn't trying to fool you. The first night in the club, when I realized it was you, you still hated me. I thought you would always hate me, and I would have no other chance to have you in my life, so I took it. I'm sorry. You don't have to believe me, but I promise I never meant to hurt you," I cry, and she's joined me, wiping the tears angrily from her face.

"Your promises don't matter at all, Jack. You lied to me. You hurt me and took advantage of me. We were together, and you *lied*," she screams. I open my mouth to try to find something to say when the last voice I want to hear right now pierces the tension in the air.

"What's going on in here? Jack? What's Margot talking about, the two of you were together?" Henry asks, placing the gift baskets he was carrying down onto a side table.

Nobody moves. I'm unwilling to break the silence, and I don't even have anything to say if I did. The thing I always feared, the anxiety that kept me up at night, is about to crash over me like one last lethal wave. The only family I've ever had is about to cease to exist, and I'm the one to blame. The fact that it's happening on Ledger's son's birthday is something I'll always regret, and I doubt the child will ever hear the name Jack Carter.

Henry is objectively a genius, and it doesn't take long at all for him to connect the dots. I see everything click into place behind his eyes, and I wish I wasn't looking. I've never seen such a combination of hate and disgust. *I don't think I'll be leaving this hospital intact.*

"You were together?" Henry asks in a low whisper, stalking slowly toward me like a panther approaching unsuspecting prey. "I know too much about you, Jack Carter. So either you cheated on my baby sister..."

"I would never." I squeak out.

"Or my *baby* sister was the woman who you came to me for advice on *how to dominate*!"

I've never heard Henry raise his voice, and I'm shocked into silence. Margot's face pales in my periphery as she realizes that neither of us is in control of this situation now. We're both just along for the ride.

"You asked me, in detail, how to *properly punish* my *baby sister*. You told me and my brother, to our faces, that she was your *natural good girl!* Did you know it was her? This is your chance to live. Did. You. Know?"

"Yes," I choke out, and before I know it, he's grabbed me by the neck and has me shoved against the wall on my tiptoes. Margot could probably end my life here if she wanted to, by clarifying that she *didn't* know, but she stays silent.

I'm so focused on how Henry is holding me up with one hand and trying to breathe, that I never see the punch coming—heavy and right in my ribs. I crumple to the floor on a wheeze. I'm being pulled up, and I have a feeling the next one is coming for my face, and I deserve it. I see Margot over Henry's shoulder, tears streaming down her face and a hand over her mouth as he pulls back.

"Henry, wait!" she cries, but she's interrupted by Ledger bursting in.

"It's a boy!" He's sobbing, tears of happiness wetting his shirt. Everything that was happening in the room before he came in stops, and all of us shift our focus immediately to the new dad. We're in one big group hug, Henry grabbing me around the waist and digging in a little extra on the side that he punched. Margot beams, and even eye contact with me doesn't dim her smile.

"He came about an hour and a half ago. I'm sorry I didn't come out sooner, but we were doing skin-to-skin time and taking pictures. He breastfed for the first time, *which is fucking hot, by the way—*"

He laughs as Henry interrupts him with a disgusted, "Jesus, brother."

"Mom is in there now. Margot, do you want to go?"

She pulls her bottom lip between her teeth and looks at me, wondering if I'll make it out alive without her here. I give her a subtle nod, and she turns to go. This is my mess to deal with, not hers.

Wincing, I take a couple of steps back as Henry and Ledger face me shoulder to shoulder.

Ledger notices and gives me a concerned look that hurts because I know it's about to shift into something else. "Jackie, are you okay? What happened, man?"

Henry doesn't beat around the bush. "Margot was Jack's sub. He knew it was her the entire time. He's done something to betray her and break her trust. She's very upset."

If I thought that hurting Margot and Henry, and losing their trust, was enough to break my heart...seeing my best friend, the man who's always been closer to me than a brother, look at me with disappointment...God. I can't live with this.

"You were fucking Margot? And you knew you were?" he asks, pain evident on his face, like he can't believe I would do something like this. I can't believe it, either.

I nod, once, and brace myself for the hit that quickly follows across my jaw. I know it's not as hard as he's got or my jaw would be broken, but my ears ring all the same, and I slump backward into a plush armchair.

Fuck, I'm losing it. I can't stop crying, my head hurts, and I see black spots in my vision. I think that asshole concussed me. They can beat me if they want to, and ship me off to wherever they want, never to be heard from again. But I'm not going one more second without my cards on the table. Time to say my piece.

Chapter Sixty-Eight

"I'm going to be your favorite auntie. I promise to spoil you *even more* than your daddy, or Grandma, or your uncle Henry, or even your uncle Jack," I say, swaying the sleeping baby in my hands. Sloane agreed to let me take him on a little walk to find Ledger while Mom helped her get cleaned up. And following the sounds of his shouting, it doesn't take me long...he's landing punch after punch as Henry holds Jack steady for him.

"I love her."

Jack's quiet sob stops their progress across the room, and they wait, hands on hips, for him to say more.

I'm in too much shock to do anything but freeze in place in the entrance of the room. I've been too angry to listen every time Jack's tried talking to me, but watching him spill his heart to my brothers is an out-of-body experience, and I can't help but hide partially behind the door as I watch the scene unfold.

"It wasn't about fucking her. I did hurt her because I'm a selfish bastard, but my goal has only ever been to love her. I've known for a long time that she's it for me, and I tried to stay away out of respect for the family. I tried so damn hard."

Ledger still looks furious, but Henry's gaze has softened slightly. "You've known for a long time? How long? You always stayed close to her growing up..."

"No. Nothing like that growing up. I just wanted to protect her. Not like a brother, but I always felt like her bodyguard, like I was responsible for her, you know? Nothing happened until after your wedding, Ledger. I failed. She was too perfect, and I failed to resist her. But I immediately knew I had put us all at risk, and I tried to make her realize there are better men out there than me. I sent her to Paris thinking she'd find someone better. When she came back to New York and hated me, I figured I had completely fucked my chances, but I was willing to do anything. You have no idea how much I knew I fucked up as soon as I let her go..."

Ledger has turned to face away from him now, hands on top of his head as he processes, but Henry hasn't stopped staring at Jack this entire time.

"I made a mistake with the club that I'll pay for the rest of my life, but my motivations were the same as they've always been. I wanted any piece of her that she'd give me. In any capacity, no questions asked. And I wanted her to be happy, regardless of what that meant for me. None of that's changed. If she wants the real Jack, he's hers. If she only wants me in a mask, she'll never have to see my face again. If she wants me to dance in a monkey suit 24/7 for her, that's fine.

"If she wants anything from me, ever again, it's hers. No questions asked. I fucked up royally, worse than I hope either of you ever know, but I'm convinced I have the capacity to make her happier than any other man on the planet. She's certainly the only woman who will ever bring me an ounce of joy. I'm going to grovel, on my knees if she wants, for as long as she'll let me, and be in her life any way she'll let me. I tried to ignore it so I wouldn't upset or disappoint you all for too long. I wasted time with her. I won't do it again. I love her so fucking much. More than anyone else ever will. More than either of you do."

Punch.

"The fuck you do!" Ledger yells, hitting Jack in the ribs this time instead of his already bleeding face. "Don't you sit here and tell me you love my own goddamn sister more than us after the stunt you just pulled. You don't deserve to *crawl* on the same fucking ground as her. You're lucky I don't kill you right here, you fucking *traitor.* You were a brother to me. *Fuck,* you were closer than a brother. "

Punch. Punch. Punch.

"But I *do,* "Jack breathes, spitting blood on the floor before continuing. "I'm so fucking sorry, Ledger. But I love her too much. She's worth it. I'd choose her over you every time. Over all of you. I won't apologize for that."

Ledger goes to lay another hit, but Henry pulls Jack away, saving him from the impact. "Wait, Carter, I'm going to have to agree with my brother that you don't deserve to breathe the same air as our dear sister. I don't give much heed to empty declarations of love, but I'll give you one chance to convince me yours are not."

I feel myself moving closer to Jack, drawn to him as he shifts his gaze between my brothers.

"Henry, I mean this with the utmost respect, but I don't believe you've experienced a love like I have for your sister to be an adequate judge. But you, Ledger, your love for Sloane might come close to how I feel…"

"Again with those fucking insinuations that you could possibly know what it's like to care for someone like this."

This time, the bite in Jack's voice mirrors that of Ledger's. "Don't I? I've watched *you* fumble through life with your pitiful little *poor me* existence, not giving a damn about anyone who cared about you for so long. And then I watched you do a complete one-eighty when you met Sloane. You straightened up, changed your bachelor pad into a home, got married, and started a damn family. And you really want to tell me you don't want that for me too? Because the only way I get that is with Margot. I want the home, I want my ring on her finger, I want…*That!*"

I realize as we lock tear-filled eyes, that I've made my way to be standing right behind my brothers, who both turn to look at me holding little LJ in my arms.

"You want to know that I mean to do well by your sister?" he asks the men beside me, all the while never breaking eye contact with me. "I have the property ready to build whatever house she wants. *Three of them.* Enough acres for a compound by each of your houses and beside Blanche's as well, so she can choose where to live. Or hell, I'll build her a mansion on all three with my own hands. I've had a ring for a while now, and I would love nothing more than to have her signature on a piece of paper, legally binding her to me the way our hearts have been bound for years. As far as children go, it would be my greatest honor in life to raise a family with her. To hold our own baby in my arms, the tangible combination of our souls."

"Jack..." I breathe, handing LJ to his dad so I can wipe the blood about to fall from Jack's eyebrow.

Before I can reach him, Mom comes marching into the room. "Ledger Sinclair, your wife *who just gave birth* is looking for you...Oh good heavens!" She pauses to take in the state of everyone. Ledger with bloody knuckles, Jack with a swollen, bloody face, me with puffy red eyes, and then of course, Henry, looking as suave as ever. "When we agreed to wait until after LJ was born to tell your brothers, I wasn't counting on it being *immediately* after he was born."

Everyone's attention snaps to Mom. "You knew about this?" Henry asks.

"Why, of course I did."

Henry just shrugs, but Ledger doesn't let it go. "And you knew Jack had been dominating her in a sex club with a fucking mask on?"

"God forbid someone has a kink or two." Mom rolls her eyes. "And really, Ledger? I wouldn't expect you to have such a problem with that."

"I wouldn't if she had known it was him behind the mask. All the while, he knew exactly who she was. He lied to her for *months,*" he says, his nostrils flaring at the reminder of what Jack did.

"Oh, even better!" she says, fanning herself with her hand.

All three men groan, in agreement for the first time today, pulling a laugh from Mom. "Ledger, why don't you take LJ back to his mama while Henry and I go fetch us all some proper food," she orders, placing a hand on both of her sons' shoulders and guiding them gently out of the room, leaving Jack and me alone at last.

"Marg…"

Before he can finish my name, I've tackled him to the ground, stealing what little breath he had left after his beating from Ledger with a kiss. I'm not a particularly clumsy woman, but as I try to straddle him without moving my lips from his, I end up kneeing him in the ribs, causing him to whimper into my mouth. *Oh fuck, I'm sure Ledger cracked his damn ribs. I'm going to end up really hurting him.* I make a mental note to both punch and thank my brother for beating Jack to a pulp, then slowly get off him, helping him up as I go.

He lets me help him sit down in one of the hospital chairs in our little private waiting room but pulls me onto his lap when I go to sit beside him.

"Princess, I'm so fucking sorry. I didn't…"

"Shhh," I say, covering his mouth with a finger, then cupping his face, wiping away the blood that's still falling in some spots. "I know, Jack. I know."

I'm trying to be gentle as I finally straddle his lap, but he doesn't share my concern as he wraps his arms around me and squeezes with such fervor, I feel like *my own* ribs are going to break. "I love you *so goddamn much, Margot,* and I *swear to you* there isn't anything else I'm keeping from you. There isn't anything else I'll ever do for the rest of our lives that will ever cause you an ounce of pain. No more secrets, baby girl, I promise."

I look down and start fidgeting with the hem of my sweatshirt. If he would've had some other woman's lips on him, I think I would've wanted to know. "Well, in that case, I do have one thing to tell you. Michel and I did, um..."

He lifts my head so that our eyes meet, a half smile on his face. "It's okay if something happened, baby. I wouldn't ever hold that against you."

"I tried. I just wanted to forget you for a night," I admit, brushing his damp hair from where it's stuck to his face before gently kissing his forehead the way he always does me. "But I couldn't do it. I couldn't even kiss him, Jack. The only thing he did last night was convince me that you and I were meant to be. He made me promise to forgive you and live happily ever after."

One of the most beautiful smiles I've ever seen lights up his bruised face. "God, I went from wanting to kill Michel to wanting to kiss him."

"That could be arranged as long as I can watch," I say, not able to stop my smirk as he rolls his eyes. "Jack, did you mean all those things you said?"

He holds me to him once more, just letting our hearts beat in tandem as we melt into each other. "I meant that and so, so much more. I pinky promise, Princess. I'll spend the rest of my life proving it too."

Epilogue 1

"Jack!" I hear my princess yell from the living room. She was in there feeding LJ last I checked, and I'm not sure I've ever run so fast as I left the bottles I was sterilizing, leaped over the island, and raced to her side. I knew when we agreed to babysit LJ at Blanche's house so that Sloane and Ledger could go celebrate her "six-week clearance," I should have hired security. Knowing I'm responsible for the safety of Ledger's firstborn has had me on edge all weekend. We've cleared the air, and I feel like our brotherhood is stronger than ever. He told me last week that he can't imagine trusting anyone else with his sister, and we had a very manly hug and cry.

"What? What's wrong?" I ask frantically, sliding to a stop in the living room and realizing too late that I didn't even bring a knife from the kitchen to neutralize any threats. I've been training with Ledger, though, so I feel pretty confident in my ability to take most guys down. I look for an intruder, but only find Margot giving me a bemused look, holding LJ as he gazes up at me calmly with his big gray eyes.

"Don't be dramatic, we're fine. But I did just find something very interesting on your phone while I was trying to find the PDF of the legal agreement between the club and La Reine that Marco sent. What exactly is this?" She hands the phone to me, going back to snuggling an increasingly sleepy LJ, and I look down to see what she's found. I damn sure don't have any more secrets for her to find, so I have no idea what she's talking about. It's a document saved in my miscellaneous folder on the cloud, and I can feel my face turn beet red when I see what she's been reading...

I can feel you starting to panic, and I can't wait to see how your brilliant mind finds yourself a way out of this. I know you will. Speaking of panic, I bought our wedding bands this week to match the engagement ring I've had for years. I can't live in a world where I don't believe I can earn you back anymore. I can't. So I'm out here like an idiot doing everything I can in the meantime to convince myself that I will. Earn you back, that is. I'm also working on a few backup plans, currently ranging from hiring someone to kidnap us both so that you fall in love with me again via trauma bonding to buying a private island and acting like we're shipwrecked with no communication devices. My ideas are all forced proximity for now, but I'm sure I'll think of more. Last week, I bought the estate that borders Sloane and Ledger's house, and the one that borders your mother's, so that we can live close to whoever you want. Or both. I'm hoping...ah goddammit, Margot. Of all the things you could've done, why did you have to choose sucking on my fucking neck? Such a smart girl. Too smart for your own good. Fuck baby. Fuuuck. You were supposed to have ten more minutes, but I don't think I can do this. Bye for now, Princess. I have to go spank you, then fuck you into next year.

Now I'm beet red with a painfully hard dick. I cough out a laugh that I hope comes across as nonchalant, then end up choking on my spit in the most *chalant* way possible. Margot offers me her glass of water while I try to recover my ability to breathe, and then quietly waits for my explanation, trying not to jostle the sleeping baby with her own shaking shoulders.

"Uh, well...so," I begin, not really sure if she's going to want to talk about the club at all. "All those times that, uh, well. I had you, preoccupied and um. I said I was working. I was really just basically typing my stream of consciousness and manifesting getting you back."

"There are pages and pages of this, Jack."

"Yeah, I, uh, printed it out once just to see, and it was eighteen pages, I think. Front and back." I sigh. "I'm sorry. I know we haven't talked about the club, and it's a ton to unpack. We don't have to discuss it if it's mostly negative feelings for you."

"Come here, Jackie. Sit," she says softly, and I obey her immediately, tucking myself half behind her on the couch, wrapping one arm around her shoulders to softly play with the wisps of LJ's blond hair as he sleeps in the crook of her arm.

"I told you that I forgive you, and I meant it. It doesn't upset me to think about the club. I've actually wanted to bring it up myself, but I've been too nervous."

Pausing my path tracing the baby's tiny eyebrows, I turn my head to look at her. "You've been nervous? Why?"

Now it's her turn to blush, and I can't wait to hear what she's got to say. "Well, okay. I'm just going to say it, but please don't be mad. We've been having tons of really hot sex, and if we never change a thing, I'd be satisfied our whole lives. But I kindofmissyoudominatingme. Not that I want all our sex to be that way. But if we still played sometimes, maybe…" She bites that damn lower lip and looks at me with those sparkling blue eyes.

Oh, *fuck yes*. It's Christmas and the Super Bowl all wrapped up in one. My princess misses being my pet. I could make her repeat it, but I'm literally salivating at the thought of putting her back on her leash, so I put her out of her misery and make it very clear that I've been missing it too. Threading my fingers through her hair, I scratch at her scalp for a few passes before fisting a handful at the nape of her neck and locking her in place, facing me.

"You've missed me, pet?" I purr, and her eyes roll back in her head.

"Yes, Sir," she whimpers, and I'm about to tie her to this couch with anything I can get my hands on when LJ wakes up and fusses. I kiss her temple and go to prepare a bottle, but this conversation is far from over.

After dinner, she's burping LJ and resisting putting him in his crib when I walk into his nursery. As she rocks him back and forth, humming under her breath and pressing tiny kisses to the top of his head, I'm struck by what a natural she is. Finally she puts him down in his crib, cozy and safe in his sleep sack. Turning, she startles a little at me standing in the doorway and smacks me with the burp cloth before we double-check all the monitors and close the door. Not that he's sleeping for too long at once yet, but still. Routine is crucial, according to Ledger.

Settling into the couch with a fire fading in the fireplace, we curl up in the quiet, enjoying each other's company.

"You're a natural with him, you know," I say, playing with her hair and breathing in her soft exhale. "Nobody would ever believe you're the baby of the family. It looks like you've taken care of babies all your life."

She shrugs. "He's an easy baby to love, and I don't know. It feels right. Even if I haven't taken care of that many, I always loved playing with baby dolls as a kid. I'm sure you remember, old man."

I roll my eyes and give her a tiny pinch. "Yes, darling, I remember. I also remember holding *you* as a baby, so don't sass your elders."

We laugh, but then she's biting her lip again, telling me she's got something else on her mind that she doesn't want to say. Finally, she turns, fully straddling me so she can face me head-on and see my full reaction to whatever this is about to be.

"We haven't talked about it since the hospital, but that note reminded me. You were serious about the properties?"

I can't stop a half grin from appearing on my face, giving an embarrassed laugh. "Uh, yeah, Princess. I bought them all back when I wrote that note. We can look at them while we're down here, if you want, or I can sell them. It's the hundred acres west of your mom's house that used to be the Brown's and the Smith's. They were both selling so I combined the lots. I think the best spot for a house would be maybe five minutes from here on a golf cart. Then the spot at Ledger's is the thirty-five acres directly north of their house, up against the forest, probably a walkable distance from their place but not visible because of the trees. The lot neighboring Henry's is smaller, but I have no doubt we can make it into whatever you want. Why?"

Margot takes a deep breath and meets my eyes. "I'm supposed to pick up my new birth control pack from the pharmacy tomorrow."

I furrow my brow in confusion. "That's fine. I can pick it up tomorrow when I go grab lunch. Is there anything else you need?"

Laughing, my princess shakes her head before putting both her hands on my face. "No, Jack. I...don't think I want you to pick it up. I don't think I want to take it anymore."

My brain short-circuits as all my blood flows south to my dick. My gorgeous, perfect woman wants my baby. I think. And I think she wants it now. I might pass out. "Why did you ask about the land?" I ask, probably sounding like an idiot but trying to keep up with what she's saying.

"Well..." She laughs, leaving me distracted by her smile, lighting up the room and fighting for my attention with her words. "I was hoping that maybe we could pick our favorite and start building a big house." She leans in and gives me the softest kiss. "Keeping LJ for the weekend has been a dream, and I just...I want one. Maybe with blue eyes," she continues, like she doesn't see me fighting for my life, holding back tears. "Sloane said they're starting to try for another right away so that hopefully they'll be close in age, and if we started now, all the cousins could grow up together."

At some point, my brain reboots, and I feel like I'm back in control of myself. Grabbing her waist, I grind her down on my painfully hard cock so that she can feel exactly what I think of this proposal. I'm completely on board. *Fuck.* I was content to have her to myself for a few years first, but I'm equally content to make a mini version of us, taking our love and turning it into a new precious life.

She gasps, and it's intoxicating. Oh yeah. I'm gonna have fun with this.

"Is this what you want, Princess?" I ask, and she whines. "Eyes, Margot. Look at me when I'm talking to you." They snap to mine, and they're blown with lust but still mischievous. I almost forgot how fun it was to play with her like this.

"I have to make sure I understand what you want so I can give it to you, baby. You want this dick, right? You want me to come inside you, so fucking deep, that it wouldn't matter if you were on birth control or not, don't you?"

"Yes, please. Jack, I need it. I want it. I want your baby," she pants, and I groan, forcing her to slow. Doing this isn't going to help our quest at all. I pull her down to my chest so that I can purr directly into her ear.

"Maybe I'll show you where I've been storing the breeding bench I had made for you, pet. I can leave you spread open all day for me and give you as much cum as you can keep inside that greedy little pussy, hmm?" She whimpers again, desperate and writhing on my lap.

"I'm gonna track my ovulation and make sure we have the best chances," she whispers, cut off when my hand gently but firmly wraps around her throat and brings her attention back to me as I laugh darkly.

Looking straight into her eyes so she sees how serious I am, I tell her the truth. "I'm not going to need a schedule to get you pregnant, Princess. Now that you've told me what you want, I'm going to give it to you. You don't have to worry about anything else." I capture her mouth in a deep, languid kiss, and I'm about to tell her to go wait naked on the bed for me on all fours when the baby monitor goes off. Pressing my forehead to hers, I kiss her nose, then stand and put her on her shaky legs.

"I'll take this one. Go get ready for bed and get comfortable, darling. You won't be sleeping much." I punctuate my statement with a smack on her ass as I go to get LJ and a bottle. Might as well get a little more baby practice in while I can. If I have anything to say about it, it won't even be a year before we're snuggled up with our own.

Epilogue 2

"Flynn? The F stands for *Flynn?* John Flynn Carter?" I ask, looking down at where Jack has just signed our marriage certificate. I'm not sure why that surprised me, but I expected something older and fancier.

We're still planning on having a huge, and I mean *huge,* wedding after the twins are born, but Jack insisted we go ahead and get married. "*You've already agreed to marry me, and we know we want to spend the rest of our lives together, so why would we wait?*" And he's right, there's no reason not to go ahead and make it official.

Handing the clerk our completed paperwork, he turns to me with a contagious smile on his face, before kissing my head and leading me out of the courthouse. "Nope! Not anymore! Now it's John Flynn Carter *Sinclair.*"

I remember how it felt when he admitted to me he wanted to take my name after proposing. In fact, the memory of that whole night is crystal clear when it plays in my mind...

The moment two pink lines appeared on the stick, Jack went crazy. After squeezing me so tight I couldn't breathe and kissing every inch of me from my womb to the top of my head, he started frantically going through my closet, pulling things off the hangers like a madman before laying out several options for me on the bed.

I think I was in so much shock myself that I didn't question him once during the entire drive, until we pulled up at the house we grew up in, which Henry now occupies when business leads him back this way. "Jack, what are we—"

I'm cut off by him scooping me out of the car and walking me to the old clearing near the back of the property, where we would spend so much time playing as children. I know he's in impeccable shape, but damn, it's hot for him to walk a half mile, holding me like it's nothing. I don't even think to question him until he sets me on a branch of the tree I've always considered special.

"Jack, I'm pretty sure that's not what this means, but I just have to make sure. You do know when women say they nest when they get pregnant, that doesn't actually involve a bird's

nest, right? Because I do appreciate that you would stake my favorite tree, but continuing to fix the house up is really what that means..."

Before I can continue, he drops to both knees in front of me, as if this tree was my throne and he was kneeling at my feet. "Margot Sinclair. I... Would you...It's just..." He looks up at me with tears already falling down his face and reaches in his pocket to pull out a little pink velvet box. "Princess, you always said you were going to marry me. Do you still mean that?"

When he opens the box to showcase the exact pink diamond ring I used to obsess over, my demure sniffles turn into plain ugly crying.

"Margot Sinclair, will you marry me?"

"Jack Carter, if you don't get me out of this damn tree right this minute and put your ring on my finger, I'm going to die!*"*

As commanded, my very own Prince Charming stands and places the diamond on my left ring finger. Lifting me from the branch, he twirls me around and around in the process. "Does that mean you'll marry me, baby?" he asks as he gently places me on my feet, his arms still wrapped snug around my waist.

"Yes, yes, a million times yes! Jackie! Umph..."

His lips crash into mine with a force that would knock me over if he wasn't holding on to me so tightly, as our kiss deepens into something magical. Like the last piece of a jigsaw puzzle clicking into place, it dawns on me how I really did get my happily ever after. I'm going to marry the love of my life, we're going to have a baby, and we're going to grow old together surrounded by the family we create.

"Hmm, Margot Blanche Sinclair-Carter? Or Carter-Sinclair? I don't think I want to drop my last name

completely," I say, looking down at my finger as he guides me back to the house, still in a post-proposal haze.

"How about just Margot Blanche Sinclair?" he suggests, spinning me to face him, and cupping my chin to pull my attention from the pink sparkly diamond to his deep blue eyes. "How about we just drop the Carter?"

My brows furrow as he stands there smiling softly. "You don't want me to take your name?"

"Actually, I want to take your last name. If you'd let me."

Before I know it, he's holding me with my legs around his waist. "Jackie, I would love that."

I'm still grumbling because he never lets us take the golf cart anymore when we go to Mom's house. We decided to move in beside her, partially because this house needed fewer renovations and partially because I want her closer when the babies get here. Not that Jack isn't already lining up multiple nannies and doulas to help get us through the newborn stage with twins. We still travel to New York occasionally, but for the most part, we've stepped back from the day-to-day with our jobs and have just been enjoying life for the first time in years.

"I know you love it, Princess, but you know why we can't. Regardless of having to get on the road or not, it's not the absolute safest mode of transportation for the babies."

My only response is an eye roll as he helps me out of the car to go to our celebratory dinner. Confetti flies through the air as we walk through the door as a small choir of "congratulations" fills the air from our family, immediately lightening my mood. I don't know if I was just too tired during my first trimester, but as soon as I hit twelve weeks, my mood swings have been out of control. Mom is sure it's because we're having a boy *and* a girl, but we'll have to wait a couple more weeks for the anatomy scan to be sure.

Henry is the first to make contact since Sloane and Ledger are busy entertaining LJ. "Welcome to the family, officially, Mr. Sinclair," he says, holding out a hand for Jack to shake before pulling him into a bro hug.

"Hell yeah! Welcome, brother!" Ledger chimes in, leaping up from the floor and pouncing on Jack, nearly bringing him to the ground in the process.

It didn't take my brothers long to move past everything, especially with a little help from Mom. Henry was the first to get over himself, and the free babysitting really helped our case with Ledger. They still try to steer clear of the R-rated discussions that used to take place way too often, which I can't say I'm upset about. There are things you just don't need to know about your brothers. Or your parents for that matter.

"It's mighty big of you to forfeit your Carter IV for a Sinclair Jr.," Henry teases, ruffling Jack's hair, a move that's annoyed him all his life.

Rolling his eyes, he wraps his arms around me, resting his hands on my swollen belly. "Yeah, well, if we are lucky enough to get one of both, we'll have an MJ and a JJ."

"Margot Blanche Sinclair Jr.?" Ledger asks, and you can practically see the light bulb glowing above his head.

"Yup! And John *Flynn* Sinclair Jr.!" I say, emphasizing Jack's middle name.

Henry chuckles, but Ledger is locked on Sloane. "Nope! Don't even think about it!" Sloane says, looking up from her son and reading his mind like a book the minute they lock eyes. "We are not naming our daughter *Sloane Jr.!*"

They are due about the same time as us but went ahead and did the blood test to find out the gender this time. I'm really not sure who's more excited to have a little girl between the two of them. It definitely makes me hope we have one of each as well, so nobody will be outnumbered. Not that growing up with three brothers—*well, two brothers and a Jack*—was so bad, but poor LJ if he ends up with three little Sinclair girls.

"Oh, why not, darling?" Mom asks, kneeling beside Sloane to play with the baby. "The next could be Blanche Jr.! We could have an LJ, a JJ, an MJ, and SJ and then a BJ!"

The last name gets everyone's attention as we all break out in simultaneous rounds of laughter.

"Okay, okay, no Blanche Jr.!" Mom says between breaths.

I'm clenching my legs together to hold my bladder, and when I look at Sloane, she's doing the same. I've reached the point in pregnancy when I pee every time we laugh or sneeze, and as silly as it is, it's nice to have someone close going through it with me. And as competitive as our husbands are, I have a feeling this won't be the last time we find ourselves experiencing this together.

When Ledger found out we were having twins, his excitement lasted all of ten seconds before he realized his best friend put *two* babies in his woman and punched a hole through the wall. *Then* he realized that woman was his sister and punched Jack. The two of them have basically declared a breeding war against each other, not that I mind. I've always wanted a big family, so the more, the merrier.

Ledger finally gives up his dream of a little SJ and "Wait, did you say Flynn? The F is for *Flynn*? All this time I thought it stood for *fucker*. Especially after you knocked up my damn sister."

"Ha. Ha. Ha. Very funny," Jack says, with a clap between each for emphasis. The gleam in his eye turns more devious by the second. "It actually stands for 'fucked her so good it's twins,' so."

"Here we go again," Sloane mumbles under her breath as she finally gets up off the floor to distract her husband with kisses as I slap mine across the chest for egging him on.

"Alright, alright, let's eat before dinner gets cold," Mom says, leading the pack of us to the dining room with LJ in hand.

Ledger isn't fuming anymore, but he's still side-eyeing Jack like prey when I wrap him up in a bear hug. "I love you, brother," I say, kissing him on the cheek before going to sit next to my *brand-new* husband at the dining table.

Mom is at one end of the table with Henry on the other. LJ sits between Mom and Sloane and a glance reveals the three matching high chairs against the wall behind him. Ledger sits across from me with his arm behind his wife. And Jack is as close to me as he can get with a hand on my swollen womb. I put my hand over Jack's and look around the table at our growing family, realizing I really did get everything I ever wanted.

Missing the Sinclairs already?

Missing our favorite lovers already? Sign up for our newsletter for an exclusive *Masked in Deception* bonus chapter and find out how Jack and Margot continue to have fun with their newly found kinks!

https://dl.bookfunnel.com/zdhyzydm74

Be the first to know about T.K. Drake's new releases and receive exclusive content!

www.tkdrake.com

Instagram: @tkdrakeauthor

Also By T.K. Drake

Available now!
Ledger and Sloane's story
Redeemed in Crimson
Book One in Sinclair Affairs Series

Henry's story is next!
Book three in Sinclair Affairs Series
Caged in Desire
Coming November 2025

"I said. I will not be marrying an eighteen-year-old. However, we will not be carrying forth this contract any further. I will fulfill it. Come see me in a year. Send any necessary paperwork to our counsel in the meantime. And leave the dossier on the girl for our review."

Taking a deep breath, I meet my mother's assessing gaze and see her looking at me with admiration and a touch of melancholy. There's no time for her emotions now, though. All I'm interested in are facts.

"Mother," I growl out. "Explain."

Still to come...

We aren't stopping there! The Sinclair story continues with book four in January 2026 and book five in spring 2026!

Acknowledgments

Thank you, Universe, for giving two best friends the chance to live out a dream. Thank you, childhood obsessions, for leading us into the arms of all of our book boyfriends. Thank you to everyone who helped us bring these characters to life.

And the BIGGEST thank you to all of our readers. You've already changed our lives.

About the Authors

T.K. Drake is a dynamic duo of best friends who couldn't find the perfect romance novel and decided to write it themselves. As only children, they spent their childhood entertaining each other with elaborate stories and games. Reuniting as adults has inspired them to unleash their creative energy into contemporary and dark romance, bridging gaps in the genre and writing books they longed to read. Based in the Southeastern United States, when not writing they are usually reading, lounging on the beach, or planning their next international vacation.